PRESIDENTIAL ORDER OF SUCCESSION

This is the United States government's ultimate fail-safe.
Imagine a day when it comes into play . . .

1. The Vice President
2. Speaker of the House
3. President Pro Tempore of the Senate
4. Secretary of State
5. Secretary of the Treasury
6. Secretary of Defense
7. Attorney General
8. Secretary of the Interior
9. Secretary of Agriculture
10. Secretary of Commerce
11. Secretary of Labor
12. Secretary of Health and Human Services
13. Secretary of Housing and Urban Development
14. Secretary of Transportation
15. Secretary of Energy
16. Secretary of Education
17. Secretary of Veterans Affairs
18. Secretary of Homeland Security

Praise for Michael Palmer's THE LAST SURGEON

"Prepare to burn some serious midnight oil."

—*Boston Herald*

"Highly suspenseful and compelling."   —*Booklist*

"Palmer has always been a good writer but he has never crafted a story as suspenseful as this one...This is the kind of book you read with a bright light on and all the doors locked...Franz Koller is one of the most deadly villains to grace the pages of a novel since the introduction of Hannibal Lecter."   —*Huffington Post*

"Should please...all those who enjoy their suspense mixed with medical characters and settings."

—*Library Journal*

"The thrill of the non-kill...[is] chilling."

—*North Shore Sunday*

"More twists and turns than a sociopath's psyche... inventive and effective, an entertaining and engaging read."   —*California Literary Review*

THE SECOND OPINION

"A heart-pounding medical thriller...satisfying, expertly paced [with] enough suspense to keep readers happily turning the pages."   —*Boston Globe*

"The novel is not merely a thriller but also an exploration of its central character's unique gifts and her determination to communicate with her comatose father despite overwhelming odds. Another winner from a consistently fine writer." —*Booklist*

"A splendid novel." —*Globe and Mail* (Canada)

THE FIRST PATIENT

"An exciting thriller that is full of surprises and captures the intense atmosphere of the White House, how the medical system works, and how the 25th Amendment could be brought into play. I thoroughly enjoyed it." —President Bill Clinton

"An incredibly realistic, frightening thriller that is every White House doctor's nightmare."
—Dr. E. Connie Mariano,
White House Physician 1992–2001

"Endlessly entertaining…the roller-coaster ride of a plot builds to an undeniably shocking conclusion."
—*Publishers Weekly*

THE FIFTH VIAL

"An ingenious medical thriller, suspenseful and cleverly plotted." —Kathy Reichs

"A terrifying vision of the Hippocratic oath gone very wrong."
—*Entertainment Weekly*

"Palmer taps a real medical issue for storytelling thrills."
—*Boston* magazine

"A tale set at the very edge of our medical knowledge. I loved it!"
—Tess Gerritsen

"Palmer is adept at tapping into people's natural fear of disease, doctors, and hospitals and converting that fear into unnerving suspense...If medical thrills are what you're after, he delivers."
—*Booklist*

"In his entertaining twelfth medical suspense novel... Palmer, himself an M.D., does a good job of informing the reader on an important ethical issue."
—*Publishers Weekly*

"Palmer is adept at reaching into the psyche...and knows how to wield a scalpel...chilling."
—*Ottawa Citizen*

"Gripping and topical."
—*Toronto Sun*

"Palmer's latest has thrills and chills aplenty, while conveying a sobering—make that *terrifying*—message. Not only is this one heck of a medical thriller, it's a scary wake-up call to what could happen if a few individuals decided to play God, a premise that scared the daylights out of me. Could this happen? Palmer makes you think so." —Sandra Brown

"*The Fifth Vial* is a nail-biting thriller you don't want to miss." —Catherine Coulter, author of *Whiplash*

"Michael Palmer delivers a complex plot, fascinating characters, and plenty of action. *The Fifth Vial* is a roller-coaster ride that winds its way through the United States, Africa, India, and Brazil on the way to a terrific surprise ending." —Phillip Margolin

"Brilliant storyteller Michael Palmer is at the top of his game, and gives us a compelling and thought-provoking tale that will have you looking over your shoulder. It's both realistic and terrifying, and it will keep you up all night!" —Iris Johansen

"There's a compelling truth at the center of this high-octane thriller. The twists keep you reading and the questions Palmer poses keep you thinking all night long." —Tami Hoag

"Michael Palmer, perhaps the best of our medical-thriller writers, has penned an action-packed tale that will have you checking all your body parts for days afterward." —Terry Brooks

Also by Michael Palmer

The Last Surgeon

The Second Opinion

The First Patient

The Fifth Vial

The Society

Fatal

The Patient

Miracle Cure

Critical Judgment

Silent Treatment

Natural Causes

Extreme Measures

Flashback

Side Effects

The Sisterhood

A HEARTBEAT AWAY

MICHAEL PALMER

St. Martin's Paperbacks

This is a work of fiction. All of the characters, organizations, and events portrayed in this novel are either products of the author's imagination or are used fictitiously.

A HEARTBEAT AWAY

Copyright © 2011 by Michael Palmer.
Excerpt from *Oath of Office* copyright © 2011 by Michael Palmer.

All rights reserved.

For information address St. Martin's Press, 175 Fifth Avenue, New York, NY 10010.

Library of Congress Catalog Card Number: 2010039321

ISBN: 978-0-312-58751-2

Printed in the United States of America

St. Martin's Press hardcover edition / February 2011
St. Martin's Paperbacks edition / August 2011

St. Martin's Paperbacks are published by St. Martin's Press, 175 Fifth Avenue, New York, NY 10010.

10 9 8 7 6 5 4 3 2 1

*To my editor at St. Martin's Press, Jennifer Enderlin,
and to my agent at the Jane Rotrosen Agency, Meg Ruley*

How blessed can a writer be?

ACKNOWLEDGMENTS

When writing a novel, help comes in many, and often unexpected, ways. In addition to my editor and agent (see the dedication), deepest thanks to:

Dr. David Grass, neurology

Dr. Geoffrey Sherwood, hematology/oncology

Dr. Connie Mariano, White House medicine

Paul Weiss, power specialist

Robin Broady, LICSW

Jessica Bladd Palmer

Pilot Dave Pascoe

Steve Westfall, biocontainment

And to my main men always and forever:

Daniel, Luke, and Matthew, the McGuffin Guy

To anyone I might have missed, thank you, too. Promise I'll catch you next time.

PROLOGUE

The last thing Eddie Gostowski was thinking about on Thursday evening, the twenty-second of May, was that he was going to die.

For the first hour or so of his 11 P.M. to 7 A.M. shift as a security guard for the NYISO power distribution giant, he had been thinking about the Yankees, and wondering if they had enough pitching to win the American League East Division again. For the second hour, he had debated whether to buy flowers or candy this year for his beloved Mary's sixtieth birthday.

Eddie had been patrolling this particular control facility for most of the eleven years the New York Independent System Operator had been in existence, and nothing out of the ordinary had ever happened—absolutely nothing . . . not once. He understood his job and he understood what was at stake should the NYISO somehow shed its entire load at once—a massive blackout of almost indescribable proportions, engulfing everyplace from Albany to New York City and Long Island. It was his job, along with others in the chain of virtually fail-safe checks and balances, to ensure such a disaster never occurred.

But nothing out of the ordinary had ever happened at his control facility—absolutely nothing . . . not once.

As he had every night at this time, Eddie set a timer for fifteen minutes and prepared to take a nap. But first, one last check of things. It took him a few seconds to realize that several of his gauges had gone out of whack. The unmanned substations serving Marcy to Albany and Albany to Leeds had gone off-line.

Curious.

Eddie began ticking off all the possible explanations for the weird happening, and came up with little. If the gauges were right, and there was no way they could be, there was no longer any power going to the capital district, which surrounded and included Albany.

Still more bewildered than alarmed, Eddie moved to his left. His equipment told the same story for other substations. Dunwoodie to Long Island and Ravensbrook in Queens had also been tripped. Goethals and Farragut, controlling the power to large portions of New York City, was down as well. Assuming the readings were all correct, the whole system was unstable, and the largest city in the country was on the verge of something massive and horrible.

Eddie's first move was a call to the nearest manned station 150 miles north in Albany. Seven rings and an answering machine.

Even an explosion at the facility in Albany would not cause this sort of power loss. Since its inception, NYISO had been closing loopholes in its system to the point where an almost inconceivable number of events had to occur simultaneously to cause any major degree of problems.

But incredibly, those events were happening.

As far as Eddie could tell, his control station was now the only thing standing against a blackout that would engulf most of eastern New York including Long Island and the five boroughs of New York City.

He raced to the phone, got the emergency number of the FBI from a chart on the wall, and began dialing.

That was when he felt the point of a knife press against the back of his neck.

"Set the receiver down, sport," a man's husky voice said in an accent that sounded British.

The knife point felt as if it were going to slice straight into Eddie's spine.

"P-please. That hurts."

"What's your name, sport?"

"Eddie. Eddie Gostowski. Please."

"I'm going to lower the knife, Eddie, but unless you do exactly as I say, you're a dead man. Got that?"

"Yes."

"I SAID, HAVE YOU GOT THAT?"

"Yes! Yes! Now pl—"

"Okay, sport, we don't have much time. You're going to turn around and look me in the eye. If you fuck with me in any way, any way at all, I'm going to slit your throat. Is that clear? Okay, now swing around."

Eddie did as he was ordered. Towering above him was a man—six foot three, maybe more, with shoulders that seemed to block out the room. He was dressed in black—watch cap, jeans, and a turtleneck—with black greasepaint covering his face. His eyes were dark and cold. In his hand was a bowie knife—broad and curved at the tip—ten inches long at least.

Behind the man and to his right, arms crossed, feet apart, stood a second man in identical dress and grease-paint.

As frightened as he was, Eddie couldn't get the notion out of his head of the disaster that would ensue should the brownout that was already in effect be allowed to progress. As if responding to his thoughts, the big man placed the tip of the bowie knife beneath Eddie's chin and lifted his face up.

"No arguing with me now," he said. "I want you to use whatever you have here to trip this unit off-line."

"But—"

The huge man drew the razor-sharp blade across Eddie's gullet like a violin bow, slicing open a shallow gash from one side of his jawbone to the other.

"I said don't argue with me, sport! Now, do as I tell you and you won't be hurt any more. Mess with me and you'll die in pieces, and we'll still find the trip switch to take this place off-line."

He pulled a handkerchief from his back pocket and passed it to Eddie to stanch the flow of blood.

Shakily, Eddie crossed to the adjacent room, hesitated, and then threw the trip. Instantly, the substation went black. Moments later, a generator kicked on and the lights returned.

"Anything else we need to do?" the big man asked the other.

"All four teams have reported in. No problems at all."

They motioned Eddie back into the control room and down onto his chair.

"That your emergency line, sport?" the man asked, gesturing to a red wall phone.

"Yes," Eddie managed, continuing to put pressure on the gash. The handkerchief was sodden with blood.

"Is it monitored?"

"Yes, but with the blackout I'm not sure anyone is there."

"I'm sure this call will be recorded, though, right? I said, 'RIGHT?' "

"R-right."

"Okay, then. This the number?"

"Yes. . . . Yes, sir."

Only then did Eddie realize the man was wearing latex gloves.

The intruder fished out a sheet of paper from his back pocket and unfolded it. Then he dialed. Eddie could hear the taped message go on. At the beep, the man held up the paper and read, with some unevenness, what was typed on it.

"In the beginning God created the heavens and the earth. Then God said, 'Let there be light.' Now, Genesis has taken that light away. This is the beginning."

"Okay, sport, you've been a big help—a real big help."

"Thanks," Eddie said meekly.

The man turned to go. Then, with a sudden, vicious backhand swipe, he slashed the huge bowie knife through Eddie Gostowski's throat.

"Maybe I should have told him that sometimes I can't be trusted," he said.

CHAPTER 1

"Madam Speaker, the President of the United States."

At the words from the sergeant at arms of the House of Representatives, the audience rose to its feet as President James Allaire entered the House Chambers to thunderous applause, mixed with cheers. Allaire glanced at the two Secret Service agents stationed opposite each other just inside the entryway, standing as straight and still as the black and gold Ionic columns dividing the wall behind the tribune. Sean O'Neil, head of the presidential Secret Service unit, shadowed Allaire as he glad-handed his way down the long, royal-blue-carpeted corridor.

The president's heart responded to a rush of adrenaline as the clapping neared the decibel level of a jet engine on takeoff. He stopped every few steps to shake hands or exchange modest embraces with men in dark suits wearing carefully chosen ties, and with impeccably dressed women who smelled of exotic perfume. Ahead of him, he could just see the nine justices of the Supreme Court, and the five members of the Joint Chiefs of Staff.

Allaire sensed O'Neil move a step closer behind him as a congressman from Missouri exuberantly pumped his hand and then shouted, "Go get 'em, Mr. President! You're going to wow 'em tonight!"

That's right, Allaire thought. *I* am *going to wow them.*

There had been many occasions during the beginning of the first term of his presidency when Dr. Jim Allaire privately wondered about a decision he was forced to make. The weight of a single act, benign as it might at first seem, often carried with it surprising ripples and unintended consequences that added to his graying hair and the crow's-feet at the corners of his gray-blue eyes.

However, delivering the first State of the Union Address of his second term was not one of those moments of self-doubt. He had won reelection by a fairly wide margin over Speaker of the House Ursula Ellis, and now, despite lingering sub rosa enmity between the two of them, it was time to cast aside politics and get some business done.

For the past hour, Allaire had paced inside the office of the minority leader of the House, sipping Diet Pepsi and having makeup reapplied for the cameras, all while trying to contain his nervous energy. The feeling he got before a speech of this magnitude reminded him of his days playing quarterback for the Spartans of Case Western Reserve, where he also earned his M.D. degree.

Between his college football career and years spent working as an internist at the Cleveland Clinic, Allaire had learned the importance of balancing confidence with a respectful fear of failure. Viewed as a man of the people, the genuine caring that had made him a respected physician contributed to his consistently elevated job approval rating as president. With the world's problems getting progressively more complex and domestic terrorism on the mind of every American, the people needed a leader they could believe in—a man of poise and dignity in whom to invest their trust. Tonight, Allaire vowed to reaffirm that he was that man, and to give them a speech they would all remember.

The president reached the podium, where his head speechwriter, visibly more nervous than he was, had placed two leather-bound copies of tonight's carefully guarded address. He turned and presented the first copy to Vice President Henry Tilden in his capacity as president of the Senate, and then the other to Ursula Ellis, who strained to maintain eye contact, and whose handshake held all the energy of a mackerel on ice. The president stifled a grin, although he suspected Ellis knew what he was thinking—fifty-three to forty-four—the margin by which he had beaten her in the election.

Allaire had practiced the speech dozens of times and could probably have delivered it flawlessly without the aid of the transparent teleprompters set on either side of his lectern. The crowd kept up its applause. With the American flag serving as his backdrop, he faced the people and waved his appreciation. Then he set his hands on the sides of the podium as a signal he was ready to begin. His eyes met briefly with those of his wife of twenty-seven years, the much-loved first lady, Rebecca

Allaire, and next to her, their only child, Samantha, whom he still could not believe was a senior at Georgetown, already set for Harvard Law.

The clapping continued. Speaker Ellis rose from her chair and banged her gavel several times. At last, a profound hush fell over the seven hundred in attendance.

On the cornice overhead, the clock read exactly 8:00 P.M. Allaire's thoughts flashed on the motto inscribed in the frieze—IN GOD WE TRUST. It was a running joke about doctors that their M.D. degree really stood for M. Diety. Allaire had a deep faith, and had never felt comfortable with the notion of physicians as gods. But he did know that at that moment, he was closer to being God than any doctor had ever been.

Thanks to the recurring deadly attacks by the apparently domestic group calling itself Genesis, the first order of business for the night had to be terrorism. People were on edge. The four attacks orchestrated by the group had been bold, ruthless, arrogant, and very dramatic. Still, there had as yet been no demands made—only the damage and the deaths. He was going to start strong with a warning to Genesis, whoever they were, of American solidarity, and a promise that their capture and successful prosecution was the top priority of his second term.

Allaire had been assured by Hank Tomlinson, chief of the fifteen-hundred-officer Capitol Police force, that security for tonight's speech was the most extensive ever, employing state-of-the-art magnetometers, camera after camera, and manual bag checks in addition to advanced X-ray screeners. Now, it was up to the president and his speechwriters to convince the American people that they were as safe and secure in their homes and personal lives as those here with him in the Capitol of the United States.

Allaire's speech materialized on the virtually invisible teleprompters.

"Madam Speaker, Vice President Tilden, fellow citizens: As a new Congress gathers, I am reminded of and humbled by the sacred honor you, the American people, have invested in all of your elected officials. So, before I begin tonight's State of the Union Address, on behalf of all who have been blessed with your trust, I want to offer my bottomless thanks for another term of what my father would have called good, steady work."

Allaire paused, waiting the perfect number of beats to let the laughter subside before resuming. It was a strategic opening that he had argued for with his speechwriters, all of whom felt it important to start on a more somber note. As usual, he was right. The State of the Union was a wonderful opportunity to showcase his humanity, in addition to imparting to the electorate his resolve and courage to do what was right and necessary.

"But with this responsibility comes great challenges that we must strive together to overcome. Our economy is growing stronger now, but there is much to be done. Unemployment is at its lowest level in more than a decade. Slowly, we are winning the war against poverty. Our optimism that we as a people can master any difficulty and achieve unparalleled peace and prosperity throughout the world has never been greater, and the state of our union is strong."

Allaire beamed as those on both sides of the aisle, and in the gallery, rose to their feet as one, cheering loudly. He could hear whistles over the applause, and hesitated long enough to draw in a slow, deep breath. The next several crucial minutes of his speech would focus on international and domestic terrorism. The crowd settled down. Allaire scanned their faces. He would know when they were ready for him to resume.

As a dense silence enveloped the room, the president suddenly heard a disturbing noise—a popping sound, immediately followed by something that, to him, sounded like the plink of breaking glass. The sound came from somewhere in the crowd to his right. Allaire and many others turned and watched as California Senator Arlene Cogan opened up the purse that she had stowed beneath her chair. Instantly, a thin, white mist wafted out from within it, covering her heavily made-up face like a steam bath. Within seconds, Cogan and those nearest to her began to cough—and cough vehemently.

Allaire immediately gave a prearranged signal to the coordinating technical director, ordering the man to implement antidemonstration procedures and shut down the network pool controlling all television feed from the Capitol.

Murmurs from among the crowd escalated as another pop occurred across the chamber from the first, followed by another, and another, each accompanied by the breaking of thin glass, white mist, and more coughing. The murmurs gave way to shouting. Another briefcase and a purse were opened, releasing identical thin clouds.

"Don't open it!" someone hollered.

"I can't breathe!"

"For God's sake, that's you! That's your pocketbook!"

"Get out of here! Let's get out!"

The popping and breaking glass continued.

Two more . . . three . . . four . . . five.

Allaire could see that mist was even arising from some bags that were unopened. He quickly counted fifteen plumes scattered about the room, maybe more.

"Do not open your briefcase or purse!" Allaire shouted into his microphone. He slammed his open palm on the podium. "Everybody, please remain calm!"

Secret Service agents rushed the stage and quickly surrounded him. They attempted to escort him to safety, but he struggled against them and continued to call loudly for order. At that instant, Allaire caught sight of something on the two teleprompters in front of his podium.

His blood turned cold.

The speech, which seconds ago was easily legible in fourteen-point Helvetica font, had disappeared from the screens. In its place were three lines of text. Allaire's breathing nearly stopped as he read the message.

On THE FOURTH DAY
God created the sun, the moon, and the stars.
And Genesis released WRX3883.

CHAPTER 2

WRX3883.

Jim Allaire knew immediately what had happened. Genesis had struck a mortal blow at the government of the United States and at the very heart of the country. Every soul in the U.S. Capitol building, including himself, the vice president, and nearly the entire line of succession to the presidency, was in danger. If there was to be any hope of averting an even more unprecedented disaster, he had to take control of the situation. He felt his chest tightening and wondered if it was just fear settling in, or something far more horrific—something in his bloodstream, already at work, attacking his body.

WRX3883.

For a moment, the magnitude of the evolving crisis held Allaire immobile. From his vantage point on the rostrum, he could see that panic had already begun to overtake many of the seven hundred who had gathered for his address. Self-preservation was replacing civility.

Men and women alike, some of whom he had known for decades, were shoving their way toward the exits, some of them viciously. Job one, Allaire decided, would have to be to secure all the doors.

In the center row of the balcony, Rebecca and Samantha stood immobile, side by side, looking down at him. Even at a distance, he could make out the pallor in their faces and the fear in their eyes. Before he could act, though, several agents took him by the shoulders and began moving him away from the microphone. Others stepped in and began helping to guide him toward the rear emergency exit.

"No!" Allaire shouted. "Tend to the doors! The doors!"

He could see, to his horror, that people were already nearing the exits from the chamber, and he knew they would all have to be brought back in, by force if necessary. Several more agents arrived.

They're just trying to get me to safety, Allaire told himself. *But they don't realize that there is no place safe to go.*

There wasn't time to explain.

Allaire twisted his body hard to the right, breaking the hold of the agent positioned directly behind him, while simultaneously seizing the lapels of another agent's suit jacket. He pulled the man to within inches of his face, making certain his orders would be heard over the escalating din.

"Call and get the exits out of the chamber secured right now! Lock them down!"

"But sir, we need to evacuate."

"Listen to me! Nobody is to leave this building. Absolutely nobody! Get everyone who leaves the chamber back inside right now. It is life and death. Do you understand?"

"But—"

"I said, do you understand?!"

"Yes, sir."

"Then I want guards posted at every exit. Shut down the elevators to the gallery level, and block those doors as well. Have guns drawn if need be and use them if you have to. Nobody gets out. No exceptions."

"But sir . . ."

"Dammit, do it now or go sit down!"

The president's face was flushed. He could feel the arteries pulsating in his neck. The agents guarding him peeled away, as if from a football huddle. Chief agent Sean O'Neil was just a few feet away, barking orders into his radio.

"Sean," Allaire said, motioning the man closer, "we've got a lethal situation on our hands. A virus. Get three of your guys to the press gallery and confiscate all cell phones, pagers, and anything that might record or transmit. Use force if you have to. Tell them I'll explain soon."

O'Neil hesitated, a shadow of doubt darkening his face.

"Mr. Pres—"

"Don't challenge me, Sean! Move now!"

The cries of those in flight intensified as Capitol Police and Secret Service agents moved into position and began the difficult task of herding them back inside the

House Chamber. Allaire estimated that no more than twenty-five or thirty had actually made it out the doors to the vestibule. His wife and daughter remained in front of their seats, two of the few who weren't in motion. Then he saw Rebecca cough several times. Further down the row she was in, a congressman from New Hampshire was also coughing.

Allaire searched for the plumes of smoke nearest to his family, but by now, the mists had almost totally dissipated.

I am responsible for this, he thought, forcing his way back to the rostrum. *I should never have allowed it to happen.*

"You can't block these exits!" a senator's familiar voice boomed. "Let us out!"

"They can't do this!" a woman cried. "They can't trap us in here like this!"

"What the hell is going on?"

"I won't go back in there. I won't!"

Sweat, something Allaire had felt certain would not be an issue tonight, cascaded down his brow, stinging his eyes, then salting his lips.

"Mr. President—"

Allaire turned toward the voice, which came from the center aisle, along which, just a few minutes ago, he had made his grand entrance. The architect of the Capitol, Jordan Lamar, a portly African American man, was pushing toward him through the dense crowd.

"Mr. President—" Lamar called out again.

Allaire motioned for the man to hurry. Together on the rostrum they were joined by Hank Tomlinson, chief of the fifteen hundred men and women of the Capitol Police force.

"What the devil is going on, Mr. President?" Lamar asked. "We've got to get you out of here."

"I'm not going anywhere. No one is. Now, listen. I need every person back in his original seat immediately. Make sure every door leading to the outside is sealed. No one gets in and no one gets out. I mean *no one*."

It was hard to hear over the clamor behind them in the main chamber and a story above in the gallery. Now there were also some shrieks as word spread that the ways out were being sealed.

"Sir, I don't understand," Tomlinson said. "What's happened?"

Allaire struggled to maintain his composure—seldom a difficult task for him. Behind and above the Capitol Police chief, he could see that Rebecca and Samantha, along with some others, had instinctively sat back down.

"I'll tell you, Hank. I'll tell everyone," Allaire said. "First, though, we need order in this room, and we need it now."

"But how . . . ?"

Allaire had heard enough. Gripping Tomlinson firmly by the lapel, he pulled the man close to his body, distracting him long enough to extract the officer's gun from his shoulder holster. Allaire had learned how to fire the semiautomatic SIG P226 as part of Operation Keepsake, a long-standing Secret Service program. As an emergency security precaution, Operation Keepsake was designed to impart Special Forces combat training to the president of the United States, or as he was commonly referred to by the agents, the POTUS. Before Tomlinson could react, Allaire raised the gun high above his head.

Four shots, fired in rapid succession and amplified by the sound system, exploded from the black-steel barrel. The discharges echoed deafeningly inside the enclosed chamber. Plaster from the ceiling where the bullets struck dropped onto several startled attendees. Silence quickly followed. Allaire wasted no time taking advantage of the change. He grabbed the microphone, turning up the volume until he heard feedback.

"This is the president of the United States. Please return to your original seats—precisely your original seats. I am commanding the military, the Secret Service, and the Capitol Police to see to it that there are no further attempts to leave this building. All exits have been secured. Right now, I need each and every one of you to sit down at your original seat immediately. You must be seated exactly where you were prior to the disturbance. This is a direct order from your president. As soon as you are back in your seats and have quieted down, I will explain what is going on."

At first, only a few dozen seemed to be responding. Then Allaire dispatched two more shots, and within half a minute, nearly all the seats were filled. The few who refused to comply with the demand were roughly deposited in their places by the nearest soldier or policeman.

Allaire's eyes swept across the rows of dignitaries, many of them among the best and the brightest his

country had to offer, many of them his friends, all of
them now in grave danger. Rebecca and Sam were together in the seats his staff had earlier reserved for
them. For a moment, Allaire held his wife's desperate
gaze. Then he mouthed the words *I love you* and touched
his finger to his eye, and next to his heart, before pointing it at Sam. It was a sign of affection they invented
when their daughter was a child. She and her mother,
in return, made the same gesture to him. Allaire could
not think of a time that he loved them more.

As the president panned the faces in the crowd, a
single thought would not let go. Never had he seen so
much fear.

And yet, the seven hundred had no idea just how
afraid they really should be.

CHAPTER 3

Allaire stood with his hands pressed firmly on the lectern, trying to construct what he was going to say and how he was going to say it. His eyes, nearly unblinking, gazed forward. His mouth was dry. He had always loved being a physician, but after fifteen years as a practicing doc, he felt as if he wanted to do more, and turned to politics. How many times over the years before he left medicine had he sat with patients and given them the horrible news that barring a miracle, they were going to die from their illness? He used to feel that, because his sensitivity and empathy were genuine, he was reasonably effective at it.

Not this evening.

The crowd's attention remained fixed on him. The anxious quiet was beyond tense, interrupted only by scattered volleys of coughing. Allaire knew it was time. These people wanted—needed—explanations, but he felt strongly that if he disclosed the whole truth about the virus, there would be no way to contain the ensuing panic.

"What's happening?" a man suddenly shouted, pre-empting Allaire from the gallery.

"Does this have anything to do with Genesis?" a second man called out.

"Yes," he heard his voice say with forced calm. "Yes, unfortunately, it does."

The first act of terror for which Genesis had taken credit was the Great New York Blackout, eight or nine months before. THE FIRST DAY, the terrorists had labeled it in a call to the FBI. *God said, "Let there be light," and Genesis said, "Let there be darkness."* Something like that. Three men were brutally murdered during the sabotage of several substations, and another hundred people were estimated to have died as the re-sult of the three-day power outage. No demands were made by Genesis.

THE SECOND DAY, creation of the sky, was marked by an off-hours explosion that destroyed a wing of the San Diego Air and Space Museum. Three killed—hundreds if the blast were six hours earlier. Again, no demands.

Also no real suspects, despite the most intense FBI/CIA/ATF investigation since 9/11.

THE THIRD DAY, just two months ago, represented the creation of dry land and the bringing forth of plants and fruit-bearing trees. On it, the spectacular all-glass National Horticultural Building was leveled by a power-ful blast, killing twelve and injuring fifty more.

Now, more than seven hundred, including Allaire

himself and his wife and daughter, had their necks in a noose.

It was THE FOURTH DAY.

Without warning, the president coughed.

His chest tightened as panic washed over him. He risked a peek at his palms, praying that no red blotches or discs would be there. *Is it happening already?* No, his palms were unmarked and unremarkable. He let out a relieved sigh, which the microphone broadcast to all. Just a tickle in his throat. For now, just a tickle.

A woman, seated in the gallery, dead center to the president, stood up, clutching the hand of a boy no more than thirteen years old, whom Allaire presumed to be her son.

"Are we in danger?"

The president inhaled deeply and exhaled slowly.

"I don't have enough information to answer your question at this moment. It is possible," he went on, choosing his words carefully, "that we might have been exposed to a pathogen—a virus. As a protective measure, until I have more information, I am asking that everyone stay calm, and more importantly, that everyone remain seated. I will speak more precisely about the situation when I have discussed what we know with my advisors. Until then, as your commander in chief, I have ordered the security forces here to use any measures necessary to keep you in the room and in those seats. Now, please be patient. I must review these developments with my advisors."

At that, a dozen or so people leapt up and began shouting questions at once. It was Georgia senator Saul

Kennistone who caught the president's eye. Kennistone opened his mouth to yell something at him, but a sudden, body-shaking fit of coughing choked back the senator's words.

So, it has begun, Allaire thought.

His concern must have shown.

"Why is he coughing?" someone shouted. "Is that the virus?"

As if answering the question, several people around the chamber joined in the chorus of dry, hacking coughs.

"We are investigating," Allaire said over the noise. "That is all I can say at the moment. Now, please, in addition to my Capitol Police Chief Tomlinson, Agent O'Neil, and Vice President Tilden, the following are to come to the podium immediately for a briefing."

The president summoned White House Chief of Staff Megan McAndrews; Department of Defense Secretary Gary Salitas; Health and Human Services Secretary Kate Broussard; Homeland Security Secretary Paul Rappaport; Capitol Architect Jordan Lamar; and Admiral Archibald Jakes, Chairman of the Joint Chiefs of Staff. Dr. Bethany Townsend, Allaire's personal physician and longtime family friend, was the last one called forward.

The room erupted again in an anxious commotion, punctuated by continued sporadic coughing. Those occupying the floor area, reserved for officials from the Senate, House, Supreme Court, the president's Cabinet, and diplomatic corps, obeyed the president's edict and remained seated. Those individuals the president had called forward stood and made their way to the rostrum.

People in the upper gallery sections, however—those now-unlucky souls who had scored a coveted ticket to the State of the Union Address, as well as members of the press and broadcast network teams—were less compliant. Not a mass exodus, Allaire observed, but enough people to draw his attention decided to head toward the exits. The president watched with irritation and immense sadness as people were forcibly turned back by the guards stationed at all the doors. One particularly aggressive man, clawing at a uniformed security officer, was whipped into submission by the butt of a pistol.

Allaire gripped Sean O'Neil by the shoulder.

"Sean, please clear the area around us."

O'Neil engaged three agents to back people away from the group. Then he quickly returned to the POTUS's side.

"We've got to make sure nobody leaves the House chamber," Allaire said urgently.

"We're doing that, sir."

"No, I mean make *absolutely* sure."

"Sir?"

"Dammit, Sean—" The president quickly composed himself and leaned forward to whisper, "This virus is viciously contagious. If it gets out of here, there's no telling what might happen. Have your people and the other guards immobilize anybody who tries to force their way to the outside. Use whatever restraints and force are necessary."

"Yes, sir."

O'Neil, tall and lean, and emotionless in every way

except for the alertness in his dark eyes, delivered the president's directive via secure radio. Allaire returned to the lectern. He leaned forward until his lips brushed against the metal mesh of the microphone.

"Ladies and gentlemen. Please settle down. Please. Quiet down this instant!"

It took several additional calls for quiet before the room settled into an uneasy silence. All eyes were now directed upon him. Allaire made a furtive glance toward his wife and daughter. In seconds, the concern etched across their faces forced him to look away.

"I must be very clear," he said. "Until we know more about what we may have been exposed to, I cannot allow anybody to exit the House Chamber. I promise to share what information I have as it becomes available. For now, I'm requesting your cooperation."

"And what if we don't!"

The unidentified man shouted his thinly veiled threat from somewhere in the upper gallery.

"What we've been exposed to could be highly contagious," Allaire's amplified voice boomed out. "Until we have more information, I cannot risk a public health crisis. To ensure public safety, I've authorized the use of extreme measures against anyone who attempts to exit the building. That is a nonnegotiable order from your president. Now, please, you must excuse me. I'll return shortly with additional information and our proposed next steps after I speak with my staff."

Once more the room erupted into chaotic chatter. The White House chief of staff, intense, intellectual Megan McAndrews, was the first to approach.

"Mr. President," she whispered, "you neglected to include the speaker of the house."

McAndrews tilted her head in a nearly imperceptible gesture toward Ursula Ellis, in her seat atop the tribune.

"If I didn't call somebody," Allaire said, with an edge, "either I don't need them, or I don't trust them."

CHAPTER 4

Ursula Ellis assumed Allaire had included her among the high-ranking officials he had summoned to meet with him. It took some time for her to realize he had not. Perhaps she had misheard over all the commotion, she wondered—either that, or the president's gunshots had temporarily impaired her hearing.

Vice President Henry Tilden sat beside Ellis on the rostrum. He was a tall, gangly oaf of a man whom Ellis knew would never make anyone's list of the most intellectual politicians in the land.

"Henry, did the president include me?" she leaned over and asked.

"I don't think so, Ursula," Tilden said, pushing himself up from his seat and carefully avoiding eye contact. "But I wasn't listening that closely. Please, excuse me now. I've got to go."

Yes, of course, you go, Ellis thought. *Go be the good lapdog that you are.*

Ellis remained seated in her designated chair, look-ing, she sensed, regal and composed. She had been a fourteen-point underdog when she won the nomination to oppose Allaire. A throwaway, many political pundits had called her, persisting with that notion even when she had shaved a good chunk of that lead away by the time of the election. One more month and she would have caught the bastard, she had thought over and over again.

One more month.

She concentrated on maintaining an appearance of composure. People were looking. Allaire had been an idiot firing that gun the way he did. She needed to ap-pear above it. Many out there had to be aware of the slight the man had just delivered to her. She needed the power brokers and the doubters to see a woman imper-vious to the chaos engulfing them—a true leader, fear-less in the face of impending disaster.

Ellis glanced sideways at Allaire. The sight of him churned her stomach. Perhaps now the American people would see past the smoke and mirrors of their so-called leader. Perhaps they would see that for all his cries for cooperation and unity between the legislative and ex-ecutive branches, when push came to shove, the speaker of the house was being left on the outside looking in.

Well, fine, she thought. While he was slinking away to meet with his yes-men, she was where it really counted—with the people. Sooner or later that snub might prove to be Allaire's undoing. Those waiting for him to handle whatever was going on had to have seen how his color had gone pale; how sweat dripped a rivulet of makeup down his Botox-stiffened face; how his hands shook. The man oozed weakness and uncertainty.

The moment the election results were in, the moment she had conceded, Ursula Ellis had begun thinking about the election four years from then. She had checklists in her study of her possible competition, within her party and Allaire's. None of them was all that formidable. Privately, her advisors questioned whether this might be the time for her to step back from politics and resign her seat in Congress to gather up and reform the scattered pieces of her campaign team. But she had the foresight to anticipate a virtual dead heat for control of the House, and had chosen to run for reelection to her seat while campaigning against Allaire. Now, here she was, elected in her district by a landslide, and back as speaker.

She had been guided in her decision to keep her seat by a persistent inner voice telling her the time was not right to pull back. That gentle voice, which had led her so unerringly in the past, made it clear that God had plans for her—plans to lead the country. She simply had to stay in the limelight.

Allaire surveyed the chosen ones. He looked as if he were about to faint.

This is it, Ellis thought. Whatever was happening, the president was not equipped to handle it. Sooner or later, he was going to slip—to make a profound error in judgment. And when he did, she would be ready to step forward. In truth, she felt certain her rival was misreading the situation altogether.

First, though, before she could stand in opposition to the actions he intended to take, she needed information.

Allaire was the consummate conniver. What was he up to this time? Was this some sort of demonstration—a test, like the civil defense interruptions on the radio?

Did he really believe that seven hundred of the most powerful and influential Americans were being affected by some virus?

If there was any truth at all to what he was claiming, then people needed medical evaluation and attention—food and water, not threats and isolation. But odds favored that the whole thing was some sort of scam. Allaire's leadership skills were fraying. Hers were sharper than ever. If there really was a virus, she had the intelligence and charisma to bring the people together.

It was God's will that she was in this spot at this moment.

Ellis observed that none of the president's trusted advisors now gathered at the lectern showed any physical effects from whatever had been released by Genesis. None, that was, except for the head of the Joint Chiefs of Staff, Admiral Archie Jakes, who was trying unsuccessfully to suppress his near-constant coughing. Where had Jakes been sitting when the vapor released? It would be interesting to find out—possibly very interesting.

Her body tingled with what she playfully described to her staff as her "Spidey Sense," a little surge of neuroelectricity that helped her distinguish information which had value from that which did not.

Her aide, Leland Gladstone, was a badger on any task. He needed to search out other coughers in the chamber and figure out where they had been sitting during the little explosions. Child's play for the man who would have been her chief of staff in the White House, and who still might have a shot at the position if things went her way.

Ellis then turned her attention to the more pressing matter at hand. Something tremendous had just occurred inside the House Chamber—*her* chamber, she might remind Allaire. Election opponents or not, the speaker of the house should have been a part of any closed-door briefing.

She rose and smoothed out the creases of her form-fitting black skirt. She was a trim, attractive brunette, who had once been the homecoming queen at Mississippi State. Careful not to call excess attention to herself, she approached the president, who had his back turned to her.

"Mr. President, excuse me?"

Allaire continued his exchange with Gary Salitas.

"Mr. President, can you give me some idea what's going on?"

Allaire either ignored the question or simply did not hear it over the swirling commotion. Ellis felt a rush of anger, which she quickly parried. She was not accustomed to being ignored by anyone, the president included. Allaire continued on, as if unaware of her presence, now speaking in a hushed voice to his chief Secret Service agent, Sean O'Neil. Ellis strained to pick up some words, but could not.

"Mr. President, would you like me to join the team for the briefing?" she said, louder than before.

This time, Allaire turned.

"Ursula. I'm glad to see you. Are you okay?"

"Yes, yes, I'm fine. Thank you. But I'd like to participate in the briefing, Mr. President. . . . That is if you need me."

"No. I need your leadership here in the chamber. I'll keep you informed as things develop."

Which means you won't tell me jack shit, Ellis thought.

Allaire had turned and resumed his dialogue with O'Neil.

Ellis stood behind the president, burning with hatred.

"You okay?"

Gladstone had materialized beside her. Thin and dark haired, with ice blue eyes that at times gave Ellis the shivers, the man embodied what every congressional leader sought in an aide—charm, good looks, and a wobbly moral compass.

Ellis led him away from Allaire and the others.

"I'm POed," she said finally. "How should I be?"

Gladstone patted his jacket pocket.

"Well, I assumed you would want the location of the explosions. So far I've pinpointed seven of what looks like a total of fifteen or sixteen broken glass containers. I should have the rest of them in a little while. Then, assuming you want me to, I'll start filling in the seats around them."

"Absolutely. As usual, you are well ahead of the game."

"From what I can tell so far, there's no pattern."

"There's always a pattern, dear Leland. Sometimes not so obvious, but there's always a pattern to everything. Finish filling in that seating chart, but keep your two-way radio handy. Until this situation is resolved and we are all outside waltzing down Pennsylvania Avenue, we're going to be mighty busy."

The speaker's aide headed toward the gallery while Ellis maintained her position not far from where Jim Allaire was about to retreat for the meeting with his group of sycophants. The discomfort on the man's face was a tonic. She started imagining herself sparring with him, boxing gloves on, bobbing and weaving, searching for an opening. What she needed most now, to inflict some real damage, was information. And as the president turned to go, she realized where she could find it.

Quickly moving to the right side of the group, she slid her hand around Sean O'Neil's arm and pulled him back toward her.

"I don't have time to talk, Madam Speaker," he said. "The president needs me."

"If I need you, Sean, and I do, you will make time for me."

O'Neil hesitated, and then allowed himself to be led to a spot where they would not be overheard.

"What do you want?" he asked in a pressured whisper.

"Simple. I want to know what the president says in that briefing you're going to."

"It's classified. If you're not there, you can't know."

Ellis smiled again and her thin lips disappeared inside her mouth.

"We both know that's a bad strategy, Sean. I am the speaker of the house. The American people will expect me to know what's going on. Allaire is playing politics at a time of national crisis."

"You should take that up with the president, then."

Sean turned to leave, but Ellis caught him by the arm.

"Suppose I also take up what you and that darling young White House intern were doing in the Lincoln Bedroom while the first couple was away on vacation. I'm sure the Allaires would love to see the security videos—especially the part where you so skillfully and lovingly snorted some sort of white power from between the sweet thing's breasts."

O'Neil went pale.

"How . . . ? How did you . . . ?"

"Eyes and ears, my love. I use my eyes and ears— and some well-placed friends. In fact, over the years we've been working for the American people, I've collected other useful tidbits about you, as well. The nasty custody battle with your ex over baby Duncan, for instance. How do you think this sort of revelation will help your chances, dear Sean, let alone your career?"

O'Neil looked away.

"I'll get you what I can," he muttered.

"You'll get me what I *want*, Sean. Is that understood?"

O'Neil turned without a reply and rushed ahead to catch up with the president. Ellis watched until the group had disappeared through a guarded exit.

Third.

The word echoed in her mind. She was third in line to govern the most powerful nation on earth. And all of a sudden, the two above her seemed to be on very shaky ground.

CHAPTER 5

Allaire led his team past the Secret Service agents guarding the mahogany double doors located directly to the right of the rostrum. The corridor, accessible only to members of Congress and their staff, had reinforced walls that dampened the din from within the House Chamber.

Near the end of the passageway, the president used a keycard to unlock another wooden door. Sensors detected movement inside the pitch-black room, and turned on several banks of overhead fluorescent lights.

Allaire proceeded to a keypad on the right-hand wall. Punching in his code, he waited for the hydraulics to engage. In seconds, the wall opposite him slid noiselessly downward and disappeared, revealing the Hard Room. The array of communication equipment—satellite phones, wall-mounted monitors, radios, printers, radar imaging systems, and laptop computers—gave him a brief flare of confidence that his government possessed the power to prevail against any adversary. Then he reminded himself that this was no ordinary adversary—this was WRX3883 in the hands of depraved killers, and at this moment, nothing existed inside this room, or any other, that could defeat that combination.

The large conference table in the center of the room would serve as their briefing area. Two Cabinet secretaries—Salitas and Broussard—took their seats, along with Allaire's physician Bethany Townsend; the vice president; uniformed Admiral Archie Jakes (the chairman of the Joint Chiefs of Staff); the head of the Capitol Police force, Hank Tomlinson; Architect of the Capitol Jordan Lamar and White House Chief of Staff Megan McAndrews. O'Neil, square-jawed and swarthy, remained standing against the back wall.

"Where is Paul Rappaport?" Allaire asked.

"Paul is at home in Minnesota, Mr. President," McAndrews said, "tending to his daughter."

Minnesota. Allaire groaned. He had personally approved the trip.

"Yes, of course," he said. "Sorry."

For this year's State of the Union Address, Paul Rappaport was the so-called designated survivor.

No State of the Union Address, inauguration, or other momentous occasion occurred without there being a DS—referred to by some as the Doomsday Successor. The DS was the only one of the fifteen Cabinet members officially in line to succeed the president who was deliberately not in the vicinity of Washington, D.C. He or she was chosen for the job by the military through the President Emergency Operations Center, or PEOC—the same unit with operational control of the Hard Room.

Given that every member of the Cabinet wanted to be near the POTUS during major events, the chosen DS, usually at or near the bottom of the chain, had no desire to be the one selected. Paul Rappaport's appointment, however, was a logical one—one that the former governor had actually requested.

Not only was the Homeland Security secretary a logical choice, being the most recently established Cabinet position, but just a week earlier, Rappaport's daughter's condo had been broken into and ransacked while she was in the shower. Stolen were her purse, wallet, laptop computer, iPad, cell phone, silverware, and jewelry. Even worse, the president had been informed, her underwear had been removed from her bureau drawer, cut up, and spread out on her bed. The daughter, Renee, had a history of profound anxiety and depression, and suffered a breakdown as a result of the invasion. She had just been discharged after several days in a psychiatric hospital, and was at her parents' place.

Allaire imagined that the flamboyant, furiously patriotic Rappaport, protected by a small detachment of Secret Service agents, was with his wife and only child at the moment, watching what had been the president's address, and still unaware of how close he suddenly was to history.

"Sir, I respectfully suggest we get on with this briefing," said Gary Salitas, Allaire's closest friend in Washington.

Allaire perked up. He had been quiet too long, lost

in thought as the weight of evolving events descended upon him.

"Yes, of course, Gary. Thank you. Sean, can you give me an update on the mobile device roundup?"

The Secret Service agent stepped away from his position against the Hard Room wall.

"Agents are collecting them as you ordered, Mr. President. It's a difficult assignment, though, as you can well imagine. Many of those out there aren't used to being told what to do. I doubt the press people are being forthcoming in handing over all the phones they have. We may have to resort to searching them."

Allaire sighed. The most probable scenario, and an alarming one at that, had word already spreading to the outside world via text messages, phone calls, broadcasts from network and cable television operators' mobile units from outside the Capitol, and transmissions via the Internet—all reporting something epic happening at the State of the Union, but nobody knowing exactly what. Speculation would spread quickly to every country in the world, from major cities to any remote village with even the slightest bit of communication technology.

Crisis at the Capitol.

It was likely that CNN's producers had already ordered the graphics.

The best Allaire could hope for would be to slow the spread of information and misinformation until he could work out a strategy as to how it should be presented and disseminated, and how to prevent the reaction that would ensue from any perceived lack of leadership.

He looked over at Salitas for suggestions.

"We need to think bigger, Mr. President," Salitas, a graying MIT grad, said. "We should disrupt all communications—cellular, landline, Internet, TV broadcast, for say, a five-mile radius around the Capitol."

"Can we do that?"

"We can try."

"And still allow me to broadcast to the people?"

"With any luck."

"Do it."

Salitas crossed to the communications center at the far side of the room and began making calls.

"Okay, it's time," Allaire said. "I'm going to brief you all. Soon I'll share this information with the other victims out there."

"Victims?" HHS secretary Kate Broussard asked.

"Yes, Kate. Victims. That's what we are now. All of us." He described the message on the teleprompter. "Assuming the exploding glass containers in those bags and briefcases contained aerosolized WRX3883, we must consider that every single person inside the Capitol tonight has been exposed or will soon be exposed to one degree or another."

"What on earth is WRX3883?" Broussard said.

"It's a biological agent we've been tracking for some time now."

From his position across the room, Salitas's eyes narrowed. He gave what Allaire took to be a look of warning.

"Whose biological agent? Are we talking Al Qaeda?" Admiral Jakes managed to ask between sudden spasms of coughing.

"No. Genesis has taken credit for this one. It's a virus we know about, though. Apparently they stole it."

"Why weren't we made aware of this before? What does it do?"

"I'm sorry, Archie. I chose to keep all information about the virus in house until we knew more of what we had. The microbe was ours. It was initially developed at Columbia University in New York. We took it over and were working on it at a Level Four containment facility in Kansas. About nine months ago, I pulled the plug on the project. Apparently, Genesis found a way to steal some."

"Well, now that it's been released, how real is the threat to public health?" Broussard asked.

Once again, Allaire and Salitas exchanged minuscule glances.

"This is a flu variant," Allaire said. "It . . . um . . . attacks respiratory functions much the same way a flu virus would, only more rapidly."

Broussard, a Ph.D. in immunology, frowned.

"So this is like weapons-grade flu?" she said. "That's impossible."

"It's not a type A flu virus, specifically," Allaire said, assuming Broussard would know that type A influenza was the only one of the three classes of the virus that had ever caused a pandemic.

Vice President Henry Tilden spoke for the first time.

"What can we expect? Symptoms? Spread? Outcome? Is this like SARS?"

Tilden, a former senator from Alabama, had come close to defeating Allaire in the primaries before his first election, and had been appointed as his running mate as a political concession to Southern conservatives. He was respected for his laconic wit and his cool under fire, but like most of the vice presidents before him, had all but disappeared from sight during his first term.

"I don't know, Henry. I intend to contact our experts at the Centers for Disease Control."

Hank Tomlinson, the sturdily built Capitol Police chief, pushed himself to his feet.

"And just how did somebody manage to sneak this virus inside the Capitol and detonate fifteen weapons?" he asked. "There was only one entrance open, and we had our most sophisticated screening equipment in operation. In addition, we did an inspection of every bag or briefcase."

"Well, Hank," Allaire said, "as head of the security unit here, that's something I expect you to figure out."

"Yes, sir," Tomlinson muttered.

He took his seat and kept his eyes fixed on his hands.

"We've got to tackle this like any crisis situation," Allaire said, "and that means first things first. I promise you, we will overcome this challenge. And we'll do it together."

"What do you need us to do, Jim?" Tilden asked.

"While we're in this waiting game for data about the virus, we need to focus our efforts on two fronts: people and communication. The perception that the entire U.S. government is in imminent danger will send the global economy into a tailspin. We need to minimize that as much as possible."

"What do you suggest?"

"Craft a message, Henry. You can use my speech-writers if you need them. Let the world know that we're going to be okay, but until we're absolutely sure there is no immediate public danger of the virus spreading, we're going to err on the side of caution. You can say there was an exposure to a highly contagious pathogen. But our microbiologists are hard at work identifying it, and breaking it down. Let the people know that we're going to be okay, but we need time to complete our thorough assessment."

"Got it," Tilden said, seeming actually buoyed to have been given the responsibility.

Allaire watched as the man furiously wrote down notes.

"Work with Megan on this, Henry. Let me read what you have when you're ready. We'll use Connie Lawson from NBC to break the story. She's got the right demeanor to keep facts ahead of emotions."

Admiral Jakes raised his hand.

"Mr. President, I will mobilize—" He stopped to cough—deep and wet.

"—mobilize the military," Allaire finished for him.

Jakes, in his mid-sixties, looked gray and almost glassy-eyed. Broussard and McAndrew, seated on either side, subconsciously slid their chairs away an inch or two, and glanced over at him with mixtures of apprehension and revulsion. Allaire nodded at Salitas, who ended a phone call and brought the admiral a cup of water.

"I want to divide everybody out there into three

groups. Each group will be relocated to a different room within the Capitol complex to facilitate resource distribution. Admiral, I would like you to be the leader for the C Group. You'll mobilize in the Senate Chamber and set up operations there. Assign the other chiefs to help with each group, and also the Capitol Police."

"Who will be in my group?" Jakes asked.

"Gary and I will personally oversee the group designations. We'll need a little time to complete the list."

Uneasy looks were exchanged. Allaire sensed the team thought his chosen task was unbefitting a president in the midst of a crisis situation. But they could not know that at the moment, the assignment he had given to himself and Salitas was the most important of all.

"What should we do in the interim?" the admiral managed.

He coughed again. A sheen of perspiration had materialized across his forehead.

"Make a list of supplies you think you will need," Allaire went on. "Kate, I'd like you to lead Group B and Henry will take the A Group. A Group can stay in the House Chamber, and we'll move people assigned to Group B into Statuary Hall. Confer among yourselves as to what you think we'll need for a twenty-four to forty-eight-hour stay. Enlist help from the rest of the Cabinet and anyone else you wish. Megan will act as my liaison. I'll leave it up to you to work out bathroom usage, but it's important that we don't mix the groups as we move people around."

"Why is that?" Broussard asked.

"For inventory control, Kate. We'll manage our

supplies by group size and we don't want people thinking they can freely migrate between them."

The Health and Human Services secretary did not
look as if she were buying Allaire's plan any more than
his explanation of what they were up against.

"Yes, Jim," she said through nearly closed lips.

Sean O'Neil was instructed to mobilize the Secret
Service agents to maintain security.

"Report back to me as you make progress. Megan,
please make an announcement that in twenty minutes
I'll address the House Chamber. At that time I'll give an
update on our status and share our plans to take care of
everyone while we're sorting things out."

The White House chief of staff nodded.

"Jordan and Hank, stay here for a few minutes. You,
too, Doc. The rest of you have your assignments. Stay
calm, delegate to others, and remain in control of the
situation. You are the leaders here. I expect you to lead.
Good luck."

With the press of a button, the hydraulics concealing
the Hard Room kicked in and opened the wall.

Gary Salitas remained behind as well, though he had
not been asked. The room emptied out, and the hydrau-
lic doors closed. Those asked to remain took their seats
again.

The president sighed, then inhaled deeply and exhaled
slowly.

"Well, my friends," he began, "I need to start by saying that what I just shared in this room is not exactly the
truth."

CHAPTER 6

Angela Fletcher had ridden only half of her daily ten miles on the stationary bike when the high-def broadcast of the State of the Union Address on her new Sony went dark. Using the remote, she switched channels on her cable box, but got the same black screen on all the networks. Other channels, those not broadcasting the president's address, seemed to be working perfectly. The major networks, however, CNN, MSNBC, Fox News included, were all broadcasting the same thing, which was nothing at all.

From her perch atop the bike, surrounded by a mélange of houseplants, every one of which she could name, Angie turned her set off, then on again, and did the same with the cable box. In that time, the stations managed to display their version of a technical difficulty announcement, letting viewers know they were working on the problem.

Angie hopped off the bike and crossed her airy living

room to the kitchen, where she grabbed a bottle of vitamin-enhanced flavored water from the fridge. At thirty-eight, despite her disciplined vegetarian lifestyle and deep knowledge of herbs and nutrition, she knew her metabolism had begun to slow. The changes in her hips told her so every day, even though it was likely that she was the only one aware of them.

The bike and a set of weights were her way of battling back. Best of all, for someone who struggled to sit through most movies, plays, and concerts, the equipment allowed her to multitask to her heart's content. E-mail and riding. CNN and lifting. Reading and pedaling. Unless she were asleep, at the most five hours a night, she always seemed to be doing something, and something else at the same time. That trait had been a constant source of dismay and even annoyance to her boyfriend, Bill Collins. But *had been* were the operative words now that Collins was a thing of her past.

On her way back into the living room, Angie grabbed her BlackBerry to check e-mail. Nothing about the loss of signal had arrived in her inbox. Just the usual digital mountain of PR pitches from some of the brightest minds in science. They all wanted the same thing—a story in her paper, *The Washington Post,* and more important, for the paper's respected science reporter, Angie Fletcher, to cover whatever latest breakthrough or discovery they felt needed covering.

Angie tried the television again. Nothing new. She had voted for Allaire, as had most of her friends, and like them, she had been looking forward to tonight's speech. She loved that his background was at least as much about medicine and science as it was about politics. In addition, his oratory skills could make a laundry list sound important, so Angie felt more than a little disappointed to be missing any part of the first State of the Union message of his second term.

Figuring that Webcasts might be working, she used her BlackBerry and tried CNN.com and then her own paper's Web site. Both ran virtually identical headlines in bold lettering: *Broadcast Interruption at State of the Union Address*. Utterly curious now, Angie checked, but could not find, any links to a more detailed explanation.

It had been six months or so since she had moved from Georgetown to the refurbished brownstone in the highly desirable Dupont Circle area of D.C. Her neighbor in 2B, the unit directly below her one-bedroom condo, worked at the White House, and Angie considered asking if he had heard anything unusual going on at the Capitol. Instead, she decided to towel off and cab it.

She darted into the kitchen, still clutching her Black-Berry, then suddenly paused to grab a spray bottle from the counter to spritz her herb garden, which seemed nearly ready to harvest, at least the mint anyway. The queen of ADD, Collins had called her, more than once. *So what,* she thought, racing into the bedroom to throw on a pair of slacks and a bulky fisherman's sweater.

She hurried back into the living room and over to Horace, on whom she kept her coat, hat, and gloves. The movers had said nothing about hauling an adult human skeleton, but she did notice them exchanging uneasy glances when they unpacked him.

Over the months she had dated Collins, a lobbyist for the insurance industry, he continually found it odd that she had a skeleton in her living room, and that her cluttered bedroom looked like a college dorm. But she assured him that Horace had everything to do with an innate curiosity for all things biological and not some Goth fetish he needed to fear, and that her bedroom was always impeccably neat—just not when he happened to be there.

Collins's lack of appreciation for Horace should have been a sign right from the start, but he was urbane, witty, and handsome as hell—clearly in the top ten of D.C. eligibles, as her girlfriends had ranked him. That was undoubtedly why she had hung on as long as she did, although ultimately, it was he who had decided they should "see other people." As tired as Angie was of dating, and as anxious as she was to connect with a mate for life, and as aware as she was of the statistics on maternal age and fertility, the breakup was a two-ton weight off of her back.

She slipped her toasty peacoat off of Horace's shoulders and grabbed the red wool cap from the top of his stand. There was something going on at the Capitol complex. She could feel it. Her instinct for news was what made her one of the most sought-after reporters at *The Post*. She understood that any story breaking on Capitol Hill would be covered by the political and national teams, and would probably have nothing to do with her expertise in science and technology. But the thought of missing out on an event unfolding in her own backyard was unacceptable, and the sudden, specific, universal loss of signal from the State of the Union screamed "Event!"

Having decided to spring for a cab, she was searching for her purse underneath the piles of stuff on her kitchen chairs, when her phone rang. She frowned at the name on her caller ID. Before she met Bill, it had been John Davis, chief of staff to one of the more powerful congressmen on the Hill. Davis had pursued Angie with such intensity that it made her at first uninterested and soon, uneasy. He had not called since her last plea just a few months ago that as nice as he was, it simply wasn't going to happen between them—especially since she was dating someone else. She let his call go to voicemail.

Then he called again.

Strange, even for someone as persistent as John, she thought. He had to know she was watching the president's speech. In fact, unless he had been fired, he had to *be* at the president's speech. Perhaps he had lost the signal and did not get put through to voicemail. When he called for a third time, she answered.

"John?"

"Angie! Thank God you're there," Davis said in a coarse whisper. "I didn't know who else to call."

It sounded as though he were afraid somebody might overhear.

"John, what's going on? I'm on my way to the Capitol right now to see why all the broadcasts have gone dead."

She located her purse, grabbed the brush on the chair beside it, and pulled it twice through her shoulder-length hair—reddish brown that day, and most of the time. Then she gathered it back in a ponytail and secured it with a scrunchie, flashing for a pleasurable moment on how annoyed Collins was when she wore it that way.

"I don't think you'll get within five hundred yards of this place," Davis was saying, "but I need your help. I think I may have been exposed to something. We all have."

"We all? What are you talking about?"

"I'm at the Capitol and I'm talking about everybody at the State of the Union Address having been exposed to something biological, a virus, Allaire said."

"Oh my God!" The news sent Angie's heart racing. "Are you all right?"

"For now, maybe. But I've started coughing and I'm really freaking out. We all are."

"Hang on a second."

She pulled on her peacoat and hat, and grabbed one of the ubiquitous spiral-bound notebooks that dotted the landscape of her life.

"You still there?" Davis asked.

"I'm here, I'm here. Now try to calm down and tell me what's going on."

"I don't know. It was some sort of biological weapon or something, we've been told. Allaire said Genesis has something to do with it."

"Damn. John, I can barely hear you. Can you speak up?"

"I can't. I don't want to be spotted. The Secret Service and Capitol Police are confiscating all our cell phones. I'm guessing Allaire doesn't want to start a panic."

"Is that why the broadcast went dark?"

"I didn't know it had."

With her phone tucked beneath her ear, Angie rubbed on some ChapStick, scribbled some notes in a shorthand only she could decipher, and turned the television back on. CNN was reporting only that something had occurred inside the House Chamber and they were working hard to get more information. Someone's grainy, shaky cell phone transmission filled the screen.

Angie heard sirens blaring in the background and watched with widening eyes as the commotion unfolding within the camera's view intensified. She remembered having the same sickening feeling when the first reports of the 9/11 attacks began trickling in. Something truly horrible was taking place now as it did back then.

"Where are you exactly, John?" she asked. "What sort of attack was it? Is anybody hurt? When did it happen?"

"Slow down, Angie. Slow down."

"Are you sure it was Genesis?"

"Angie, I'm afraid I'm going to die. I'm afraid we're all going to die."

Angie's heart beat faster.

"I want to help you, John. Just try and help me help you."

"O . . . okay."

"How did the attack occur? How was the virus delivered? Did you see it?"

Davis coughed. Angie shivered at the sound. *Was that a symptom of the infection?*

"I saw it. There were like misty plumes of smoke coming out of people's bags and briefcases and purses, from some sort of microbomb, it sounded like. Massachusetts Congresswoman Dawn Bloom, two rows in front of me, had one go off right beside her."

Angie stuffed her gloves inside her laptop case, and dropped in the ChapStick, half a dozen pens, and another notebook.

"What's happening now?"

Davis partially stifled another cough.

"The president has ordered everybody back to their original seats. He's blocked the doors with armed guards. Angie, I'm really scared. You know more about bioweapons than anybody I know. What the hell could it be? Oh, shit, I think they've spotted my phone. I'm going to keep talking as long as I can."

"John, I'll do whatever I can to find out and help." Davis coughed again—deep, moist, and racking. "John, are you okay? Talk to me!"

"They're here for my phone. . . . Listen, you bastards! This is America. We have laws. You can't do this!"

The line went dead.

CHAPTER 7

The small group remaining in the Hard Room exchanged surprised looks except for Gary Salitas, whose attention remained fixed on Allaire.

The friendship between the two men dated back nearly twenty-five years, to the meeting of a select presidential commission on drug abuse in the inner city. The meeting, one of a number of such showcases to which Salitas had been invited over the years, was also among the more frustrating, with each of the political and academic lights determined to impress or outdo the others in terms of their rhetoric and posture.

Just when Salitas had been wondering if he could endure the rest of the afternoon, a lean, angular man stood up without asking to be recognized and began to speak. His name plaque read JAMES ALLAIRE, M.D.; CLEVELAND, OHIO, and he was angry. He was angry that people were speaking of Latin American cartels and minimum prison terms, of deposing dictators and passing stiffer new laws; of more presidential select commissions. But not once had anyone mentioned the abject hopelessness of inner-city children. Not once had anyone suggested a connection between drug use and classroom size. Not once had anyone offered the blueprint for a partnership between business, industry, and programs designed to provide every one of those children with a computer.

Allaire spoke for less than five minutes that day, but his eloquence, conviction, and the power of his words were unforgettable. And by the time the physician from Ohio had finished his remarks, gathered his notes, and strode from the room, Gary Salitas had vowed to hitch his wagon to the man's star.

To this day, not once had Salitas regretted that decision.

"I will explain as much as I can in a moment," the president began. "First, though, I want to be certain you know Jordan Lamar." He nodded toward the stocky, baby-faced man several seats to Salitas's right. "Jordan's official title is architect of the Capitol. Jordan, this is my personal physician, Dr. Bethany Townsend, head of the White House Medical Unit."

"We've met," Lamar said, shaking Townsend's hand and making certain that she knew the fifth member of the group, Hank Tomlinson, the chief of the fifteen-hundred-member Capitol Police force.

"Okay, then," Allaire said. "Between the two of them, these men know every detail of the Capitol complex, from the surrounding topology to the nature and location of the facilities, passageways, and points of entry and egress. As of this moment, I am ordering a joint operation, to be conducted between the Capitol Police Board, represented by Jordan and Hank, and the military, coordinated by Secretary Salitas. It will be known as Operation Guardian Eagle, and its goal will be the neutralization of what Genesis has done here tonight."

"And what does that have to do with the military?" Tomlinson asked.

"The remaining Joint Chiefs of Staff will assist us with Guardian Eagle. But they will be strictly on a need to know basis, and my orders will be transmitted to them through Secretary Salitas. As of now, the only people to be made fully aware of Guardian Eagle are seated right here in this room. Is that understood? Good. Gary, I'm authorizing you to deputize any military, National Guard, or other federal law enforcement officials you deem necessary. FBI, NSA, CIA—you have all of our personnel and resources at your disposal."

"Yes, sir," Salitas said.

"I want a secure perimeter established around the entire Capitol complex. Station sharpshooters and flamethrowers facing every exit. Jordan will make sure you don't miss any. Use barricades to establish a secondary perimeter to keep the public back. Use force if need be to accomplish that."

"Understood."

The president turned away momentarily, gathering his composure. When he turned back, his jaw was set, his lips bloodless.

"One more thing," he said. "Anybody who leaves this building, and I mean *anybody,* including every one of us, is to be given one verbal warning and only one to go back inside. Then they are to be shot dead on the spot, and their body immediately incinerated and disposed of as biohazard."

CHAPTER 8

DAY 1
11:10 P.M. (EST)
Shoot to kill.
   Incinerate the bodies.

Allaire understood, as did the others in the Hard Room, that the president of the United States had just used his power as commander in chief to authorize the cold-blooded murder of civilians. Disbelieving stares penetrated his defenses, and for a moment he sensed he might be close to breaking down. He flashed on a photograph of John Kennedy during the Cuban Missile Crisis. From the many accounts he had read, it seemed that the young president handled the defining event of his administration with a steely outward resolve. Judge Prime Minister Nikita Khrushchev correctly and save the planet. Misjudge the man and millions get consumed in a nuclear firestorm.

But this crisis wasn't about missiles. This was about WRX3883. And although President Jim Allaire's decision to quarantine the Capitol had the potential to save millions from a raging pandemic, in all likelihood, he and his family weren't going to be among them.

If only he had quashed the idea at the very beginning. If only he had simply listened to Dr. Sylvia Chen's proposal and sent her away.

Allaire hoped that he looked like a man of strength and assuredness. If he lost control and the crowd in the House Chamber started to surge toward the exits, there was no telling what the virus floating in the air and taking root in their bodies would do in the outside world.

He could not allow that to happen.

He had to select words that would keep the crowd at bay. He had to choose how much information to share, and just how to say it.

But at the same time, he had to trust someone.

Kennedy had his brother Robert, members of the National Security Council, and the Joint Chiefs of Staff. Jim Allaire had the people in this room: the president's physician, an architect, the head of the Capitol Police force, and Gary Salitas, who, along with the president, was the only one who knew the whole truth. Some of Allaire's newly formed inner circle still looked stunned at his order for an instant kill. If they possessed full knowledge of the peril presented by the rogue virus, and they were about to, Allaire had the utmost confidence that each of them would take exactly the same course.

That logic, however, offered only cold comfort.

"Hank, I'm giving the Capitol Police full operational authority over our outer perimeter. This place has got to be sealed and sealed tightly. The virus we're dealing with is highly contagious and infectious. There's no telling what the consequences would be if it got loose."

Tomlinson nodded, as did Jordan Lamar.

"With all due respect, Mr. President," Tomlinson said, "you haven't given us much information on what's really happening here. I'll do whatever is necessary to protect and serve our country, but sir, please, we can't fight what we don't understand."

"Yes, of course, Hank." Allaire again paused to solidify his composure. "What I am about to share with you goes beyond any security clearance for top-secret information. I'm trusting you to keep this confidential. To do otherwise could result in a panic with the potential for an incalculable loss of life. Can I trust you on this? Do I have each of your words?"

The group exchanged looks in a silent poll.

"You have our word, sir," Tomlinson said.

Allaire nodded. For the first time since the previous group was assigned tasks and sent from the Hard Room, the president directly addressed his personal physician, Dr. Bethany Townsend.

"Dr. Townsend, do you recall the Kalvesta files?"

Bethany Townsend, petite, with a pretty smile and weathered face, creased her brow in thought.

"Yes, of course," she said. "That goes back almost two years. You asked me to review the pathologist's report. It was a family of five if I recall. No, six. A husband, wife, and their four children, all of whom expired at some point in their sleep. Carbon monoxide had been quickly ruled out as a possible cause."

"Correct. They lived in a house that we supplied for

them in Kalvesta, Kansas. The husband, Army Lieutenant Colonel Jeremy Jackson, worked at a top-secret Level Four biocontainment facility in Kalvesta. None of the Joint Chiefs of Staff out there is aware of the existence of such a facility. Gary?"

The defense secretary took up the narrative.

"There was limited and tightly controlled operational knowledge of our efforts in Kalvesta. Lieutenant Colonel Jackson's wife believed her husband held a position with the Kansas Department of Wildlife and Parks. In reality, he was part of a team developing a new biological agent for the United States government. Because of the military implications of our work, I was the only Cabinet member fully informed of Kalvesta."

"Go on, Gary."

"If word of this research got out prematurely, we would have had a public relations nightmare on our hands. The biological agent we were developing had that much implication for our national security."

"And just what agent was that?" Townsend asked, her expression suggesting she had just come upon the answer to her own question.

"WRX3883," the president replied.

CHAPTER 9

DAY 1
11:20 P.M. (EST)

Dr. Bethany Townsend's expression was equal parts disbelief and fear.

"Are you implying that what killed the Jackson family is the same biological agent that we've all been exposed to?"

"Unfortunately, that is exactly what I'm saying," Allaire replied. "Both you and the pathologist failed to pinpoint the cause of death because we intentionally kept you unaware of Project Veritas. But we did learn a great deal from your findings about how WRX3883 attacks the body."

"Excuse me, sir, but Veritas?" Townsend asked.

"Veritas for truth. Even Vice President Tilden did not know about it, although I was going to tell him at the time I decided to pull the plug on the project. But by then, after funding was stopped and the whole project was shutting down, there seemed no need to tell anyone."

"A little too late for the Jackson family," Townsend said.

Allaire bowed his head. Salitas, sensing the president needed time to gather his thoughts, spoke up.

"The people at Veritas conducted a close inspection of Jackson's biocontainment suit and found a tiny opening by the wrist, probably from bumping against a syringe or scalpel," Salitas said. "At the time, Dr. Chen's team was working with a new strain of the virus, trying to increase its potency and effectiveness. That pinhole-sized leak in Jackson's suit turned him into a carrier. He went home feeling fine and spent the night with his family. He infected all of them without his knowing he was a walking hot zone."

"Jesus," Hank Tomlinson murmured.

"The Veritas team immediately destroyed the viral line and resumed work on an earlier strain. They augmented it and controlled how fast it acted when administered. But they never perfected it. Then the president shut down the program."

"What happened to the Jacksons?" Tomlinson asked.

Allaire looked at Salitas through reddening eyes. The defense secretary walked to the water cooler and returned with water for both of them. Allaire drank his cup dry in a single swallow, then was able to continue.

"They were tightly quarantined, and treated as best our doctor knew how with massive doses of IV antiviral drugs. But nothing worked. They died in just a few days."

"My God. And that virus is what we have been exposed to?"

"That or a variant, yes. We were all devastated by what happened to the Jackson family, but we had to weigh that tragedy against the possibility of ending the war on terror."

"Ending the war on terror? Mr. President, just what does this virus do?" the police chief asked.

"The target organs of the germ are a group of structures in the midbrain including the hypothalamus, the anterior cingulate cortex, the amygdala, and the limbic system. These structures in the gray matter of the brain influence many functions, but taken as a whole they control the will—the ability to make voluntary decisions, the uniquely human ability to lie. When the microbe was first brought to my attention by Dr. Chen, a professor at Columbia, her animal studies had shown that cats infected with the virus would swim without resisting. Hard-core carnivores could be trained to eat a mix of vegetables and vitamins. Mortal enemies could quickly be taught to live in the same cage."

"So? Since when did we get into the development of biological weapons?"

"Since terrorists flew airplanes into the World Trade Center buildings," Gary Salitas said, returning to the table. "That's when. And I wouldn't call WRX a weapon. This country is pockmarked with cells of enemy combatants who don't feel much like sharing their plans with us."

"And you're suggesting this virus will make them?"

"That was the idea," Allaire said. "With the liberal press holding a constant magnifier on our techniques of interrogation, we have a very limited toolkit when it comes to extracting information from these . . . individuals. We were developing and testing the virus in hopes of making them share what they knew without resorting to more stringent measures, or having to move ahead based on their version of the truth. And for a time it looked as if Veritas was going to be a success."

"But even with the new strain, there were still side effects," Salitas added.

"What sort of side effects are we talking about here, Mr. President?" Bethany Townsend asked, her tone cool.

"I had been assured by Dr. Chen that the results from the new variant strain were most encouraging," Allaire said. "But as I read through her reports it became increasingly clear that the germ still had some serious problems. It was unstable in terms of mutation, and there had been no progress made in controlling how it spread from host to host. In fact, the data suggested that the highly contagious nature of the virus had gotten worse."

"So that's when you shut down the program?" Tomlinson asked.

"In retrospect, I wish that were the case, Hank. Even with the setbacks, we still believed we had a silver bullet with WRX3883. I kept Vertias operational. Until the theft."

"Theft?"

"Yes. Nine months ago, a presumed terrorist, working in the lab, stole five canisters of the virus. At least that's how many we recovered from a compartment in the wall of his basement when we arrested him. Shortly after that I finally ordered the project shut down."

"Did we have test animals at this Veritas lab?" Townsend asked.

"Yes. Mostly primates. Those were the research animals of choice for Dr. Chen. But she brought another virologist to Kansas with her—a scientist who was staunchly against animal testing and experimentation. His approach involved the use of advanced computer models of the virus and various treatments. He claimed his methods were capable of simulating, with near ninety-nine percent accuracy, the nature of the virus's mutation patterns, as well as the effect of different antiviral drugs."

"Ninety-nine percent sounds a bit optimistic," Townsend said. "Especially given that his methods didn't seem to work any better than Chen's. So, what are we all in for here?"

"I'll debrief you all about our exposure and what we can expect in a moment," Allaire said. "But I can tell you that as far as contagion goes, the penetration statistics are daunting. Bethany, I know you're angry. But I really need you. If you can, I'm putting you in charge of organizing our containment strategy. Veritas was headquartered in an underground facility. The lab had Level-Four containment, and aside from the insider theft I told you about, there were never any incidents. Gary will get you the contact information for the former director. Meanwhile, get in touch with the CDC and anyone else you need and have them help you. Try to maintain some control over who you tell what to. We're going to need a whole bunch of containment suits and a safe way of getting food, medication, and personnel in here."

For half a minute, Townsend simply sat there. Then, with painful slowness, she stood and crossed to the communications center.

"As you wish, sir," she said.

"As for the rest of you," Allaire went on, "I need you to be patient. Be as calm as possible. I've trusted you with this information because I think you can handle it, and because I need your help. We can't risk starting a mass panic. Our hope now is that we develop a way to neutralize the virus and contain it inside the Capitol. All our energy and focus must be directed toward those efforts. And most importantly, I need you to support me and my decisions one hundred percent." Allaire turned to architect Jordan Lamar. "All hell is about to break loose, Jordan. This building is going to be our home for a while. I'm counting on you to make it as comfortable for everyone as possible. Even though it's the middle of winter, I'm worried that with seven hundred of us, the rooms are going to warm up fast from body heat, so we might need to boost the air-conditioning levels."

"Yes, Mr. President."

"Gary, I need you to help me make two calls."

"Yes, Mr. President."

"First get me Paul Rappaport in Minnesota."

"No problem. And the other?"

"I need the warden at the supermaximum federal penitentiary in Florence, Colorado."

CHAPTER 10

The guard's riot stick, slamming against his cell door, intruded into Griffin Rhodes's nightmare, but failed to drive it completely away.

The recurring dream was especially vivid this time, intense sounds and colors . . . and pain, like daggers thrusting through his eyes.

The dreadful ache was in his abdomen, too—a powerful cramping as if his intestines were strangulating. Griff felt his bowels let go, and knew the gush beneath him was blood.

Marburg virus! I . . . have . . . Marburg virus. Let me die! Please just let me die.

He tried to cry out the words, but there was no sound—only the terrible cramping.

Griff pounded impotently on the wall by his head.

"Dr. Rhodes. . . . Can you hear me? . . . Dr. Rhodes?"

The voice in the dream was a woman's—a Kenyan

physician named Marielle—Dr. Marielle. She had been incredibly kind to him.

How long had it been? How many days? How many weeks?

More of the slamming against the steel cell door. It was one of the guards' favorite ways of tormenting him.

He was standing in front of his bathroom mirror now, supporting himself on the edge of his rusted sink, staring at the expanding bruises on his face and at his eyes. It was Marburg. His horribly bloodred sclerae told him so. He had feared becoming infected from the day his fascination with deadly viruses began. Now, it was happening. Marburg—most likely the Ebola variant. Hemorrhagic fever. Sweats. Unimaginable muscle aches. Blood spewing from the nose and GI tract. Blood in the tendons and the skin. Blood on the brain.

Eighty percent death rate.

Blood.

For years he had been fearing this encounter, waiting for this attack, or something like it. For years he had anticipated the moment when his precautions would not be enough, when living on the edge would prove disastrous—when he would go from being the hunter to being the victim.

Finally, because of a stupid miscalculation outside of a jungle cave not far from Kisimu on the eastern rim of Lake Victoria, he was going to die, and die viciously. The best he could hope for before he was gone was to have the cave sealed, and to have Level 4 precautions instituted at all the surrounding hospitals . . . provided he survived long enough to do so.

The devastating cramps intensified. Now he was on his hands and knees in a field. Blood was pouring in two steady streams from his nostrils, falling to the parched ground in thick, angry drops. In the distance he could see the outline of his lab, a sprawling, cinder-block monolith, cutting a broad, rectangular chunk from the azure African sky.

Overhead, airplane-sized vultures circled. One of them glided to the ground, landing awkwardly and waddling across toward him, intent on pecking at his flesh.

Not yet, dammit! Not yet!

Once again, his eyes began to throb. Griff had always wondered what Ebola infection would feel like. Now he knew. His imagination had hardly done the virus justice. Praying for death was about the best he could do.

"Dr. Rhodes . . . Dr. Rhodes, can you hear me? . . . It is Dr. Marielle. . . . I swear he opened his eyes. . . . Did you see that? . . ."

The clanging on his steel door resumed, echoing through the cinder-block hell of his solitary confinement cell.

Which was worse, the nightmare or his reality?

The vulture was joined by another, then another— huge black shadows with fiery eyes, drifting down to gnaw on him. Each bite brought pain—pain and more blood. Griff thrashed on his cot and tried to bat them away.

Help! . . . Help me!

The vultures were unrelenting now, tearing away huge chunks of his flesh, challenging him to wake up.

Facedown on the blood-soaked ground, Griff continued flailing at the mammoth birds.

The sudden clang of his cell door finally caused the nightmare to loosen its grip. Reluctantly, the lurid images receded.

"Rhodes . . . Rhodes . . . Hey, asshole, wake up! . . ."

Donald Spinelli, the huge, heavy-lidded guard, stood across the room, by the naked toilet bowl, impatiently smacking his riot stick against his own thigh.

Griff rubbed his eyes, turned away from the unadorned cinder-block wall, and peered briefly across at the man. Then he rolled back onto his side, again facing the wall, utterly drained. The nightmares arising from his battle against Ebola weren't an every night thing, but even after a decade, they still occurred frequently enough, and as vivid and inexorable as ever.

The guard moved to the side of Griff's institutional cot and slapped him with force on the bare sole of his foot.

Unwilling to give the brute the satisfaction of hearing him cry out, Griff clenched his teeth against the stinging and gripped his heavy beard. He had practice dealing with pain. It would take more than a smack on the foot to get a reaction from him. Much more. Over the nearly nine months he had been in solitary confinement, all of the prison guards had been abusive to one extent or another. But Spinelli had been the worst. If physically possible, there was no way he would give the sadist any satisfaction. Still, it wasn't worth provoking him.

"What do you want, Spinelli?"

"Put on your Sunday best, Rhodes. You're leaving."

"What?"

"Just what I said. You're out of here."

"Nine months in this cell with an hour a day walking in the yard alone, and all of a sudden, just like that, I'm out of here? This your idea of funny?"

"I wish. It's real. Straight from the warden."

"What's going on?"

"I got no idea. When you get out there—" he motioned to the small barred window overlooking the exercise yard, "why don't you ask the guys in that chopper?"

CHAPTER 11

DAY 2
1:20 A.M. (EST)

Senator Harlan Mackey had seen enough. Fear and chaos were erupting around him like Mount Vesuvius. People rushing for the exits were being forcibly turned back. And exactly where was America's leader now? Gone. Vanished into a back room with his disgracefully inept Cabinet, looking like the reincarnation of Boss Tweed.

The Kentucky senator and majority whip would not tolerate Allaire's gross mishandling of this situation one second longer. Mackey's well-known motto—*No way, no how!*—applied to this crisis the same as it did to any legislation he worked to defeat. And how dare Allaire violate the sanctity of the House Chamber—firing off a gun as though he were Wyatt Earp taking over some lawless Western town. People were ill, and from what Mackey could tell, they were only getting sicker. They did not need Jim Allaire. They needed medical care.

At least Mackey could feel grateful that his son's math teacher had refused to reschedule an exam. Because of the man's inflexibility, Jack and his mother had passed up their pilgrimage to D.C. for the State of the Union Address. Lucky them.

Many people had begun grudgingly to return to their seats, although a number of others were still milling around the aisles and shoving toward the doorways, demanding with escalating vehemence to be let out. Mackey wondered how long it would be before somebody got hurt—really hurt—by one of Allaire's Capitol Police goons.

And what, exactly, *had* they been exposed to? Was Genesis really responsible? Did they really pose a threat worthy of Allaire holding the Congress and so many others hostage? If so, why didn't they just quarantine the coughing people and let everybody else go? The closest puff of smoke was many rows away from where he was sitting, and Mackey had yet to feel any symptom at all. God knew at least a third of the chamber had that hacking cough now. If Mackey were in charge, that's exactly what he would have done. Keep the sick away from the healthy.

Goddamn Allaire.

Did the man think they were all stupid? Of course he did. Allaire's arrogance defied all boundaries. Well, if he thought Harlan Mackey would be a good little soldier and sit tight inside a potential death trap, then he grossly underestimated this senator's resolve.

People continued to mill around Mackey, who decided then and there that he would escape this nightmare.

"Senator Mackey! Senator Mackey!"

People continuing to converge into the center aisle, yelling at the security guards, coughing, and crying, made it hard for Mackey to spot Frost Keaton, a junior staff assistant from his office, waving his arms and calling his name. Poor Frost. For his exemplary job performance, Mackey had awarded Keaton Jack's much sought-after SOU ticket. Keaton pushed his way through the crowd and, typically, seemed more concerned for his boss than he did for himself. Dumb kid.

"What's going on, Senator?" Keaton asked. "Is it true that Genesis is behind this?"

"I don't know, son. Like you, I'm waiting for the president to return. I'm sure we'll all know something soon enough."

"Well, I had some new ideas for our highway bill. I guess I'll just work on those while we're waiting."

Mackey felt a brief pang for the twenty-two-year-old American University grad and his endless supply of optimistic energy.

"Are you worried?" Keaton said.

"Me? No. Son, it takes a lot more than all this to worry this old farmer."

Mackey flashed on the idea of taking Keaton with him. But just then, the boy coughed.

Are there more people coughing now? the senator wondered. If so, he would have to move even faster.

"Look, son, you stay here. I'm going to see if I can learn what's going on. I'll let you know what I find out. For now, just sit tight and wait for me to come back."

The young aide stifled another cough.

"Thank you, sir," he managed.

Mackey served as one of ten on the Capitol Complex Appropriations Board. The committee handled everything from human resources for the Capitol's extensive operational staff to routine maintenance issues. Few knew all the secrets of the Capitol complex. Thanks to that committee, Mackey knew nearly every one of them. Every way in, and most important, every way out. At least now those insipid hours spent haggling on that wart of a committee might prove to be worthwhile.

The speaker of the house, Ursula Ellis, had left her seat and was making her way around their party's half of the hall. She was an incredibly capable woman, and given another month or so, she just might have won. Now, hopefully, she was mobilizing people to take a stand against Allaire, regardless of what position he took.

Nobody was standing near the podium, and the crush of people was moving in the opposite direction. *Perfect.*

Mackey walked past the rostrum to a spot in the corridor twenty feet beyond. The trapdoor beneath the carpeting was nearly invisible. It had been constructed to reach a maintenance area on the next level down, which housed the workings of the lift that provided wheelchair access to the tribune.

Nobody noticed as the senator quickly descended the stairs and closed the door behind him. The darkness surrounding him was nearly total. He found the wall switch and located a dank, seven-foot-high tunnel, dimly lit by a series of unadorned, wall-mounted fixtures, running in an east-west direction from the base of the lift. Mackey followed it to where he knew it would split into two passageways.

The longer of the two tunnels, tiled, better lit, and cleaner, would, after some distance, connect with a flight of stairs to a hallway linking the Rayburn House Building to the Capitol. A solid, wooden door opened only from that side. Mackey suspected that the Rayburn tunnel would be guarded at its entrance, as many in Congress used it to bypass the security lines in the visitors' center. Instead, his plan took him into the darker tunnel, on the left.

Moving slowly, after five minutes, he came to the door of an unmarked exit, which he knew was only a hundred yards or so from the Capitol's First Street entrance. The architect of the Capitol, Jordan Lamar, had at one point requested funds to upgrade the tunnel and the door, but Mackey's committee had tabled the petition and never gotten back to it.

Cautiously, the senior senator from Kentucky pushed the door open. The night was cloudless. The air was cold, but manageable, even without an overcoat. He would hurry up Delaware for a block or two and take a cab to his condo in Georgetown. There he would pour a tumbler of Jim Beam and watch Allaire embarrass himself in high-definition.

He allowed the door to ease closed. The hardware echoed in the still air as it locked. He hesitated, then took two tentative steps across the shadowed alcove. Nothing.

Had he turned and looked upward at the window one floor above, running along the Rayburn hallway, he would have seen a shadow silhouetted against the darkness. But his concentration was fixed ahead.

Another two steps.

Still good.

Suddenly, from somewhere across Constitution Avenue, a powerful spotlight hit him squarely in the face.

"Turn back and reenter the Capitol at once," an amplified voice called out. "We will not ask a second time."

Squinting against the intense glare, Mackey reached behind him. But he knew the heavy door was locked. He turned back and took a single step toward the light, his hands raised to shield his eyes.

"Wait," he cried out. "Wait. It's me, Senator Harlan Mackay, from Ken—"

At that instant, he was punched in the center of his forehead—or at least that was what it felt like for a split second. During the rest of the second, the punch became a searing pain. From somewhere out in the night he heard the crack of a gunshot. At nearly the same instant, he flew backward, his head snapping into the metal door. He was neurologically dead by the time his knees buckled, although his heart was still beating as he slumped to the frigid pavement.

By the time an approaching team of three soldiers stopped thirty yards away, Senator Harlan Mackey was dead by virtually every criterion.

One of the soldiers aimed the nozzle of his M2A1-7 portable flamethrower.

"I know we're not supposed to question orders," he said to the sharpshooter next to him, "but I sure hope

those guys have a damn good reason for what they're
doing."

Without waiting for a response, he adjusted his gog-
gles and hit the trigger. A prolonged, brilliant spear of
burning napalm sliced through the night into the inert
body of the man they had just killed. The corpse's clothes
vanished immediately, and the skin beneath them boiled
and bubbled, and then charred. The stench of burning
flesh mixed with the powerful odor of the napalm. For
five seconds, ten, fifteen, the stream of incendiary remained fixed on the blackening body.

The corpse of their victim was now ash. Wearing a
gas mask, the third soldier approached the smoldering
mound and waited for it to cool enough. Then, using a
tapered shovel and a metal broom, he swept up the senator's remains and dropped them into a biocontainment
canister. Another team would arrive shortly to complete
the disposal.

Without looking back, the three men retreated and
resumed their positions. In less than three minutes, the
containment vehicle had come and gone, and all was as
it had been.

Ursula Ellis's aide, Leland Gladstone, was no longer
able to hold back the bile. He whirled to one side,
dropped to his hands and knees, and vomited onto the
cement floor. He was a suburban prep-schooler with a
degree from Yale, and had never even seen a dead
person, let alone watched one be murdered in such a
gruesome manner.

Ursula had known something big was about to happen. She had noticed Harlan Mackey vanish behind the speaker's podium.

"Do you still have your BlackBerry, dear Leland? Or did Allaire's robots take it from you?" Ellis had asked.

"I still have it."

Gladstone patted his back, where he had concealed the device underneath his white dress shirt and secured it in place using his belt.

"Can it record video?"

"It can. Better than most camcorders too."

"Follow Mackey. See where he goes. I don't know what Allaire meant by extreme measures, and O'Neil didn't come back with anything useful. All O'Neil told me is that Russians or Chinese may be behind the attack, and that they're preparing us for an extended stay. Supposedly whatever we've been exposed to is some type of flu virus. Not that lethal, but presumably very contagious."

"That sounds like useful information," Gladstone had said.

"Perhaps. But O'Neil wasn't the last to leave the debrief and my instincts tell me there's more Allaire's hiding than he's sharing."

Gladstone, who knew the myriad tunnels of the Capitol nearly as well as did Ellis, chose to follow the passageway one story above the one Mackey had taken. There was only one place the senator could be going. Camera poised, Gladstone knelt by the sill of the window and watched the heavy metal door swing open beneath him. The well-known, distinguished man's death, incineration, and removal had happened so quickly, and with such organization, that the events had barely registered in Gladstone's mind while he was recording them.

Now, the aide stumbled back from the mess he had made and used the wall to push himself upward. The military had murdered Harlan Mackey, almost certainly on orders from the president.

Gladstone wondered if Ellis had known her colleague and loyal campaign supporter was in peril. *Did she sacrifice him to satisfy her own curiosity about Allaire's true intentions?* he wondered. Regardless, Gladstone's video was all the motivation he'd ever need to maintain his devoted support of Ellis. And the speaker of the house would certainly know what to do with this new information . . . and the video.

CHAPTER 12

"Move it, Rhodes!"

As Griff stepped onto the packed dirt of the Florence federal prison exercise yard, guard Donald Spinelli forced him forward using the butt of his nightstick and a single, well-placed jab against his lower spine. Griff stumbled, but fierce winds from the whirling blades helped to keep him from going down. Dust shooting into his eyes stung like sandpaper.

In the months since Griff had last worn his favorite pair of blue jeans, they had gone from comfortably snug to barely staying over his hips. The rotor-driven winds plastered his plaid flannel cowboy shirt against his once wiry, now near-skeletal frame.

The twin-engine helicopter lifted off the yard, touched down again momentarily. It was clear to Griff the pilot was in a rush and not about to stop the rotors. During his virus-hunting days, he had chartered helicopters from time to time back in Africa, but those were ragged machines, better equipped for falling than flying. This aircraft, though, reminded him of images he had seen of Marine One, with its dark green body and white top, American flags emblazoned on the engine casings.

UNITED STATES MARINE CORPS was painted in white on the chopper's tail. Griff's gut had knotted as soon as he realized his removal from the so-called Alcatraz of the Rockies might be a military action. It had been just over nine months since he had last been the focus of another military operation—his final moments of freedom until now.

So many changes.

His beard, a tangled mess of black streaked with gray, immediately collected a fine coating of prison yard dust. He wondered if, in addition to his dark memories of nine months in solitary confinement, that dirt would be all he would ever take away from Florence. It had to be. No matter what lay ahead, he wasn't going back. Nine months chopped out of a life that had been built around doing the right thing and accepting the consequences for his decisions, such as the Ebola infection. Nine months during which there had been no human contact other than with guards bent on causing him pain. Nine months of confusion about why he had been imprisoned, or what future, if any, he had in store. Nine months during which the only clue he had in that regard was the label *Terrorist.*

Griff had barely stepped inside the helicopter bay door when he felt the aircraft begin to lift. A soldier, dressed in well-pressed military camouflage, handed him a jet-black flight helmet, then guided him into an unpadded seat. Griff strapped himself in and took one last look out the helicopter's oval window at Florence, shuddering at the gun towers and concrete block, framed with barbwire, now fast fading from view. He wondered if anyone watching from inside except for the warden and a few guards even knew his name.

Terrorist.

The built-in radio inside his helmet allowed Griff to hear the soldier seated across from him over the engine's roar.

"Dr. Griffin Rhodes, my name is Captain Timothy Lewis, with the United States Marine Corps. By order of the president of the United States of America, it is my honor to welcome you aboard this VH-60N aircraft."

"Tell the president that nothing he does is going to get me to change my vote."

The marine smiled. "I think you'll get the chance to do that yourself, sir."

"Actually, now that I think about it, I never got the chance to vote at all. In fact, I don't even know who won the election."

"I'm sorry, sir. It was President Allaire. He won again, by quite a wide margin, too."

Allaire.

Griff stared out at the blackness. Of all the theater of the absurd scenarios he had lived through, this military removal from solitary confinement in a supermax federal prison had to be the most bizarre. But now, learning he was up here at the behest of the president topped them all.

"Thanks for the info," he said. "Any idea why he's sent for me?"

"Sir, the president will be radioing in at oh two hundred hours eastern standard time. My orders are to transport you to Tinker Air Force Base in Oklahoma. From there a plane will take you to Washington, D.C."

"Washington? What for?"

"Sir, that's for the president to explain. For now, just relax and enjoy the flight. There are snacks on board if you'd like some."

"Fresh fruit?"

"Yes, sir."

"Hostess cupcakes?"

"It's possible."

"I'll take both plus some bottled water."

"Done."

The soldier handed Griff a bottle of Dasani from a cooler.

"And a Butterfinger or Heath bar if you have them," Griff added. "Make that two of each."

Surprisingly, the captain filled the order right down to the cupcakes.

"Enjoy the trip, sir," he said, setting a cardboard tray on Griff's lap.

Enjoy the trip.

Those were the exact words another soldier had said nine months ago, right after he had kicked Griff viciously in the ribs and then manacled him with a heavy pair of chained cuffs.

Enjoy the trip.

It had been a quiet Sunday night in Kalvesta, Kansas,

when the front door to Griff's house shattered open. As usual, he was at his computer, poring over data. In fact, except for the rare occasions when he was playing bridge or chess online, he was always poring over data. His research centered about experiments in modifying viral mRNA—messenger RNA. The thrust of his work was getting a particular virus to incorporate a foreign sequence of nucleotides when it replicated. The result would be germs incapable of further reproduction.

The data, based on a model he had begun developing years before in Africa, had recently started showing some serious promise. Best of all, every bit of his work was done using CGI—computer-generated imagery and advanced data processing. No live subjects. That had been Griff's long-standing pledge to himself. No animals. Slowly, steadily, he was closing in on a potentially revolutionary antiviral treatment. He could feel it.

Simultaneous with the disintegration of his front door, the power was cut to the house. In total darkness, Griff could hear, but not see, his windows shattering. Suddenly flashlight beams cut swaths in all directions as soldiers, military police, and members of SWAT, all wearing gas masks, swarmed inside like ants on a sugar mound. Guns were drawn. There was so much shouting that Griff could make out little of what was being said. That is until the soldiers came at him.

"Get down! Get the fuck down! Facedown, now!"

They pointed their weapons at him. Three soldiers forced him onto his belly. A boot, pressed firmly against the back of his neck, driving his face against the oak *floor. That was when he received the first of many kicks—this one to his side. His organs seemed to loosen as the air rushed out of his lungs.*

"Where is it?" one of the attackers demanded.

"Where is what?" Griff managed.

Another kick. This one harder. The toe of a boot plunged between his ribs. Pain exploded throughout his body and he gagged for air.

"Tear the place apart!"

The lights came back on. Two men forced Griff to stay facedown. All around him he heard the sounds of destruction—glass breaking, fabric ripping, objects crashing. Every so often a soldier would roughly pull his head up by his hair and demand to know where "it" was.

"I don't know what you're talking about!"

That was when they would kick him again. Always in the same spot, maximizing the pain.

Interminable time went by before a woman called out from his small, partially finished basement.

"I've found it! Captain, I've found it!"

Griff heard footsteps racing up his basement stairs. Hands grabbed at him and yanked him up by his shirt. He saw a petite brunette soldier holding a green cylindrical metal canister bearing several biohazard decals on it.

Impossible!

Griff knew the canister well. WRX3883. It had come from the Level 4 containment zone of the lab where he was working—the most secure containment area in their system. He studied it for a moment, unwilling to believe that it had just been retrieved from the basement of his house. If the canister held the virus from Level 4, still growing inside its tissue culture, then it also held death—horrible, slow, inexorable death.

"How many did you find, soldier?" the ranking officer barked.

"Five canisters total, sir," she replied. "They were in a cubby, hidden behind the basement wall paneling."

"Secure him," the captain ordered.

Two soldiers standing behind Griff pulled him upright and pinned his arms to his back. The officer in charge then stepped forward and punched Griff hard in the stomach, not once, but twice. The room began to spin. The soldiers holding his arms in place now had to prop Griff up as well. In addition, they kept shouting at him, demanding to know if they had all the canisters.

"Were there more than five?" he heard them say.

"Sylvia Chen . . . my boss . . . speak to her. . . . I didn't take those canisters. . . . Find Sylvia . . . she'll vouch for me. I'm just a researcher, I—"

Another fierce punch to the gut cut off his words. He dropped to his knees and retched. Soldiers surrounded him and dragged him outside into a crisp, star-drenched Kansas night. Again, they rudely pulled his arms behind his back. He cried out in pain. Handcuffs closed tightly around his wrists, cutting into his skin.

"Too tight," Griff said.

"Too bad," a soldier responded.

They pushed him into a camouflage-painted Hummer. Soldiers were seated on either side of him.

"Where are you taking me?" Griff asked.

"To prison," the soldier answered. "Enjoy the trip."

Nine months with no answers, no explanations. Nine months of isolation and filth and abuse. Nine months of self-regulated push-ups on a concrete floor and yoga positions in the grimy corner. Now, suddenly, an open cell door, a final series of blows from one of the guards, and a helicopter flight at the invitation of the president of the United States. He might have felt exultant. He probably should have.

But he didn't.

Instead, Griffin Rhodes had a sinking feeling that he might have just replaced one layer of hell for another.

"Sir, I have President Allaire on the sat phone," Captain Lewis said. "He's ready to speak with you."

The marine passed over a bulky, stainless steel case with a satellite phone inside. Griff had to take off his helmet to speak. The constant churn from the rotors made it hard to hear, but not impossible.

"Dr. Griffin Rhodes? This is President Jim Allaire," the voice, distinguishable despite the background noise, said.

"Mr. President."

Griff knew all about Allaire's involvement with Project Veritas. But only Sylvia Chen and a few higher-ups had any direct contact with the man. Griff suspected he might now come to regret having joined the ranks of those accorded the honor.

"Dr. Rhodes, there has been a massive exposure to WRX3883," Allaire said.

Griff's jaw tightened. Captain Lewis apparently felt

the tension and turned away to look out the window. Bad news could wait, Griff imagined him thinking.

"Where? How bad?"

"We have reason to believe Genesis is behind the attack."

"Who?"

The president paused.

"You don't know about Genesis?"

"Well, I haven't exactly been given a wealth of reading material for the last nine months."

"Understood. I can explain that later."

"Where was the exposure?"

"It occurred during my State of the Union Address."

"Pardon?"

"Yes. You heard correctly. In the chamber of the House of Representatives. Fifteen separate exposures around the hall."

"How was the virus released?"

"Exploding glass cylinders. Widespread. Somehow, the containers were inserted into purses and briefcases, and then detonated, probably by radio signal."

"Have you locked down the building?"

"Yes."

"Tightly?"

"No one in, no one out. The chamber has been sealed and the building as well. Plus there's an absolute perimeter set up fifty yards outside the Capitol. One man—a senator from Kentucky—tried to sneak out of a little-used exit. He was taken out by a sharpshooter, and his body incinerated."

Griff breathed a deep sigh. *At least they had done that.*

"Sir, were you directly exposed?"

"It's been five hours. We've all been exposed—or will be."

"You authorized Veritas. You know about the progressive mental deterioration?"

"I know. That's one of the reasons why I ultimately suspended the research and closed down the lab."

"When?"

"About eight or nine months ago."

Griff felt himself sink. He had warned Sylvia Chen that the project was too dangerous, the virus too unstable in terms of mutation. He had warned all of them.

"You know we don't have any treatment," he said.

"That's why I'm bringing you to Washington, Dr. Rhodes. I need you to come up with one."

Griff respected Allaire's acumen for biology and physiology. According to Sylvia Chen, the president had not only read Griff's lengthy scientific reports, he understood them as well. The president must have been aware of his slow progress toward an antimicrobial treatment for WRX3883, which meant he also knew he was asking the impossible.

"Mr. President, before we go any farther, there is something I need to know."

"Go ahead."

"Were you the one who authorized my arrest?"

There was a prolonged pause.

"We had evidence," the president said, "irrefutable security film of you stealing canisters of the virus on which you were working. Under the provisions of the Patriot Act, you were a terrorist. What would you have done?"

"I am no terrorist and I stole nothing. Now tell me, did you authorize my arrest?"

"Will my answer affect your decision about helping us?"

I can't help you because there is nothing I can do before you and the others are dead.

"Regardless of what you say, I will do what I can. But I want the truth."

"The truth is, yes. Yes, I did authorize your arrest, and I would do it again."

"And the solitary confinement?"

"I was convinced you had turned. I believed you were a terrorist and a severe threat to the United States of America. I did what I thought was in the best interests of our country. Our plan was to isolate you, and then eventually—"

"To torture me."

"There were those close to me who wanted to do it immediately," the president said.

CHAPTER 13

DAY 2
3:00 A.M. (EST)

Allaire had done all he could. Despite his obvious contempt for Rhodes, the man was now en route to Washington. The first of two planned portable airlocks with connecting tunnels was in place. Boxes of supplies were now being sent into the Capitol along a bed of metal rollers. At last report, the second tunnel was nearing completion.

The military continued to request expanded access to the Capitol, but Allaire was keeping them at bay. Until Griffin Rhodes had a chance to evaluate the situation and provide a preliminary assessment, the Capitol would remain off-limits to anyone who wasn't absolutely essential.

Using House Chamber surveillance video, Allaire and Salitas sorted out the group assignments faster than either thought possible. They used the location of the fifteen aerosol blasts to define the breakdown. Group B, those with moderate exposure, numbered just above three hundred. Group A, lowest exposure, were allowed to remain in the House Chamber. There were sixty people whom Allaire marked as having the heaviest exposure. Those individuals were assigned to Admiral Jakes's C Group.

They would be the first to die.

Gratefully, Rebecca and Samantha were As.

Sylvia Chen's reports detailing how WRX3883 spread from host to prospective host gave Allaire the idea to establish the quarantine groups. Chen had presented compelling evidence that extended exposure to carriers with later-stage infection increased the amount of virus passed to a new host. Allaire had good reason to believe those with heavy exposure to WRX3883 would speed up the progression of symptoms in people with less virus in their system.

The president understood that he was largely responsible for this disaster. He should have pulled the plug on Veritas sooner. Perhaps he should have taken more people into his confidence before authorizing the program in the first place. He always felt his job was about being true to himself and standing up for what he believed in.

But this time, he had been wrong. His closest friend and advisor, Gary Salitas, had been wrong. And worst of all, given his background as a physician, the scientists he had decided to believe in had been wrong. They had convinced him that the power of WRX3883 could be harnessed—that the adverse effects of the virus could be eliminated. Now, by having supported their view, he had, in all likelihood, signed his own death warrant, as well as those of his wife and daughter, and many, many others.

The report of crusty Harlan Mackey's grisly demise had been a terrible jolt. Now, death from the virus had a face—probably the first of many.

At the president's request, Gary Salitas, Jordan Lamar, and Dr. Bethany Townsend remained in the Hard Room. Allaire strained to get his mind around the enormity of what lay beyond the door. This wasn't the time for remorse and self-pity. Now, more than ever, he had to connect with what it meant to be presidential, knowing his actions might be among the last of his administration.

The others watched and waited.

"How much are you going to tell them?" the defense secretary asked finally.

"I don't know. I'd like to hold back on talking about Mackey."

"Agree. So long as no one starts making a big deal about where he is. And even then I think we can just speculate. What about the virus?"

The president shrugged. "Bit by bit might be best," he said.

Townsend looked at the two friends curiously, but said nothing. She had been the Allaires' physician since the man was first nominated, and was widely respected for her candor with the media, and her loyalty to the first family. She had grown comfortable issuing warnings about rising cholesterol levels in the most powerful man on earth, but in this situation, she felt helpless. She was a Group A, but how long before the horrific symptoms that claimed the Jackson family materialized inside her? She could not access the Kalvesta, Kansas, files from within the Capitol, but she could recall specifics from the case in gruesome detail.

Townsend's vision blurred as a bolt of pain hit just above the bridge of her nose. Another migraine. They occurred infrequently, usually under tense situations, but nobody really knew about them. Or could it be the virus, attacking her body in unexpected ways? From now on, every twinge, every cough or pain would be seen as a possible harbinger of debilitation and death.

Townsend had decided to resign her position as first doctor following Allaire's initial debriefing. The revulsion she felt over biological warfare of any kind cast doubt over her ability to support the president as his physician, his friend, or even, for that matter, as a fellow citizen.

Then, as he spoke to her, one to one, and requested she remain with him in the Hard Room—he knew her well and sensed her revulsion at his decision to develop WRX3883, and he needed her scientific brilliance and insight, as well as her deep compassion—her anger began to lessen. She had often tried to imagine herself in his position, making gut-wrenching choices on a daily basis that had the potential to affect millions, even billions of lives. In the end, she had learned to think carefully before second-guessing his decisions.

"Gary, what's our ETA on Rhodes?" Allaire asked.

"He'll be arriving here at Bolling AFB at approximately oh six hundred hours, Mr. President. We've got a chopper standing by to bring him here."

"Good. I want you to coordinate his entry into the Capitol. How are we progressing in getting ahold of the guy Rhodes wanted?"

"That would be his former lab assistant," Salitas said, consulting his BlackBerry. "Forbush . . . Melvin Forbush. We're ready to set up a call when Rhodes arrives."

"Do we have anything on the guy? Do you think he was involved in the theft of the virus?"

"The answer appears to be no. We're checking into all that again right now."

"And where is he?"

"He's still at the lab in Kansas."

"But we closed the place."

"He's the only one there, Jim. Sort of a caretaker."

"But why?"

"Apparently no one else wanted to stay. There were just a couple of dozen in the whole lab installation to begin with. Now, with their only project shut down, it's just Forbush. We keep the place ready because we don't have that many Level Four containment facilities, and you never know when we might need one."

"What a mess. We throw one guy into prison for bioterrorism, and we leave his assistant in charge of the lab."

"It's just a shell of a lab, sir."

"I don't care. I don't trust Rhodes, and if this Forbush worked for him, I don't trust him either."

"That's understandable."

"But Rhodes is our best hope for finding a treatment, or . . . or a cure."

"I believe that's true, Jim."

"Our best chance to survive this nightmare."

"I understand."

Salitas paused and pursed his lips.

"Jim, if you believe he might in some way be responsible for the attack, may I ask why you think he's cooperating?"

The president glanced over at Townsend and Lamar, then back at Salitas.

"I don't know that he *is* cooperating," he said. "Before I brought you in on all this, Gary, I met in secret with Dr. Sylvia Chen."

"The Dragon Lady. I know. Smart woman. WRX3883 was her baby."

"Well, in one of our first meetings she told me about Griffin Rhodes, who was working in her lab developing a vaccine or an antiviral drug that would counter infection with the WRX virus."

"Go on."

"Some years before that, he had been working in Africa—Kenya to be exact. From what she told me, he was a cowboy back then when it came to tracking down the sources of outbreaks of the deadliest viruses known to man. Fearless. Like the guys who ride bulls for a living. He was also a computer whiz, who frustrated people around him by refusing to use animals in his research—only computer models.

"Well, according to Chen, back in his Africa days, he was after the source of an expanding outbreak of Ebola infection, which was moving down a mountainside toward a densely populated village. Rhodes found a cave loaded with bat guano that tested strongly positive for the virus. He brought up a crew and sealed several side openings to the cave. Then he dynamited the main entrance closed.

"On the way down the mountain, he came across a hut. Blood was everywhere inside it. The whole family was dead from hemorrhagic fever. Everyone, that is, except one child—a small girl cringing out back beneath a pile of refuse. She was just beginning to show signs of the disease. Rhodes sent all the workers down to the village to avoid them being exposed. Then he carried the child five miles down to the hospital. Seven days later, the girl died and Rhodes developed full-blown symptoms of Ebola."

"I hadn't heard any of that," Salitas said.

"My fault for neglecting to tell you. The proof against him in the theft of WRX3883 was overwhelming. He stole that virus, purely and simply. We had videos of him doing it plus the pile of corroborating evidence you know about. But in the back of my head, I couldn't get rid of that story Sylvia Chen had told me."

"Is that why you opted against any kind of torture to find out who he was working with?"

The president shrugged.

"I don't know. Maybe. From what I knew of the man, and I had never met him face-to-face, I decided the only logical explanation for his actions was that he had gone crazy. I couldn't bring myself to torture him for that. Remember, that was before Genesis surfaced. I wouldn't have connected Rhodes and them anyhow."

"Unless he *is* Genesis. So, do you trust him now?"

"No, I don't trust him. How could I? But we're in real trouble, Gary. Hours? Days? Maybe a couple of weeks at the most. People are going to start dying soon. You know how contagious that damn germ is. But I also know Griffin Rhodes is the only card we have to play."

"Yes, sir."

"Now, I want a team on the man at all times, and I want you to organize it. Top secret, small numbers. The best we have. From the moment he sets foot off that plane, I want your people to be on him. Can't be anybody from inside though. Because we've all been exposed, we can't count on anybody to be reliable for long."

Townsend, who had been silent, finally spoke up.

"Excuse me, sir? I . . . don't understand that last statement."

Allaire and Salitas exchanged looks.

"I'll fill you in more later, Bethany," the president said. "But suffice it to say, it's why I need you here with me right now."

"And why is that?" Townsend asked.

"Thanks to that virus, it is only a matter of time, possibly very little time, before I will no longer be mentally competent to be president."

CHAPTER 14

Dr. Bethany Townsend turned and walked away, struggling to regain composure before she could face the president again.

"No more games, Jim," she said finally. "No more half-truths and dammit, no more outright lies. As your physician and friend I expect full disclosure, right now, or consider this my resignation."

Allaire encouraged his physician to take a seat and poured her a glass of water.

"I agree. Promise. Bethany, I need you to devise a means by which we evaluate my mental state."

"By 'means,' are you talking about some sort of test? I know from the Kalvesta files what the virus did to the Jacksons' central nervous systems. But I thought that danger had been taken care of. Are you implying that there are mental status side effects of this incarnation of the virus as well?"

"Not exactly side effects. After the Jacksons' disaster,

before we stopped the Veritas project altogether, the virus had been working perfectly. You know what interferon is, yes?"

"Of course."

"I remember the name," Salitas said, "and I know certain anticancer protocols use it, but I don't remember what role it plays here."

"Interferon is a protein made naturally in the body," Townsend said. "It's produced in response to certain infections, and also to attacks by cancer cells—particularly those cancers caused by viruses."

"Sort of like an antibody," the president added.

"Only not nearly as specific and probably not as powerful. Think about cold sores or other herpes infections. The outbreak happens, then goes away, but the virus is usually not completely removed from the body. Instead some of the germs remain in the skin or along nerve roots in a dormant state. Then a stress or other some factor awakens them. There's an outbreak, and the cycle is repeated again. We believe that interferon is one of the natural chemicals that drives the virus underground, so to speak. It is manufactured in response to an outbreak."

"Got it," Salitas said. "So common colds might be good for us if they stimulate interferon production."

"Exactly," Townsend replied. "The interferon produced in response to a common cold could be protective against viruses that cause leukemia. That possibility is still being investigated."

The president took over the explanation.

"Well, it appeared as if the WRX3883 virus was

held in check or even destroyed by interferon and antibodies. . . . Until it wasn't."

"Mutation," Townsend said in more of a statement than a question.

"All of a sudden Dr. Chen and her team just couldn't keep it in check. It was as if the virus had become immune to interferon. Remember what I told you about their clinical trials—getting cats to willingly swim across a pool, or mother monkeys to stop feeding their young?"

"Yes."

"Well, just as Chen thought the virus was under control, her animal subjects, mostly monkeys, began to undergo a progressive neurological degeneration— dementia, erratic mood swings, serious aggression, weakness."

"Jesus," Townsend muttered, shaking her head. "I can't believe this is happening."

"There was no reversal once their animals began to come apart. The virus continued to replicate and attack their brains. Death was due to seizures and central nervous system shutdown."

"So you think we're all headed for dementia and death."

"I do."

"And you want me to come up with a psychological test that will demonstrate when you are mentally no longer able to be president."

"Yes."

"And what then?"

"Gary, is Paul Rappaport in a secure location now?" Allaire asked.

Salitas nodded.

"He's being transported to the 934th Airlift Wing, Minneapolis-St. Paul Air Reserve Station on the north side of the Minneapolis-St. Paul International Airport. They have an encrypted line. Actually, he may be there already."

"Good. Get ahold of him for me, please."

"Yes, Mr. President."

Salitas's return to formality was his way of asking Bethany Townsend if she was in or out in terms of unencumbered support for her patient.

"Mr. President," Townsend said by way of response, "what can we expect with this virus now? How will it manifest?"

"Working that out is your second assignment, though I want you to stay clear of Group C—Chief of Staff Jakes's group. We have to assume they'll soon all be causalities."

"How so?"

"Anybody at ground zero, say within ten feet of any of the blasts, will initially suffer several hours of uncontrollable coughing, vomiting, dizziness, profound headache, loss of balance, lethargy. Within seven to ten days the bleeding will start due to the destruction of clotting factors. In that respect, WRX3883 is like the Marburg hemorrhagic fever viruses, specifically Ebola. Massive bruising will develop, along with bloody diarrhea. The victim's skin will begin to loosen and detach from the underlying tissues. The sclerae of their eyes will turn bright red. Black, soupy vomiting will hail the end. Death will occur from dehydration and hemorrhage anytime between ten and fourteen days after infection."

"Mr. President, Group C is over sixty people. Is there anything we can do for them—anything at all?"

"I've sent for the virologist who was in charge of developing a treatment for WRX. Hopefully he'll be able to come up with something. Meanwhile, Dr. Broussard is arranging for every antiviral drug we have to be delivered here in large quantities. You and she will be responsible for coordinating their administration. It's your decision, but I would focus on groups B and A. I don't think we have the means to kill this bug, but maybe you'll be able to slow it down."

"What can we expect neurologically?"

"From what I got from Dr. Chen's report of her animals, with moderate exposure there will be a period of progressive confusion and emotional lability, followed by a loss of will and profound suggestibility. That somewhat stable period will last for two or three days. That's when the infection was supposed to subside."

"After that?"

"Neurologic deterioration—staggering, grunting, salivating, uncontrollable arm and leg spasms, progressive dementia, violence, and finally grand mal seizures, high fevers, and death."

"Damn. So the three of us are in Group A?"

"Gary is close to being a B, but yes."

"So how long have we got?"

The president shrugged.

"Two weeks. Maybe three. Eventually, death will be due to seizures and central nervous system shutdown."

"So while I'm testing your mental status," Townsend said bitterly, "who's going to be testing mine?"

"Mr. President," Salitas cut in, "I have Paul Rappaport on the line."

Allaire flashed on Rappaport's daughter, the reason his Homeland Security secretary had asked to fill the role of designated survivor. He had met her at Rappaport's swearing-in ceremony. She was a pale, rail-thin, somewhat mousy woman. The people who had vetted the nominee reported her as having two past hospitalizations for anxiety and depression, but Allaire saw no reason her psychiatric history should lead to withdrawing his support for what was otherwise a nearly spotless résumé. In fact, if anything, Rappaport's devotion to his daughter was a mark in the man's favor.

Over the first four years the one-time governor of Minnesota had been in the Cabinet, he had overstepped his bounds from time to time. But by and large, he had been a good and loyal soldier to the president.

Allaire took the satellite phone from Salitas, set it on speaker, and sat down on the high-backed oxblood leather chair at the head of the conference table.

"Mr. President," Rappaport began, "is everything okay? Media speculation is that there was some sort of terrorist attack using a biological weapon."

The president gave Rappaport a full briefing. No half-truths. No withheld information. Afterward, there was only silence from the man. Allaire wondered if their connection had dropped.

"You still with me?" he asked.

"I am, Mr. President. I'm at your disposal and ready to do whatever is necessary." There was a force behind his words, a confidence that was actually startling to Allaire. "What's next?"

The president cleared his throat.

"Dr. Townsend will devise a test to evaluate my mental function—to assess if my will or intellect have in any way become compromised."

"How long?"

"Given my level of exposure, two weeks. Maybe more, maybe less."

"What are you suggesting we do, sir?"

"After the Kennedy assassination, Lyndon Johnson was sworn in aboard Air Force One. When it's time, we'll send transportation out to bring you to the White House."

"When it's time?"

"When my physician says so, and assuming no one ahead of you is in shape to succeed me, you will take the presidential oath of office."

"My God. That is quite a lot to absorb, Mr. President."

"A man does what he must—in spite of personal consequences, in spite of obstacles and dangers and pressures—and that is the basis of all human morality."

"John F. Kennedy."

"Very good, my friend. Let's hope your moment doesn't come, but if it does, I trust you to do what is right and just."

"Thank you for your confidence."

"What's your security situation there, Paul?"

"I have two Secret Service agents with me and my family. That's all."

"Not good enough," Allaire said. "You have twenty-four hours to get your family settled and safe. By then I want your home secured as if it were the White House. Biometric scanners. Infrared perimeter alarms. Video surveillance, the works. I'll get Gary Salitas to work on that for you. We'll send a detachment of Secret Service agents out there ASAP."

"No need for the security measures, Mr. President," Rappaport said. "Except for the Secret Service protection. Through my office of Homeland Security I have access to the best systems professionals in the world. I'll phone Roger Corum. He's the CEO of Staghorn Security and has connections to all the major players in the industry. He's already an approved vendor, and he's done a lot of work for us."

"Very well. Good luck, Paul. We'll be back in touch soon."

"Yes, Mr. President. And sir?"

"Yes?"

"If the time does come, I promise I'll be a great president."

CHAPTER 15

DAY 2
6:30 A.M. (EST)

The VH-60N banked smoothly to the right and eased toward the ground. Griff sat motionless in a plush leather seat, staring out at the granite buildings of D.C. This helicopter, though the same type that had lifted him to freedom hours earlier, had a fully finished interior, and was clearly used for transporting high-profile passengers. He was on the last leg of a journey from solitary confinement in a maximum-security penitentiary to a meeting with the president of the United States.

Just another typical day.

Griff had made the trip east, from Tinker Air Force base to Bolling, in an eerily empty C-22B transport plane. Flight time took less than three and a half hours from takeoff to landing with different military teams escorting him at each step of the two-thousand-mile, three-stop journey. Now, with the beginning just ahead, he pressed his forehead against the small portal window, and allowed images of people and places to flow through his mind.

From the earliest days of his remembered life, he had one and only one guiding force—the desire not to be normal. His parents were gray, conservative, hard-working Midwesterners, both of whom died early—his mother of cancer, and his father in a construction accident that left Griff and his older sister Louisa set financially. He was a rebel in school—a wiseass many called him—well coordinated but disinterested in sports; brilliant, but with a history of underachievement that was well on the far side of arrogance. The boys respected and feared him because of his reckless disregard for danger and his body. The girls, with few exceptions, kept their distance. The cops only saw him as a troublemaker—a brawler who, as often as not, would end up in the ER pummeled by someone twice his size.

Then Louisa died.

Meningitis, they told Griff. Meningicoccal meningitis. Within one hour of her first symptom, a headache, she was in a coma. Less than thirty-six hours later, without ever regaining consciousness, she was dead. She was twenty-four at the time. He was seventeen.

Griff watched the ripples sent across the Reflecting Pool by the powerful rotors. Escorted by several military aircraft, the chopper had passed unhindered through restricted airspace, touching down atop a cordoned-off area of frozen lawn between East Capitol Street and Capitol Driveway. Griff had studied maps of the Capitol complex en route, and knew they had landed near the entrance to the recently constructed visitor center.

Emerging from the belly of the chopper, his legs felt stiff, his muscles ached, and his temples were beginning to throb. Fatigue? Dehydration? Stress? Perhaps just the transition to freedom from twenty-three hours a day for nine months isolated in an eight-by-eight concrete cell.

He wondered what symptoms the seven hundred or so inside the Capitol were experiencing. Certainly there would already be some coughing. A good percentage of Sylvia Chen's monkeys who had been dosed with WRX3883 by aerosol had rapidly developed a dry, hacking cough, accompanied by an outpouring of mucus. Several of the animals had died even before the virus could have taken hold in their nervous systems, probably from sudden airway obstruction, but possibly from some sort of allergic reaction to the germs themselves.

Several times, Griff had called the vet working for Chen, and insisted she treat the animals. But the woman, surly and arrogant, admitted that although she was a D.V.M., she was a specialist in pathology, paid more to autopsy the subjects than to keep them going.

Giant mobile spotlights illuminated the predawn darkness with enough wattage to turn midnight into noon. A camouflage field jacket, supplied to Griff earlier, protected him against the crisp morning air. He rubbed at his eyes and reflexively tugged at his tangled beard. Hours earlier, the flight crew on the C-22B had handed him a heavy scissors, a package of Gillette disposable razors, and a can of shaving cream, but he declined their offer.

The president needs to see the man he's made.

Shielding himself against the wind from the rotors, Griff took in his new surroundings with interest and awe. A mishmash of barriers—concrete blocks, low steel gates, wooden sawhorses, and barrels—formed a secure perimeter along all the roadways bordering the Capitol that he could see. Uniformed soldiers, police officers, FBI agents, and combat-ready personnel from SWAT patrolled the makeshift perimeter, their guns ready. At periodic intervals, there were sharpshooters standing beside the tripods that bore their long-range rifles.

Well behind the soldiers and police, the curious lined the perimeter, in places standing five or even ten deep. Griff estimated the crowd to be a thousand or more, with people still arriving, the vapor from their frozen breath swirling in the rotors' wash. Some had impressive cameras and appeared to be from the media, others were using cell phones and camcorders to capture whatever might be transpiring.

History in the making.

If they only knew.

In addition to the military and the crowd, several large trucks were offloading what almost certainly were cartons of provisions into a large tent. Power cords snaked across the lawn from thrumming generators, providing illumination and heat. Griff took in the remarkable, surreal scene, juxtaposing it against the stark, unadorned walls of his cell at the Florence penitentiary, where he had started this day. He was impressed with the organization and the speed with which the military was responding to the crisis. But he also knew there was no way they were going to wade in and out of this logistical morass without a disaster.

Sooner more likely than later, WRX3883 was going to escape.

The crowd nearest to where Griff debarked noticed him right away.

"Who is that, the Unibomber?"

"Is there anyone else coming out of there? . . . Nope, he's it. . . . He's it?"

"Maybe he's the prime minister of someplace."

"I can't believe they're going to let him in there without giving him a bath."

"Looks like the ghost of Howard Hughes."

Griff battled back the urge to stop and tell the growing crowd that if they knew what was going on inside, none of them would want to be within five miles of the place. Instead, he pulled up the hood of his field jacket and trudged ahead, flanked by a cordon of soldiers, all wearing similar military camouflage.

Behind him, the rotors slashed to a stop. Ahead, a tall, ramrod-straight man, bareheaded with a gray flat-top, emerged from the visitors' pavilion. He was dressed like the other soldiers, but Griff could tell right away he was brass.

"Dr. Rhodes, I'm General Frank Egan, head of the U.S. Northern Command," the man said, extending his gloved hand. His steely gaze remained fixed on Griff's face, clearly taking measure of him. "I am under orders from the president to get you inside the Capitol complex and to escort you to the House Chamber as quickly as possible."

"Well, then, escort away," Griff said.

"We've had our best people here for a few hours now. There's a staging tent set up over there for you and the others who will be changing into field biological gear. They are Racal spacesuits, positive-pressurized, HEPA superfiltered air supply, with redundant battery power. There are more on the way. I believe that's what you requested."

Griff nodded grimly and smiled inwardly at the fact that the highly technical descriptions were like something from a child's primer to him now. No one who had been around him during the weeks following his sister's death would have ever predicted the transformation that was about to occur.

As his sullenness and oppositional behavior had intensified, the powers in his high school met with his aunt and uncle—his only remaining relatives. They in turn brought in their minister, and after that, the police community relations officer, who had done his best but failed to reach the brooding, disenfranchised teen. Throughout the meetings, Griff had sat stoically, staring at the wall or out the window, saying little. Then, after a three-week absence from school, spent sleeping on the basement couches of friends, or in abandoned buildings that for years had been his haunts, he suddenly marched into class and aced an exam in a chemistry course he had never attended.

"Is this the team who will be escorting me in?" Griff

asked Egan, pointing to the six soldiers who stood confidently at ease behind the general.

"Yes, they are."

"I'm guessing they aren't biocontainment experts."

"You are guessing right."

"They armed?"

"Does it matter?"

"Allaire wants me to save the day, but he doesn't trust me, is that it?"

"I have my orders, Dr. Rhodes. These soldiers are prepared to sacrifice their lives for this mission. They will suit up and accompany you every step of the way."

Griff just nodded. The general surprised him though, when his hard eyes suddenly softened.

"Dr. Rhodes," he said, "I don't know what in the hell is going on inside, but it's an understatement for me to say that your being flown here as you have been is of the utmost importance to the people in there and to our country. The president has shared with me some of where you've been for the past nine months and why. All I can say is please do your best to help him and those people with him."

"I will do that, General," Griff said, his mouth unpleasantly dry.

Egan studied him.

"I believe you will," he said finally.

"General, one more thing."

"Yes?"

"I hate to be a pessimist here, but you need to prepare yourself for the worst."

Griff flashed on his work with Project Veritas, specifically on his computer models, which he had been working on for years in his efforts to steer clear of experimenting on animals. His latest programs rendered flawless CGI animations of various combinations of the ribonucleic acid (RNA) pattern of the WRX3883 virus, as well as other, related RNA viruses like SARS and hepatitis C, and many deoxyribonucleic acid (DNA) viruses as well.

His programs, the most promising of which he had code named Orion, could generate countless three-dimensional combinations of the molecules that formed the backbone of the submicroscopic germs. But they could not, to this point at least, develop a sequence that would effectively kill them.

At that moment, however, he did not need a computer simulation to tell him what he already knew. Within fourteen days—twenty-one at the outside—everybody inside the Capitol would die in a manner as horrible as his worst Ebola nightmare.

Over the years before his arrest, despite all the financial support and equipment he could ask for within the tight security of the Veritas project, Griff had failed to uncover the missing link in his RNA sequencing that would create an effective viral kill-drug. It was naïve of Jim Allaire to believe that within fourteen days, the answer would suddenly appear.

"Looks like I've traded one cell for another," Griff said, gesturing at his escorts.

"Think of them as bodyguards," the general said.

"Is that how President Allaire described them to you?"

"Not exactly."

Not ready to deal with Egan and his militia, Griff turned and walked back toward the crowd. Immediately, a second helicopter, hovering two hundred feet overhead, turned a powerful spot directly down on him. The glare hurt his eyes.

"Guess they're worried I'm going to run for it," he said to no one in particular.

He slowed, but continued walking away, enjoying the sense of freedom, however artificial. Behind him, no one followed. The spot remained on—Egan hedging his bets. As Griff neared the crowd, which seemed to have doubled in size since his arrival, people again began shouting.

"Hey, crazy man!"

"You with the beard!"

"Can you tell us what's going on?"

"Here, over here. Let me get a picture of you. Just one shot."

Flashbulbs popped.

In the clamor and cacophony of voices, suddenly one stood out—a woman's voice from somewhere deep within the crowd. It was enough to make Griff peer ahead, looking for her. But every minute was crucial, and with the spotlight glaring off the sea of frozen breath, there was no chance. He turned and walked back toward where the head of the U.S. Northern Command stood waiting. As he reached the man, he heard the woman's voice once more above the din.

Of all those voices shouting at him, hers was the only one calling him by name.

CHAPTER 16

Griff lifted the vinyl flap of the camouflage-colored field tent and stepped inside. At this point, he decided, there was no sense in trying to explain to the head of the Northern Command that he had a lingering issue with the military.

The walls of the deceptively roomy tent rippled with the gusting January wind. There were seven tall metal lockers, evenly spaced along one of the walls. Set against the opposite side was a portable sink and head-high shelving unit stocked with army-issued towels. Portable gas heaters kept the space warm.

Griff and his Special Forces bodyguards wasted no time getting undressed. There was no banter, no extraneous talk. They exchanged their street clothes for green surgical scrubs, folded neatly inside their lockers. Griff found it a challenge to pull the drawstring tight enough to hold the pants up around his depleted waist. Finally, he pulled his field biological suit from the tightly packed locker and spread it out on the floor. With well-practiced moves, he stepped into it feetfirst, then slid his arms into the sleeves, extending his fingers until his hands fit snugly inside the attached gloves.

"You guys know to be extra careful with the hands, right? One tiny puncture could kill you."

"We know how to take care of our gear," came the terse reply.

"I gotcha," Griff said, raising his hands defensively.

The other soldiers eyed him coolly. He reminded himself that to them, he was a convicted terrorist. In fact, there would be no one he encountered this night who believed otherwise. No bands. No banners. No ceremony proclaiming welcome to freedom, Griff.

"I don't know how much experience you've had in a hot zone before," he said. "This virus is lethal. Aren't you the least bit curious as to what they've thrust you into?"

"No one thrust us into anything," the soldier to his right said. "We volunteered. Our orders are to shadow you every step you take, and to protect you if anyone tries to . . . to—"

"Go ahead, say it."

"To take you out."

"Well, I'm sure you'll do great in there," Griff said. *Just as I'm sure you're not all coming out alive.*

Griff pulled the flexible butyl hood over his head. What little vapor condensed on his visor evaporated as soon as he got the PAPR breathing system running. Without a built-in microphone, he had to raise his voice to be clearly heard. Even though the gloves and boots were essentially welded to the suit, he still wrapped his wrists and ankles with tape. None of the soldiers took that added precaution.

"I'm taping up," he said. "I'd suggest you do the same."

"Why?" one soldier asked.

"To shore up your weak points, that's why."

The soldiers stared at him numbly.

"I don't see any weak points."

"Wrists and ankles. Look, this virus doesn't care how careful you think you're being. It has one mission, just like you do. Its mission is to find a way into your bloodstream, locate the organ it was born to make its home in, and replicate. If it were a perfect organism, it would use you up just enough to keep you and it alive forever. It would be so much easier that way. But this virus isn't perfect, so it will kill you whether it wants to or not, and in ways you can't even imagine."

The soldiers eyed each other. Finally, one nodded. Griff tossed him the roll of duct tape.

"I'm ready when you are," Griff said.

Minutes later, the seven emerged from the field tent and made their way across the frozen ground toward the visitor center entrance. Spacemen on the move. As always, the suit made Griff feel mildly claustrophobic, despite it being loose-fitting and pliable. He had no doubt that the sensation was brought on in part by the invisible assassins separated from him and unimaginably violent death by only four mils of vinyl.

He scanned the faces of the soldiers flanking him, checking them through their clear plastic visors for signs of distress. Clearly they were tough and focused, but then again, none of them had contracted a Level 4 virus like Ebola or WRX3883 before. In all likelihood, that fact would change before too long.

As they walked, Griff could again hear spectators shouting at them, though his hood muffled their voices. Suddenly, he heard the woman's voice calling his name—once, then again. But before he could locate the source, General Egan emerged from behind an armored troop transport vehicle. He ordered the guards to halt a few feet shy of the portable airlock.

"Sergeant Stafford, you'll keep me informed of your progress by radio."

"Yes, sir."

The husky soldier, who introduced himself to Griff as Sergeant Chad Stafford, draped the bulky radio, tethered to a low-hanging strap, around his neck. Three others were handed M16A4 assault rifles, and two were given high-powered flashlights. Griff noticed that none of them was given a first-aid kit.

"Be sure to leave all this gear inside when you return," Egan said.

"General," Griff said, "those weapons will just add to the risk of a suit puncture."

"With all due respect, Dr. Rhodes, I'll be the judge of that," Egan said. "Our orders are to keep an eye on you and a lookout for anyone who might cause you trouble."

Following the general's order, two soldiers guarding the airlock entrance stepped aside. Griff paused to make a careful inspection of the hastily built structure.

The unit had two distinct parts—the airlock and a connecting tunnel. Both were comprised of vinyl panels set upon heavy-duty integrated aluminum frames that formed a transparent enclosure. The airlock was large enough to accommodate all seven of them. The tunnel, however, which was accessible through a vinyl door inside the airlock, required them to walk single file to reach the entrance of the Capitol.

The airlock met Griff's standards for safety, but only for a Level 3 or less microbe. Neoprene cell foam gaskets sealed the frame-to-frame connections. Ceiling-mounted HEPA air filters produced the optimum negative pressure airspace. There were three portable chemical showers inside the airlock chamber itself, which they would use to decontaminate before they could exit.

The rudimentary structure, designed to allow entry into the Capitol with the minimal risk of viral escape, was not up to the safety standards of a BSL-4 containment facility. But despite his reservations, Griff knew the setup was better than nothing and best for these circumstances.

Once inside the airlock, he used the gauge he had requested to measure microns of airborne contaminate. As soon as he got three satisfactory readings, he pulled open the door sealing the airlock from the tunnel. On the way out, each of them would be required to take a twenty-minute chemical shower, following which Griff would measure the air quality again. Three more safe readings and he would risk opening the airlock door for them to exit.

Simple enough.

"The visitor center entrance to the Capitol should be unlocked," Sergeant Stafford yelled. Griff could barely hear over the noise of the ceiling-mounted air purifiers lining the tunnel walkway. "You'll be met by the president's personal physician and escorted to President Allaire by his Secret Service people."

"Roger that," one soldier replied.

The team entered in single file. No one spoke as they passed through the visitor center door. Once inside the Capitol, Griff paused, adjusting his senses to the new environment. All was silent.

Deadly silent.

After a delay of two minutes, a team of four agents appeared—two men and two women. Their expressions suggested they hadn't been briefed to expect the biocontainment suits. Or maybe it was Griff's Unibomber appearance.

"Where's the doctor?" Sergeant Stafford asked.

"Detained. People are starting to get sick. We've got medicine and supplies coming in by tram to the House subway station."

Griff turned to the agent.

"I'll need access to those tunnels so I can sample the atmosphere. We might have to seal them off. We have no idea about their air flow patterns."

"What is this virus?" an agent said.

"Nothing good," Griff answered.

The agents introduced themselves, but Griff paid no attention to their names. Instead he studied them for signs of strain. Then he asked to check their hands.

Chen's test animals had reportedly developed bizarre patterns of redness on their palms as their infections intensified—crimson swirls or concentric, targetlike lesions. Of the four agents, only one of the men, tall and angular, had a slightly increased respiratory rate. He could have been hyperventilating because of the tenseness of their situation, or he could have been incubating virus.

It had been just over ten hours since the initial exposure.

"Why are you wearing jackets?" Griff asked. "It's hot inside these suits and we have fans going. You guys must be baking."

"We're wearing shoulder holsters," one of the women said. "The people in there are upset enough without having obviously armed guards parading about."

"What's the room temperature?"

"No idea, but it's up there. We just got the AC running again. It already shut down on us once. We're trying to keep the House Chamber and other rooms cool. Body heat wants to turn the place into a sauna."

"Well, radio somebody right now and tell them to shut that AC off. It's bad enough there are openings around every window in this creaky old place. We're talking viruses here, as in small—unimaginably small for most people. And like I said, we don't know about airflow or how the germ will spread. Let's not help it along through the ventilation shafts."

The Secret Service agent sent the order on via radio, and the biocontainment team and their guides resumed their descent into hell. They crossed a polished marble floor and then headed down a short flight of stairs into Emancipation Hall. From there, they passed the model of the Statue of Freedom and up some stairs before emerging into the Great Rotunda. Griff took little notice of the splendor of the dome, lined by cream- and gold-colored toruses, with the Brumidi frieze and stunning fresco at its top. The way things were, the Great Rotunda, and the rest of the Capitol for that matter, had become nothing more than an ornate coffin.

They crossed under the dome in silence, but from up ahead, Griff heard voices. The clamor grew louder as the team approached Statuary Hall.

"Isn't everybody still inside the House Chamber?" he asked, visualizing the floor plans he had studied on the way across country.

"We've moved some people. President's orders."

"Varied exposure levels?"

"No one's told us. They just said who to move and where."

Griff's containment suit was sweltering, but still, the scene in elegant Statuary Hall sent a chill through him. Entering between Washington and Jefferson, the team stepped into a large, two-story semicircular space, crowded with people. Many of them were lying on blankets, spread out across the richly polished checkered floor. Others were propped against the pedestals displaying the busts of heroes from each of the states.

In a bizarre, unsettling juxtaposition, those comprising the miserably uncomfortable assemblage were decked in their finest evening wear, much of which had been ripped in response to the heat. A Civil War infirmary scene was Griff's first impression—minus the bloodied bandages and hand-carved crutches.

Portable lighting augmenting that from the chandelier bathed the scene in an eerie glow.

There were several cots set up in a row along one wall, bearing mostly older men and women with IV drips in their arms. Near them were several large trash cans, filled to overflowing with rubbish, and beside the cans were columns of cartons, stacked five high, with stenciled lettering on the side that read: US ARMY RATIONS.

The voices fell into a deathly silence as Griff and the others made their way into the room. A number of the detainees, haggard, shirts open, hair undone, slowly rose to their feet and followed Griff's movements with their eyes. Then, without warning, a small, frustrated mob, ten or twelve, with madness in their eyes, rushed him. Some clawed at his suit. Others tried getting at his mask.

"What's going on?" a woman shouted. "Tell us!"

"Help us! Please!"

"Who are you?"

"For God's sake, do something! Get us out of here!"

The violent reaction was totally unexpected. One break in his suit, one microscopic tear in the seal between his mask and hood, and he was dead. Griff batted away at their arms. The soldiers and Secret Service agents, also taken by surprise, delayed several seconds before finally wading into the crowd, shoving some people aside and others to the floor. The agents pulled their sidearms and two of the soldiers swung the barrels of their M16s, gashing open a distinguished-looking gentleman's face. A woman came at Griff from the side. Her hair was matted down with sweat and her makeup had run rivers along both cheeks.

"Please," the women begged, "I have a son. A husband. If it's just a flu virus, why can't we leave?"

"Flu?" Griff repeated. "Is that what you were told?"

"Yes."

Griff clenched his jaw and pushed his way past the woman, being led and followed closely by those assigned to protect him.

"Wait," one of the soldiers behind Griff said.

The group turned. He was an African American, with the broad shoulders and narrow waist of a serious weight lifter. Now, the soldier stood motionless, holding his right arm out. The tape safeguarding his wrist had been torn away, and the weld between the hand and arm was ripped, exposing his skin.

"I'm sorry," Griff whispered, placing his arm around the shoulders of the man who had quite possibly saved Griff's life at the cost of his own. "I'm really sorry."

Without a word, the soldier set his rifle down, placed his helmet beside it, turned, and head high, walked back into Statuary Hall.

For a time, no one could speak.

"Let's hope you're worth it, pal," one of the other men said finally. "Let's hope you're worth it."

The group was led down a hallway to a nondescript door just outside the House Chamber.

"The president is waiting for you inside," an agent said.

Griff inhaled deeply, then exhaled and opened the

door. From his seat at the desk inside the small office, James Allaire rose. For a time, the two men stood several feet apart, sizing each other up.

"You're lying to these people."

"I'm the goddamn president of this country. I do what I feel is necessary to maintain order and protect the citizens. I'm counting on you to save their lives."

"You were wrong about me. You know that? I'm not a terrorist."

"Well then, prove it."

CHAPTER 17

The exterior of the S&S Trading Co. mirrored the other garages and rundown brick warehouses lining a quarter-mile stretch of K Street in southeast D.C. Reports of decreased violence in the notoriously high-crime neighborhood amounted to little more than the city's well-connected Economic Council responding to a steady inflow of landlord payoffs. Homicides were up, prostitution was up, and tax revenues were down. Agitation was increasing to clean up the area in preparation for gentrification, and sooner or later there would be a big-time crackdown.

But not that night.

With every cop in D.C. summoned to the Capitol, patrols were essentially nonexistent, and the street people were out in force. Teenage drug dealers and over-the-hill hookers strolled past the S&S Trading Co. without giving the building a second thought. From the street, they could not see the sophisticated array of satellite dishes set dead center on the roof. Beyond the massive steel sliding door, painted a nondescript reddish brown, two men sat at opposite sides of a folding table, smoking cigars, drinking coffee, and playing cards. The men, one African American, the other Caucasian, were dressed in military fatigues.

A naked bulb dangled from a cord suspended a few feet above them. Smoke drifted through the shaft of light. Seated to one side of the dimly lit space was a third man, copper-skinned and wiry, with a once-handsome face that was marred by a spectacular scar running from his forehead through his brow and down his right cheek. He was paying no attention to the others. Instead, wearing headphones, he was fixed on a wall-mounted bank of a dozen video monitors.

The images on each of the screens automatically changed every three minutes, along with the sound associated with it. A joystick enabled the man to adjust the angle and distance of the views projected by the concealed cameras, positioned throughout the United States Capitol building. There were several of them he could zoom in close enough to read the number plates on the seats in the House Chamber, and he could rotate another pair 360 degrees to observe the chaos unfolding in Statuary Hall.

There was room for a second operator at the bank of screens, but at the moment one man was handling them by himself.

Suddenly a speaker, mounted on the wall just above the monitor bank, crackled to life, disrupting the quiet, and actually startling the man, whose name was Alex

Ramirez. Ramirez, an electronics expert who had soldiered in a dozen or more wars around the globe, glanced up at the cameras he had installed—cameras that were now monitoring him and the others in the S&S Trading Company.

"I don't pay you goof-offs to play cards," a disembodied male voice boomed out. "Get back in the garage and work on the equipment. Ramirez, where's Fink?"

The other men stopped playing cards and redirected their attention toward the monitors on which they were featured.

"Fink's catching some Z's in the back room," Ramirez said.

"Well, wake him up," the voice barked.

Ramirez swiveled his chair around.

"Hey, goof-offs, on your way back to the garage, can one of you guys go and wake up Fink. Tell him it's Cain."

Ramirez had recognized Cain's voice.

"If you men follow orders," he had said that first day, "you'll be rewarded to the degree that Matt Fink discussed with each of you. If you question our patriotism or refuse to follow any directives, you will be permanently and painfully retired from this unit and from your life."

The wall-mounted speakers became active again.

"Ramirez, take manual control of camera nine and queue it up for Fink," Cain said. "I want him to see what's going on."

The man spoke with the confident authority Ramirez had grown accustomed to obeying over his years in various armies.

Cain, Genesis—cute. As always, Ramirez chuckled at the notion of how his Bible-toting, God-obsessed mother, had she lived past fifty, would have taken to his working for people who based their operation on the scriptures, and in particular on Genesis, her favorite book of the Old Testament.

Poor, deluded old gal.

Through a number of missions together, Ramirez had developed complete trust in his friend Matt Fink. First, though, he had to survive nearly having his throat slit for making a casual remark about the mercenary's name.

"It was my father's name and his father's name before him," Fink had said, holding Ramirez a foot off the floor with one hand, and brandishing his huge knife with the other. "The first man I killed thought it was a good idea to make fun of it."

Initially, Ramirez had doubts about this particular job. For a time after signing on with Genesis, he kept those doubts to himself. Then the first payment hit his Swiss bank account and his apprehension vanished like the darkness of the first day. As long as those payouts continued, he decided, he would gladly light a frigging candle on his knees if that's what Genesis wanted.

How's that, Mama?

Matt Fink's heavy footsteps echoed in the spacious, high-ceilinged warehouse as he strode over to where Ramirez sat. Fink always slept lightly, and never far away from a weapon—most often his bowie knife or his Luger, and at other times, both. The men liked to joke that sometime, during a nightmare, the giant would shoot himself and slit his own throat. By the time Fink reached the screens, he was wide awake and fully alert. He waved up at the camera.

"Hey, there, Cain, old sport. What's up?"

"Are you aware of what's happening at the Capitol?"

"There have been no reports of any incidents that jeopardize our mission."

"Ramirez, zoom camera nine in on the group in the biosuits. They entered the building a little while ago."

Ramirez pressed a button on his control panel. The monitor labeled CAMERA NUMBER NINE flickered as the image auto-focused on the targets. The recording showed seven individuals dressed in biocontainment gear making their way like lunar explorers across the polished marble floor.

"They're military," Fink said. "We expected this would happen. It does nothing to compromise our efforts."

"Six of them are soldiers," Cain replied, "but who in the hell is the one with the beard?"

Fink peered at the screen, then leaned forward and took over control of the camera himself.

"Let me get a decent close-up of him," Fink said.

"Don't move that apparatus too much. I don't want them to know they're being watched until it's time."

"Anything you say, sport."

"And stop calling me sport."

"I'm from bleedin' South Africa. We'd call the Pope sport."

"And while you're working on that," Cain said, "can

you guys explain to me how we lost visual of the president for over forty-five minutes?"

"There must be a dead space where our cameras can't pick him up," Ramirez offered.

"Impossible," Cain shot back. "We had every inch of that building covered. Someone screwed up."

"Couldn't have been you," Ramirez muttered.

"What?"

"Nothing, boss. Sorry if we missed something."

"Good. Now, get me a shot through the visor of the guy with the beard."

Fink continued to maneuver and position the camera until the bearded man's weary face came into better focus.

"Good. Very good," Cain said. "We can use facial recognition software to find out who he is. If we need to, we can even remove the beard. Fink, we'll provide you with a detailed background on this man after we get a match. I have a feeling I already know."

"We'll be waiting," Fink said.

"Meanwhile, I want you to get over there and mill around with the crowd. Bring two men with you. Ramirez will keep an eye on Mr. Beard—or maybe I should say *Dr.* Beard—and we'll be in touch when we know something for certain."

"You've got it sp— Mr. Cain, sir."

"They're wearing portable breathing systems that are battery powered. Sooner or later he's going to have to come out."

"Count on us to be there when he does," Fink said.

CHAPTER 18

"Okay. The way I understand it, if I do my best to find a way to beat this bug, I'm free, whether I succeed or not. No strings."

"That's the deal," the president said.

"Even though you still believe I stole that virus from my own lab."

"The security cameras picked up several perfect shots of your face behind your visor. Particles from the floor of the deepest level of the lab were on your boots, and we found the canisters hidden in a recently constructed compartment behind your basement wall. The gym bag you used to transport the canisters was found in your bedroom closet."

"It wasn't me."

Griff's meeting with James Allaire was in a conference room that did not appear on any of the floor plans Griff had studied. The president of the United States was one chair to Griff's right at a vast mahogany table.

The secretary of defense, Gary Salitas, sat several places to Griff's left, next to Dr. Bethany Townsend and a man introduced as the Capitol architect. Two Secret Service agents stood against the wall behind them, presumably ready to save the president from the terrorist in the blue biohazard suit. The rest of the room was empty.

Griff felt his anger toward this man, who had stolen nine months of his life, simmering very close to the boiling point.

"Do we have any chance?" Allaire asked, clearly unwilling to enter into a debate around Griff's guilt or innocence.

"If it *was* the flu, like you're telling all those poor people out there, the answer would be yes. But it's not."

"We've decided to share the true facts a bit at a time," Salitas said.

"Well, a bit at a time, I don't think they're buying your flu story, Mr. Secretary," Griff replied.

"Look," Salitas snapped, "if you're going to be a wiseass—"

"Easy, Gary," Allaire said. He took a deep breath to reset himself and exhaled. "Okay, Dr. Rhodes, this is a real mess we've gotten ourselves into. We don't have a hell of a lot of cards to play. In fact, at the moment you're about our only hope."

"Sorry if I sound a little out of joint, sir," Griff said. "But I hope you'll understand if at the moment you're not on my list of favorite presidents."

Salitas made a move toward him, and the guards responded in kind, but Allaire stopped them with a raised hand.

"I understand," he said. "Tell me, Dr. Rhodes. When—when you were put in prison, how close were you to coming up with something that would kill WRX3883 or at least keep it in check?"

"I would say I had a shot. I had completed my computer model of the virus twice. Both times, though, something changed in the germ."

"Mutation."

"Precisely. We were after reverse transcriptase, one of the enzymes the virus makes to help replicate itself. If we could administer a drug that would disrupt the formation of that enzyme we could possibly neuter the little buggers before they could reproduce. Just like taking your pooch to the vet."

"Why were you having so much trouble?"

"The virus mutates faster than I've been able to modify the transcriptase. There's something missing in my sequencing, but I hadn't been able to figure out exactly what when you pulled the plug on me. Did you know that the solitary confinement cells at the Florence penitentiary are eight feet by eight counting the toilet? That's less than the length of this table."

"How long will it take you to figure out what you were doing wrong?" Salitas asked, his jaw nearly clenched.

"Did you know that aside from the guards calling me a terrorist while they were beating me with their clubs, no one ever told me why I had been imprisoned? No dime to make a call, no attorney, no hearing. Nothing."

"Enough!" Salitas barked, slamming his fist down.

"Gary, please. Dr. Rhodes is angry with us. He

doesn't see our responsibility to the people of this country the way we do. And at the moment, that's okay. We need him, Gary. We all need him. . . . Dr. Rhodes?"

"We need to be thinking *if*, not *when*," Griff answered. "I have no real basis for guessing what this virus does in people. We've had some contagion disasters with Dr. Chen's monkeys, but never any leaks involving humans."

The exchange of queer looks between the president and his defense secretary lasted only a moment, but Griff caught it, and wondered about it.

Did they know something he didn't?

He filed the unasked question away. Allaire and Salitas had already shown themselves capable of lying if they deemed it necessary. Griff felt certain they would not hesitate to lie to him.

"My lab," he asked. "What's the status?"

"Your man Melvin Forbush has been serving as a watchman at the lab. We just got ahold of him. He's started getting the place operational."

"We have a support team of CDC virologists being deployed to the Veritas lab as well," Salitas said.

"Cancel them," Griff replied curtly. "I don't need anyone's opinions but my own. What I need are blood samples from twenty or thirty infected hosts. All exposure levels. Between Melvin, my computers, and the lab, if it can be done, it will be done. It's my work. I'm the only one you need."

"I'm afraid I can't allow that," Allaire said. "We have your lab notebooks. I'm sure our scientists can do something with them."

"In that case, I want Sylvia Chen to head up the other team."

Again an exchange of glances.

"Um . . . Dr. Chen disappeared . . . two days after your arrest," the president said. "We haven't heard from her since. We suspected she might have been an accomplice of yours, but we still really have no evidence to support that."

"Have you had people out looking for her? The FBI?"

"Of course."

"And are they still looking?"

"Some are."

"Some?"

"A few officers are still on the case."

"Damn. I just spent a significant percentage of my life locked in a concrete box while you stop looking for the one person who might—"

"I've heard about enough!" Salitas exploded, leaping to his feel and charging toward Griff. His cheeks were flushed, the veins in his neck protruding.

"Gary! Dammit, leave him be! He has a right to be upset about this one. I'm sorry, Dr. Rhodes. Sylvia Chen's trail was ice-cold, and I needed every agent looking for Genesis."

"Tell your pal there to spend a couple of days in solitary at the Alcatraz of the Rockies," Griff said. "Then he can come at me, provided he has the strength left to do so. Do you have any idea what this Genesis wants? Is it a group or a person?"

"Almost certainly a group—domestic, most likely.

No idea what their agenda is except to sow fear and discord."

"Religious fanatics?"

"Maybe. We're betting some sort of fundamentalists. . . . So, do we have an agreement or not?"

Griff doodled for a time on a sheet of yellow legal paper.

"So, you've got scientists to make sure I do the work," he said finally, "and military guard dogs to make sure I don't make a run for it. Is that right?"

"Yes. That's about it," Allaire said. "I'm prepared to set you free no matter what the results of your research, provided our people tell me you put in the effort. A full presidential pardon."

"And if I say no?"

"Then I'll put you back in prison, and you'll have the blood of seven hundred people on your hands while you rot there."

The force behind Allaire's words seemed to shake the room.

"Then I have one demand of you," Griff said. "Since we really don't trust one another, I want everything I do to be documented by a third party—someone unassociated with your administration. A reporter. That way there can be no misunderstandings or covert efforts to change fact into fiction. Consider it an insurance policy on your word."

"I'll make some calls."

"No need," Griff said. "Get me Angela Fletcher."

"The science reporter for *The Post*?" Allaire asked.

"She's reported from hot zones before."

Allaire and Salitas silently conferred and agreed.

"I'll see if we can track her down."

Griff flashed back to the scene outside the Capitol, the chaos of the gathering crowd, and the disembodied woman's voice that kept calling his name.

"No need for that, Mr. President," he said. "I believe she's outside the Capitol right now."

CHAPTER 19

"I knew it was you, Rhodes!" Angie cried out. "I knew it!"

Griff was there as she entered the Capitol through the airlock, his military entourage a respectful distance away.

"Welcome to hell," he said, reaching out to take her gloved hands in his.

"You know, I almost didn't bring my binocs with me, but at the last moment I threw them in my bag. All it took was one good look through that visor of yours and I knew it was you, despite the Rip Van Winkle beard."

"It's a long story."

Through the visor of her butyl hood Griff could see that, if anything, Angela Fletcher was even more beautiful than the woman in his memory—wonderful skin; sensual, truculent lips; velvet, deep brown eyes. It was hard to believe it had been twelve years since they first met in Kenya. She must have been a baby.

"If *you're* here," she said, "things must be really bad."

"Worse than you can imagine."

She set her hand on his arm.

"Whatever they want of you, Griff, I know you can do it. I'm pleased to see you're back in the game."

The temperature inside his suit went up several degrees.

I know you can do it.

He had heard those exact words from her before. First in Africa, then again, years later, on his houseboat in the Keys.

I know you can do it.

She always had more faith in him than he did in himself. He had never told her, and probably never would, but Angela Fletcher was the only woman he had ever loved.

The canvas backpack Angie wore contained blood collection supplies. Strapped over one shoulder she carried a lightweight video recorder and a digital SLR camera, accounting for all the items Griff had requested.

"How's the suit, kiddo?" he asked.

"It's a little tense in here, but nothing I can't handle."

"Some claustrophobia at first is expected. But now's the time to turn back if you're feeling panicked. Believe me, no one will hold it against you, least of all, me."

"I'm a reporter. This is the story of the century. I'm not going anywhere. Besides, I might be able to help."

"You already have."

"You going to tell me the story behind that beard?"

"When we have time. You ever draw blood?"

"I worked as a phlebotomist in college before I

switched out of premed. But I don't think I ever did it with bulky gloves on."

"We've got the president's doctor to do some of the drawing, and we'll see if there's a corpsman here. I can do the rest. In case you couldn't guess, a puncture in these suits is highly undesirable. Let's walk."

"So what do you know about this virus?" Angie asked. "And how did you end up here? The last thing I remember was when I found you on that houseboat of yours vowing to the heavens that your Ebola encounter had done you in, and you were through with viruses."

"Things happen, people change," he said.

It had been just another day in an unending sequence of fishing, naps, and Jack Daniels when Angie showed up on the deck of *Sanctuary,* the moss-colored sixty-eight-foot Sumerset houseboat Griff had bought at a Drug Enforcement Agency auction and set up in a sleepy little marina in Key Largo. Seven years had passed since the two of them had first met in Kenya—six years and nine months since Griff, with little explanation, had ended their intensely passionate love affair and gone off chasing after the source of an outbreak of deadly Lassa fever.

Angie had come to Africa on assignment to report on virus hunters for *Science Times Digest.* "Cowboys of the Jungle," the article would eventually be called. She was young, beautiful, bright, brash, and ready for adventure. The whole package. It was difficult to say which one of them fell quicker . . . or harder. Griff's sudden pullaway was nearly as surprising to him as it was to her, although it didn't take him long to work out the reason.

After waiting more than a week for him to return or at least to make contact, Angie finally left for the States. Friends told him that she did so hurt and angry, and never knowing why he had taken off the way he did.

Griff was dozing on the stern deck of *Sanctuary* when she came aboard carrying a houseplant, and knocked on the wall of the cabin.

" 'It's not you, it's me,' " she said. "Couldn't you have come up with a little more inventive note than that?"

Griff felt his throat close.

"Creative writing was never one of my strong suits," he managed, grateful that there was a half-filled glass of Jack Daniels on the table.

"I guess it wasn't," she said.

"It's a little late, I know, but for what it's worth, I'm sorry."

She sat down next to him. Her scent was dizzying.

"Just a few months ago I was working on a story about an Ebola accident, and I heard from one of the cowboys I interviewed about what happened to you."

"Tweren't nothin'. . . . You married?"

"Engaged. You?"

"I like to sit here and fish and drink, and watch the sun pass by. Women tend to want more out of a husband than that, I think."

"You were afraid you were going to die. That was the reason you took off on me, wasn't it?"

"Almost. I was never afraid of dying. I was afraid of what my dying would do to you. You didn't deserve that."

"You might have let me in on the decision."

"I didn't feel I could. I was always going to lose, Angie. It was just a matter of where and when, and how much of me was left when the battle was over."

"You once said you were going up against near-perfection. I never quite knew what that meant."

"But you do now."

"I think so, yes."

"I should have been a matador, Ange," he said, absently tossing a pebble into the still water. "Bigger opponents."

"But you'd have to kill the bulls and you don't kill animals."

"I'd sing them to sleep."

They talked through the night and into the next day. Angie was working on an article for *The Post* on researchers who were bypassing animal experimentation and testing, but still getting answers. Griff's seminal paper on the subject was referenced more than any other.

By the time she had gathered her notes and prepared for the drive back to the airport in Miami, he had given her enough material for a whole series. In between scribbling page after page in her remarkably illegible shorthand, she had managed to clean the galley, change the sheets, catch a fish, clean it, and poach it, accompanied by the contents of what seemed like a bunch of near-empty boxes, and a mélange of refrigerator leftovers.

"Why have you stayed away from the lab for so long?" she asked, packing her briefcase.

"Too dangerous. Them viruses never forget. Like elephants."

"Come on, Griff. I'm serious. People need you. Science needs you."

"Do you need me?"

"Dammit, Griff, don't make this difficult. I love the memories of what we had. I don't want to have to shut them out."

"Sorry."

"You can get back to your research. I know you can do it. Why can't you see how much you have to offer to the world?"

"I don't know. I guess nearly dying has a way of getting inside a man. Every day while I was in Africa I felt as if I were totally prepared for the inevitable. I guess I wasn't."

"You weren't meant to spend your life this way. If you need help, then dammit, go and get it. Take meds if you have to. But don't deprive us all of what you have inside you—especially your fearlessness."

Griff thought about her visit every day after she left. He had promised to call her and let her know what was happening, but he never did. Still, the moment she stepped off his boat and drove away, he had sensed something inside him begin to change.

"I'll take that backpack, Angie," Griff said.

The pack, filled with blood-collection gear, was light, but the decreased mobility of the biosuit made it cumbersome to tote. Angie followed him through Emancipation Hall, with the soldiers close behind. Aliens on the move. As they walked, Griff did his best to explain the circumstances leading up to this moment, especially the nine horrific months he spent in solitary confinement for what was clearly a frame-up.

Her proximity to him was distracting, even more so when she shared that not long after she left him on the Keys, she had finally accepted that she wasn't in love with her fiancé and had broken off their engagement.

"So, what's happened since then?"

"Not that much. I've become a paragon of serial monogamy. But I remain eternally optimistic, just like always."

Griff's pulse accelerated as they neared Statuary Hall. He became determined to share his feelings with her . . . as soon as the time was right.

Along the wall to their left, racks of comfortable clothing, probably from local department stores, were being sorted by Capitol police in preparation for distribution.

"Angie, it's not going to be a pretty sight in there. People are very anxious. Some of them are already getting ill. Earlier a group of them charged at me and tore one of my protectors' suits. Just stay focused and move ahead steadily. If people try and get near you, we'll stop them."

If she heard him, she did not respond. The moment they came through the archway bordered by the statues of Jefferson and Washington, she fell off the pace and stopped just inside the expansive room.

"Angie, don't get distracted now!" Griff whispered urgently. "Keep moving. Dammit, keep moving!"

But Angie remained where she was, surveying the

frightening, pathetic scene. She took in the people sprawled out upon the floor, and those slumped over with their backs leaning up against the wall. Then she knelt down beside one particularly distressed woman. The woman, in her forties and probably quite pretty, was wearing a black evening dress that had been torn in places against the oppressive body heat in the hall. Her hair was disheveled, and makeup was smeared across her face. The large amethyst brooch that had held her neckline together had come open. Her back was pressed to the wall, and she was sobbing uncontrollably.

Seemingly without thought for herself, Angie knelt down, wiped the woman's makeup and perspiration away with a piece of cloth, smoothed her hair, and then, to Griff's horror, dexterously refastened the brooch.

"We're here to do what we can to help," Angie said softly.

The woman regained an ort of composure.

"I'm frightened," she sobbed.

"I know. I know. You're going to be okay. What's your name?"

"Emily. Emily Wells. My husband's a congressman from Utah. First term. He was ill tonight and gave me his ticket."

"Well, why not try and do what you can to help some of the others, Emily. It will make the time pass more quickly. I'm Angela Fletcher, from *The Post*. This man behind me is a world-famous virologist. He's here to help figure this whole thing out." Angie took the woman's hand. "Be strong. There are a lot of people working to get you out of here."

"Th . . . thanks."

Angie helped Emily Wells to her feet and guided her over to where several others were dispensing rations.

Griff saw that some of those approaching them from the left were among the group who had come at him earlier. Quickly he led Angie away, but not before she could reassuringly pat several people on the shoulder and help one older, disoriented man find a bottle of water. The soldier whose biosuit had been torn moved in and helped control the angry, frustrated crowd.

"You're doing fine, ma'am," he said to Angie, in response to her unasked question about him.

"Remember what I said," Griff implored her as they retreated from the hall. "Don't get distracted."

"There are so many of them."

"That's only one of three rooms. We're going to do everything we can to help them, Ange, but you won't be able to help anybody if they tear your suit like they did to that poor soldier back there. Now, let's go see Allaire."

"What did you tell him that got him to bring me in?"

They were led into the waiting area by the Hard Room.

"I told him that you were here as a neutral party to document my movements. Our deal is that even if I don't come up with anything, he'll pardon me provided you report that I tried my best."

"I'm not exactly a neutral party, Dr. Rhodes. Does he know about us? Our past, I mean."

"No. I just told him that our paths had crossed before and that you have the knowledge and awareness I need, in addition to a public approval rating that is probably higher than his."

"So he doesn't know a thing?"

Griff glanced over at the soldiers and felt confident they were too far away to overhear them.

"Nope. Believe me, he's got more important things to worry about."

At that moment the Hard Room wall glided open and President Allaire stepped out. He looked worn.

"Miss Fletcher, my pleasure," he said, extending his hand and then introducing her to Gary Salitas. "I've very much enjoyed your work over the years—especially as an M.D. and something of a science nerd."

"Thank you, sir."

"Are you still seeing that insurance lobbyist? Collins, right? Bill Collins?"

Angie paled at the notion that the president would know such personal details of her life.

"We stopped—um—dating several months ago. How did you—?"

"Your friend Dr. Rhodes, there, became a person of interest to our government when he started working on a top-secret virology project. Then, nine months ago, when he was videotaped stealing canisters of the virus that was eventually to get us into this mess, he became a person of what we call *extreme* interest. We know more about him than he probably knows about himself, and as you are a well-known media person associated with Dr. Rhodes, we made it a point of getting to know you, too."

"Well, now," Angie said, realizing that Allaire was

issuing a thinly veiled warning to both her and Griff.
"I find that just a little unsettling."

"Please don't worry, Ms. Fletcher. Knowledge about
the people we're dealing with is what keeps our government strong. The professionals who are paid to do
this for us are very good at their jobs. If we had to, we
could probably pull up what Dr. Rhodes had for breakfast on the day of your last birthday, which happens to
be—" Allaire checked a sheet of notes on the table in
front of him "—May twenty-ninth. We also know
about your time together in Africa, as well as your visit
a few years ago to see him on his boat in Key Largo.
You were researching a story and stayed the night."

"I don't like this," Griff said, feeling his face hot and
flushed beneath his hood.

Allaire leveled a steely gaze at him.

"Rhodes, I frankly don't care what you like or don't
like. To me, until you prove otherwise, you're a terrorist who, for whatever reason, has placed your interests
above your country's. Do you think you could have just
picked someone to report to us and we would blithely
invite her in here? We know enough about Ms. Fletcher
to trust that unlike you, she is likely to place the needs
and security of her country above her own. Am I wrong
about that, Ms. Fletcher?"

"No, sir," Angie said, with firm conviction. "No,
you're not. What I report back to you will be what is
happening. But I want to say again how unpleasant it
feels to learn my life has been investigated to such an
extent by my own government."

"Objection noted," Allaire said dismissively. "Okay,

then, Dr. Rhodes, I hope I've made my point about the measures I am willing to take in the interests of national security. With that in mind, I am giving you one warning and one warning only: If you want to stay away from the inside of that cell at Florence, then don't fuck with me again."

CHAPTER 20

The only virus poisoning the Capitol, Ursula Ellis believed, stood on two legs with his hands resting on the House of Representatives lectern. She glared down at Jim Allaire from her perch atop the tribune and felt her hatred for the man shift into overdrive. Looking away, she made eye contact with Leland Gladstone, who was already in position on the House Chamber floor. Her aide gave her a discreet thumbs-up sign. She tried to suppress her smile. A nod to Gladstone was the signal that his message had been received.

Soon enough, Ellis thought. *Soon enough.*

Allaire ordered the three hundred people held captive inside the House Chamber to retake their seats, and Ellis delighted in seeing how his usually unflappable demeanor had waned. He looked gray and pinched. The mood in the room was reflecting his plummeting popularity.

"I promised you an update as soon as I had information to share," Allaire said through the PA system. "At this very moment, there is a team of specialists on site, who are experts in all facets of the virus we may have been exposed to."

A senator jumped to his feet.

"You said 'may,' sir. Is there doubt that we've been exposed? Could this all be for nothing?"

The question rattled Allaire, who fumbled with his words before correcting himself. "We've almost certainly been exposed to something," he said. "The nature of the pathogen, however, is still in question. Cultures and other attempts at nailing down the germ are under way."

Ellis silently applauded the representative from South Dakota for asking what she herself had long been thinking. Allaire prattled on. Half-truths and outright lies.

"The biocontainment suits you have seen are being used as a precaution," Allaire said in response to a specific question. "In addition to examining some of you, this team of specialists will be taking blood samples. Those samples will be used to assist in determining a timetable for our release. We have to be certain there is no widespread public health threat before we give the green light to evacuate the Capitol. In the meantime, we're working on removing seats to provide for more adequate sleeping arrangements. Also, I know the lines to use the bathroom have been long, so we'll be providing portable waste facilities as well."

"What about contacting our families? My cell phone

is useless. What in the hell did your people do? . . .
And why?"

The man stood on his seat, waving his cell phone de-
fiantly. The crowd cheered until he was quickly subdued
by two Secret Service agents, who clearly had not been
told that transmission had been blocked on those cell
phones they hadn't already confiscated. Ursula watched
with pleasure as the agents pried the device from the
man's grasp.

The mood inside the Capitol was worsening. Everybody wanted out—everyone, except perhaps for Ellis,
who needed Allaire to keep the crowd imprisoned
inside. Politics 101 dictated that the more people felt
oppressed, the easier they would be to turn. It was her
duty to expose the truth about this man, and Allaire's
mounting paranoia played perfectly in her favor.

"I understand you're very concerned about your
families," Allaire was rambling on. "We're working on
that issue, but it's going to take some time. Rest assured,
my White House staff is getting word out to your
families as I speak, informing them of the situation
and sharing my personal commitment that we will resolve this crisis as quickly and efficiently as possible.
Soon you'll be able to make calls yourself. We're working on setting up a phone bank and bringing in medica-
tions for those of you who need them. For national
security reasons there will be limits on the sort of information you can share."

Ellis cringed. This was America, dammit, not some
backwater third world dictatorship. Allaire's wife and

daughter sat center to the president on the chamber floor, gazing lovingly up at him. Ellis wondered what their expressions would be in another couple of minutes.

"I know this isn't the update that you wanted," Allaire continued. "I know you were hopeful I would say that the crisis has passed and we can now all go. It is my deepest regret to inform you that is not the case."

It was time. Leland Gladstone stood and raised his hand. Ellis's heartbeat responded to an adrenaline rush.

"Mr. President," Gladstone called out, "I found medication belonging to Senator Harlan Mackey in the bathroom. I went to give it to him, but could not find the senator here in the House Chamber. Has he been relocated to another part of the Capitol, sir?"

Ellis held her breath. She wondered what might happen to Gladstone in the aftermath of what was soon to follow. Whatever Allaire might to do her aide, Ellis would make it her first priority to undo.

"Yes. Senator Mackey has been relocated," Allaire said. "You can provide the medication to my physician, Dr. Bethany Townsend, and she'll see that he gets it."

"Oh, good," Gladstone said. "So the video I have isn't of Senator Mackey."

Ellis bristled from the same sense of pride she felt whenever her own gifted children excelled at something special. Allaire took a staggered step backward, but soon regained his composure.

"What video?"

"Here, I'll show you."

Gladstone hit the power on the digital projector he had hidden underneath his seat. He had found the projector inside a locked cabinet in the press gallery, precisely where Ursula said it would be. Sean O'Neil had provided her with the key, and Gladstone found cables there to connect the machine to his BlackBerry.

The stiletto of light filled a portion of the House Chamber's side wall. The grainy image was of the Capitol's east exit walkway at night.

"What is this? What is the meaning of this?" Allaire thundered, his face reddened.

Gladstone bore in.

"In the initial confusion after the outbreak, I somehow ended up on the second floor of the Capitol. I was taking some video of this ordeal when . . . well, when this happened."

Gladstone pointed toward the makeshift screen, which now displayed footage of a man stepping into the frame. The man took a few steps forward. His back was turned to the camera. But the moonlight and glow from streetlamps lining the walkway bathed him in a dim light. Those who knew Mackey could easily match the build of the man in the video to that of the senator.

Mackey took another step forward, and then paused and swung around so that he was facing Gladstone's camera. The focus wasn't sharp, but some in the chamber gasped at the man they knew was Mackey. He called out something, but there was no sound on the recording. The BlackBerry camera angle tilted down to capture the man trying, and failing, to pull open the locked exit door.

"Stop this at once!" Allaire cried out.

Several Secret Service agents charged down the aisle toward Gladstone.

Mackey took a step forward and raised his hands to shield his face. Just as the agents reached Gladstone and the projector, Mackey's head snapped back. A spray of blood exploded from a lemon-sized hole that materialized on the back of his skull. The picture bounced wildly and then went dark.

The agents snatched the projector from Gladstone, then looked sheepishly at the president for guidance.

Ursula Ellis took that as her cue to act. She leapt to her feet and reached for her microphone.

"Mr. President," her forceful voice boomed out, "I believe it is time for you to tell us the truth."

CHAPTER 21

James Allaire and his advisors had absorbed a direct hit.

Flanked by Secret Service agents, he left the House Chamber to a chorus of appalled cries from those who had watched the murder of Harlan Mackey. Through the microphone, he had promised to provide a full explanation, but his words were nearly drowned out.

The moment he got clear of the lectern, he ordered Sean O'Neil to detain both Gladstone and Ellis for questioning. It was a decision Gary Salitas staunchly opposed.

"You're going to divide the people into camps by doing that," Salitas warned, "and not just by party affiliation. If you isolate Ellis, you're just going to give her that much more power."

Allaire grumbled under his breath.

"Well, what do you suggest I do, Gary?"

Salitas reaffirmed his loyalty by placing a gentle hand upon Allaire's shoulder.

"I suggest we figure out a way to explain what that punk just broadcasted. But tread lightly here, Jim. Ursula Ellis is not someone to be underestimated."

Allaire grudgingly rescinded his order. Then he bit back his anger at the House speaker, and returned with his team to the Hard Room. There were other pressing matters on which they needed to focus.

"So what you're saying, Hank," he said to the chief of the Capitol Police force, "is that you've rechecked the official attendance list for possible fraud."

Tomlinson nodded.

"I have, sir."

"And you found no anomalies, nothing out of the ordinary."

"That's correct," Tomlinson replied.

"And the security cameras? You're suggesting playback showed no suspicious activity inside the chamber prior to the start of my address."

Again Tomlinson nodded.

"Yes, sir. There was no suspicious activity whatsoever."

Allaire gritted his teeth. He felt his anger at Tomlinson growing, and drew in several calming breaths. WRX3883 could cause erratic behavior and even serious aggression. Was he just upset at Tomlinson's lack of progress, or was he experiencing a physiological change? He shuddered at the possibility. Subtly, he checked for telltale markings on his palm.

Nothing.

What would he do if they suddenly showed up?

"Well, where does that leave us, Hank?" he managed.

"These aren't phantoms we're dealing with here. These are real flesh and blood terrorists. We need to know what vulnerability of ours they exploited. It may be our best way of tracking them down."

"My team is open to suggestions, Mr. President," Tomlinson said. "We want to catch who did this as much as everyone here."

Cameras monitoring the space outside the Hard Room picked up the arrival of Griff and Angie along with the six armed men accompanying them. Allaire motioned for Salitas to let the group inside. Griff and Angie entered, each carrying a box of what Allaire assumed would contain the collected blood samples. A sea of blue biocontainment suits followed Griff and Angie into the secret room. For several tense moments the hum of breathing apparatuses punctuated an otherwise silent gathering.

"What's the status of C Group?" Allaire asked Griff.

Griff turned toward the president. Though Griff's face was partially obscured by his suit's visor and thick beard, Allaire could see the distress brewing in the man's eyes.

"They're starting to show signs of respiratory difficulty and disorientation," Griff said. "No fatalities to report, but it's still early."

"And Admiral Jakes?" Allaire asked.

"He's not well. None of them are."

"Thank you."

Griff hesitated a moment, then added, "I heard about what happened in the House Chamber. I heard about a video—"

Allaire raised his hand.

"Not now, Dr. Rhodes," he said. "We're trying to figure out how these terrorists got the virus inside the Capitol in the first place. You know this virus best. Any theories how it could have been done?"

"I've been trying to figure that out myself," Griff said. "I have to believe there's a connection between Genesis obtaining WRX3883 and my being framed for the theft." Griff paused there. He and Allaire held an uncomfortable stare for a moment before he continued. "As to how they pulled this off, well, I have no good theories at this time."

The president rose from his seat and turned his back to the room. Allaire stayed silent while his mind worked feverishly to concoct a plausible scenario. Then he spoke aloud, uttering a Latin phrase, one his medical school professors often quoted.

"*Res ipsa loquitur,*" Allaire said. He repeated the phrase twice more, once with his back to the room, and again after turning around to face them all.

"What are you saying, Mr. President?" Tomlinson asked.

There were other confused looks.

"*Res ipsa loquitur* is Latin. It means 'the thing speaks for itself,'" Allaire explained. "In malpractice lawsuits, prosecuting attorneys who successfully argue *res ipsa loquitur* are guaranteed a significant payday. You see, our court of law is based upon the premise that we're innocent until proven guilty. *Res ipsa loquitur* turns that premise on its head. It says, because something happened and normally that something shouldn't have happened, you, the accused, are guilty of causing it to happen. Therefore, you are guilty of malpractice. *Res ipsa loquitur.*"

Jordan Lamar appeared even more confused.

"I'm sorry, Mr. President, I don't see how that helps us."

Allaire turned his back again and walked over to a three-foot-high black metal filing cabinet. He opened the cabinet, which was stocked with just-in-case office supplies.

"It helps, Jordan," Allaire said, reaching inside the cabinet, "because it means that the attack speaks for itself. It happened. That's the given, just like an attorney can argue that the patient entered the operating room for a toe operation and left with one leg missing." Allaire stood up, still with his back turned to the room. "Tell me," he said, "what did Genesis do that speaks for itself?"

Allaire turned around, and though he had reached for something inside the cabinet, he held nothing in his hands. He waited for somebody to speak.

Bethany Townsend finally responded.

"Genesis placed the vials of WRX3883 inside the bags of select persons attending the State of the Union Address," she said.

"Exactly, Doctor," the president replied. He stood in the center of the room, his arms folded across his chest. "That's precisely what they did. The thing speaks for itself."

With that, Allaire lowered his crossed arms. A wooden ruler, measuring one foot in length, slid out from where he had hid it up the sleeve of his suit jacket. The ruler clattered noisily on the wooden table before settling with the inch markers up.

There was no triumph in Allaire's expression.

"Hank, I want a full accounting of your security personnel. I am sure you'll find that one of them is missing."

Tomlinson still looked puzzled. "What are you suggesting, sir?" he asked.

Allaire was patient.

"Somebody working our security checkpoint wasn't looking for contraband being brought into the Capitol," he said. "He was using his post as a means of bringing the vials inside and inserting them into the bags as he was searching them."

Tomlinson lit up as the new realization took hold.

"On it right away, Mr. President," he said.

Quickly, the room emptied out. Griff was the last to leave.

"Nice going," he said, turning back at the doorway. "I would have every inch of this place swept for cameras. These people have been preparing for this for a long time."

"Dr. Rhodes, how do you think I should handle the Mackey situation?"

"You sure you want the opinion of a terrorist?"

"Doctor, you and I are up against it enough without clawing at one another like this. We need to call some sort of a truce."

Griff studied the man, who seemed to have aged years in just a few hours.

"In that case," Griff said, "I would consider separat-

ing what you know from the customary rules of politics.
Hard as it may be, that means no more lying."

Allaire held his gaze.

"I'll consider it," he said finally.

CHAPTER 22

Despite his smoldering anger at being denied due process following his arrest in Kalvesta, Griff grudgingly had to admit admiration for James Allaire's ability to remain composed in the face of monumental decisions.

Some years ago, Griff had reviewed a journal article analyzing the nervous systems of professional tennis players. The hypothesis of the paper was that given the normal rate of nerve conduction, and the speed of a tennis serve, the serve would have been in the screen behind the receiver before he could react and return it. And yet, return serve they did—again and again. The conclusion of the researchers was that the speed of nerve conduction in the top players was some sort of anomaly— a mutation, perhaps.

Watching Allaire operate, wondering about the often historic consequences of his actions and decisions, Griff found himself speculating if the man's nervous system functioned differently than the physiologic "normals" of the world. While those with normal decision-making processes were deciding what to do, the president of the United States had already done it.

At Allaire's order, a quiet but thorough search of the Capitol had been conducted. The sweep disclosed cameras concealed in every room—at least two dozen units in all.

But none in the Hard Room.

Allaire's counterattack began with architect Jordan Lamar's casual brush past Griff. It took several seconds for Griff to realize a note had been pressed into the palm of his glove.

All correspondence from me will come through Lamar. J.A.

One by one, each of the president's team received instructions. The Hard Room would be the only safe area for communications, but that space was to be used only for emergencies. Cameras would either be dismantled or left on as decoys.

Doc, one of the early notes read, *we must assume Genesis knows who you are and why we've brought you here. YOU ARE NOW A CONSTANT THREAT TO THEM . . . stay away from the House subway line until we tell you. That's going to be your way out of here and back to your lab. J.A.*

Griff felt his stomach drop. He had entered the Capitol complex fearing and not trusting the president. Now, it appeared, he was the target of Genesis as well.

Not safe, he wrote back. *No decon zone. Risk outside exposure.*

Help us make it safe. Many lives at stake. Military will help. J.A.

A team headed by Salitas discovered six cameras expertly concealed inside smoke detectors in the hallway outside the subway. The state-of-the-art video equipment was providing a window into the supply delivery route running from the underground entrance into the Capitol complex.

Allaire ordered half of the cameras inactivated and the rest redirected and left in place. None of them was to be in a position to record any unusual increase in activity.

The cameras were not the only discovery made during the next few hours. Hank Tomlinson had been unable to locate one of his officers, a five-year veteran of the Capitol Police force named Peter Tannen. Tannen had been assigned security detail at the breached checkpoint and was now assumed to be a part of Genesis. The FBI was dissecting the man's life with the intensity of their 9/11 investigation. Suspicion already was that he might no longer be among the living.

Griff and Angie slipped into the subway tunnel. Their mission was to get out of the Capitol and back to the lab at Kalvesta. Griff glanced over at a nearby wall-mounted clock and made a mental note of the time following the initial exposure.

Twenty-eight hours.

In another forty-eight, the first fatalities might be reported. He did not need a clock to tell him that the deaths would continue until there was nobody left in the Capitol to die.

The military team with him was Special Forces, trained to be first responders following a bioterrorist attack. Before the operation got under way, Griff briefed the group on the dangers of WRX3883.

"We're used to working with anthrax," one of the operatives said at the conclusion of Griff's brief presentation. "This shouldn't be that different."

"If you get infected with WRX3883, you'll wish it were anthrax. Be careful, but work as rapidly as you can."

Two hours later, the team leader for the Special Ops unit approached Griff in her blue biocontainment suit. He could see through her visor that, like himself, she was drenched in sweat.

"We're ready for your inspection," she said. "Whoever that Angie is, she's a hell of a worker."

"I know."

They were well ahead of the timetable.

"Good enough," he said, nodding his approval of what was really impressive work.

In amazingly little time, the Special Ops team had created a reasonably safe, fully functional decontamination zone between the House side of the Capitol and the subway line connecting the complex to nearby office buildings. He overheard one of the soldiers say that they had just built a doorway between life and death.

Time to head for Kalvesta, he wrote to Allaire.

A lot of people are counting on you, the president's return note read. *Don't let us down.*

Angie materialized beside him.

"How'd we do?" she asked.

"The Special Ops people want to adopt you."

"Thanks. They were ready to walk through fire for you. More and more you're reminding me of that cowboy in Kenya that I took such a shine to."

Her eyes seemed to light up the space behind her visor.

"Are you ready to decontaminate?" he asked.

"Are we ready to go?"

"As soon as Allaire says we are."

"Lead the way."

"Simple," Griff said. "First, we're going to take an ultraviolet bath."

He pointed to an area that contained several large saucer lights mounted on tall metal stands. The lights were plugged into a running generator.

"What will they do?" Angie asked.

"Kill any virus still clinging to our suit. From there, we'll shuffle into the portable airlock." Griff gestured toward the clear plastic cube erected beside the entranceway separating the Capitol from the subway line.

"Won't bad air get out when we go in?"

"The airlock is negative pressurized," Griff said, "so that poisoned air from the Capitol won't leak out into the tunnel."

"And who's gonna drive the train?"

"The system here uses a driverless car to shuttle members of Congress and their guests between the Capitol and the Rayburn building," Griff said. "One less person to decontaminate."

"Are you going to be the first through?"

"No, you are," Griff said.

"Why me?"

"Well, all the women are going first."

"Why's that?"

"After the light bath you're going to take a chemical shower. Then you'll need to strip naked. There will be a change of clothes waiting for you on the train. You'll put your biocontainment suit in the red toxic waste bags provided and leave them on the Capitol side of the air-lock."

"You couldn't set up a divider, huh?" Angie said.

"I told the team that to save time we'd just turn our backs."

"Anything for our country."

Angie squeezed his hand and left to join a group of three women at the ultraviolet bath station.

CHAPTER 23

DAY 3

5:00 A.M. (EST)

Griff was the last person to pass through the airlock. He came through naked, but rather than feel self-conscious, his thoughts were keyed on the seven hundred people imprisoned in the building he was leaving. This was already hell for many of them.

It was going to get much worse.

He reflected on the remorselessness of Genesis, whoever they were. Death at power stations in New York. Death in a museum in San Diego. Death in a public garden in D.C. And now, death on a truly grand scale. His own passions ran deep in many areas, but none were even close to being intense enough to kill for. He could intellectualize terrorism, but he had never really been able to understand it.

And now, he had been placed squarely in the path of the extremists to whom cause was everything and killing was nothing. Even if he somehow managed to survive, even if it all came together for him in Kalvesta,

Genesis might be damaged, but their hatred and their cause would endure. They would come up with something else. Some new demonstration of their commitment and resolve to accomplish—to accomplish what?

And along the way, more people would die.

The best he could hope for was to stay alive and try to disrupt their plan . . . this time.

Griff stepped onto the waiting train and Angie, facing away, handed him a towel and a set of hospital scrubs.

"We're going to have to get some meat back on those bones, Doc."

"You peeked. Well, I did yoga and calisthenics almost every day while I was locked up in solitary, but I guess my equation for staying in shape was missing useful nutrition."

"When we get to Kansas, I'll handle the cooking. For the past few years I've been on a Chinese kick. You'll love it. There's more calories in those bean sprouts than you think."

"There were times when I considered chowing down on one of the guards."

"Ugh!" She made room for him on the bench next to her, and instantly he felt stirred by her closeness. "Griff, tell me something," she said. "Given the status of your research when they arrested you, do you think you can do this?"

"I was getting pretty close to something useful. That may be why they came after me. But at best, what we're facing is a long shot. I've been running through some hypothetical figures while I was waiting for the shower.

I came up with a two percent chance of solving the design problems that were there when the militia came and hauled me away."

"Two percent doesn't sound like much."

"Okay, make it three. I'll be restarting cultures from the blood samples in those containers. In addition, Allaire said he was having a line of the virus flown up from the CDC, where they have it in storage."

"When you come up with something, I'm going to have one hell of a story."

"When you get started beefing me up with your cooking, be sure to stir in some of your optimism."

The team was relieved to be free from the biocontainment suits—especially, it appeared to Griff, those who finally got to cradle their assault weapons in ungloved hands.

"We're ready to roll," Sergeant Stafford radioed in.

Moments later, the fiber-optic backbone controlling the Automatic Vehicle Operation engaged, and the fully enclosed trolley moved silently ahead. The car came to a gentle stop at the Rayburn building subway station, and the doors swooshed open.

"I've never been to Kansas," Angie said.

"Just imagine Lake Victoria in Kenya, and the lush jungle surrounding it, and the cries of countless wild beasts, and then flip the scene over to the reverse side."

Stafford and the other soldiers surrounded Griff and Angie and led them through a maze of corridors and stairwells on their way to the surface. Once outside, Griff took a grateful breath of the cool, early morning air, and held it until he needed to exhale.

The Capitol was to the north of them now. Even from a distance, Griff could tell that the crowd levels outside the barriers had increased substantially, as had the military presence maintaining some semblance of order. There were three ten-person vans waiting with their engines running. The vans had black tinted windows and Griff assumed they were bulletproof, too.

"How many are coming with us?" Griff asked Stafford.

"Eight."

"That's a lot of vans for eight people."

"Two are decoys. Let's go. Move it."

The side doors to one of the vans slid open and Griff and Angie were the first inside. One of the soldiers carelessly swung Griff one of the refrigerated cases containing the blood samples.

"Easy with that!" Griff admonished the man. "Unless you want to be responsible for finding out just how dangerous these bugs really are."

The soldier just grunted and continued loading gear into the van. There was heat in the van, but not enough to enable Griff and Angie to remove their camouflage field jackets. Angie slid in beside Griff and pressed her body against his. He took hold of her hand. She glanced at him curiously, but made no attempt to pull away.

"I heard Allaire mention something about a second team working in tandem," she said. "Is that true?"

"We're not exactly working in an atmosphere of mutual trust, as the guardians, here, will attest. There's a Bio Level 4 facility in Alaska someplace. Allaire has enlisted my assistant, Mel Forbush, to set up a data-sharing network between us. As long as they don't slow me down, it won't be an issue."

"Thank you for asking them to send me with you."

"I don't trust Allaire to keep his word, and he doesn't trust me not to bolt. You're like the proctor."

The last soldier stepped inside and the van door slammed shut. Stafford sat in the front passenger seat, his radio pressed to his lips.

"We're moving," Stafford said. "Launch the birds."

He lifted a pair of high-powered night-vision binoculars to his face.

Griff felt suddenly edgy.

"What's going on?" he asked.

Angie seemed to sense it too. Her grip on his hand tightened.

Stafford passed the binoculars back.

"What am I looking for?" Angie asked.

"The doctor's decoy," Stafford said.

"My what?"

"Griff, he's right," Angie said, as she fiddled with the focus. "There's a man, thin, bearded. I can just make him out getting into a helicopter."

"What are you talking about?"

The driver shifted the van into gear and the quick acceleration pushed Griff back into his seat. They were headed toward Canal Street. The two other vans split off and headed in opposite directions on C Street. Griff stiffened. He did not need binoculars to see the black silhouette of the chopper, rising above the treetops after takeoff.

"Stafford, what in the hell is going on?"

"President's order," Stafford said. "We use this protocol or something like it to protect him. Now it's been instituted to protect you. When it comes to saving the country we don't leave things to chance."

Barely able to breathe, Griff kept his gaze locked on the helicopter as it grew smaller on the horizon. Suddenly, a trail of fire burst into view, seemingly from out of nowhere, and began to chase the climbing chopper.

"God, no!" Griff whispered. "No!!"

He screamed the word.

There was an explosion, and a patch of dark morning sky erupted into a bright ball of fire. The van shook from the force of the explosion. Griff watched through the window as fiery pieces from the helicopter fell to earth like meteorites.

CHAPTER 24

Griff stared at the contrails of black smoke streaking the spotlit sky.

Jim Allaire and his advisors had created a decoy of him, and now that man was dead.

"I want to speak to the president," Griff demanded. "Now!"

Stafford did not bother to turn around, nor did he respond to the request.

Griff rose from his seat, pushed past Angie, and yanked open the van's side door. They were traveling at forty miles per hour, along empty roads that police cars and motorcycles had cleared of traffic. Cold air swept into the cabin. Other armored vehicles had joined in their procession, including an ambulance and a USSS Electronic Countermeasures Suburban, which was following several car lengths behind.

"Sergeant?" the driver called out to Stafford.

"Keep driving," Chad Stafford said, drawing his sidearm and turning in his seat.

"Griff, what are you doing?" Angie shouted.

Griff was clinging to the frame of the open door, barely able to fight the rush of air.

"Get the president on that radio, now!" he screamed.

He held on, his body partway outside the moving van. His long, tangled hair snapped about like an unfettered sail in high winds.

"Get back inside the van this instant. That's an order!" Stafford commanded.

One of the soldiers scrambled over Angie and grabbed Griff by the collar. But the husky young man was lacking the leverage to pull him back inside.

"Get me the president on that radio, or I swear to you, I'll jump."

Stafford motioned the driver to slow.

"Don't slow the van down!" Griff yelled out. "Don't do anything but get me Allaire on that goddamn radio."

"Okay, okay, pal," Stafford said. "Just pull it together and come back inside. That was a tough one. None of us expected it. I'll get you the president."

Griff allowed Angie and two of the soldiers to haul him back to his seat. He was hyperventilating and shaking. The van pulled to the curb and stopped.

Stafford turned back until his face and Griff's were inches apart. He had holstered his sidearm.

"The president considers you an enemy of the United States," he said. "I have orders to kill you if you try to escape. Don't give me the pleasure."

Griff snatched the radio away. There was a brief silence followed by a burst of static.

"What is it, Rhodes?" James Allaire snapped.

"Nobody told me you were sending a double out like that."

"Because that's not your concern."

"That man and . . . and the pilot just died because people thought it was me."

"*Two* pilots," the president corrected. "Did you think this is some sort of game, Rhodes?"

"I can't stand the killing. You set them up to die. You knew what was going to happen."

"Correction. We *suspected*. That's why we left some of Genesis's monitors in place—so we could feed them whatever information we wanted them to have."

"I don't believe this."

"Now pull yourself together, Rhodes. You're not the only one appalled by death. We all are. You have your job to do. We have ours. Do you want to come back here and watch seven hundred more people die? . . . Do you?"

"No."

"Well, then, never forget that these people we're up against are resourceful and well financed enough to pull a missile out of the trunk of their car and shoot down a helicopter. The war on terrorism is just that. A war. Because it's a war, people die. We didn't choose our enemy, here. They chose us. Our only hope is that the casualties our people sustain will ultimately have some meaning. Right now, whether or not that happens, whether or not there is meaning to those deaths, depends on you. Is that clear?"

"If your plan is to sacrifice more people to keep me alive, count me out. Regardless of what you think, or why you had me thrown into prison, I'm just not in the business of killing."

"That's why those men and women are there along with you. Now, you have your job to do. I suggest you keep your concerns limited to that."

The connection went dead.

Griff sank back into his seat. The van accelerated. Angie set her hand on his knee.

"They have no way of knowing the number of lives you've saved," she said softly, "or the personal risks you've taken to do it."

"But that was my life at stake, and my choice to risk it." Griff turned away and stared out the window.

"The men in that chopper made their choice as well," Stafford said.

"And what did sacrificing their lives accomplish?" Griff asked. "Clearly Genesis knows who I am and they probably know where I'm going. So what did giving up those men accomplish?"

Stafford turned to him.

"You really don't know?"

"Enlighten me."

"Genesis isn't after you anymore, Rhodes. Thanks to those men and their heroism, the enemy thinks you're dead. Now you damn well better pull it together and do your part."

CHAPTER 25

"Hey, buddy, can you spare some change?"

The panhandler had set up camp on the front steps of the S&S Trading Co. Matt Fink had to suppress the urge to kick him across the street. Instead, he tossed a dollar onto the urine-soaked blanket that was probably helping to keep the grizzled old man from freezing to death.

"I've had a good day," Fink said, hands on hips, "and I'm feeling generous. But if you don't take your lazy, begging ass somewhere else, I'll crush your windpipe and watch you drown in your own blood."

Grinning, the giant watched as the beggar wheeled away his rusted shopping cart. Then he used an electronic key to unlock the massive steel sliding door that concealed the electronic center and warehouse of Genesis. His eyesight adjusted to the dim interior. Alex Ramirez, his bodybuilder's shoulders bulging beneath a cut-off sweatshirt, sat in front of the bank of monitors. Most of the screens were black.

"So, how many cameras do you figure they got?" Fink asked.

"They missed a few, but I think they're still looking."

"Men's room?"

"Actually, two in the men's rooms and the two in the ladies' rooms are still operational."

"I told you they'd be among the last to go."

Fink guessed that 90 percent of the cameras Ramirez and his "workmen" had installed over the two months leading up to the State of the Union Address had been discovered by the increasing surveillance sweeps, and had been rendered inoperative. It had been Fink's idea to place equipment inside the washrooms, a brainstorm that netted them some serious dividends. Not only were those units still operational, the conversations they recorded provided the intelligence that Cain had used to order the missile strike.

Fink had done the rest.

"I wanted that shot," Ramirez said, as if reading his mind.

"Ah, it was a thing of beauty, my friend. Absolute perfection. I promise you the next one, whatever it may be. Meanwhile, get me Cain."

"Where are the others?"

"Still disassembling the pickup out back. One shot. One hit. Now that's what I call perfection."

"You think anyone saw the launch?"

"Doubtful. By the time the bird was in the air, I was back under the tarp. We drove along, business as usual. The streets were largely empty, too. Everybody is either outside the Capitol, or home watching it on TV."

"I'm holding you to your promise, Fink. One of these other jerks can work the monitors. I need some action."

For emphasis, Ramirez reached down beside his chair and hoisted a fifty-pound dumbbell half a dozen times.

"I'll make sure Cain knows," Fink said. "This little success should have him pleased as punch."

"It does." Cain's voice crackled from the wall-mounted speakers.

"Ah, Cain, old sport, good to hear your voice."

Fink considered elaborating on the complexity of what he had done, especially given the short lead time to plan, but he knew Cain would have been unimpressed. He had worked for the man long enough to know that success was an expectation.

"Did you have strong visual of the target?" Cain asked.

"Dead on," Fink said. "Beard. Thin. He's the bloke we saw arrive in the Marine chopper, all right. Heavily guarded, too, right until he entered the helicopter. Then he got aboard alone and the bird carrying him lifted off from the south lawn just as you told us it would. We were in position prior to liftoff and engaged without incident."

"Nice work," Cain replied. "That man had the potential to be a serious fly in the ointment."

Fink chuckled.

"You pay for the best, you get the best."

"We have a couple more pieces of business on our plate. The first of them involves our inside man from the Capitol. His name's Tannen. The president knows now that he was working for us."

"None of this would have been possible without him."

"That's true," Cain said, "but now I'm afraid he's become something of a liability."

"Funny coincidence," Fink said, punching his cohort on the deltoid. "Señor Ramirez, here, was just telling me he's starved for action."

"In that case, you guys work something out. Tannen's stashed in a Motel Six south of Alexandria. He's expecting a ride west. He has a place in the Smokies and a cousin there who's going to help get him out of the country. You'll both split Tannen's share once he's dealt with."

"Sweet," Ramirez said.

"No hill without gravestones, no valley without shadows," Fink said, quoting a South African proverb he had learned from his father. "You said there were other pieces of business?"

"It's time we moved to phase two, and let the president know what our demands are in exchange for a truce, and maybe even the treatment for that virus."

"I thought there was no treatment for that virus."

"As long as Allaire believes there might be, we're in a good position. And now, thanks to that shot of yours, his options have been greatly reduced. In fact, I believe that at the moment, we're now the only hope he has."

"If there's anything we can do to get those demands to them, just say the word."

"Well, as a matter of fact, there might be. Before the cameras and listening devices went dead, Ramirez, there, picked up enough chatter to know that the chaos inside the Capitol is increasing. He also sent me enough audio and video segments so that we are certain President Allaire has picked himself up an enemy—a serious, powerful enemy, who is bent on bringing him down. Once you two have taken care of that business at the Motel Six, get back to me. We're putting together a package that we've decided to get to that person. From what you've seen, do you think you could get close enough to send it inside the Capitol?"

"I believe so," Fink said. "Right now, the chaos inside the building can't be any worse than the chaos we encountered outside. That's all we need."

"Excellent. The package should be waiting when you and Ramirez get back from Virginia."

"Mind if I inquire who the package is for?" Fink asked.

For several seconds there was silence. The mercenary feared he might have overstepped his bounds. Cain paid his salary and those of his men, but the man made it clear at the outset that Genesis would share information only on a need-to-know basis, and would respond harshly to any employee who questioned them.

"Well," Cain replied finally, "you've done well by us, Fink, and you, too, Ramirez. Our new ally-to-be, and spokesperson, provided we can get her to cooperate, will be Ursula Ellis, the speaker of the house."

"Quite a looker, that one," Fink said. "I know exactly who she is."

CHAPTER 26

DAY 3
12:30 P.M. (CST)

The corrugated steel hangar was carefully constructed to conceal the entrance to the Kalvesta Biosafety Level 4 facility. In one of its previous incarnations, the massive Quonset-style structure had been part of an Air Force training center. The government left behind the skeletons of a few decommissioned aircraft to convince any trespassers who snuck by the small security contingent that the facility contained nothing of any great interest.

Griff and Angie walked briskly across the hard-baked clay and gazed at the newly installed chain-link fencing. The perimeter was guarded by a team of heavily armed military personnel—the third such security checkpoint through which they had passed. The setup was nothing like the sleepy installation where less than a year ago, Griff and the rest of the Veritas team had sought to establish a biologic pathway into the will center of the human brain.

"How in heaven could Genesis have snuck the virus past all these guards?" Angie asked.

"They couldn't, is my guess," Griff replied. "But back before my arrest, there wasn't this level of security in place. In fact, there was hardly any security at all." He pointed past Stafford and his squad to a squat, concrete building that stood in close proximity to the hangar. "That was our topside security. We had one guard on duty at all times, and there was a collection of sophisticated electronic monitoring inside, but that was it."

"So at least now we're safe."

"I think these troops are here as much to keep track of us, and to keep us penned in, as to keep anyone from getting at us."

"Especially now that Genesis thinks you're dead."

Griff assured himself that there was no levity in Angie's remark, and then nodded. At some point, he had vowed, he would learn about the men who had given their lives to foster the deception that he was dead. Perhaps their families could use some help.

Anxious to sever the connection to his decoy, Griff used up an hour of the flight to Kalvesta cutting off his beard, and then shaving his face clean. Now, the wintry afternoon breeze felt strange on his skin. Angie had given the transformation her approval.

"Still handsome after all these years," she said.

As the pair neared the hangar, several of the soldiers standing guard tensed. The Army corporal in charge stepped forward and introduced himself first to Griff, next to Angie, and last to Stafford and his men.

"Do you know where Melvin Forbush is?" Griff asked the man. "I was told that he'd meet us topside."

"Forbush has sent up word he will meet you in the lab, sir. He's been below ground since we arrived here. We haven't even seen him yet."

Griff laughed and Angie gave him a puzzled look.

"Melvin is as good a microbiologist as you'll ever find," he explained, "but he is also, how should I put it, a little eccentric."

"Oh, I love eccentric—at least I usually do. Will I love Melvin?"

"I suspect you might. I do. He's an absolute fanatic about his work, but he's even more of a nut about Hollywood. Melvin is inevitably only one of two places—working on his equipment, or watching movies. I'm not surprised he hasn't been above ground. Listen, corporal, I know my way around, and also the biosecurity protocols. Sergeant Stafford and his men will wait around here. They worry about us, so you can assure them that this is the only way in and the only way out of the lab."

Before Stafford had the chance to respond, the corporal nodded toward the security guard. The razor-wire gate slid open on a track and Griff and Angie entered the hangar, a building about the size of two football fields set side by side. The ground beneath the arcing metal was hard-packed dirt, frozen solid by the Kansas winter. However, where once the hangar was a huge, nearly empty shell, now it was filled with military vehicles—Humvee battle buggies, Jeeps, transports, two ambulances, and a tanker. The trucks were parked in rows along the hangar walls and two more vehicles pulled in through the rear entrance while they were watching.

"I guess Allaire's taking this all pretty seriously," Angie understated.

"Impending death has a way of spurring people to action."

Kalvesta's dramatic, busy transformation was ironic given the size of the microbe at the center of it all. When Griff first arrived from New York with the team from Sylvia Chen's lab, the BL-4 facility had been a tawdry oasis in the high plains desert, consisting of a dozen or so bungalows spaced along some ill-defined dirt streets, a rutted landing strip, and a dilapidated basketball court.

Of course, the real story of the place lay in the gleaming laboratory far below the surface.

The ingress to the lab was unchanged since Griff's forced departure. Mounted on the wall beside the hangar entrance was a Kronos 4500 time clock. The corporal swiped his security card through the clock's reader slot. Instantly, a rust-speckled Cessna T-37 Tweety Bird, secured by wheel chocks and parked in the center of the space, began to move.

The aircraft, once a trainer for the USAF, glided aside, along with the perfectly camouflaged ground beneath it, to reveal a flight of circular steel stairs that descended fifty or sixty feet to a grated metal landing and elevator bay.

"Impressive," Angie said.

"Only the beginning," Griff replied.

On the way down to the landing, their footsteps echoed off the polished steel walls. The elevator was small. Griff's stomach knotted up the way it did whenever he was inside the claustrophobic atmosphere of what he used to refer to as a human incubator. In his world of killer germs, a healthy fear was a vital tool for staying alert, and therefore, alive.

The elevator traveled slowly. The 250-foot journey down took thirty seconds. They exited into a long, fluorescent-lit corridor with a seven-foot ceiling. The hum of powerful air-conditioning and purification units echoed throughout the space. The smooth, whitewashed concrete walls were unadorned, save for several framed safety posters, each a reminder that death was never farther away than a moment of inattentiveness. At the end of the corridor was a closed steel door, painted fire engine red, and stenciled SECURITY CHECKPOINT ONE in white lettering. There was a six-inch wire-mesh porthole in the center. To one side, another sign warned that the door was alarmed, and that access through it required authenticated biometric scans.

"How many of these checkpoints are there?" Angie asked.

"Three or four depending on what you count. There's this one, which leads to several cool zones including offices and our library. Down the hallway, beyond another doorway, things get serious. There's a pair of parallel, secure portals leading to the Kitchen."

"The Kitchen?"

"Our cheery name for the WRX3883 laboratory suites and tissue culture incubators."

"Where the beasties get cooked up."

"Exactly."

"One floor below the Kitchen, on the very bottom level of the facility, also secured off by one or two doors, is what I call Hell's Kitchen—Sylvia Chen's animal lab. Twenty or so monkeys and some cats. I almost never went near the place because I hated it so much and because none of my research involved her animals."

"But the space is empty now?"

"I assume. If it's not, then Hell would not be a strong enough word."

Angie pointed in the direction of a security camera fastened to the ceiling above a hand and retinal scanner.

"Is that the camera they used to film you stealing the virus?" she asked.

Griff nodded. "One of them. There are state-of-the-art security cameras throughout this place. Don't ask me how they got footage of me, though, because I haven't got a clue."

"Will the system let me in?"

"The security system requires identification to enter *and* to leave the lab. But Melvin is a super-stickler for details, so he'll probably unlock the door from the inside and then get us passes. Look, there he is. Oh, one warning—he hates being called anything other than Melvin."

Griff motioned to the porthole. Beyond it Angie saw a tall—very tall, actually—gangly man in a knee-length lab coat advancing toward them. There were no more than six inches between his unruly mop of auburn hair and the ceiling. Melvin completed his biometric scans and the door separating them opened with a loud click.

At six foot six or so, the virologist had to hunch to pass beneath the metal threshold without hitting his head. He was clean-shaven, with rounded, childlike features and thick tortoise-shell spectacles.

"I once suggested that Melvin try growing a mustache just to make him look a little more professorial," Griff told Angie. "His response was that unless he could grow the exact one that Daniel Day Lewis had as Bill the Butcher in *The Gangs of New York* it was simply not worth the effort."

"I might call that eccentric."

"He's also a bit unpredictable. A mastery of social skills has never been one of his strengths."

Typically, even though he and Griff had worked shoulder to shoulder for years, Forbush did not open his arms for a welcoming embrace. Instead, he offered a somewhat tepid handshake.

"Good to see you, my friend," Griff said. "I'd like you to meet Angela Fletcher. She's a reporter from *The Washington Post,* here to write about our efforts."

Forbush took hold of Angie's outstretched hand, but rather than shake it, he rotated her wrist in various directions, carefully studying it.

"Nicole Kidman," he said, finally. "Narrow hands, long fingers. I can show you some stills from her films and you'll see that your hands and hers are a near perfect match."

Angie laughed.

"Thanks, Melvin. She's one of my favorites, especially in *Moulin Rouge* and *To Die For*. She was nominated for an Academy Award for that, yes?"

"Actually, no. She won an Oscar in 2002 for *The Hours*."

"Sorry."

"Don't be. I know a lot about the movies, so if someone gets something wrong, I just tell them. Then, if they keep thinking they're right, I just show them. Film can be doctored, but it really doesn't lie, so if I say I'm right, I always am." He handed out specially coded access cards. "So, are you two ready to create your biometric profiles?"

"I already have one," Griff said.

"No, you don't. Right after they took you away, everything that said you existed vanished. Then Dr. Chen disappeared not long after that."

"But you stayed."

"The truth is I didn't have anyplace to go. You and Dr. Chen were the only ones who could have written a recommendation for me. Believe it or not, in the past, prospective employers have thought I was strange."

Griff set his hand around the taller man's shoulders.

"Your kind of strange is a good kind of strange, Melvin. I'm glad to see you again."

"After it was clear neither you nor Dr. Chen was coming back, Sam, her animal guy, and I sold her animals to other labs, and Sam got a job with one of them. Then I just cleaned up and accepted the government's invitation to stay around. I just now found out where you've been. No one would ever tell me. All they would say was that you had stolen WRX3883. I knew that wasn't possible."

"Well, I'll tell you, it wasn't pleasant, either. The president had me thrown into solitary confinement at a federal prison in Colorado."

"Now he wants you out here working again?"

"Go figure."

"You have the spirit to fight back but the good sense to control it," Forbush said. "Your eyes are full of hate. That's good. Hate keeps a man alive. It gives him strength."

"I'm not even going to try and guess what movie that's from," Griff said.

"*Ben-Hur,* actually. Jack Hawkins playing the slave master Quintus Arrius."

"Melvin, you're amazing," Angie said.

"Glad you think so, Ms. Angela. This man here understood me. He's the best."

"I'm sort of figuring that out."

"How anybody could think he was guilty of stealing our virus is beyond me. I tried to tell them that it was impossible, but nobody would listen."

"What was impossible?" Griff asked, his interest suddenly peaked.

"You being the one to steal the WRX3883 cultures. I told Dr. Chen and the others why it never could have happened the way they said. I even showed her proof that it wasn't you. But she didn't do anything about it. Then when she disappeared, so did anybody I could raise the issue to."

"I don't understand, Melvin," Griff said. "What do you mean you showed her that it wasn't me?"

"Just what I said. I brought her to my theater and showed her why I know you didn't steal the virus."

"Well, everybody thinks that I did. I realize that knowing I'm a good guy is enough to convince you it couldn't have been me, but you can't show somebody a person's character."

"That's true," Forbush said with a wry grin, "but I can show them the film. And like I said, film can be doctored, but it doesn't lie."

CHAPTER 27

After all they had been through, Griff was obsessed with the need to reopen his lab and get to work. But there was no way he could put off seeing exactly what evidence Forbush believed he had. He felt sickened by the notion that his friend had tried unsuccessfully to convince people that he had been framed.

But he wasn't surprised.

Had the president simply not cared, or were the people who had set him up that good?

Hate keeps a man alive. It gives him strength.

As Forbush led him and Angie down the passageway to the lounge area, Griff felt his bitterness and anger grow. How deep did the conspiracy to get him away from Veritas go? If Allaire was in any way involved, he had better hope that Griff never found out.

Forbush had his choice of bungalows outside the hangar, but it seemed as if he spent little time in any of them. Instead, he had converted two small underground offices into a sleeping area and a rather sophisticated movie theater, outfitted with five stadium seats and an antique popcorn machine. The seventy-inch movie screen, DVD player, and state-of-the-art home theater projector were, as Forbush put it, enlightened gifts from the United States government.

"You mean they bought this stuff for you?" Griff asked.

"Well, define *bought*. I filled out some paperwork, and marked certain items as research materials. It took some time, but ultimately they shipped me exactly what I ordered. And when I leave government service, Uncle Sam will get to watch movies and make popcorn."

"The Pork Barrel Cinema," Angie said. "We should have a marquee made up."

"Just don't put a photo of it in your newspaper. So, do you want me to pop up some buttered corn, or do you just want to see what I have?"

"I can't believe this," Griff said, slumping into one of the chairs in the front row. "Nine months in a goddamn cell."

"Be tough," Angie said. "What goes around comes around."

Forbush extracted a video from the middle of an entire wall of hundreds of carefully aligned video and DVD cases. Then he held up the cover.

"*Gaslight*. Have you seen it?"

"I know the word," Griff said. "It's a verb, and it means to sabotage someone's life to make them think they're going nuts."

"And this is where that word came from. Ingrid Bergman won the best actress Oscar in 1944, playing the naïve singer Charles Boyer sets out to drive crazy. It's about things not being as they look on the surface." He extracted the tape from the case. "I give you the surveillance video from security cameras twenty through twenty-four. It was never nominated for a Oscar, but it could have been—for best special effects."

"Does it say why they chose me for the leading role?" Griff asked glumly.

"No, I can't explain why they picked you," Forbush said, "but I think I have a good idea who played you."

He worked his way around to the projector and queued up the video.

Angie locked her fingers in Griff's as an image of the lab appeared on the wide, white screen.

"I've spliced a couple of camera views together," Forbush said. "The timing's in the lower right."

Nine months, Griff was thinking. *Nine months of my life gone.*

Images of the sadistic Florence penitentiary guards flashed strobelike through his mind.

At the bottom of the surveillance footage was the fuzzy lettering of a date and time marker that indicated the recorded events occurred some nine and a quarter months ago, at a few minutes past midnight.

"Since this is a silent film, I'll provide the narration," Forbush offered from his seat behind them and to the right. "For Ms. Angie's benefit, what we're looking at here is footage from the WRX3883 culture lab."

"Actually, Melvin," Griff said, "Ms. Angie knows this stuff. She's written pieces about hot zone virology, including a couple about me."

Angie stood up and pointed to a large cabinet on the right side of the scene.

"What's this?" she asked.

"That's one of the biosafety cabinets we use to work with hot agents," Forbush answered.

"No, I know that. I mean this incubator or whatever it is next to it."

Forbush sounded genuinely impressed.

"That's Big Bertha. We custom built her to mimic a human host in various stages of WRX3883 infection—body temperature, natural defenses, that sort of thing."

"So you've got virus growing in some sort of nutrient bath, incubating in a way that simulates the host organism's response. Amazing."

"Well," Griff said, "when your boss is the president, and you've got Dr. Sylvia Chen running the show, research expense is never a big concern."

"Okay, audience," Forbush broke in, "in our next scene, you'll see Griff enter the lab. Security access logs will document that it was him, even though it wasn't."

"How did you get this, Melvin?" Griff asked. "We don't archive surveillance video."

"After I learned about your arrest I archived the footage myself," Forbush explained. "I wanted to see with my own eyes what they said you'd done. It wasn't until I watched it on the big screen twenty or so times that I figured out what was wrong."

The video showed an empty lab for two more minutes before someone dressed in a white biocontainment suit entered the frame. The suit was bloated from air pumped through an attached yellow hose that descended from the ceiling. The intruder moved like Neil Armstrong on the moon.

"Now, with his back to the camera, we can't tell who this is. The only clue that it's Griff is the canvas bag he's carrying,"

"That's my bag all right," Griff said. "But that's not me."

"In ten seconds, you might think otherwise," Forbush replied.

As soon as the tenth second ticked past, the suited person turned and faced the camera directly. Griff and Angie uttered gasps of astonishment. It was easy to see Griff's face through the hood's clear plastic front shield. If this was a double, it was a perfect one.

"How in the hell did they do that?" Griff asked.

"How did James Cameron make all those beautiful, tall, sexy blue Na'vi in *Avatar*? How do you and I manage to re-create human RNA out of thin air?"

Mesmerized, they watched as Griff carefully removed tissue cultures of WRX3883 from the incubator and placed them inside six seamless aluminum canisters.

"Those canisters are custom designed to permit safe transport of cultured virus from one lab suite to another," Griff explained. "We can sterilize the outsides without harming the virus."

"For the first few viewings I wondered why you didn't do anything to disable the cameras," Forbush said. "Then

I realized you didn't have to. It would be perfectly normal for you to make this specimen transfer."

The next sequence cut to Griff, still carrying the black canvas bag, but now dressed in his street clothes and on his way out of the lab. He traveled through a maze of concrete corridors before he came to a stop at Security Checkpoint Two. The video showed him place his hand upon the biometric scanner and ended when he opened the security door to exit.

"Is that it?" Griff turned to Melvin and asked. "I thought you said you had proof. You show that in a court of law and I'm gone for good."

"What do you mean?" Forbush asked. "That is proof. Proof positive."

Griff and Angie exchanged bewildered looks.

"I don't get it," Griff said, an edge of irritation in his voice.

"What? You're telling me you didn't see that. Look again."

Forbush reran the last minute of footage. He froze the frame just as Griff set his hand on the wall-mounted biometric scanner.

"I still didn't see anything," Griff said.

Forbush sighed.

"Do you know that there are people like me who live for finding goofs in film? And trust me when I say there's not a movie without them. Hollywood even hires continuity specialists to make sure that if a character is wearing a hat in one shot, she's got the same hat on the same way if there's a change in the camera angle."

"So you found a goof that clears me?"

"More than a goof," he said. "Look at the screen where I froze it. What do you see?"

"My hand on the scanner," Griff replied.

"Which hand?" Melvin asked him.

"My left," Griff said. "It happened so fast, I wasn't even looking for it."

"You're right-handed. That's your primary hand. That's the hand your security profile was built from. The scanner is set up so that either hand can be placed in the indentation. In other words, it has two thumbs. Since the mold is to the left of the door, a left-hander would just set his—or her—left hand in place. But a right-hander would have to step across the indentation to set their hand in it. We each scan one and only one hand when we are creating our security profile—our dominant hand. You couldn't have possibly exited through that checkpoint using a left-hand scan, which means—"

"It wasn't Griff carrying that bag," Angie finished for him.

"No. But it was somebody," Forbush continued. "Whoever did this probably used other security footage of Griff to cobble together a perfect digital forgery. It's really flawless. Well, except for that one little gaffe."

"And you showed this to Sylvia?" Griff asked.

"Oh yeah, I showed her. I didn't come right out and confront her, though."

"Confront her about what?" Angie asked.

"Sylvia Chen's biometric profile. She's one of the three left-handed primaries that we have in the system. I would bet the thief was her."

"Maybe that's why she disappeared," Griff said. "The president told me that at one point there were dozens of FBI agents—I think he actually said *hundreds*—out looking for her."

"Maybe it's worth trying some more," Angie said. "Does Sylvia have an office down in the lab?"

Forbush nodded.

"We'd have to suit up, but I can take you in there. A couple of agents have already searched there, though."

"If neither of them were women, we ought to look again."

"Why?"

"Most women have a special talent built onto their X chromosomes. The talent to find things. If we want to find out who's behind Genesis, that office is the first place we should look."

CHAPTER 28

Griff had gone ahead to get his lab operational, and had left Angie and Forbush to get started in Sylvia Chen's office. Angie held her security card up to the reader and the red light above the palm scanner turned green. Standing off to one side, Forbush next had her set her hand on the opaque plate that initiated the biometric scan sequence. As she was waiting for approval, Angie suddenly found herself imagining Sylvia Chen approaching the door from the other side, carrying Griff's canvas bag, and knowing that she was setting up an innocent man who had been her friend and coworker for years.

Prison . . . Possibly torture.

The woman had to have known, Angie thought. She had to have known what was in store for Griff. *Who paid her to do it? Why? Where had she disappeared to?*

A sweet, computerized voice announced, "Biometric scan approved for Angela Jane Fletcher. Guest pass seven-oh-seven, security level Alpha Hotel Alpha. Please proceed to iris scan."

Angie set her chin in place and readied herself.

"Who supplies all this equipment, anyway?" she asked through clenched teeth.

The scan failed and a loud warning buzz followed.

"Please clear the optical scanner and try again," the voice demanded.

"You can't talk during a scan," Forbush said. "The algorithms that handle the matching are very precise. Keep your chin pressed in and your head as still as possible."

"Sorry."

Angie repositioned herself.

"The equipment comes from different vendors," Forbush explained. "Staghorn Security from Indiana handles the ordering and then puts the system together and installs it. If every one of the companies dealing with the government were as efficient and detail-oriented as Staghorn, half the national debt would probably vanish. Those guys know what they're doing and they know how to do it."

This time the scan worked and Angie lifted her chin from the cup.

"What about the cameras?" she asked.

"Those came from Staghorn also."

"Maybe we should talk to them. If they know the equipment inside and out, perhaps they'll have some idea how Genesis and Sylvia managed to pull off the scam. The computer graphics don't seem like they would be that easy to do."

"If you know how, you know how," Forbush replied

matter-of-factly. "Griff is in his lab right now. After we go to Sylvia's office, maybe he'll show you what he does in that arena."

"You really care about him, don't you?"

"I trust him, if that's what you mean. He's genuinely concerned about people. I suppose you've already picked up on the fact that sometimes I have trouble . . . um . . . getting along with others. He and I have never had one disagreement." Forbush considered his words for a moment, then added quite seriously, "Even though I'm smarter."

Angie waited on the other side of the door for the man, then headed down the corridor toward the cool zone of offices, and beyond that, the Kitchen. Data transferred wirelessly to a computer chip automatically unlocked the next secure metal door with a loud click.

"Do you know the Staghorn folks, Melvin?"

"I've done some work with them. Nice people. Smart. Anxious to please."

"I would imagine that sometimes you're not so please-able."

"You imagine correctly."

As they approached the hot zone changing area, Angie sensed an increase in the tightness in her chest. In spite of herself, she was beginning to panic. They were two hundred feet underground approaching the area where, less than a year ago, dreadfully powerful microbes were being developed, including a virtually invisible germ that would soon begin killing scores of people in the Capitol.

"Is there any living virus left down here?"

"You mean in the Kitchen? I suppose it's possible. We don't take any chances. Besides, Griff has those blood samples from Washington. He's suited up, working on them now to reestablish tissue culture lines."

The band around Angie's chest grew stronger. Her breathing felt strained.

"I need a minute, Melvin," she said.

"Don't be embarrassed. We all feel claustrophobic and endangered from time to time down here, especially when we stop to think about how few particles of WRX3883 it would take to kill us."

"That makes me feel much better."

"Good," Forbush said, clearly missing her sarcasm. "You said you wanted to start with Dr. Chen's lab office. You're going to have to suit up."

"I've done that before."

"So you know that breathing in the suit takes some getting used to."

"Yes."

"The air can feel like molasses at first."

"I understand."

"And we'll have to talk real loud to be heard over the air compressors."

"Melvin, let's go."

"Change on the other side of the lockers, then go through the security door. I'll meet you in the Kitchen. This is the door to the locker room. Once you pass into the first staging area, the light above the locker room door will turn green."

Willing herself to calm down, Angie pulled on the door handle. It was difficult to open.

"Negative pressure," Forbush said. "Helps keep any loose virus particles from—"

Before Forbush could finish the explanation, Angie clenched her teeth, yanked the heavy door open, and stepped inside.

"Don't forget to remove all jewelry," Forbush's voice continued through a speaker on the wall. "And remember to tape your wrists and ankles. . . . This is a little like the lab in Michael Crichton's *The Andromeda Strain,* but not exactly. . . . Arthur Hill played Dr. Jeremy Stone in that one. One of my favorites. He's Canadian. Not Dr. Stone, but Arthur Hill."

Several years before, Angie had written a three-part story on the autism spectrum disorder called Asperger syndrome. Unless her research was way off base, Melvin Forbush was a poster child for the neurological condition. *Delightful, but at times exasperating,* she had written. *Often brilliant, yet frequently unaware or out of step. Obsessed with details provided they are interested in the subject.*

He and I have not had one disagreement, Forbush had said about Griff.

It was another tribute to the man already hard at work in the lab ahead of her—the man charged with saving the lives of the president of the United States and seven hundred others. Angie had never fallen in love with the same man twice. Now she found herself wondering.

Twenty minutes later, she was ready. Dressed in a biocontainment suit, she exited the locker room and entered the next staging area, which glowed purple from ultraviolet lights. Finally, she entered the airlock to await her guide. The rush of air after she connected her hose was initially like going ninety in a convertible with the top down.

"Are you doing okay?" he asked.

"I'm fine. This is what my brain feels like most of the time. I sort of like the rush."

As Angie waited, once again her thoughts focused on Sylvia Chen. Griff had given her a capsule summary of the woman and her life. Born in China, and brought to the U.S. by her mother at a young age. Now speaks with minimal or no accent. No mention of her father. Graduated from Yale at twenty. Ph.D. from Columbia at twenty-six. Tenured by age thirty-eight. Briefly married. No children. Tireless researcher. Driven by ambition. Passed over for what would have made her the youngest department chief at Columbia, and so took her research on WRX3883 to the government. Author of literally hundreds of books, articles, and scientific papers. The anti-Griff in terms of her belief in the importance of using animals for her research—primarily chimpanzees or other smaller primates. Nevertheless, she had great belief and trust in Griff and his work. An opera buff and chess master. Meticulous, serious, intense. Owned a black Porsche, and in the wide, flat spaces of southwest Kansas, drove it extremely fast. Coveted a Nobel Prize, and had hitched her wagon in that regard to WRX3883, but believed it was bad luck to dwell on that desire.

The airlock door opened and closed, depositing Forbush behind her. Together, they entered the hot zone identified by a wall-mounted placard as the Kitchen.

"Do you want a tour?" Forbush offered.

"Later, maybe. I want to see Dr. Chen's office and lab."

"I tell you, it's already been gone over several times."

"Then this shouldn't take too long."

Next to the placard were detailed instructions on how to handle an exposure event. Beside the instructions was a sign reading simply BLACK ZONE, with an arrow pointing straight down.

"Explain," she said.

"We never used it, but it's a small bunker down below near the animal facility, with a couple of beds and a TV. If you get exposed to WRX, that's where you would go to die."

"Nice."

"Sort of like the submarine in *Das Boot*."

"Chen's office?"

"Down the hall."

"Favor, Melvin. Can I do this myself?"

"I suppose. What do you think you're looking for?"

"I have no idea. Something . . . anything. Ten minutes. Just give me ten minutes."

"Miss Marple."

"Pardon?"

"Agatha Christie's detective—*Murder at the Gallop*; *Murder Most Foul*. That's who you remind—"

"Ten minutes, Melvin."

She thanked him with a pat on the shoulder.

Sylvia Chen had gone to great lengths to insert some hominess into her windowless space. The walls were whitewashed plaster, with either Chinese artwork or bookshelves filled with scientific tomes. There was a wooden desk in the corner—perhaps walnut—and incandescent lamps designed to mimic natural sunlight. The largest painting, framed in black, was an appealing watercolor of Angel Falls in Venezuela, and across from it was a small table, featuring an inactive water fountain made of bronze. The floor was foot-square off-white tiles, largely covered by a circular oriental rug in rich blues and reds.

After a slow inspection of each wall and shelf, Angie stood in the center of the rug and closed her eyes. Sylvia Chen was there. This was a woman who cared desperately about her appearance and her surroundings—a woman who needed to be appreciated.

When Forbush returned, Angie was seated at Chen's desk, gazing first at one wall, then at the next.

"Are you done yet, Miss Marple?"

"Not yet. I'm just getting a sense of Sylvia."

"Not much here, is there?"

"More than you might think," Angie said over the rush of air in her helmet.

Griff appeared to Forbush's right.

"Like what?" he asked.

"Oh, hi, there, Doctor. How's it going?"

"Looks like we're live. We've got virus and we've got cells to grow 'em in, and the two seem to be getting along."

"So let the games begin," Angie said. "Have you budgeted any time for sleep?"

"Do you think those people in the Capitol are sleeping?"

"Point made. I'll pick you up some maximum-strength NoDoz at the commissary as soon as they build one."

"You were saying there's more to this room than one might think."

"Like the way that table over there is turned at a forty-five-degree angle to the wall, and the reason Chen chose a circular rug and not one with corners."

"I still don't get it," Forbush said.

"Melvin, how much do you know about feng shui?"

CHAPTER 29

Griff made his own cursory exam of Sylvia Chen's office, but saw nothing more unusual than a supremely organized, uncluttered workspace.

"You need to look with your mind, not your eyes," Angie urged.

Griff stood with his faceplate nearly touching hers to hear above the constant rush of air flowing into his pressurized suit.

"Okay, educate me."

"I would say that my life has been an endless series of phases. Some of them don't stick, like racquetball and SCUBA and contra dancing, some of them do, like vegetarian cooking and pilates. My feng shui period only lasted until I realized I was far too scattered and disorganized to ever pull it off. But knowledge is never wasted, and by the time I stopped my adult extension classes and daily studies, I had learned a great deal."

Griff and Melvin followed her over to the framed picture of Angel Falls—the tallest waterfall in the world.

"Feng is wind, shui is water. It's a Taoist explanation of nature that stresses the importance of energy flow. The simple idea of the science—and like most things Chinese, it can be examined on any number of levels—is that a clear energy flow improves fortune, health, and happiness."

"Energy," Griff said. "Got it."

"For instance, this room is divided into zones. I can tell without a compass that this is the north wall of the office because of the water elements Chen has placed here." She gripped the back of a narrow chair positioned directly beneath the framed picture and pulled it a few inches away from the wall. "This chair and the blue throw pillow on it feature the colors that best energize this zone."

Griff pointed to the adjacent wall, which was also the entrance into the office.

"What zone is that?" he asked.

"That's the east zone. The inside of the office door is painted green."

"You know, I actually remember her saying that the color of her door helped her to think better," Forbush said.

"No surprise. This area is characterized by the wood element. Green colors dominate and improve optimism, contentment, and spiritual growth."

"I'll bet you got an A in your course," Griff said.

"Actually, I almost got kicked out. Dr. Huang, the instructor, said I needed to sit still during class or I couldn't stay."

Griff set his gloved hands on Angie's shoulders and turned her to him.

"All interesting," he said, "but I don't see the relevance, and I've got a lab to get up and running."

"We want to know where Sylvia might be, right?"

"If she's still alive," Forbush added.

"Well, the office layout and décor tell me that she adheres to at least some traditional Chinese beliefs."

Angie turned to Chen's desk and held up a framed five-by-seven photo.

"That's Sylvia," Griff said, believing he had answered the question Angie was about to ask. "Although I am sure it was taken some years ago."

Instead, Angie pointed to the other woman in the photograph, an elderly Chinese woman dressed in a white floral-patterned blouse and black skirt.

"How about her?"

Griff shrugged.

"No idea."

"It's her mother," Angie said. "Facial structure, eyes. I'm virtually sure of it."

"So?"

Angie pulled the photograph out from the black frame and held it up so that Griff could see the date and time stamp the digital camera automatically applied to the print.

"This was taken four years ago."

Griff shifted impatiently.

"Listen, Angie, I'm fascinated by all you're saying, and I don't want to sound rude, but we've got to focus on getting some experiments started. Where are you going with this?"

"If Chen is alive, I would bet dollars to donuts that she's going to be near her mother."

"That's quite a leap from a painting and a chair. How could you conclude that?"

"Traditional values. The mother/daughter bond is strong in most cultures, but it's especially so between Chinese women and their mothers."

"Is that it?"

"Actually, no," Angie said. "Listen, Griff, I know you guys are in a rush, but I think there's something here."

"Where?"

Angie summoned them across to the bookcase.

"The dominant element in the west zone is metal. Silver and gold colors and the metals themselves enhance this zone's energy."

Griff stooped to examine some of the titles.

"I don't see how books like *Pathogenesis in Clinical Virology* would improve anybody's health," he said.

"Unless that person had just contracted Marburg," Forbush quipped, laughing unself-consciously at his own dark humor.

Angie pulled out books from the bookcase, glanced quickly at the covers, and instead of shelving them, tossed them aside one by one.

"Hey, Ange, slow down. There might be something sharp that could puncture your suit. What are you looking for, anyway?"

"This!" Angie exclaimed, holding up a tall, thin volume with a colorful cover.

Griff read the title aloud.

"*The Power of Peach: Recipes Fit for Kings and Emperors*. I don't get it."

"Me neither," Forbush added.

"Given the other titles, and the relevance of almost all the books to Chen's work, this one is out of place. There's no other one like it here."

"Go on," Griff said, suddenly interested.

"The peach is symbolic of long life, and plays a significant role in feng shui."

One by one, Angie turned the pages of the cookbook, fumbling because of her gloves. As she neared the middle, a trifold brochure slid out and fluttered to the floor. Angie picked it up with some difficulty, unfolded it to its full width, and held it up for Griff and Melvin to read.

"Riverside Nursing Home. And here's a letter from them written three years ago thanking Dr. Chen for her inquiry."

"What are you thinking?" Griff asked.

"I'm thinking Sylvia's mother might well be a resident in this facility. And if Sylvia is still alive, she's somewhere near this place, or at least she visits there."

"How do we prove that?" Griff asked. "We don't have phones or even Internet access unless we're being monitored."

"I wouldn't try that anyway. Too dangerous. Especially if we're the only ones who suspect this might be where Sylvia is. Until we know who Genesis is, and how they knew to blow up that helicopter, it's unwise to trust anyone but ourselves. You two have to stay in this lab, but I don't. Melvin, I need your help in sneaking me out of this place."

"Your wish is my command," Forbush replied. "Where to?"

"The nearest decent-sized airport." She pointed to the address on the back page of the brochure. "I'm going to New York City. Chinatown, to be precise."

CHAPTER 30

DAY 4
9:00 A.M. (EST)

With the bang of her gavel, Ursula Ellis called to order the first meeting of the newly formed United States House Special Committee on the Death Investigation of Senator Harlan Mackey. Ellis possessed profound knowledge of congressional history and could not recall an instance where a special committee resolution had been drafted and voted on in such a compressed timeline. Most unusual too, since President Allaire had endorsed the committee that could ultimately destroy him.

Ellis reflected on the formation of the special committee, and the moment when Allaire, in all his arrogance, agreed to allow it to happen. The president had returned to the House Chamber after a lengthy absence conferring with his cronies, his face drawn and the color of fog. The mood in the hall was bordering on hysteria. Some members of the legislative and judicial branches were demanding to see the video of Mackey's death again, but as the presiding leader over nonlegislative

House activities, Ellis acted within her authority to deny the request. The video had served its purpose, and to rebroadcast it would offer no gain. She had already gotten what she wanted. Jim Allaire was on the ropes.

"What are we going to do about this, Ursula?" Allaire had asked.

They sat facing each other behind the rostrum, Allaire in the vice president's chair, and Ellis seated across from him in her own.

"Well, Mr. President, you'll need to be more specific than that."

"You know damn well what I'm talking about," Allaire snapped.

On the House floor, a cordon of Secret Service agents, Sean O'Neil among them, blocked access to the rostrum and ensured a private exchange between the two adversaries.

"Sir, there was evidence presented inside this chamber that suggests you may have condoned or even ordered murder."

"Well, obviously that's not the truth, and you know it."

"All I know is what I saw on that videorecording," Ellis said. "Answer one question for me, Mr. President."

"Go on."

"Did you authorize the military's use of deadly force?"

Allaire's eyes narrowed.

"No," he had said.

"Well then, I'd like to form a special committee to establish independent corroboration of that claim. I assume you'll vigorously endorse such a measure. Unless, of course, you have something to hide . . . sir."

"And just how do you propose going about organizing such a committee, Ursula?"

"Simple, Mr. President," Ellis had said, her tone syrupy with confidence. "At my last count, we have two hundred and eighty voting members of the House of Representatives, all confined by your orders here inside the House Chamber. You have not made it clear whether or not I have access to the ones who are *not* here."

"And your point?"

"Constitutionally speaking, whether or not we get the others, that gives us a quorum to conduct business."

Allaire went from calm to livid in a blink.

"You want to hold an official House vote in the middle of this crisis? Are you insane?"

"With all due respect, sir, if your intention is to maintain order, you'll need to reestablish trust. I believe this is the best way to proceed in doing that."

"Let me get this straight," Allaire said. "The purpose of this special committee of yours is to investigate *me*?"

Ellis could almost feel the man's desire to wrap his hands around her throat. The notion made her smile.

"Oh, not you specifically, Mr. President. The committee will focus on Senator Mackey's tragic death. Naturally, I'd expect your full cooperation when the committee calls key witnesses to testify under oath. Yourself included."

"And if I refuse my support?"

Ellis did not hesitate to respond, although given the

jubilation she was feeling, it took effort to maintain an outward expression of gravity.

"In that case," she said, "I'd request that the House Judiciary Committee consider evidence of wrongdoing. The Constitution does grant us the authority to impeach you for high crimes and misdemeanors. I'd say that murder falls under the former of those transgressions. Wouldn't you agree?"

"Ms. Ellis," Allaire said, "given the threat to our nation posed by these circumstances, what you are doing borders on treason."

"We have only one Constitution, sir, and I will be only one of those committed to protecting it."

The anger on Allaire's face had quickly yielded to stoicism.

"Conduct your hearing and call your vote," he said. "You'll have my support."

"Thank you, Mr. President."

Leland Gladstone crafted the first draft of the resolution to form the special committee. Ellis edited much of it. Still, she was impressed that her precocious aide's prose demonstrated a remarkably mature acumen for the craft of politics. Multiple possible interpretations for every statement. Copies of the resolution were made in the media room, and were distributed to each voting member. Then Ellis called the quorum together. The measure passed with near unanimous support.

Ellis appointed herself chairperson, which did not violate House rules given the committee's lack of a legislative agenda. Her next task was to select the fourteen committee members from a candidate pool of

more than five times that number. The resolution called
for equal representation from both parties, though Ellis's presence ensured that deadlocks would be broken
in her favor. She purposefully picked several Allaire
loyalists. After they turned against their beloved leader,
which Ellis was confident they would, the shockwaves
sent through his supporters would be that much more
profound.

Access to nearby meeting rooms was not permitted,
so Ellis's newly formed Select Committee met in a
cordoned-off section in the upper gallery. Despite the
frigid temperature outside, body heat was threatening
to convert the chamber into a sauna. And of course,
not only were the windows locked shut, but the air-
conditioning had been disabled. Shipments of utilitar-
ian clothing had finally been distributed throughout
the three groups, and as a result, morale was slightly
improved.

"Before we commence with committee proceedings, I want to personally thank each of you for putting
aside extremely valid concerns for your own health and
safety to focus on vital congressional business," Ellis
began. "I would have not pushed to create this select
committee had I not believed it was of the utmost importance to the health and safety of our most pressing
responsibility—the welfare of the citizens of the United
States. Through your courageous vote, you've shown
your support in the most significant of ways."

Silver-haired Barbara Crain, a many-term representative from Delaware, whose ashen complexion cried
out for fresh air, spoke first.

"To be honest, Madam Speaker, any action at this time is a welcome distraction. We are feeling impotent and stifled here."

Many nodded agreement and Ellis graciously thanked them all again. She kept her attention focused on the body language of Allaire's hardliners, and asked Gladstone to do the same. As she expected, they initially appeared ready to stonewall progress and vociferously defend Allaire to the end. Their postures would change soon enough.

"Just a procedural note," Ellis said. "My aide, Mr. Gladstone, will be compiling complete and detailed reports of all committee activity. However, under the Open Meetings and Hearings rule, clause two of House Rule eleven, we've voted these proceedings will remain closed. Therefore, I'll remind this committee to refrain from recording any of what is discussed here."

A congressman from Ohio, overweight and perspiring profusely, scoffed, "We don't even have anything to record with. Allaire's damn Nazis have made sure of that."

That led to a volatile exchange. Ellis banged her gavel to reestablish order.

"A reminder that we will conduct this committee with established House rules for special investigative committees. The chair recognizes herself for five minutes to deliver an opening statement." Ellis had written out her remarks, but could have easily recited them from memory. "Today, we are faced with one of the greatest and gravest threats our country has ever known. I am of the opinion that this is a threat from within. By within

I mean not only from the terrorists calling themselves Genesis, but from our own government, and, yes, from the president himself. It will be the business of this committee to ascertain the validity of my disturbing claim.

"Let us begin with an examination of the facts, such as they might be. Genesis, a known terrorist organization, has allegedly penetrated our extensive, state-of-the-art security to infect us with a virus of some sort. How did they accomplish such a feat without assistance from the very forces assigned to safeguard us? Why have we been prevented from participating in the response to this devastating attack? Why is the executive branch of our government not giving us, the legislative branch, the chance to do the job for which we were elected?"

Ellis paused and let her gaze linger longest on several of the staunchest Allaire supporters. Gladstone checked his watch and held up two fingers to signal Ellis the number of minutes she had spoken.

"As the gentleman from Ohio sadly pointed out," she continued, "under presidential order, you no longer have phones to contact your own base of support. Why is that? Let me ask: How many of you have a major university in your congressional district?" Half the hands were raised. "And don't these major universities have scientists? There are vast resources at our disposal that could assist in ameliorating this crisis, and yet we're denied access. Why?" Again Ellis paused. She had learned that a question often carried more persuasive weight than a claim of fact.

"I propose that there is more to this situation than meets the eye. I further propose that by an exhaustive exploration of Senator Harlan Mackey's tragic and horrible death, to which we have all borne witness, a new truth will emerge. This select committee must act with the interest of the country above the interest of any individual . . . or any president. We need to know what Genesis has demanded, not only with this terrifying attack, but with those that preceded it. Surely such demands have been voiced. Surely President Allaire must know what they are. Why has he not shared this information with the people through their duly elected senators and representatives? This committee must be prepared to deal with any and all possibilities—even charges that the president of our country has chosen to keep us in the dark as to what Genesis wants, and has resorted to murder to protect his self-interest by keeping those secrets from us. Does any member have an opening statement?"

A deeply entrenched Allaire supporter raised her hand.

"I have a statement."

"The chair recognizes the congresswoman from Kentucky," Ellis said.

"You've raised some interesting points, Madam Speaker, that have perhaps altered my thinking. Our dear colleague Senator Mackey appeared to have been executed for simply stepping outside. If this virus does not pose an extreme risk to the populace, as the president so asserts, why did Senator Mackey pay such a steep price for what would seem to be a minor transgression?"

"What are you suggesting?" Ellis asked, as a way of urging her on.

"I'm asking of those present at this proceeding, who believes this virus represents a minor health threat?" A majority of hands were raised. "In that case," she continued, "we should be able to shortcut this investigation simply by getting somebody on this committee to volunteer to leave the premises and walk the same path Senator Mackey took. President Allaire assured us the shooting was accidental. We believe the virus threat is negligible. A quick trip outside should prove both claims quickly."

"So said," Ellis replied. "Do we have any volunteers willing to take up the congresswoman from Kentucky's suggestion?" Not a single hand went up this time. "If you doubted the importance of our committee before, perhaps those doubts have now been erased."

There was movement to Ellis's right. She turned to see a Secret Service agent approaching, carrying a large, bulky manila envelope.

"These are closed proceedings," Ellis said. "I'm sorry, but you are not permitted here."

"My apologies, Madam Speaker, but this package arrived for you with our last supply delivery. I'm in charge of package security, so I had to have it scanned, but I did not feel the need to open it. It's apparently from General Egan himself, so I thought you might want it right away."

"Much appreciated. I'm sorry to have snapped at you."

The agent handed Ellis the package, nodded to apologize for the intrusion, and left in the direction from which he had come. Ellis studied the delivery. It was a padded envelope sealed with clear plastic tape. The outside markings she recognized as official U.S. Army insignias, and it was stamped URGENT in bold red lettering. Ellis banged her gavel one time.

"The chair recognizes her right to call a thirty-minute recess."

Ellis rose and maneuvered past the members of her select committee. To this point, the hearing could not have gone much better. As far as doing any significant damage to Jim Allaire, she was still feeling her way along. But the man was lying and concealing vital information, and she was far too much of a pro not to keep probing until something in his shaky façade gave way.

She knew who General Paul Egan was, but had only met him briefly at some sort of official affair. Almost certainly he wasn't an Allaire supporter. Whatever it was, she sensed this package could only be good. Clutching it, she headed off in the direction of the ladies' room.

CHAPTER 31

> General Paul Egan has nothing to do with this package. We used his name to be sure the security monitors took the delivery seriously and brought it to you. The members of Genesis believe that you are someone fit to lead this country. Reply to this message if you agree and would like to learn more. The code to open our messages will be the security login password of your Bank of Virginia online banking account.

Ellis took in a sharp breath as she read the text on the display screen of a handheld messaging device that had been carefully enclosed in protective wrap. It was as thin as a BlackBerry, but somewhat larger. The display on the screen was sharp.

Password? The device prompted.

Impossible, she thought. There was no way Genesis could have gotten ahold of her personal banking password. She purposely typed in an incorrect code, and the device immediately refused to proceed. She then typed in the correct numbers and was directed to two typed sheets, carefully hidden between the bubble wrap of the envelope and its manila outer shell. Printed on the first sheet were the words GENESIS DEMANDS.

Ellis took the package into a stall and secured the door. On first reading, the demands—radically antiestablishment—bordered on the absurd. But Ellis pushed aside her initial impression by reminding herself of the brilliance the organization had displayed thus far, as well as their unbridled ruthlessness.

Who is behind Genesis? she typed.

The response appeared less than a minute after she pressed Send.

We represent everybody who values true freedom. That is all you need to know. These messages are encrypted and secure. These transmissions cannot be detected. Have you read our demands?

Ellis reviewed the sheet of demands again, and then sent a message, which read simply: I have.

The device buzzed in her hand after Genesis returned a reply.

We have communicated these demands to the president and he has ignored us. The virus you

have been exposed to is real and lethal. We alone
have the treatment that will save your lives. The
president, by not responding to our demands, has
sealed your fates.

Ellis typed: What do you want from me?

This time there was no immediate response. *Can
this all be some sort of trick on Allaire's part?* She had
after all threatened him with impeachment. Could he
be trying to set her up as one willing to negotiate with
terrorists? It was possible.

If Allaire wasn't behind this, then why were they
reaching out specifically to her?

Ellis warned herself to tread softly until the picture
became clearer. If the message were really from Genesis, then Allaire had not only ignored their communications, but kept them secret as well. If so, he had placed
everyone in the Capitol in mortal danger. Suddenly, the
device buzzed in her hand.

See to it that legislation is passed that will make
our demands law. Do so and we will give you and
you alone the antiviral treatment. You will be responsible for saving the lives of seven hundred
of the most important people in America.

Ellis did not need Genesis to explain the potential
impact of her being the one to end this crisis. She was
more than fit to lead the country. It was her destiny to
do so. What Genesis was offering was the path to that
inevitability. She thought of William Jennings Bryan,

who wrote: *Destiny is not a matter of chance, but a matter of choice*. At that moment, her choice was to prove that the opportunity indeed was for real.

What is this virus? Ellis typed.

WRX3883.

What is that?

Ask your president. He'll know. He made it.

Interesting, Ellis thought. But the exchange proved nothing. Were she to confront Allaire with specifics about the virus, it might only confirm that she had taken his bait. She needed more certainty than that to proceed.

Ellis typed: The president has brought in a virologist and tasked him to develop an antiviral drug. He may succeed before I get your bill passed, in which case, you have no leverage.

She wondered how Allaire, assuming he was behind this sham, would respond.

The virologist is dead. Killed when we blew up his transport helicopter. You have no other option.

Not only was that an interesting response, but a most unexpected one as well. Ellis knew all about the helicopter disaster. The explosion shook the chamber walls and incited some panic among an already jittery group.

"Nothing about the explosion will derail our plans for a rapid resolution to this challenge," Allaire had told a meeting of the leaders of Congress.

Ellis wouldn't believe him until she had questioned Sean O'Neil. It took a little prodding, but finally the agent revealed that the explosion had killed a pilot, copilot, and a decoy of the virologist who had been chosen to develop an effective treatment for the virus that was threatening them.

Clearly, the president had nothing. His iron-fisted quarantine was born out of panic, which meant that Harlan Mackey's death was no accident.

Ellis tensed. This *was* Genesis who was contacting her. She felt absolutely certain of it. If they were to provide her with the cure, she would assume the stature of a savior.

Destiny.

Ellis studied the sheet of demands again. They were ridiculous—over the top. Under normal circumstances, any lawmaker championing a bill with these provisions would be committing political suicide. But these were hardly normal circumstances.

Genesis had organized the legislative demands into three broad categories: national security, immigrant rights, and privacy.

The national security mandates called for the immediate cessation of unchecked spying on ordinary Americans, as well as the abolishment of the Patriot Act, and a rewrite of the ECPA, the Electronic Communications Privacy Act. The impact of such a bill would be profound. It would make it illegal to monitor communication on the Internet. Wiretapping, in all but the most extreme cases, would be abolished. And the legislation currently in committee to establish a national ID program would be scrapped.

Who are these people? Ellis wondered again.

In addition to the security demands, they called for the dismantling of the immigration and naturalization service, ending all discrimination against immigrants, along with sweeping changes that would essentially erase our borders with Mexico and Canada. They also insisted on the installation of consumer privacy protections, which would make surveillance camera footage a civil rights violation unless it was related to preventing robbery.

This was truly toxic legislation.

But what we have all been exposed to was equally toxic as well.

These demands were coming from Genesis, Ellis concluded. And although she did not personally support any of their proposals, given the circumstances and the stakes she could champion the effort nonetheless. Flexibility was at the very heart of good politics. Once she was sworn in as president, the country would see only a hero—a hero who had done what their elected leader could not.

Even if I were to succeed in passing this legislation, Ellis typed, you could not meet your obligation. I am not the POTUS and therefore, not elected to lead the country, or sign this bill into law.

You are third in the succession order, came the reply. With our help, there will be no one for you to succeed.

Ellis felt another jolt of adrenaline. Her mind danced with images of her taking the presidential oath—images of such vivid and glorious detail that she believed, for just a moment, they had actually occurred. Genesis sounded as if they had the resources to make it happen. She had to take the ride. There was, however, one glaring problem that still needed to be addressed.

It must be me who secures the treatment, she typed.

The exchange that followed occurred in rapid succession.

Genesis: Your job is to get the legislation passed. We'll provide the drug. You can decide how to explain where it came from.

Ellis: But this will take work. What if Allaire's virologist succeeds before my legislative work concludes.

Genesis: We told you, the virologist is dead. We saw to that.

Ellis: That is incorrect. He is very much alive. You succeeded in blowing up a helicopter. But with a decoy on board, not him.

Genesis: Interesting. In that case, we know the man's location. The matter will be resolved. And you will become the president. Bank on it.

CHAPTER 32

Matt Fink had been a pilot in the South African Air Force before he became a mercenary, opting for more close-up work and much more money. Now, he banked a sharp right turn, extended the Learjet 40XR's landing gear, and then rechecked his instrument panel for any needed course corrections. He slowed to 140 knots and extended the wing flaps to decrease the aircraft's stalling speed. The Lear was a joy to fly compared to the stiffer JAS Gripen fighter he had piloted in the service.

Clear skies and no strong crosswinds made for perfect flying, and a bright Kansas sky gave Fink a clear view of the runway. He repositioned his headset microphone to continue the arrival sequence with air traffic control at the Garden City Regional Airport.

"Garden City Tower, LXJ183 is eight miles out entering a left downwind for the visual three-two," Fink said.

"LXJ183 is cleared to land runway seventeen, winds three-four-zero at five to ten."

"Cleared to land, LXJ183," Fink repeated the instruction.

The wheels touched down with barely a bump and Alex Ramirez, who had passed the flight from Baltimore in the copilot's seat, stood with the aircraft still in motion.

"I'll head back and get the weapons and gear ready," he said.

"The Cessna's waiting for us," Fink answered. "I want to be airborne within an hour."

The two men had worked together for years, and had handpicked the team for the Genesis job. Ramirez, who'd had his face cut nearly in two in Rwanda, was sharp and dependable, and the absolute best with any sort of electronics, or any kind of garrote. He was also a vicious infighter, who had disposed of the Capitol security guard Peter Tannen quietly and efficiently, thus earning himself this trip to Kansas.

Fink taxied to a smooth stop at the location assigned to him by the controller. Then he powered the engines down and confirmed the cockpit radio was off as well. Cain expected him to check in, and that conversation was not one he could afford to inadvertently broadcast to Garden City's air traffic tower.

He made contact with his employer through a high-tech push-button phone.

"We've landed at Garden City Regional, ready for phase two," he said.

Seconds later he heard a beep and Cain's baritone voice.

"What's your ETA to Kalvesta?"

"We're forty miles west. Once we get the paperwork done, we should have our first visuals of the facility within an hour."

"Very good," Cain replied. "You'll be able to send me photographs?"

"Yes. Cain, let me go in. I know I can get to Rhodes and finish this once and for all."

"Negative," Cain said. "This is a reconnaissance mission only. We dismantled our surveillance of the facility after the lab was closed down. I need to see how it's been resurrected before we make our next move. But I promise you, Fink, you'll get your chance soon enough. We can't have Rhodes messing things up at this stage."

"Roger and out."

The mercenary snarled and returned the phone to the front pocket of his fleece-lined flight jacket. The blown missile strike at the Capitol wasn't totally his fault, but he was the one with the visual, and he was the one who pulled the trigger. He took great pride in his near-perfect record of mission successes. He would wait for Cain's kill order, but not for too long.

Ramirez had unloaded the duffel bags of equipment and weapons, and was waiting for Fink on the tarmac when he deplaned.

"Stay here, sport," the older man ordered. "I'll go sign for the Cessna."

Five minutes later, the killer was seated in a small wood-paneled office in an outbuilding near the air traffic control tower. The portly rental agent across from him, Jim Kinchley according to his desk plate, turned down a small portable television that was broadcasting the latest CNN news report from the Capitol.

"Crazy stuff happening out there," Kinchley said.

"Crazy," Fink agreed.

"Well, I got your fax and was able to get started on the paperwork. Just need to finish up the rental agreement is all."

The documents Fink had used to rent the Learjet from Baltimore-Washington airport included his own pilot's license with the name changed, and a master forgery of one for Ramirez, who couldn't fly anything more complex than a paper airplane, but was needed to fulfill the requirement for two pilots. Only one would be needed now for the Cessna 172 Skyhawk.

This was a stealth operation and Fink took every precaution to ensure there were no mishaps.

"So, Mr. Keegan," the agent said, "how long will you be using the one-seven-two?"

"I don't know," Fink replied. "Does it matter?"

"Have to put a specific time on this here form."

"Well then, put down two days."

Fink fixed the man with a baleful look that made him agree to the vague answer without objection.

"Mind if I ask what sort of business you're in?" Kinchley quickly pointed to a line on the rental agreement. "It's required, you see."

Another hard stare.

"Debt collector," Fink said.

With the papers signed, and an inspection completed, he taxied the aircraft over to where Ramirez was waiting. The Cessna was airborne forty-five minutes from when they had touched down. Not wanting to burn fuel on a long ascent, Fink leveled out at four thousand feet, and proceeded on an easterly course that took him over a barren, flat patchwork of square and rectangular brown fields flecked with snow.

The Kalvesta facility came into view forty minutes after takeoff. Ramirez peered through the lenses of his high-powered Brunton binoculars and made some initial observations while they were still several miles away.

"I'll need to get closer to take any useful pictures, but from what I'm seeing we've got ourselves a mini Fort Knox," he told Fink. "Lots of manpower, lots of guns, and lots of fencing."

Fink retrieved his phone to report that initial assessment to Cain, when his cockpit radio sparked to life.

"Unidentified aircraft, you are flying in restricted U.S. military airspace. Alter course heading two-seven-zero and maintain at least ten miles from point north thirty-eight degrees, three minutes, thirty-four seconds; west one hundred degrees, seventeen minutes, eleven seconds."

It was not a smart move to have passed so close. Clearly with so much at stake, including his own life, Allaire was moving quickly.

Fink altered their course without hesitation.

"Roger that and all apologies," he said into his

headset. "Was unaware of any military activity here. Changing to a heading of two-seven-zero as instructed."

"Thank you, aircraft. And have a pleasant day."

Fink switched the radio to intercom mode, cursed out loud, and then spoke to Ramirez via their headset microphones.

"For now is right, there, sport," he said. "We're going to have to make this a ground operation."

"No problem," Ramirez replied, with the binoculars still pressed to his eyes.

The Cessna completed its sharp turn to course correct and again leveled off. Ramirez no longer had visual of the facility that was now directly behind them. But moments later, he tapped Fink on the arm because something else had caught his attention.

"Take a look," Ramirez said, passing over the binoculars.

The heading change had put the Cessna directly above a red Ford Taurus that was pulled over on a particularly barren stretch of road, just five miles from the entrance to the Kalvesta facility. Fink piloted the plane with his knees as he studied the scene below through the binoculars.

"You see?" Ramirez asked.

Fink nodded.

"Not a lot of traffic on this road at this hour," he said.

"Or any hour, I would bet."

"Not every day you see somebody being helped out of the trunk of a car either."

"Not every day," Ramirez agreed. "Doesn't look like she was in there unwilling either."

"Not if after you get out of the trunk, you jump into the front seat like she just did." Fink handed the binoculars back to Ramirez. "Can you get a plate number from here?" he asked.

"I can."

Fink took out his phone.

"Cain, it's Fink. You read me?"

"I'm here," Cain answered.

"Can you run a license plate for me?"

"Give me the numbers."

Fink kept the Taurus in view while he recited the plate numbers to Cain. The Taurus had pulled back onto the road and was continuing west on Route 156. A few minutes later, Fink's phone beeped.

"The car is registered to the Kalvesta lab tech Melvin Forbush," Cain said. "What's going on?"

Fink explained the situation.

"Follow him. The no-fly zone tells me enough about security. Getting to Rhodes is going to take some planning."

"Roger that."

Fink increased the plane's altitude, but not so much that he lost sight of the car as it traveled past Garden City and turned south onto U.S. 50.

"Anything of interest on Fifty South?" Fink asked.

Ramirez checked his map and said, "The only thing between here and Cimarron is Garden City Regional Airport."

"Well then," Fink said, "it looks like we'll be returning the plane sooner than we planned."

CHAPTER 33

DAY 5

11:00 A.M. (EST)

Angie's odyssey from Denver was something of a nightmare. Engine problems delayed the flight for several hours, and then canceled it altogether. By the time she arrived in Midtown Manhattan it was nearly eleven in the morning. She used the time before her noon meeting with Sliplitz to buy some toiletries, makeup, a large Giants T-shirt, and a pair of yellow sweatpants, which she packed inside the carry-on she had borrowed from Melvin.

She slept in short bursts on the flight from Denver, awakening damp with perspiration from dreams reliving her clandestine departure from Kalvesta. The adventure began with a problem—Melvin reported that all vehicles leaving the compound were being inspected. After scouting the search procedure for more than an hour, he came up with a plan based, not surprisingly, on something he had seen in a movie.

The key was timing. In fact, she and Melvin practiced their maneuver half a dozen times in a secluded corner of the parking area. They were down to less than ten seconds beginning to end when she finally proclaimed they were as good as they were going to get.

First, Angie, holding an armload of blankets as an excuse in case someone stopped her, concealed herself against the wall of the bungalow closest to the main guard post. Melvin, positioned by the hood of his Taurus, waited for the trunk to be checked and closed, and then began coughing violently, and crying for help. Academy Award–worthy, he would later call his performance.

"My asthma!" Melvin called out, pounding on the hood. "I'm choking. . . . Inhaler . . . in glove compartment. . . . Help me!"

The soldier conducting the inspection set aside the mirror he had been using to examine the underside of the car, and raced to Melvin's aid. At that moment, Angie moved quickly across the fifteen-foot space separating the bungalow from the rear end of the Taurus. Keeping low, she unlocked the trunk with Melvin's spare key and opened the trunk eighteen inches. Then she shoved in the blankets and followed them through the small opening.

"Damn," she murmured reverently, when she felt the car accelerate and realized that Melvin's plan had worked.

Six miles in the trunk—that's what Melvin told her it would be. Six short miles before he felt comfortable they would be clear of the facility and any patrols, and he could get her out and into the passenger seat. Despite being propped with pillows and the blankets, and having tested the space out, Angie felt the gnawing pangs of claustrophobia set in the moment she closed the trunk from the inside.

There had to have been a better way, she was thinking one moment.

I can do this, she was thinking the next.

Her discomfort would have been even more acute had she known that five minutes out, Forbush's cell phone had lost any signal.

By the time they had passed what Angie felt had to be the six-mile mark, her dry-mouthed anxiety had mushroomed into an air-hungry panic. She began to hyperventilate. *He forgot the deal! Melvin's going to drive the whole way with me in here!*

She tried calling him and then lit her flashlight, which had only a brief calming effect. Next she pounded on the trunk's underside. Nothing. The car motored on, jarring her from side to side as her breathing grew even more rapid and shallow. At one point, they slammed in and out of a huge pothole, snapping her teeth through the inside of her cheek.

More time passed and she began imagining terrible things—being buried alive and smothered to death; being kidnapped, and even raped. When Forbush finally released her from the trunk, she learned that they had traveled less than two miles when they hit the huge pothole, nothing near the five miles she had guessed.

Never again, was all she could think as Forbush helped her to her feet and into the passenger seat. *Never again.*

Angie fought back the urge to call Griff. They had little doubt that nearly everything they did at the lab was being monitored. She shuddered at the notion of how compressed her world had become. The constant scrutiny, the airlocks, the elevator, the biohazard suit, the trunk. The claustrophobia of what had recently been a carefree existence in one of the most fascinating cities in the world had actually shaken her confidence. She expressed those feelings to Melvin, who did his best to be supportive. But there were obvious limits to the man's ability for empathy. For now, she would have to gain strength from Griff's final words to her.

I believe in you.

In contrast to the sleepy Garden City airport, the terminal at JFK was a near gridlock of travelers. Angie was jostled by several of them as she followed the signs to ground transportation. One of them, a lean and swarthy man wearing sunglasses, had been on the flight from Garden City to Denver, as well as on the flight from Denver to New York. He muttered an apology as he passed her, then hurried away, a cell phone pressed to his ear.

From a small television set embedded into the back of the cabby's seat, Angie watched the latest Fox News report from the Capitol. The broadcast reporter was a sharply dressed woman in her late twenties, and behind her were hundreds of television cameras from other news outlets jockeying for the most eye-catching shot. Despite the reporter's complete confidence in her story, Angie knew the information she was reporting was woefully inaccurate. Allaire's PR machine had done a masterful job categorizing the virus threat as flulike and explaining the extensive security measures as precautionary only.

Angie turned the volume off, unwilling to listen to any more misinformation. She knew the truth—hell, she had the story of the century to report. All she had to do was direct the driver to any of a number of media outlets in New York, and in no time she'd be given her choice of plum jobs and probably a seven-figure book deal as well. But the country was at stake, and for the first time in her professional life, she opted for perpetuating a lie over printing the truth.

When she arrived at her Midtown destination, Angie paid the fare plus tip in cash. Genesis had found ways to frame Griff and to bypass the security system at the State of the Union Address. There was no reason at this point to underestimate their resources, creativity, or viciousness. It was hard to believe her credit card transactions were already being monitored, especially given that Genesis had no reason to know who she was or how she was involved with Kalvesta, but there was no sense in taking chances.

Angie had never lived in New York City, but she always felt at home there. Once on Broadway, she located Sliplitz's number, and rang the buzzer to apartment 3E. Seconds later, she heard the intercom click on.

"Da?" said a man's voice.

"Gottfried, it's me."

"Ah, zis gloomy day is suddenly brighter," replied the heavy German accent.

Angie quickly opened the outside and inner doors, entering the dreary foyer before the buzzer shut off.

She walked up to the third floor, carrying her small suitcase rather than bouncing its wheels against every stair. Her energy was returning—the fog that had slowed her down following the horrible ride from Kalvesta had lifted. She was back on the job. This was what she lived for. Her ADD personality was made for the frenetic, unpredictable world of reporting.

The man who answered the door to 3E was short, fat, bearded, balding, and, he had told her over the phone, recently divorced for the fourth time. Of all her professional contacts, Gottfried Sliplitz had proven to be one of the most useful. When they first met, Sliplitz was an analyst with the Health and Human Services Agency in Rockville, Maryland. Angie was research-ing a story about salmonella contamination at a local drug manufacturing plant, and Sliplitz was a source. Within minutes of her concluding their first interview, the affable German professed his love for her. To prove it, he falsified documents that gave her unprecedented access to plant employees and corporate records.

The story of greed gone bad and public safety ig-nored was nominated for a Pulitzer Prize. It didn't win, but she came close to winning a jail sentence for con-tempt of court, for not giving up her contact at the HHSA. She knew never to turn on a source—especially one like Gottfried Sliplitz. As a result of that code, she had come perilously close to jail for contempt on sev-eral other occasions as well. Now she needed the man's help again. And with his adoration for her still in bloom, he was more than willing to oblige.

"You look vonderful, *liebchen*. Can you come in for

a while?" Gottfried asked, his eyes begging the way a puppy might plead for a pat.

"Thanks for the offer, Gottfried, but I don't have time. Were you able to get me what I need?"

"I am chief analyst for ze New York City Department of Health and Mental Hygiene," Gottfried said. "Big step up from Rockville. Good money, too."

"Strange name, though."

"It could have been vurse. Ve are also responsible for dog licenses, developmental disabilities, und STD prevention, to name just a few."

He extracted a manila envelope from a drawer and handed it to her. "With these papers, you are officially an investigator in our department."

Angie kissed Sliplitz on the cheek and hugged him.

"You're the best, Gottfried. I promise, soon as I can I'll make it up to you."

"On a date?"

She smiled at him.

"I've just started seeing a terrific man. Besides, I need to keep our relationship professional. Think of what could happen if we turned sour? I would lose a dear friend and an invaluable resource."

"I'll take ze risk."

"But I won't. Look, I have lots of friends I can hook you up with," she promised. "Just not right now."

"You break my heart."

She kissed him again on the cheek.

"Luckily, you heal quickly. Between us, right? Nobody knows about this?"

"Between us," Sliplitz confirmed.

Angie gave the man a final embrace before she departed. As she headed down the staircase she passed a man on his way up. He was wearing dark sunglasses, and grunted a greeting as he brushed past her.

Once on the street, Angie flagged another cab. As they pulled away, headed downtown, the driver of the Town Car parked behind them set his cell phone aside and followed.

CHAPTER 34

Angie stepped from her cab into a world as far from the rolling plains and bison ranches of western Kansas as imaginable.

Chinatown.

The lower Manhattan neighborhood featured pungent odors, tightly packed shops and apartments, cracked sidewalks, brick buildings with red-painted fire escapes, double-parked trucks casually blocking traffic, and nerve-shaking noise from blaring horns and a dozen active construction sites. Storefront signage was in Chinese with a smattering of English subtitles. Many of the goods displayed in windows underneath neon signs were unlikely to be found in any other part of the city. Fruit stands, fish markets, and shops selling knickknacks to tourists lined the narrow, winding, overcrowded streets.

Angie stood in the entrance of a redbrick building she guessed might have once been a tenement. There was no sign identifying the nursing home, although she confirmed the address was the one on the brochure she had found in Sylvia's office. She pressed the only button on the building's facade and a high-pitched voice on the intercom said something in Chinese.

"Department of Health and Mental Hygiene," Angie said, holding up her fake ID badge to the security camera installed overhead. The photograph laminated into the card was one Gottfried Sliplitz had taken from her Facebook page.

There was a lengthy pause before the door buzzed. She entered into a cramped, poorly lit hallway, dominated by an ornate, rickety wooden staircase that ascended steeply in front of her. The unmistakable odor of cooked fish and salt drifted down from the floors above.

Stepping into character, Angie hid her suitcase behind the stairwell. She looked around for an elevator, but saw none. Curious. Surely a nursing home had to have one.

Eschewing the stairs, she headed down the hallway, which turned once to the right and ended at a heavy metal door that was locked. It was possible there was an elevator somewhere behind it, but that made little sense. Perhaps the nursing home had been merged with the building next door and that was where the elevator was.

Finally, she returned to the front hallway and trudged up the steep stairs, still wondering how a nursing home could exist without some sort of transport for disabled and wheelchair-bound residents. As she ascended, the sound of voices grew louder. She stopped on the fourth floor, where the chatter was the loudest, the odor the strongest. A small sign nailed to a shuttered door read RIVERSIDE beneath its corresponding Chinese characters.

Angie paused to catch her breath, then knocked. A haggard, middle-aged Chinese woman responded. She had short dark hair streaked with gray, and wore a black blouse with a swirling, orange floral design. Angie held up her Health and Mental Hygiene identification card, and was suspiciously invited one step inside. She felt slightly foolish at having come so far on such little evidence. If she were wrong about Riverside, she would be flying back to Garden City by morning.

"Does a Mrs. Chen reside here?" she asked.

The woman shook her head, shouted something into the space behind her, looked quizzically back at Angie, and shook her head again. Angie wished that she had the picture of Sylvia and her mother to show, but Griff had warned her that the chemical and ultraviolet decontamination process required to remove it from the Kitchen would have ruined the image altogether.

"May I come in?" she asked.

The woman nodded, spoke again in Chinese, and then motioned for Angie to enter. They stepped into a narrow, oak-floored hallway that featured rows of doors with numbers, but no glass, presumably residents' rooms, extending in both directions. It was more dormlike than any nursing home Angie had ever visited, but the corridor was also remarkably clean and fairly free of clutter. Several walkers and wheelchairs were pushed up against the wall, plus an empty hospital bed provided the only visible clue as to the building's function.

Angie followed the woman until they came to an

open, brightly lit common area. There were two dozen or so elderly Chinese women and men seated on couches and easy chairs, or clustered around foldout bridge tables. Many of them were talking, seemingly at the same time. Some of the residents were playing games— backgammon, cards, and Mahjong. Others were watching television. A few were simply staring off, perhaps at their memories.

Angie scanned the room for Sylvia Chen's mother. Lack of any possible candidates continued to erode her confidence in her conclusions about the place. Had she put Gottfried at risk for nothing? Melvin too? Suddenly the nonlinear thinking of her ADD, which had so often helped her break a story, seemed childish, misguided, and even worse, potentially dangerous.

A stunning young Chinese woman approached from across the lounge, requested her credentials, and examined them with care.

"Hello, Ms. Donna Prince," she said finally, in perfect English. "My name is Wu Mei. Please call me Mei. I am the floor manager and duty nurse in charge. My aunt told me you are looking for someone."

"Yes. I'm looking for a woman. Her family name might be Chen. I have reason to believe she's a resident here."

"We have several Chens living here," Mei said with a brief laugh. "It is a very common Chinese name. Perhaps if you could be more specific."

Again, that photograph.

"Her daughter's name is Sylvia if that helps."

"I'm sorry," she said. "Is there some sort of problem?"

"We have reason to believe Mrs. Chen's daughter may have come in contact with a very contagious virus, and then visited her mother here," Angie said, retelling the story she had conjured up during the flight from Denver. "We are searching for both the mother and the daughter. I'll need access to all the rooms in this facility."

"Goodness!" Mei replied, setting her hand to her lips in a show of genuine alarm. "Nothing like what's happening in Washington, I hope."

"Possibly. We need to find these women to do some blood work."

"I'll be happy to help you look," Mei said. "This floor is for our low-acuity residents. Higher-acuity patients are on the upper floors."

"I appreciate your cooperation. It will be noted in my report."

"Right this way."

Mei led Angie back to the stairs.

"Pardon me, Wu Mei, but I went to take your elevator up here and could not find one on the first floor. I wondered how you transport your residents from floor to floor and down to the street."

Mei did not reply immediately, and in fact, kept walking to the stairs. The silence was awkward. Suddenly, the nurse stopped and turned.

"Could I see your credentials again, please?" she asked.

Angie felt herself go cold. Her backup plan, which probably could have been her first choice all along, was simply to tell the truth. But with the FBI failing to find

Sylvia Chen, and Genesis eerily prescient, some sort of deception seemed called for.

Now, it appeared, she had been caught.

She handed over her ID.

The young nurse, looking genuinely distressed, scanned it briefly and handed it back.

"We have one," she said gloomily. "At the back of the building. But we don't use it very much, and I believe my aunt and uncle, who own this place, have had a long-standing arrangement of some kind with the building or the nursing home inspectors. Please, please don't say anything about it in your report. The elevator is very old, but I have heard my uncle say that the cost to replace it and the structural support around it would force them to close down. And there is really nothing like this place for our Chinese elders."

"I understand," Angie said. "You have nothing to worry about from me."

"Oh, thank you. Thank you so much. I was going to walk you up to the sixth floor. Why don't we ride instead?"

Angie kept the visage of Sylvia's mother clear in her mind as she followed Mei down the hallway and to the right. The elevator—truly ancient—was precisely where she had guessed it would be. Mei lifted the wide, double doors and Angie stepped inside the darkened car, turning around and then instinctively backing a step toward the rear wall.

"Stop! Don't move any more!" Mei cried out in alarm. She pointed behind Angie at a gap of about two feet between the steel elevator floor and the wooden back wall. Immediately, Angie took a precautionary step forward. Mei closed the doors, then used a key to engage the motor. The car clattered to life and traveled slowly upward, with Angie wondering how close this lift might be to the original one built by Otis in the mid-nineteenth century.

"How long has Riverside been in business?" she asked.

"Since the nineteen forties. My great-grandparents opened the place because too many Chinese were forced to send elderly parents to facilities that did not respect our traditions."

The elevator came to a hard stop and Angie momentarily lost her balance. Mei turned the key once more to lock the system, then lifted open the door, and motioned for her to follow.

They started with the room closest to the elevator, and immediately, Angie felt a jolt of excitement. Her search was over. Seated on a small vinyl-covered chair, in the corner of a stark space illuminated by light coming through a small, grimy window, and also from a bedside table lamp, was a woman probably in her eighties. But as Angie introduced herself, knelt down, and studied the woman's deeply etched face at closer range, her certainty faded as quickly as it had come.

She could be Sylvia's mother, Angie thought—*but just as probably, she is not.* The eyes, the vague expression—there was something about them that made Angie now feel that her initial reaction had been wrong.

"That's Mrs. Li," Mei said, not bothering to move away from the woman. "She is one of our Alzheimer residents. She drifts in and out of lucidness, but as a matter of fact, she does have a daughter who visits."

"Go on, please."

"Well, first of all, her daughter has been badly scarred by a fire, and keeps her face covered, so I really can't describe her."

"That's all right," Angie said, feeling a nugget of suspicion materialize around what seemed like something of a coincidence.

"Let's keep looking," Mei said.

Three floors and sixty room checks later, they were back where they had begun.

"And you're sure that nobody's off-site?" Angie asked. "Visiting with family? Out shopping?"

Mei shook her head.

"Not at so close to dinner. And no, I checked the books after we finished in the rooms at the change of shifts. All of our residents are on the premises."

Angie felt a wave of frustration wash over her.

What now?

She asked to see Mrs. Li one more time, but the visit was again unproductive. The woman was significantly older than the one Angie remembered from the photograph in Chen's office. For a moment, Li seemed to brighten at the mention of the name Sylvia, but just as quickly the glimmer went away.

"Well, I want to thank you again for your cooperation," she said. "You've been extremely gracious with your time."

"If I come across anybody named Chen with a daughter Sylvia, I'll be sure to contact you, Ms. Prince."

"Thank you," Angie said, though she knew the phone number on the business card Sliplitz had made for her would connect to a nonworking number.

Back to Kansas.

Angie retrieved her suitcase and stepped outside into a biting, late afternoon wind. She searched for a cab, saw that none were coming, and trudged off in the direction of Houston Street, where more were sure to pass. She crossed the alley dividing Riverside and another brick building, which brought her in front of a Chinese restaurant. It was only then that she realized how long it had been since she had last eaten.

The aroma wafting from the modest-sized place beckoned her inside. Even at this hour, the restaurant was busy, mostly with Asians—the indicator Angie had always, without any hard evidence, come to associate with quality, authentic Chinese food. There was an open table near the kitchen. She maneuvered through narrow gaps between chairs and dodged the hustling waitstaff on her way to a seat.

How will Griff take the news? she was wondering.

In one inspired burst she had failed to find the only link to Genesis and the ultimate proof of his innocence.

"It was still worth it," she said aloud, though her words lacked conviction.

Lost in thought, she did not notice the waitress standing beside her table. The woman turned over Angie's teacup and filled it from a steaming, metal pitcher. Angie glanced up and her breathing stopped.

The waitress was Professor Sylvia Chen.

CHAPTER 35

DAY 5
4:00 P.M. (EST)

"You wish something drink or you like order?" Sylvia Chen said in a heavy accent.

She was rail-thin, with dark eyes that were nearly lost in shadow, but Angie had no doubt whatsoever that it was she. Her uniform, a black dress shirt and black slacks, was a size too large. The nametag above her breast pocket read simply BAO.

"Sylvia," Angie whispered, "please don't react. I know who you are and I know why you are here. I need to speak with you. I came from Kalvesta to find you."

The steel pitcher in the waitress's hand began to shake. Dollops of brown tea splashed out from the spout and stained the white tablecloth.

"No understand," Chen said, avoiding any eye contact.

"Stop it," Angie said harshly. "This is urgent."

The color drained from Chen's face. Her body stiffened.

"No . . . please . . ."

Her eyes were wild with fear as she made a furtive scan of the restaurant. Either she was searching for an exit, or perhaps, even more terrifying to her, Angie's accomplice.

"Easy," Angie said. "Please don't call attention to yourself. I'm not here to hurt you."

"Are you police? Military?"

The words were said softly. The accent was gone.

"No, I'm not. Trust me."

"Are you them? Are you Genesis?"

The woman kept trembling.

"I'm a reporter with *The Washington Post*. The Capitol has been quarantined. Griffin Rhodes has been asked by the president to develop a treatment for WRX3883. I'm helping him keep a record of everything that he does. We know about how he was set up before, and we know you were involved. The president has gotten him out of prison and reopened your lab. There is little time. People are dying from the virus."

Chen's knees buckled, as though mention of the past had placed too much stress on her joints. Angie reached up, supported the woman by her arm, and encouraged her to sit down. Chen refused, straightened up, and pointed to the menu on the table.

"Is there any chance that you were followed?" she asked.

"I don't see how," Angie said. "I flew in from Kansas earlier today via Denver."

"Genesis is very resourceful. I should never have agreed to cooperate with them, but they knew all about my work, and they knew that their financing was the last chance I had to keep my research going. They are also very dangerous. I am a loose end for them now. All they want is the virus. They don't care about controlling it. They tried to kill me, but I escaped and came here. If they find me, I assure you, both my mother and I are dead."

"I can help you, Sylvia. That's why I came to New York—to help you and to see if there is any way to control the virus. I'm working with Griffin Rhodes at your lab."

"He's out of prison, you said?"

"Yes, he's been out for just a few days."

"That is wonderful news. Listen, stay here. Study your menu."

Angie did as she was asked, but went on red alert in case Chen bolted.

The Ph.D. scientist went to service a table of four, then returned.

"I'm going to ask you again. Is it possible you were followed?"

"I know the people who are after you are resourceful," Angie replied, "so I suppose anything's possible. But I really don't see how."

Chen looked unconvinced.

"How did you find me?"

"The brochure in the peach cookbook," was all Angie needed to say.

"Did my mother tell you I was here in the restaurant?"

"I didn't find your mother. Where does she live?"

"Riverside. I thought you knew that."

"On close inspection, the woman I thought was your mother—a woman named Li—didn't look like her."

Angie's puzzled expression seemed to clarify the mystery for Chen.

"Ah. Li is the name I made up for her. Her real name is Chen, same as mine. Chen Su. You went looking for the woman in the picture on my desk, yes?"

Angie nodded. "I checked every patient in Riverside."

"Do you know how Alzheimer's disease can ravage the body? Alter the appearance?"

"I do. How long has your mother had Alzheimer's?"

"It's been progressing for several years. She still floats in and out, and is sometimes quite lucid, but it is getting worse. The woman in the photograph in my office is the woman I want to remember. This is what my mother looks like now."

Chen fished out a picture from her pocket and handed it to Angie. Then she went off again to take orders. When she returned, she set a steaming bowl of some sort of seafood soup in front of Angie.

"This is the best thing on the menu," she said, "especially on a cold winter's day like today. I hope you like it. You just came in here by chance, then?"

"I was starved and this was the closest place to the Riverside. Mei, the nurse there, said the daughter who visits Mrs. Li was badly scarred by a fire."

"When I go there I am wearing a hat. My face is covered by a scarf. My hands are hidden by gloves. I lie to protect my mother and myself."

"You have to help us," Angie said.

Chen paused for a time.

"I know," she said finally.

She took another nervous look about the restaurant, and even glanced several times out the front windows. Droplets of perspiration had appeared like condensation on her brow.

"So you will help us?"

"I've done terrible things," the virologist said in a shaky voice. "I did not know they would do this. The attack on the Capitol. How could I have known?"

"What were you told would happen? Do you know who these people are? Do you have any idea how we can stop this?"

Chen shut Angie off.

"Eleven o'clock the restaurant will be closed," she said. "It is too busy here for the rest of the evening. Too dangerous to talk now. Come into the alley at the back of the restaurant. Red door with Chinese lettering on it. Knock three times so I know it is you. I have some papers that might help. I'll tell you everything that I know then."

"Eleven o'clock," Angie said.

Chen nodded grimly, turned, and vanished through the swinging kitchen doors.

CHAPTER 36

DAY 5
10:00 P.M. (CST)

Sleep.

Griff's eyes stung with a persistent gritty burn that he knew only sleep could relieve. He felt desperate to rub at them, to coax some moisture out of the tear glands, but the plastic face shield on his biosuit made it impossible, and the forty minutes it would take to remove his helmet, massage his eyes, and get suited up again were an unacceptable waste of time. Relief would have to wait. The same with sleep.

Thirty-six hours straight now since his last nap.

Gratefully, the concentration involved with his work eased the time along.

His limbs felt leaden, and his joints ached inside the bulky protective suit. Every twenty minutes or so, he took a brief walk through the Kitchen to Sylvia Chen's office, and back to his own. Perhaps he had gone without sleep this long during his months in solitary confinement, but it was hard to track time in such an utterly monotonous place. Here, more than two hundred feet underground, he had the added reminder of wall-mounted digital clocks in every room.

He took a break, went online, and looked up the record for continuous sleep depravation. Eleven days by a seventeen-year-old student in the sixties. Guinness had subsequently closed the category for fear of causing serious health problems in those attempting to get their bit of immortality, although no adverse effects were reported in the high schooler.

Back to work.

Griff adjusted the electron microscope until it projected crystal-clear images of WRX3883's submicroscopic world onto an attached television monitor. Despite the screen's high-definition resolution, he had to strain to keep the image in focus. Forty-five minutes slid by. He rose from his chair, but knew it had been too long. His knees had gone to Jell-O and he stumbled twice before managing his brief walk.

I'll just close my eyes for a few seconds, he decided. . . . *Just a few seconds.*

Griff's head dropped forward onto his arms, and in moments, his thoughts began to fade. Then, just as suddenly, they reappeared, centering about horrific images from the Capitol—snapshots of people whose lives he had vowed to try and save. As if he were at the wheel on a long-distance drive, he snapped his head from side to side until he produced a jet of renewed consciousness that did the trick—at least for the moment. If he had to stay alert for another thirty-six hours, he would do it.

It had taken several hours of painstaking effort to get his lab operational again, but things seemed to be working remarkably well. The computers had sparked back to life and were picking up where he had last left off some ten months ago. Cultures of the blood brought from the Capitol were cooking in cell lines Melvin had prepared.

WRX3883 was a hearty, rapidly multiplying microbe, and after several hours of growth, they were able to move samples of the virus from the incubator to the electron microscope's airless vacuum chamber. Griff proceeded to collect data from those samples, which he then input into his software application. From there, he could simulate the response to variations of his antiviral treatment. The end result, if successful, would be a new approach to interfering with WRX3883 replication.

During the early days in Sylvia Chen's lab at Columbia, flushed with a series of successes, he had nicknamed his program Orion, in honor of the legendary great hunter of Greek mythology. Griff's Orion had only one mission: hunt WRX3883 to extinction, without harming the host. For now, Orion was computer-generated, but if Griff could map out the right RNA design, it could be synthesized in a lab or even inserted into a cell line.

For a time, the excitement surrounding his work was dizzying.

Then, the failures began.

In every computer simulation he ran, WRX3883 battled his creation with the same lethal ferocity of the gods' assassin, Scorpius, the scorpion, who eventually felled the great hunter Orion.

This scorpion's lethal weapon: mutation.

WRX3883 was as quick as it was deadly. From a germ with effects limited to the deep central nervous system, suddenly there were computer indications of disastrous damage to tissue cultures grown from blood and gastrointestinal cells as well.

Again and again, Griff's attacking protein seemed close to working. But in this battle, Orion's near successes were still the equivalent of abject failure. The missing link, he knew, might be something as close as a minor RNA sequence modification, or something as distant as Orion, the constellation. No matter how close the breakthrough was, according to Griff's models the result for the infected host remained the same—death.

Another stroll through the Kitchen, and he shifted his attention from the television screen of magnified WRX virus to Sylvia Chen's laboratory notebooks, which were laid open and stacked atop one another on the stainless steel table beside the electron microscope. He flipped through pages of notes dictated into a computer program, or written in his former boss's small, irregular hand, but as with the images generated by the microscope, exhaustion blurred the words. He'd come to the last of the three-ring binders, and was flipping through old lab notes searching for anything of interest to his work, when one report in particular caught his breath.

The report, titled simply "The Macaque Incident," and dated a year and a half ago, detailed the most horrific account of animal testing Griff had ever seen. A simple protocol mistake by an animal keeper in Hell's

Kitchen—Sylvia Chen's animal lab—infected thirty Rhesus monkeys with exceedingly high doses of WRX3883. Their decline, stunningly rapid, was captured on video for later study.

Chen's documented account was disturbingly graphic, and evoked in Griff memories he had long wished to forget. It was his policy never to go near the animal lab unless he positively had to. But the cries for help from the caretaker had brought him down there. He tried to help the animals with a variety of antiviral drugs, and even one of his more advanced serums. But there was nothing he, or anybody, could do to save them. He could still hear screams of dying monkeys, some so sick that they used their rapier-like nails to slice their own bodies to ribbons, trying to scratch the virus out.

The disastrous Macaque Incident notwithstanding, Sylvia Chen remained convinced that her work with primates held the answer to terminating a WRX3883 infection before the microbes could mutate. Griff constantly considered incorporating elements of Chen's research findings with his own, but could not bring himself even to appear to endorse her methods. Now, as much as it sickened him to read through her notes, he knew they might contain useful nuggets that could help uncover Orion's missing piece.

Griff had read a survey in which 90 percent of the general public accepted the use of animals in medical research, so long as that research involved serious medical conditions, and all alternatives had been fully considered before sacrificing the experimental subjects. He argued that WRX3883 was a weapon, without any true medical gain to be had. He also pushed his own methods as a viable alternative.

Chen's only concession was to keep him employed and provide him a platform for proving or disproving his hypotheses.

Forbush entered the lab and set a box of pipettes on the counter by the stainless steel sink.

"After Sylvia vanished, the FBI wanted to take those notebooks," he said. "Two guys who looked like Michael Douglas and Harvey Keitel searched her lab and office. They hated the biosuits and ended up knocking over just about everything that wasn't screwed down. When I told them they couldn't take anything out of here, they were really upset. They read the notes in Sylvia's office, but I don't think they got much out of them. How about you?"

"There are things here and there that might be useful, but I just don't know if I want to study them. It makes me sick to have to relive that monkey disaster."

"Now that you mention it, my friend, you really *do* look a little sick. Can you take a break?"

Griff rejected the suggestion, even though his stomach felt hollow and his body as though Novocain had been pumped in as a replacement for his blood.

"We've got to push ahead, Melvin," he said, "at least for a few more hours. Then maybe I'll take a short break."

"Good idea. When you walk, you're starting to look like Boris Karloff in *Frankenstein*."

Arms out front, Forbush dramatized the remark.

"Thanks, Melvin," Griff said. "You know, I've been wondering. What if Sylvia had the wrong animals?"

"How do you mean?"

"She tested on Rhesus monkeys, but never on chimpanzees, partly because she knew I would have drawn the line at that and left the project. Their immune system is closest to our own. I wonder now if that would have made a difference."

"I can get the chimps," Forbush said. "Just say the word. It may take a little while, though."

The notion of working on chimpanzees soured Griff's stomach. Even assuming Melvin could procure the animals reasonably quickly, Griff would have to abandon Orion to chase another path—one that could prove costly in terms of time, just to satisfy some SWAT—a Scientific Wild Ass Theory.

Would it be worth it?

CHAPTER 37

DAY 5
11:00 P.M. (EST)

The alley behind the Sechuan Hop smelled of rotting vegetables. Frozen towers of cardboard boxes, stacked taller than Angie stood, abutted two Dumpsters overflowing with garbage and refuse. Dense overcast and the buildings themselves obscured any moonlight, and steel fire escapes protruding from the buildings made the narrow passageway seem even more foreboding.

Angie pulled the red knit hat she had bought from a street vendor down over her ears to shield them from a biting wind. At precisely eleven o'clock, as instructed, she knocked three times on the cold steel of the restaurant's alleyway entrance. On the second knock, the door budged. On the third, it swung open several inches, grating on rusted hinges. Angie took a cautious step inside and glanced about the basement, which was minimally lit from a source ahead and to her right. No one was there to greet her. She was unwilling to close the door any further.

"Sylvia?" Angie called out.

Nothing.

She was forced to clear her throat to speak again.

"Sylvia, are you here?"

But for the wind down the alley, the silence was absolute.

Floor-to-ceiling metal shelving, stocked with dried goods and restaurant supplies, created the feeling of claustrophobia that Angie had recently found so disturbing. Ahead of her, the shelves split to form three narrow aisles, two of which were dark. Angie took a tentative step down the center one, then another. Ahead, she could now make out a bare, low-wattage bulb, suspended on a short cord. A shaft of light from the bulb cast a long, distorted shadow across the cement floor. Angie's heart was hammering now. She sensed another presence in the basement. She wanted to leave—to simply turn and run. Instead, she took another step forward.

"Sylvia? Sylvia, please. Are you there?"

The shadow ahead seemed to waver slightly. Angie could make out the shape of long arms and fingers. As frightened as she was, she was also transfixed.

"Please?" she said, her voice now little more than a whimper.

She took another half step toward the shadow, then another, pausing to listen and to check between the shelves on either side, as well as behind her. She had reached the end of the aisle. The shadow extended almost to where she was standing, although a shelf blocked her from seeing the source. Jaws and fists clenched, she peered around the shelving. Then she gasped. Sylvia

Chen was hanging by an electric cord wrapped around her neck. The toes of her black work shoes, pointing down, were several inches off the concrete. The other end of the cord had been tossed over an exposed pipe, and then secured to a nearby steel support column.

The scientist's head was bowed, obscuring her face. Angie moved numbly to Sylvia's side and took her hand. Her skin was warm.

Could she still be alive?

She lifted Sylvia's head using two fingers underneath her chin. Immediately the flash of hope gave way to anguish and revulsion. Angie recoiled at the sight of the dead woman's tongue protruding out between her lips. Sylvia's face was swollen and dark, and even in the gloom, Angie could see that her bulging eyes were spotted red with burst capillaries—a sign, she knew, of strangulation. She swallowed back a jet of bile and allowed Sylvia's chin to drop back against her chest.

Calming herself with deep breaths, Angie examined the method used to hang the woman. The overhead pipe supplied the leverage to hoist her off the ground. The knot around the pipe seemed expertly done. Was she strangled before she was hung?

Two thoughts occurred to Angie at that moment. First, that this was murder, not suicide. There was no chair or box Sylvia could have used. Somebody powerful had to have pulled on the cord to lift her off her feet. The second thought sent a chill through her. When she first stepped into the basement and listened she'd had a strong sense that she was not alone.

Instantly, Angie was overwhelmed by the need to

get out of the building and into the alley. She whirled and dashed back up the aisle.

She had made it halfway when the heavy steel door ahead of her swung shut.

CHAPTER 38

Before Angie could react, a man emerged from the shadows beside the door, and stepped into the aisle, blocking her path. He was tall—six feet or more—and thin, but broad at the shoulders. Even in the dim light she could tell that his aquiline face was probably handsome at one time. Now, dominated by a huge, jagged scar running down his forehead, across his eyebrow, and over his cheek, it was utterly terrifying. He wore a black leather jacket, black watch cap, and black leather gloves. Dangling loosely from his right hand was a meat cleaver. What little light there was glinted off its broad blade.

"Welcome to hell, Senorita Fletcher," he said, his perfect English tinged with a Hispanic accent.

React! Angie's mind screamed. *Now!*

She swept her arm across the shelf by her shoulder, sending a barrage of cans and cartons flying into his chest, belly, and groin. The impact wasn't much, but the surprise gave her what she needed—enough time to whirl and bolt back down the aisle.

"No chance, *senorita,*" the man called out in a sing-song voice.

Angie screamed for help, frantically wondering where she might find another way out. If there were a stairway, she would have to pass by Sylvia's body to find it.

"Help!" she screamed again. "Someone please help!"

"I promise it will be painless for you, *senorita,*" the man called from behind her. "Dr. Chen was kind enough to part with her papers. Now, I just need a few answers from you. Thank you for leading me to her, by the way. I've been with you all the way from Kansas, and now I feel as if we are sort of buddies."

He was close.

Angie turned her head to gauge *how* close, and slammed into Sylvia's body. The woman's corpse swung away, then back, striking Angie and dropping her to one knee. She cried out and, scrambling to her feet, shoved Chen at the killer, who was now near enough to connect with the cleaver had he chosen to do so.

Instead, he stepped to one side of the aisle, twirling the weapon like a drummer's stick. They were no more than three feet apart. Even in the deep gloom, the grotesque, irregular scar stood out like a lightning bolt. There was nothing in his expression that suggested it was worth trying to negotiate.

"Enough," he said. "We need to talk. Your friend Sliplitz understood. He answered my questions. You do the same and I promise you won't feel any more pain than he did."

"You son of a bitch!"

"Believe it or don't, Senorita Fletcher, you are not the first one to call me that. Now . . ."

Cradling the cleaver in his right hand, he took a half step toward her and reached out for her arm. Angie's response was immediate. She swept her fist overhead, shattering the lightbulb and throwing the basement into absolute darkness. In the same motion, she grasped one of the metal shelving units, bringing it crashing down on the man.

The killer grunted and cursed, and Angie felt certain he was on the floor. Instead of turning to run, she leapt forward, stepping on boxes and the shelving, and stomping on what might have been the killer's chest. Then, holding her arms out to her sides to maintain contact with the shelves, she moved ahead as rapidly as she dared, back toward the steel door.

One step through the blackness, then another.

Behind her she heard the man throwing aside the debris, and working himself out from under the shelf.

The door had to be directly ahead.

Angie was trying to visualize which side the handle was on when she slammed full face into a steel support beam. She heard the bone in her nose shatter. Blinding pain exploded through her head. Instinctively, she wrapped her arms around the post, keeping herself from going down. Her nose filled with blood. Tears flooded down her cheeks.

At that instant, the killer's hand closed on her ankle.

Fueled by adrenaline, Angie kicked frantically, and connected. The grip on her leg vanished. Dazed, she plunged ahead. Two more steps and she hit the steel door forehead first, snapping her neck back. Another blast of pain. More dizziness and nausea. More tears. She slowed momentarily, then fumbled blindly for the door handle.

Again she felt the man's hand shoot out through the darkness and close on her ankle, but in that moment, her own fingers closed on the door handle.

She jammed the handle down. Immediately the door yielded, and she was in the alley, which was only marginally better lit than the basement had been. Glancing over her shoulder, she saw that her pursuer was on his hands and knees. He had clearly lost some of his composure. His lips were pulled back in a snarl.

Angie charged ahead. The killer, scrambling to his feet, might have gotten her right there, had he not slipped and fallen heavily into a puddle of garbage mixed with freezing slush.

Still, with the man quickly regaining his feet, Angie knew the chase was almost over. She was too far from either end of the alley to make it.

"Help!" she screamed. "Someone help me, please!"

Her cries were swallowed by the dense winter night.

A fire escape seemed her only chance. The way up to the nearest one was the built-in rungs on the side of one of the narrow Dumpsters, standing no more than eight feet away.

Gasping for breath, Angie grasped the top rung and hauled herself up until she was standing on the rim of the Dumpster, six feet from the ground and another six feet or so from the steel ladder at the base of the slatted stairway.

"End of the line, *senorita,*" the man said, breathing heavily.

He reached for her ankle, but just as he did, Angie took a single deep breath and launched herself upward. The cold air and her winter jacket held her back, making the difficult leap almost impossible. She was certain she had missed, and was already wondering what she could possibly do next when the fingers of her right hand hit against the edge of the lowest rung of the fire escape ladder and curled around the metal. There was no way she would be able to hold on for more than a second or two, but that was enough. Her weight began to pull the rusted ladder down, far enough so that her feet reconnected with the rim of the Dumpster. She adjusted her grip, hooked the fingers of her other hand around the icy metal, and pulled with all her strength.

In what seemed like slow motion, the ladder swung down.

Her foot was on the second rung when she felt the killer clawing at her leg once more. This time, she pulled away easily and climbed upward toward the first landing. She screamed and screamed again for help, aware that any misstep now would mean her death.

To her dismay the windows on the building remained dark and closed. By the time she reached the first landing, the man was on the ladder. The windows facing the landing were barred. From now on it would be stairs—slatted, freezing metal that would make every step treacherous.

At the second-floor landing the windows weren't barred. She considered and quickly abandoned the notion of smashing one of them, and trying to climb or dive inside someone's apartment. The killer was way too close, and two people had already died because of her.

Keeping her hands in contact with the railing, she pounded upward past one landing, then another. Blood sprayed from her nose with every frozen breath. She pawed at it with the back of her hand and coughed it from the back of her throat. Still, the distance between her and the killer seemed to be widening. Perhaps his sodden clothes were slowing him down. Perhaps he was hurt. Perhaps it was all those hours she had spent on the stationary bike.

God, but she missed her apartment. . . .

Her dizziness was getting more intense, and her breathing was growing more difficult, but she could hear that her pursuer was laboring also. She was reconsidering smashing a window, when she looked above and saw movement. A woman was poking out from one of the windows on the next landing.

"Help me!" Angie cried out to her. "Please!"

The woman slipped back inside the room, but the narrow window remained open. Angie dove through it, landing awkwardly, hitting her already battered forehead and smearing the hardwood floor with blood. A wizened woman stood in a corner, illuminated by a small bedside lamp. Angie suddenly realized where she was. *Riverside!* She'd explored the place just hours ago. She knew the room and she knew its occupant.

It was Chen Su—Sylvia Chen's mother.

CHAPTER 39

DAY 5
11:30 P.M. (EST)

"Mrs. Chen, hide! You've got to hide!"

Angie heard the killer on the landing. It had been a mistake to lead him in here. Now she had to lead him away.

To her right, the aged woman stood placidly, her Alzheimer's disease apparently shielding her from the terror of the situation.

"Go!" Chen Su ordered suddenly. "Go quickly!"

Angie hesitated, then raced from the room at the moment she heard her pursuer climbing through the window.

"She not here! Not here!" she heard Chen cry out.

"Shut up, old woman!" the man snapped.

"Not here . . . not here . . . not here!"

Chen's room was at the end of the sixth floor, nearest to the freight elevator. The long corridor to the other rooms was totally deserted. Angie headed for the elevator, hoping to use it to escape. As she reached it and

pulled the doors apart, she remembered that Mei Wu
had used a key to start it. Counting on the relic had
been a dumb idea in the first place.

"I said SHUT UP!"

The killer's furious words echoed out into the hallway.

A moment later, Angie heard the woman get slapped
and fall to the floor.

She sickened at the sound.

It had been wrong to put Chen Su in harm's way.
Now, it was time to end it. It was time to surrender before the poor woman or anyone else got killed. Angie
took a step back toward room 603. Then she stopped.

Even without the key, the elevator could be of use.

Angie took a single step inside. The perilous gap in
the floor at the rear of the car was as she remembered.

There was a second slap from room 603 followed by
the sound of the armoire doors being yanked open.

"Not here!" she again heard Chen say. "No one here!
No one here!"

Angie set her red knit cap on the floor of the car, a
foot from the gap. Then she grabbed one of two wheelchairs resting against a nearby wall, and ducked around
the corner beyond the elevator, looking back toward
room 603. A moment later, the killer emerged, dragging
the old woman by her hair.

"Come out, *senorita,* or I kill this nice lady right
here, right now," he said. "Scream and she dies too."

Angie kept perfectly still. Then she heard the man
laugh.

"End of the line," he said.

Angie could hear him moving toward her and the elevator.

Chen Su was still continuously whimpering, "Not here. . . . Not here. . . ."

Angie took a chance and craned around the corner enough to see that the killer had let the woman go and was now approaching the gloomy elevator car with little caution. At the door, he paused, scanning inside. Then he spied her bright cap and stepped in toward it.

Angie hesitated just a beat. Then she swung the wheelchair around the corner and began a sprint toward the car. The man was on one knee, picking up the cap and then peering over the edge of the gap in the floor. He turned when she was just a few feet away, but he was twisted and off balance, and his reaction was far too late. The wheelchair slammed into his mid-back, and he went down. A second ramming, and he was into the gap.

At the last possible moment, the fingers of his gloved left hand gained a hold on the edge of the steel floor . . . then, as Angie watched from above, he swung his right hand up and those fingers tightened over the rim as well.

Glaring up at her, not saying a word, he swung one leg back and was able to gain purchase with it against the brick wall of the shaft. He pushed himself up one inch . . . then another. Now, one hand was over the rim and flat on the floor of the car.

Even at such a disadvantage, his scar was menacing.

Angie had never physically hurt another human being let alone murdered someone. Dizzy and battered, she stared down at the man. Good or bad, she was thinking, there had been far too much killing already. Far too much death.

The killer's leg continued to give him support. Now, his second hand was fully on the steel floor, inching forward.

Angie wondered how she could control him if she helped him up.

"Where did you put Sylvia's notes?" she asked.

"No . . . notes. . . . She . . . had . . . nothing."

The man's expression softened. It was as if he had gotten a read on her and knew she did not have it in her to kill.

Another inch.

Angie knelt on one knee and stared into his eyes, trying to match his fierce, defiant expression with one of her own.

"Tell me again," she demanded. "Where are the papers?"

At that instant, Chen Su appeared by Angie's side. Dark blood trailed from the corner of her mouth. Without hesitating, she cried out and began stamping on her assailant's hands again and again with surprising force.

"Wait!" Angie cried.

But it was too late.

The man's right hand dropped to his side. One final blow, and his left hand went as well.

The killer made the six-story fall without uttering a sound.

An awful thud from below punctuated the silence.

CHAPTER 40

DAY 5
10:30 P.M. (CST)

Would it be worth it? Griff asked himself.

Not surprisingly, he began thinking about his sister, Louisa, and the promise he made to himself after her death. He knew from the moment the meningitis claimed her that he would dedicate his life to hunting cures for deadly microbes. He would become the Orion of the CDC or NIH, or whatever lab would have him—a one-man crusader against death. At the time, he never considered animal testing taboo. *How many primates or sheep or cats or canines or purebred white rats would equal his sister's life?* But then, Louisa's dog—a spirited mixed breed named Moonshine—forever altered his thinking.

At Louisa's funeral, Moonshine, probably more golden retriever than anything else, sat vigil on the stairs outside the church. With the unexpectedness of her mistress's death, no preparations had been made for the three-year-old's care. But Griff knew the animal was happy, well trained, and his sister's greatest love.

"My future husband will simply have to share me," Louisa would joke whenever questions arose regarding her devotion to Moonshine.

After the funeral, there was no question Griff would take the dog as his own.

From almost the moment Moonshine and Griff returned home, she was different. Her appetite diminished, then soon all but vanished. She drank only minimally, became lethargic, and never wanted to play for long. Eventually, when her weight loss became obvious and alarming, Griff took her to a respected, highly recommended veterinarian. The vet's diagnosis of depressive disorder both shocked and saddened him. At the time, Griff had no idea canine depression was a real condition. But even more distressing, it hurt him to realize that Moonshine missed Louisa as much as he did, and that there seemed to be absolutely nothing he could do about it.

"What can I do to help?" he had asked the specialist on a return visit.

"The danger of death is very real," the doctor explained. "You've got to find a way to make life fun for her again."

And so Griff tried. He bought her toys. He took her to the dog park near his house every night. He hand-prepared gourmet food and even tried antidepressants prescribed by the vet. But nothing he did slowed Moonshine's dramatic deterioration. More and more he feared for the dog's life. That was when he called Andrea

Bargnani—Louisa's best friend, who had moved away a year or so before.

"I don't know what I can do," Andrea, a teacher, had said. "I saw Moonshine almost every day when I was living here, but since I moved, I've only seen her every couple of months."

"You were Louisa's closest friend. Maybe if you just came by for a day or so. Andrea, Moonshine's going to die from this. I'm certain of it."

When the teacher showed up at the house, the dog reacted almost immediately. She picked her head up and barked—once, and then again. It was the first bark that Griff had heard since the funeral, and the joy in the sound was apparent. Within minutes, the Shiner, as Louisa called her, was up on all fours, her tail flicking wildly. She nuzzled against Andrea's legs and tried to climb into her arms, as though she could not get close enough. Griff had no doubt at all that Louisa was somehow alive in the animal.

Andrea felt the same thing. Even though, at the time, she was living in a small apartment, she gladly agreed to take the dog.

And so, Andrea Bargnani adopted Moonshine. Were it not for the holiday cards that reached Griff every year after that, regardless of where in the world he was working, he might have lost contact with the two of them. But reach him they did. For the first two years, the picture on the front of the card showed only the woman and the dog. Soon after that, a man named Jack debuted in the photo—a tall, broad-shouldered man with kind eyes and a wonderful smile. Not long after that came a card with a baby boy. Then one with a girl. But the Shiner remained the star of every mailing, her coal-black eyes sparkling for the camera, her rich, tawny coat glowing, and her mouth open in what had to be a smile.

Griff began what became a tradition. Every year, on the anniversary of Louisa's death, he would sit with those cards and two glasses of red wine. One glass he would drink. The other he would cast into the sky of wherever he happened to be. With the ritual came the renewal of his vow to respect the connection between man and vertebrates.

Griff looked over lamentably at Melvin. *Is it time to break that vow?*

"I've spent my entire career believing I could battle any virus without killing animals in the process," Griff said.

"Do you think sacrificing primates will help us identify that missing piece?"

Griff hesitated before he answered.

"I don't know," he said.

"If it were guaranteed to make a difference?"

Griff cringed at the question and looked away.

"Given the situation, how could I not?" he asked. "It's tantamount to murder either way. But I'd feel too great a responsibility not to do everything possible to save those people."

"But at this point there are no guarantees."

"That's the problem. So we have to choose where to put our faith. Computers, or innocent animals."

"I wish I could help with the decision," Forbush said. "It would be easy if we had unlimited time. As it is, setting up another Hell's Kitchen animal facility, even a partial one, will take at least three or four days."

Griff's insides were knotted. He still desperately wanted to rub at his eyes, and to have his thoughts focus. He stared at his gloved hands, his teeth clenched.

"Do you want me to get the chimpanzee order going?" Forbush asked.

"No," Griff said with sudden, renewed determination. "I still believe my computer program is the fastest and most accurate way forward."

"I believe you're right."

"So we work," Griff said, "and we keep at it until we figure out why Orion's not doing the job I've programmed it to do."

CHAPTER 41

DAY 5
11:45 P.M. (EST)

Residents on the sixth floor of the Riverside Nursing Home eased open their doors and shuffled out into the dimly lit hallway. Their collective chatter began as a murmur, but soon escalated into loud, rapid-fire exchanges. More room doors opened in response to the heightening racket. More elderly men and women milled into the corridor. Some carried canes. Some made their way with walkers.

Angie, emotionally and physically spent, sank onto the freight elevator's unsteady wood floor. Her head was beginning to throb—a pounding bass drum behind her eyes, monitoring each heartbeat. Chen Su braced herself against the car wall opposite her. The older woman's expression was unrevealing. Her eyes seemed vacant. Angie wondered how far the terrible events of just minutes ago had already slipped from her consciousness.

Wu Mei came racing through the crowd. Two male orderlies followed her into the elevator, carrying flashlights, which they directed down into the shaft. They said something in Chinese, and Mei let out a gasp, which she quickly cut short, her hand over her mouth. The response to death at Riverside, Angie assumed, was seldom louder than a sheet drawn over a face.

"Are you okay?" Mei asked.

Angie managed a nod, although her vision was drifting in and out of focus.

"You're covered with blood. Are you cut?"

"Just my nose. I think it's broken."

"Oh, my. I will check you over, but I think we should get an ambulance. You don't look well."

With the orderlies' help, Angie rose unsteadily to her feet, and used their shoulders for balance.

"We've already called the police," Mei said. "Do you think you can speak to them about what happened here?"

"I'll try my best. . . . And Mei, I'll also do my best to see to it there are no repercussions from that gap in your elevator. After all, it did save my life."

Before tonight, Angie felt secrecy was her best hope for safety. But Genesis had found her despite all her precautions. She needed to speak with Griff and possibly with the president as well. Would it help in any way to keep Sylvia Chen's murder a secret? If so, the FBI had to contact the NYPD quickly. Without any notes from the former head of the Veritas project, Angie's mission to New York had been worse than a failure. How much should the police be told now?

Griff or Allaire would arrange a military escort for her back to Kalvesta. But first, she had to do something that she dreaded.

"Mei, I need a moment with Ms. . . . Mrs. . . ."

"Ms. Li? You need to speak to Ms. Li?"

"Yes. Can you join us? I may need you to interpret."

"Ms. Li speaks perfect English."

"I will still need you."

Once back in room 603, blotting blood with a hand towel Mei had brought her, Angie closed the window. Then she took hold of the frail, veined hand of the woman known there as Ms. Li, and motioned her to sit next to her on the bed.

"Thank you for saving our lives," Angie began, squinting against the now unremitting pounding behind her forehead. "That was a very bad man, who has hurt and killed many people. You acted bravely."

"A very bad man," Chen Su echoed.

"I have terrible news," Angie said.

"Terrible . . . news."

Angie studied the woman's face and could see the transformation more clearly now. There was natural aging of course, where fibers had weakened and skin given way to gravity. But the ravages of late-stage Alzheimer's were hauntingly evident. There were abrasions on her elbows. The skin of her fine face clung to her bones like translucent paper. The disease was progressing her life the way fast-forward speeds through a DVD. The woman looked ninety, though she was probably twenty years younger than that.

"You have a daughter."

The woman gave no response.

"Sylvia," Angie said.

"Are you Sylvia?"

Angie breathed deeply.

"Mrs. Chen, Sylvia, your daughter, is dead."

Again Wu Mei stifled a gasp.

"You are certain?" she asked.

"I am positive, Mei. I will tell you the details later."

There was no recognition from Chen Su. Not a twitch or any hint of tears to come.

"The man who died in the elevator is the one who killed her," Angie went on. "I am very sorry about Sylvia."

In fact, there was much else Angie was sorry about, starting with the papers Sylvia promised but could now never deliver. Would they have helped find the cure for WRX3883? Would Sylvia's knowledge of Genesis have been the key to stopping them?

One of the orderlies appeared at the door and spoke to Mei.

"The police are here," she said to Angie. "They want to speak to you."

Angie stood unsteadily. Then she sat back down and embraced the older woman.

"You and your daughter will be in my thoughts and in my prayers, Chen Su."

She again rose awkwardly, but managed to stay upright.

Then, without warning, Sylvia's mother got up from her bed. Her body trembled as she crossed to her scarred maple dresser. With some effort, she pulled open the top drawer. From inside it, beneath some clothes, she extracted a fine, wooden box, inlaid with mother of pearl cut in ornate patterns.

She handed the box over to Angie and said a single word.

"Sylvia."

Angie thought momentarily about explaining her daughter's death again. The vacant look in the old woman's eyes told her not to bother. Instead, Angie opened the box. Inside was an envelope.

There were four words penned on the envelope in neat, almost calligraphic printing. Angie stared at the writing, uncomprehending. The delay was longer than it might have been had she not taken such a battering to her face and head, but half a minute passed. Then, all at once, she knew. Unseen by the others, her lips tightened in a ferocious grin.

Yes! she thought. *Oh, God, yes!*

She gazed down at the writing once more.

Recipes from the Kitchen.

CHAPTER 42

The situation was getting more chaotic and more dangerous. The virus had been responsible for two deaths in Statuary Hall, and word was, several more people were on the brink. Throughout the Capitol, morale was in terrible shape. Tempers were fraying, and confidence in the leadership of James Allaire was slipping away by the hour. Ellis was putting as much pressure on the man as she could manage. She had landed some decent punches, but she knew she hadn't done enough to put him down for the count.

She needed to get the Genesis bill through Congress, and she needed to put both Allaire and Tilden out of office. There was a way, she was thinking—a piece of film that would sway the masses. Time was slipping away for all of them. No more waiting.

Leland Gladstone's hands were shaking as he scanned the Genesis document and then handed it back to his boss. He and the speaker of the house were seated in a quiet corner of the gallery level. For a time, Gladstone remained silent, his mouth slightly agape, and his gaze fixed on the floor.

"So, what are you struggling with the most, Leland," Ellis asked patiently, "my being in direct contact with the terrorists? Or are you having trouble coming to grips with being the aide and possibly the chief of staff of the next president of the United States?"

"It's all seeming like a dream. One minute it's business as usual. We're all dressed up, preparing for the president's State of the Union Address. And the next, we're locked in here, working to get him out of office and take over."

Ellis grinned.

"Well, certainly this is no worse of a nightmare than when we lost the election."

"Hardly—especially when we were coming so close. Please don't get me wrong, Madam Speaker. I believe in you, and I am on your side. All the way. I have been since the day you hired me. Surely you know that."

"Of course I do, Leland. This is the ultimate lesson I could possibly teach you—true politics in action. It's all about flexibility, about being ready to change course if necessary—being prepared to reach out at any moment and snatch the brass ring. These new developments of representing Genesis and their demands will in no way impact the work of our special committee. In fact, they make our efforts that much more important."

Gladstone still had a forlorn look.

"How so?" he asked, his voice muted.

"Have you lost faith, my Leland?"

"No . . . it's just . . . these demands Genesis wants you to support. You'll be disgraced if we try to introduce this bill to Congress."

Ellis smiled once more. Suddenly, her brilliant young aide looked very much his age.

"I'm sure," she said, "when Congress learns that if they don't vote for this bill they'll all die, mocking me will be the furthest thing from their minds."

"I'm still not completely certain I understand," Gladstone said, averting his eyes. "With all due respect, Madam Speaker, are you sure you know what you're doing here?"

Ellis understood why the question had been so difficult for him to ask. The child who loses faith in the parent also loses hope. She placed a reassuring hand on his shoulder.

"Leland, I have never been more sure of anything in my life. Why do you think it was me whom Genesis singled out? Of all the members of Congress and the Cabinet locked in here, why was I the chosen one?"

"I don't know—because you're the speaker of the house, I suppose."

"Nonsense."

Ellis glanced cautiously about the vast chamber, aware of the danger should they be overheard. In every direction, she saw only idleness, helplessness, and ennui. People fidgeted in their seats, frustrated, bored, and restless. Some had converted blankets into makeshift pillows and were leaning against the person next to them. Clusters of dignitaries congregated together, but fatigue and mounting fear had sapped much of their energy and dampened what had once been animated chatter into nothing more than scattered whispers. To Ellis they looked like the living dead. Which, according to Genesis, they were.

"They picked me because it's my destiny to lead," she responded finally. "And with your help, the world will soon see the mistake they made by not choosing me over Allaire in the first place."

"By my help, you mean by my drafting this bill?"

"That is precisely what I mean, Leland. As soon as you have completed that task, I'll introduce it to Congress and we'll get it voted on and passed."

"But . . . but even if you get the bill through Congress, Allaire will never sign it into law," Gladstone said. "Isn't that a prerequisite for Genesis giving you the antidote?"

Ellis patted her aide on the knee. His political acumen was, in many respects, far beyond his years, but in other aspects, he was still a babe in the woods.

"Thanks to the power Genesis is about to give us, our special committee work is going to be fast-tracked. Soon we'll have enough proof to impeach Allaire."

"Even assuming you can get Allaire out of the picture, Vice President Tilden will step in and veto the bill just the same."

"Well, you just leave the little stumbling block of Henry Tilden to me," Ellis said. "I assure you, he will be an impediment easily overcome."

"So you plan to impeach Allaire for Mackey's murder?"

Ellis grinned.

"That I do, my friend. Mackey's death, and how about seven hundred plus counts of attempted murder."

"And you believe the threat from this virus is as grave as Genesis claims it is?"

Ellis pointed a finger at Gladstone to emphasize that the issue he had hit upon was a significant one.

"I've been pondering that very question myself," she said. "Let me ask you something: Why do you think Allaire had us all separated into groups?"

"To help manage the distribution of resources during the quarantine period," Gladstone replied quickly.

"Ah, dear Leland. That explanation sounded lame to me when Allaire tried to foist it on us in the first place, and it sounds as lame as a three-legged hog now. Assuming it is just another one of his lies, I ask you to reason out why we were sent to different rooms."

Gladstone had to think only briefly.

"Assuming the threat is real, and Allaire knows how deadly it is, then he might be attempting to control the spread of the virus."

"Now you're cooking, Leland. And how would that best be done?"

For the first time, Gladstone firmly met Ellis's gaze with his own.

"By separating out the most severely infected."

Ellis's expression was that of a proud teacher toward her star pupil.

"Do you recall," she said, "how I asked you to map out where the explosions had occurred, and who was sitting in each area?"

"Of course."

"Let's look at that list."

Gladstone stretched his long legs to extract several folded pieces of paper from the front pocket of his tuxedo pants. Then he handed the sheets to Ellis. The speaker carefully read them over, folded them again, and returned the stack to him.

"You have about forty names here," she said.

"Those are the ones I could get. People at the center of the blasts, including those seated next to, in front of, or in back of each ground zero."

"And tell me, do you know the present location of Archibald Jakes, or Senator Cogan?"

Ellis picked two names from Gladstone's list that she had personally seen take a hit.

"I believe they're in C Group."

"Have you had any contact with C Group?"

"No," Gladstone said.

"And do you know where Group C is currently residing?"

"From what I've heard, they're in the Senate Chamber, but that's just rumor and not something I've confirmed."

"In that case, I think I should go and confirm it for myself. Is your BlackBerry charged?"

"It is," Gladstone said. "Thanks to your standing up to Allaire, I still have it."

"You look troubled, Leland. What is it?"

"You're not allowed to leave this chamber. How do you plan to get across the Capitol complex to the Senate?"

Ellis favored Gladstone with a mischievous smile.

"Because of Sean O'Neil's . . . um . . . not so minor transgressions, I still have my hand cupped around his balls. I think it's about time I gave them a good, hard squeeze."

CHAPTER 43

From the recesses of the upper gallery, Ellis watched Sean O'Neil patrol the aisles of the House Chamber. He looked ill at ease, and avoided any eye contact with the anxious faces that he passed, perhaps feeling as if he were being held responsible in some way for their plight.

Ellis felt some pity for the man. He was at once prisoner and jailer, neither of them very enviable positions. At least amid this mess, she had a purpose—some control and power over her fate. Soon enough, though, O'Neil would have some purpose as well. And once Allaire and his vice presidential toady were put in their places, once she was president, she would reward the Secret Service agent's assistance by keeping him on staff, pledged to take a bullet for her.

The speaker descended the carpeted stairwell to the chamber floor level, approached O'Neil from behind, and tapped him on the shoulder. He spun around, reaching for his gun.

"Easy, cowboy," she said. "Maybe it's time to switch over to decaf."

O'Neil glared at her.

"Next time you come up on me like that, don't expect me to stop."

"We need to talk," Ellis said.

"I'm busy right now."

"Oh? Doing what?"

"The president asked me to make some observations and report back to him."

"Observations?"

"Check and see how people are holding up."

"Oooo. Sounds important."

"What do you want?"

"I told you, to talk. Please?"

Ellis motioned to a dark corner where she felt assured they'd have a modicum of privacy. O'Neil grumbled an unintelligible protest, but followed her anyway.

"Okay," the agent said, when it seemed they were safely out of earshot of others, "what do you want to talk about?"

"Where is Archibald Jakes?" Ellis asked.

"The Navy chief of staff?"

"Is there another?"

"I don't know."

"Are we going to be difficult, Sean?"

"That depends. Are you going to keep trying to talk to me?"

"I have a Web browser on this BlackBerry," Ellis said, waving the device in her hand at waist level so that only he could see. "Do you have any pictures of your kid I can bring up? I love children, you know. Had some myself once upon a time."

"You are really a bitch."

"It's so nice how we can work together for the greater good, and still make time to share our personal lives as well."

"You keep my son out of this," O'Neil growled.

Ellis made a tsk-tsk sound, her expression one of mock sorrow.

"I am sorry, Sean," she said, "but unless you cooperate, that is simply not an option. Look, here's the deal: I need you to get me egress from this chamber, a passage that is presently denied to me."

"And then?"

"And then take me to wherever Jakes is holed up."

The agent considered the request.

"I want your word never to mention my son again."

"But—"

"I said *never*!"

"Goodness. This is a snippy side of you I never knew existed. All right, then. You cooperate and get me to Archie Jakes, and I won't say another word about your kid."

O'Neil mulled over the pledge for a second time.

"Jakes is in the Senate Chamber," he said, finally.

"I thought you said you didn't know where he was."

"I lied."

"I know. It rubs off from Allaire. So, get me in there."

"Not that simple. I don't have the key."

"A key? You mean to tell me the head of the Joint Chiefs of Staff is locked inside the Senate Chamber?"

"Yes. Along with the rest of Group C."

"Tell me Sean, have you asked yourself why that might be?"

"No."

"You're either very trusting of your president, or dreadfully uncurious."

"Both. My job is to guard, not question."

"Well, if you want that job of yours to continue, I suggest you get me inside that room."

"I can't do that," O'Neil said.

"Can't or won't?"

"Does it matter?"

"You're a really dreadful liar, Sean. Way out of your league here. I know you have a key to the Senate. I'd bet my right arm on it. That's how certain I am."

"Go to hell."

"Do you know about my recently formed special committee?"

"I do. You're investigating Mackey's death."

"Mackey's *murder*. That's right. Which means I will be having a whole lot of interaction with our dear president. Which means plenty of opportunities to let my knowledge of your extracurricular activities in the Lincoln Bedroom slip out. Perhaps if he and I mend our fences enough, he'd even grant me a temporary reprieve from this lovely chamber to retrieve the photographs of you and whatever-her-name-is that I stashed away in my office safe for a rainy day. Dear Agent O'Neil. How could you not know that everything that happens in the White House is recorded one way or another?"

O'Neil grimaced and said, "I want those photographs."

"Of course you do. But either you get me into that chamber, or Allaire and the judge presiding over your custody battle get first looks."

Ellis watched the agent's jaw muscles tighten.

"Come with me," he said in a coarse whisper.

They circled in front of the rostrum and headed along the passageway leading across the Capitol. At a doorway, two agents stood guard. Both looked extremely capable. O'Neil introduced Ellis to them.

"Jill," he said, "the president asked me to escort Speaker Ellis to the Senate."

"Didn't come over the radio," the woman replied.

"Well, he asked a while ago, but I forgot until she just reminded me."

"Lots going on," the other agent commented. "Easy to forget. Last night they ordered the security detail off the Senate doors. Now they just do a walk-by every two hours."

"Any idea why?" Ellis asked.

"Nope. Orders are orders, I guess. As far as I know, the only one who's been going in there is Dr. Townsend, the president's doc."

"That's strange."

"What isn't around here?" the guard said.

"I wonder what she's looking for."

"Well, thanks, Scott," O'Neil said.

He led Ellis forward a step, but the guards remained in place and exchanged questioning looks.

"Do you mind if we take a look at your hands?" Jill asked.

"There's nothing there," O'Neil said. "That's one of the things the president has had me looking for."

He held out his hands, palms up, and motioned for Ellis to do the same.

"What's this all about?" she asked.

"Beats us," the agent named Scott said. "But Secretary Salitas has us checking anyone who comes this way."

"Agent O'Neil, do you know what's going on?"

Her expression was serpentine.

Ellis held her palms up for the guards.

O'Neil shrugged.

"We're looking for some sort of red pattern—a circle or swirl. If we see anyone who has it, one palm or both, we're supposed to send them to Salitas."

"Interesting," Ellis said. "Interesting. When's the next walk-by supposed to happen?"

"Fifteen minutes. Right when our shift ends."

"Thanks, you two. We'll probably be back before you leave."

The two guards stepped aside and allowed the speaker and O'Neil to pass.

Ellis quickened her pace.

They descended to the first floor of the Capitol complex. Ellis was accustomed to the stairwells and corridors bustling with activity, but the only footsteps she heard now were their own. The odd silence evoked a childhood memory of being locked inside a museum after closing time. They followed the House connecting corridor through the Crypt, where Doric columns helped support the huge central rotunda, and then passed into the Senate connecting corridor. Finally, they ascended to the Senate Chamber itself.

Outside the door was a cardboard sign printed in neat Magic Marker that warned: AUTHORIZED PERSONNEL ONLY. To the right of the sign, hanging on a coatrack inside a small plastic ultraviolet chamber, was a single blue biocontainment suit. The chamber bore a label written on tape that read: DR. B. TOWNSEND.

"Only one suit for one person," Ellis said. "Don't you think that's a little strange?"

"No. I think that's a lot strange," O'Neil replied.

"Explanation?"

"Townsend doesn't want anyone else going in there except her."

"Probably so, but why the suit? She's been exposed the same as the rest of us. Could it be that the risk of exposure inside the Senate is even greater than in the rest of the building?"

A padlock connected the ends of a thick steel chain that was looped between the semicircular brass pull handles of the chamber's double doors. Ellis flicked a manicured finger toward it.

"I'm not doing this," O'Neil said.

"The problem with you, dear Sean," Ellis replied with icy calm, "is that you can't think without orders. I need to see exactly what's going on in there and why these people have been locked away. So here's my order to you: Open that goddamn door, or I swear to you, I'll make ruining your life my full-time occupation."

Reluctantly, the agent took out his key and inserted

it into the padlock. They could hear sounds coming from inside. Some of what they heard sounded like coughing. But mixed in with those sounds were what might have been screams. Then they heard a noise that was even more distinctive—and getting louder. Somebody on the other side of the door was clawing at the wood.

"I don't think we should be doing this," O'Neil said again.

"I only need a minute in there, Sean," Ellis demanded. "Turn the damn key!"

And so he did.

CHAPTER 44

Griff was asleep at one of the two tables in the small library when he was roused by a gentle hand on his shoulder. He shot upright, flailing to maintain his balance. His hand caught two tall stacks of reference books, sending them flying. Standing beside him, Forbush looked down with undisguised concern.

"You fell asleep," he said.

"The understatement of the day," Griff replied thickly. "I seem to remember you pledging to check on me every fifteen minutes."

"I did. You must have just passed out."

Griff nodded and caught a glimpse of his haggard reflection in the dark glass of the nearby videoconferencing system. His beard was making a rapid reappearance, not unlike the ground cover after the eruption of the Mount St. Helens volcano. But his sunken cheeks and hollow eyes were most disturbing, exceeding even what he remembered from his time in the Alcatraz of the Rockies.

The videoconferencing system had a direct link to the Capitol, and Allaire was expecting an update from Griff in the morning. The news Griff planned on sharing would not be well received.

"Did you at least find anything useful in these reference books?" Forbush asked.

"Maybe," Griff said. "No matter what, it was worth getting out of that suit, even for a short while. Still, I need more time to think."

"Just like Russell Crowe in *A Beautiful Mind. He* was always thinking, too."

"Didn't he turn out to be insane?"

"That all depends on your definition of the term."

"Terrific. Something's missing, Melvin. I'm thinking if we could give Orion a nudge—maybe from an adjuvant of some kind that boosts the immunologic response."

"Would an adjuvant be toxic?"

"Possibly, but certainly no less toxic than what's already inside those poor souls in the Capitol."

Before Forbush could respond, the fax machine in the corner of the library beeped that it was receiving a transmission.

"Who could possibly be faxing us?" Griff asked.

Forbush crossed to the machine.

"It could be from Ms. Angie. I gave her this number with instructions that it would be the safest way to communicate with us."

"Really? Are you sure a fax transmission can't be intercepted by Genesis?"

Melvin turned back to him and shrugged.

"As sure as I can be where they're concerned," he said. "They're a shifty bunch."

"So how can you be so confident?"

"I found a phone number on the Internet that supposedly will produce a short tone if the landline is bugged, and a longer one if it isn't. I checked, and according to that program, at least, the line was clear."

"That's putting a lot of faith in the Web," Griff said.

"Sometimes, boss, we reach the point when faith is the only thing we have left."

"Good quote. What movie is that from?"

"The one I'm going to produce when I win Publisher's Clearing House."

Forbush was chuckling as he gathered the fax pages from the printer tray. Then abruptly, he stopped.

"Griff, this fax isn't *from* Angie, it's *about* her."

Griff leapt up and crossed the small library in two steps. The logo on the fax cover sheet was from the Riverside Nursing Home in Manhattan.

"Read it out loud," Forbush said, his expression uncharacteristically grim.

Griff's throat tightened at the first lines of the note, handwritten inside the cover sheet's comment box.

My name is Wu Mei. I am the duty nurse at Riverside Nursing Home in New York City. This is regarding Angela Fletcher, who is in the hospital.

The rest of the note was typed on a computer.

"'Before Ms. Fletcher collapsed,'" Griff read, "'she admitted to forging health inspector documents to gain access to our residents. She was desperate to find a woman named Sylvia Chen. She believed Chen's mother was a resident here.

"'I am sorry to inform you that Sylvia Chen is dead. I only know that Ms. Fletcher said she was. I have no details on that. Ms. Fletcher was being chased by a very bad man when she sustained a head injury from which she eventually lost consciousness. We had her transported by ambulance to Lower Manhattan Hospital. I have no update on her condition at present.

"'The man chasing her died in a fall down our elevator shaft. Before she collapsed, Ms. Fletcher was given a box by a resident here whom we knew as Ms. Li. It now appears that Ms. Li is actually Sylvia Chen's mother, Chen Su. Inside the box was an envelope labeled RECIPES FROM THE KITCHEN, with some papers apparently belonging to Sylvia. Ms. Fletcher regained consciousness long enough to ask me to fax these pages to you. She believes this information might be critical to your work, and to what is happening in Washington, D.C. You can reach me here if necessary.

"'Dr. Rhodes, you should know that despite deceiving us, Ms. Fletcher acted with extreme bravery, and saved the life of Chen Su. I will never forget her.'

"Melvin, we've got to get a call to Lower Manhattan Hospital in New York."

"I wouldn't advise that," Forbush said. "Assuming

the man who was after Ms. Angie in New York was with Genesis, we've got to believe the leak to them was somewhere here in Kalvesta."

"What should we do?"

"That depends."

"On what?" Griff asked.

"On whether or not you have any friends in high places."

"Allaire!"

"I believe we're set up for secure communications with him. Why not go that route?"

"Put yourself in for a raise, Melvin. Listen, let me finish looking at this stuff from Sylvia, and then we'll get ahold of Allaire and see if he can insert himself on Angie's behalf—at least make sure she's getting the best care from the best doctors."

"Poor Sylvia. Mixed up with the wrong crowd and so desperate to succeed in her work. I wonder how she died. With all those people looking for her and none of them finding her, I sort of thought she might have fallen on hard times."

"Hopefully Angie's okay and can tell us what happened."

Griff flipped to the next page in the stack. Chen's lab reports followed a very consistent format, and Griff did not have to study the pages long to know that they were, in fact, written by her. But the contents of the reports were not associated with any experiments that he had ever seen.

The same title was printed on the upper right of every page.

The Certain Path

The test subjects, most likely monkeys, were each identified in a code Griff had never seen before. The reports, one sheet for each animal, included basic information about sex, cage number, viral dose, route of administration, and antiviral treatment, as well as the dates and times of each run.

Sylvia knew that Griff had drawn the line at her performing experiments on chimpanzees. But she also knew that he seldom set foot in the Hell's Kitchen animal facility. Was it possible she had somehow managed to sneak some chimps into her lab? If so, why had she taken the results away from the Kitchen—especially when they did not seem to have been any more successful than the rest of her primate work? And how did she get the sheets of paper through the sterilizing showers and UV lights?

The questions gnawed at Griff.

The recorded results noted clinical signs, along with quantity of virus injected or given by inhalation. In every instance but one, speed of death was directly proportional to the size of the inoculum.

These could have been any number of Chen's past lab reports. What made them so special? The answer to this and Griff's other questions was on the final page. As he read them, he felt his blood turn to ice.

The test animals were identified not only by code, but by first initial and last name.

Griff grabbed a legal pad and wrote down the identifying code of each test subject, then the name. Beside each name, he wrote Sylvia's recorded result.

DWM—1, S. Coughlin	*(M)*	*Deceased*
DBF—2, G. Anderson	*(F)*	*Deceased*
DBM—3, T. Geffman	*(M)*	*Deceased*
DWM—4, L. Warshalski	*(M)*	*Deceased*
DWM—5, M. Scheffer	*(M)*	*Deceased*
DWM—6, J. R. Davis	*(M)*	

Robotlike, he handed the page to Forbush, who scanned the names with the same disbelieving expression as Griff.

"This is terrible," he said, with his characteristic lack of excessive emotion.

"If it's true, Melvin, then it's worse than that."

"The certain path—the certain path to a cure, I guess. That's what the title on each page must mean."

Griff could only stare down at the report.

"I know Sylvia was desperate to keep the program going," he said, "but I never would have dreamed she was this desperate."

"No more monkeys," Forbush said, with a shrug.

"No more monkeys," Griff echoed. "She took the leap and somehow began experimenting on people."

"And they all died."

"Assuming she just neglected to mark that in next to J. R. Davis's name, they all died."

"Leaving us with one huge unanswered question."

"Where could these subjects have come from?"

"And I guess one other huge unanswered question," Forbush added. "Where did she do the work?"

CHAPTER 45

Ellis checked that Gladstone's BlackBerrry was powered on and set to capture video. She was keyed up and tense in all the best sense of the words. Jim Allaire had kept her in the dark long enough. It was time she documented what was really going on, and just how much they all had to fear from this virus.

Beside her, O'Neil looked as if his legs were about to betray him. His complexion mirrored the white of the marble floor.

Inches away, the clamor and the scraping sound on the other side of the door continued.

The Secret Service agent uncoiled the length of chain securing the Senate Chamber doors. The steel links slid through his hands and clattered into a heap at his feet. Ellis cupped her ear and listened against the door.

"Nothing," she said. "I have no idea what that sound could have been, but it's gone now."

"I think you're crazy to go in there."

"*We,* dearest. *We* are going in there. And *we're* going to be quick about it, too. In and out with a little video in between. That will be all I need. Judging from Dr. Townsend's containment suit over there, these people are infected with something pretty horrible."

"Whatever it is, we've been exposed, too."

"But I'm betting that whatever it is, these poor souls got a mega dose. It's time to see just how much your boss has been holding out on us all. Don't you want to know? I mean, it is your life, too."

"I . . . don't know."

"O'Neil, I promise you. If we stay only a minute, just enough time to let me gather the video I need, we'll both be fine—especially if we hold our breath. Now, let's go."

O'Neil sighed, and pulled the door open.

The first thing Ellis noticed as she stepped forward into the main aisle of the Senate Chamber was the smell. It was a foul stench of blood, bodily waste, and vomit, unlike anything she had experienced before. Her throat immediately tightened as her gag reflex kicked in. She wondered if the standing fans installed throughout the room were somehow keeping the powerful odor from escaping through the door cracks. The room lights were on full, and what Ellis saw as she fumbled for her camera made her cry out in fright.

The golden damask above the marbled wainscot was stained with blood and fecal matter. White marble busts of past Senate presidents, normally set in bowl niches in the gallery level, were either smashed, missing, or lying on the floor. But even more disturbing was that the one hundred mahogany senators' desks had been ripped from their footings and thrown aside, replaced by a number of cots—at least twenty or twenty-five of them, mostly occupied, and many by people she knew, now barely recognizable to her.

Some of those in the chamber wore the comfortable clothing that had been delivered to the Capitol. But there were a few others—the most debilitated—who were still wearing what remained of their tuxedoes and designer gowns. They were lying listlessly, or vomiting congealing blood into blue plastic buckets wired to the bedframes. Some were writhing in pain. Others were propped on one elbow, moaning piteously.

For half a minute, Ellis stood transfixed, the purpose of her mission forgotten.

She heard a terrible shriek and turned in that direction. The senior senator from Missouri, a genteel, dignified man in his seventies, was pressing his hands on either side of his head, groaning for the pain to stop. Blood, from a nosebleed or perhaps his stomach, stained the sheet beneath him. He screamed again, and slapped at his expansive abdomen, as though trying to put out a fire burning inside. Then, suddenly, he turned his head and vomited into the bucket—black blood, thick as oil.

Ellis managed to raise her camera and pan the scene. This was not the flu. Nor was it any other virus she could imagine.

"We've got to get out of here," she said, her voice barely able to form the words.

O'Neil was rooted. Many of these dignitaries were also people he knew well. Finally, he managed a few baby steps back toward the door. Ellis stayed close to him. Then they turned to run, but Admiral Archibald Jakes had materialized in the center of the aisle and was blocking their only way out. He was a grotesquerie. His stained dress whites were ripped in many places. The rows of service ribbons over his left breast had gaps resembling a hockey player's teeth. The sclerae of his eyes were bloodred. His cheeks were sunken and his lower jaw was in constant motion—a gnawing skull.

The admiral lifted his hands to prevent O'Neil and her from passing, and Ellis gasped.

His palms were a swirl of crimson, concentric circles, giving the appearance of having had the design branded on. On the surface of the swirls were hundreds of tiny, raised blisters, many of them broken and oozing.

"Home . . . please take me home . . . ," Jakes moaned.

His voice was a coarse whisper, and his breath was foul.

"Admiral, what's going on in here?" O'Neil managed to ask. "What's happening to you? Who's helping you all?"

"Dying . . . we're all dying." Each word the admiral spoke emerged like a hiss of steam. "Why did you do this to me?"

"No, it wasn't us," O'Neil said. "It was Genesis. It's some sort of virus."

"You lie! You lie!"

Ellis sensed movement behind her and turned to see that others in the room were now gathering behind her like zombies, blocking their only retreat from Jakes. Some of them had been friends and colleagues of hers for many years. All of them were ill—terribly, terribly ill. It was also impossible not to see the bright red patterns on their palms.

"Admiral Jakes, please," O'Neil pleaded, "let us by. We'll get you help. I promise."

The navy man's eyes were wild.

"No help. You lie! You lie!"

Jakes drove forward with surprising quickness and wrapped his fingers around O'Neil's throat. The Secret Service agent batted Jakes's hands aside, but in an instant the admiral lunged again, clawing at his face, drawing blood.

"Stop!" O'Neil shouted.

"Die! Die like me!"

Jakes continued flailing at the much younger man. Blood from the angry gouges ran down O'Neil's cheek, soaking his shirt collar.

Ellis screamed as the small crowd began folding in around them.

At that instant, the scene was frozen by a gunshot. Smoke rose from the pistol at O'Neil's waist. The chairman of the Joint Chiefs of Staff dropped to his knees, then toppled in slow motion onto his back, staring sightlessly at the high, ornate ceiling. A scarlet stain instantly began expanding from the bullet hole in his jacket. The advancing crowd pulled back as the pistol in O'Neil's hand smoked. The stench of gunpowder merged with the other odors in the room.

"Let's go! Now!" he barked at Ellis.

Clutching her BlackBerry, the speaker grasped O'Neil's coat sleeve and allowed herself to be dragged outside the Senate Chamber. The dying men and women were again moving in when O'Neil pushed the doors closed. Ellis looped the chain tightly through the handles and leaned against the doors with all her strength as O'Neil snapped the lock.

Then, gasping for air, exhausted, and rattled, the two of them slumped against the wall. The din and scratching from within had resumed, but with a difference. Somewhere amidst the mob on the other side of the door lay the body of the chief of the United States Navy.

Ellis checked her phone.

She had recorded everything.

CHAPTER 46

DAY 6

5 A.M. (CST)

"Rhodes, can you hear me?"

"Loud and clear. Listen, Angie's been hurt. Genesis somehow followed her to New York, and tried to kill her. I haven't called the hospital where she is because I really don't trust that this line is secure. It doesn't seem like anything is down here. I want you to have the FBI find out where she is and send some people to watch out for her. I'm not giving you the details, but send some men over to the Riverside Nursing Home. They'll know where she is and what name she's been admitted under. But do it quick. And make sure she has the best doctors."

"What in the hell is she doing in New York?"

"I'll tell you soon. I don't have time for this right now."

"Okay, I'll call you back."

Twenty minutes later, the video conference was renewed.

"We've got her," Allaire said. "She's in the ICU.

Subdural hematoma—that's bleeding between the skull and the brain. I have people on the way over there now."

"Surgery?"

"I don't think yet. Some subdurals don't ever require it. She's in a good hospital for trauma, but I'll get a neurosurgeon over there right away."

"Thank you, sir. I really appreciate that. So, what's going on there?"

"The situation is getting worse here by the minute," Allaire said. "What have you got for us?"

"Unfortunately, I still have lots of questions and few answers. But we're working around the clock."

The high-definition video transmission put Allaire's raddled appearance in sharp focus. Dark stubble on his characteristically clean-shaven face made his ashen complexion and gaunt expression all the more disconcerting. Griff's own image, as it was shown to him in a small square at the screen's top left corner, looked no less bleak than Allaire's.

"What's your status?" the president asked.

"As of this moment, Angie's made more progress than I have—or you, for that matter."

"What do you mean?"

"She figured out that Sylvia Chen might be in New York, and she was right. Only Genesis must have somehow picked up on where she was going. Don't ask me how they knew. They seem to know everything. They sent a man after Angie and tried to kill her."

"What about Chen? Did Angie actually find her?"

Griff nodded.

"I believe so, but she's dead. I have no details yet as to how or when. The guy Genesis sent is dead, too. It seems as if Angie managed to take him down before she lost consciousness."

"We need to ID that body ASAP."

"I assume the New York police have it."

"I'll alert the FBI right away. It might be the break we've been looking for to figure out who's behind all this. She was supposed to be there in Kansas, watching you. Why couldn't you have let me get the FBI on this?"

Griff could feel himself beginning to boil.

"Dr. Allaire," he said, with forced control, "Angela Fletcher risked her life for you and the others in the Capitol. She just accomplished in a couple of days what all those FBI agents couldn't do in a year. Let's leave it at that. I just want to make sure that she's protected."

Allaire calmed himself with a deep breath, but his eyes flashed.

"Of course," he said.

"Remember what Genesis has accomplished so far. It's like they're everywhere."

Allaire sighed audibly.

"The FBI will be at Ms. Fletcher's hospital room within the hour."

"And, I want—"

"Enough, Rhodes! How are you progressing with your work?"

Griff brushed a knot of matted hair from his forehead. He tensed as he readied himself to break the news.

"I'm afraid at this moment I'm not much closer to a solution than I was before my arrest. This virus is from hell. Maybe we should rename it Genesis because it's always a step ahead of us."

With Griff's weak attempt at levity, Allaire snapped.

His pallid complexion turned crimson in a blink. His mouth contorted, teeth bared. Glaring at the camera, he snatched up a glass of water from the Hard Room's conference table. Griff watched with growing astonishment as the man with his finger on the nuclear trigger cocked his arm back, and then sent the glass shattering against a wall.

"You cannot fail!" Allaire screamed, his face a foot from the camera. "Do you hear me, Rhodes? Do you frigging understand me? I can put you back in prison right now. Right goddamn now! I'll get someone else down there. Someone who has a clue. Give me some promise, some positive results, or I'll destroy you. Do you understand me?"

His body was shaking, his eyes wild with rage.

"Sir!" Griff pleaded. "Please! Calm down. You need to calm yourself."

Gary Salitas stepped in front of the camera, and Griff watched him place his hands on Allaire's shoulders. The president grabbed his defense secretary by one wrist and rotated it until the man cried out in pain and released his hold.

Bethany Townsend suddenly burst into view, followed by a pair of Secret Service agents. With the camera angle and all the commotion it was impossible for Griff to follow the action. When the bodies cleared, Townsend was leaning over the conference table looking directly

into the camera. The slightly built physician was breathless and flushed.

"Dr. Rhodes, we are going to have to reschedule this
call," she said. "The president is in no condition at the
moment to continue. Secretary Salitas and I will see to
it that Ms. Fletcher is looked after."

"Wait! Wait!" Griff heard Allaire shout from off
camera.

Moments later, the president returned to his seat.
Townsend hovered close by, as did the agents. Allaire
was still hyperventilating, but quickly his breathing
slowed and his color became more sanguine. He straightened his tie, and used his hands as a comb—small ges-
tures, but enough to restore some of his lost demeanor.

"Rhodes, I'm terrified my outburst is just the virus
at work," he said in a panicky, whispered voice. "It's
happening in small pockets in both A and B Groups.
Irritability beyond what should be expected under the
circumstances. Uncontrolled outbursts. Arguments.
Even fistfights."

"Sir, can you please hold your palms up to the
camera?"

Griff breathed a relieved sigh when he saw they were
unremarkable.

"We're running out of time, Rhodes," Allaire continued. "It's getting worse. But I don't have to tell you that,
do I?"

CHAPTER 47

The president's infection was becoming manifest.

Griff had no more doubt about that fact than he did about the trouble his own work was in.

The man was brittle and irascible. Talking to him was like playing catch using a ticking bomb for a ball.

"No, sir," Griff managed. "You don't have to tell me how serious this all is. You mentioned A and B Group. Any update from C?"

Allaire's expression turned doleful, his face etched by regret.

"We've had some deaths there," he said. "We've implemented increased biocontainment safety protocols to allow medical personnel continued access to the victims in C, but I'm afraid it's too dangerous to allow that to continue. The people in there are sick and many are going mad. Everyone in C Group is going to die. It's a given now. We're praying for you to save the rest of us."

"We did have one significant development," Griff said.

Allaire's voice became immediately energized.

"What is it?"

Griff had made the statement without much thought. He now decided on the spot not to reveal what he'd learned of Sylvia Chen's secret experiments. For all he knew, Allaire might have authorized them. For now, he, Angie, and Melvin were alone in this fight. It was the only way they could ensure there would be no more leaks or attempts to sabotage their efforts.

"What's the news?" Allaire demanded again.

"Some of my work is having a little effect on the computer model of the virus. We're going to experiment with adding some adjuvants."

"Those are chemical boosters, yes?"

"Exactly. I am looking to see if we can pump up the immunological response of our current treatment."

"Good," Allaire said. "Keep the people at the CDC in the loop. They might have suggestions for adjuvants that could help."

"I'll do that."

"Do you have any specific chemicals in mind?"

"Based on our results so far, there are some possibilities," Griff said. "I have Melvin doing research. We're not wasting any time on sleep."

"Do you want more help?"

"I don't have time to bring them up to speed, and I don't have the facilities. How much have you told the media and the people there in the Capitol about WRX3883?"

"I . . . actually, I haven't told them anything at all. They still think we're dealing with a variant of influenza. At least most of them do."

"Not good," Griff muttered.

"What?!"

"Mr. President, maybe the crowd would be a little easier to deal with if they knew the extent of what *you're* dealing with."

Once again, Allaire's expression began to morph. The tension in his voice rose.

"Rhodes," he said, "why don't you let me do my job as the president while you do your job as virus man and find a treatment for what's killing us."

From his spot by the door, Forbush suddenly cut into the conversation as if he was unaware that it was going on.

"Griff, I've been thinking . . ."

"Rhodes, who's there?" Allaire snapped.

Griff held a finger up to his lips to quiet Melvin, then he pointed to the videoconference monitor.

"It's me, Melvin, Mr. Allaire," Forbush said, clearly unimpressed that he had just interrupted a private meeting between his boss and the most powerful man on earth.

Griff stifled a grin. No wonder he enjoyed being around his friend as much as he did.

"This is about the list of names," Melvin said, ignoring Allaire completely. "I've been searching for death certificates, but I think that's going about it the wrong way."

"What death certificates?" the president demanded. "What are you talking about?"

"Melvin is working on Dr. Chen's animal death reports," Griff said, with theatrical exaggeration. "She gave each animal a certificate so we can easily reference them."

It was hardly one of Forbush's strengths, but Griff hoped his assistant would pick up on his expression and allow the lie to hold. Still, he turned his back to the camera so that his assistant alone could see him put his finger to his lips. After ten seconds of uncertainty, Forbush saw the light and nodded that he understood.

"Mr. President," Griff said, "I'm not sure you've met Melvin Forbush before."

Grinning broadly, Forbush bent low, put his face eight inches or so from the camera, and waved hello to the president with the fingers of one hand.

Allaire seemed to calm down a notch.

"Mr. Forbush," he said, "I want to thank you personally for your dedication and service to the country."

"It's a job," Forbush said. "I'm doing my best, and no matter how exhausted Dr. Rhodes is, he's doing his best, too."

"Good," Allaire responded. "Now, both of you get back to it. Because the way things are right now, you both need to do better than your best."

With that, the screen went dark.

"Well, that sure went swimmingly," Griff said, sighing. "I guess I'd be a little tense, too, if someone told me I didn't have much time left."

"You didn't say that."

"It's not what you say that counts, Melvin. It's what people hear."

* * *

An hour passed.

Griff spent most of it staring across the small room at nothing in particular. His exhaustion seemed overshadowed by the feelings of impotence at not being able to get more out of Sylvia Chen's recipes—her notes on what appeared to be experiments performed on human subjects.

"Hey there," Forbush said from the doorway. "Are you ready to get back to work?"

Griff sighed and stretched the tightness from his neck and shoulders.

"Yeah, I'm ready."

"Good, because I told the president of the United States you were trying your best."

"I'm suffering from brain lock, Melvin. That happens when I get real tired. It's like I'm incapable of looking at a problem from more than one perspective."

"That's strange. My problem is that I always see problems from too many perspectives. Speaking of which—"

"Yes?"

"One of the perspectives I've been thinking about, that I almost forgot to mention, has to do with Sylvia's list of names."

"Did you connect with any of them?"

"No," Forbush said. "But I've been wondering if maybe the names in Chen's lab reports could be bogus."

"Bogus?"

"A code within a code. Do you think the president knew anything about these tests?"

"I don't know what to think," Griff said.

Forbush pulled over a chair and sat down beside him.

"Well, something has been bugging me about the reports," he said.

"Go on."

"It's the heading on each page. 'The Certain Path.' "

"Why does that bug you? I assume it's just Sylvia's way of saying this is the certain path to making WRX3883 a workable agent, and keeping the lab in operation."

"Maybe. . . . Have you ever seen the movie *Dead Men Don't Wear Plaid*?"

"Steve Martin," Griff quickly recalled. "I think I saw it, but maybe I've just seen clips. It came out a while ago."

"In 1982 to be precise. Carl Reiner directed it and co-wrote the script with Martin and George Gripe, who died a few years later from an allergic reaction to a bee sting."

"We can probably do without the trivia right now, Melvin. In case you couldn't tell, we're sort of at a serious dead end."

"Well, there's a point here."

"Okay. Sorry. Don't let me take my grouchiness out on you. You don't deserve it."

"But the good thing is I can handle it," Forbush said, "so you're forgiven in advance. But listen, Griff. In the film, Martin's character is investigating the disappearance of Rachel Ward's father, a scientist named Dr. Forrest, played by George Gaynes."

"This helps us how?" Griff asked.

Forbush held up a hand to urge patience.

"Hey, easy does it," he said. "In the movie business, delivery is everything."

"Sorry," Griff said again.

"Before he disappeared, Dr. Forrest leaves lists of notes that Martin keeps on finding throughout the film. One list he titled 'Friends of Carlotta,' and the other he called 'Enemies of Carlotta.'"

"Go on."

"The big break in the case comes when Philip Marlowe, who's played by footage of Humphrey Bogart from *The Big Sleep,* tips Martin's character off that Carlotta wasn't a person. It was a place—an island off Peru."

Griff's impatience gave way to intrigue.

"So . . ."

"So, what if 'The Certain Path' isn't Chen's way of suggesting that she was on the right track, but an actual place."

Griff's eyes narrowed. He pulled his laptop computer over, opened a Web browser to Google, and typed in quotes: "The Certain Path." He clicked the first link in the resultant set, then leaned back in his chair to study the page. Moments later, a look of astonishment washed over his face.

"Well, I'll be," he said.

Griff turned the screen to Forbush, and used the computer mouse to highlight two lines of text. The highlighted words read:

The Certain Path Mission
Wichita, Kansas

CHAPTER 48

The Certain Path Mission Web site was a simple design, featuring a photograph of the building and some modest graphics. Its mission statement was prominently displayed at the top of the homepage.

DRUG ADDICTION AND ALCOHOLISM CAN BE CURED BUT ONLY BY WALKING THE CERTAIN PATH

According to the Web site's *About Us* section, the ministry's founder, Brother Xavier Bartholomew, was a recovered alcoholic/addict himself.

"It says here Brother Bartholomew was on the verge of death," Griff said. "Drugs had drained him of the will to live. And then he heard a voice, and it saved his life and guided him along the certain path to health and purpose."

"Let me guess," Melvin said. "God spoke to him

and told him to open a ministry to help other addicts get clean."

"Have you been to this Web site before?"

"I've just seen a lot of movies," Melvin said. "And as often as not, the characters in those films aren't who they seem to be. Is there anything on Brother Bartholomew that he wouldn't want posted on his Web site?"

"Like dirt?" Griff asked.

"If that's the same as skeletons in his closet."

Griff did another search, tracking a sequence of links in the search results for more information.

"Seems like we have enough dirt for a landfill," he said after a short while.

He opened a YouTube video of a Wichita TV news report. The video's title was an obvious attempt at tongue-in-cheek humor: "The Not So Certain Path." The reporter was an attractive blond woman, with a short, stylish hairdo, and a scrubbed, corn-fed glow. Griff turned up the volume on his laptop's small speakers.

"Deb Rosen, reporting from the Certain Path Mission in Wichita, where the ministry's founder, Brother Xavier Bartholomew, has been arrested and charged with multiple counts of assault and battery. The charges against Bartholomew stem from a complaint filed by this man, Karl Larson, who came to the Certain Path Ministry seeking treatment for his drug addiction."

The video showed an unshaven man in his fifties, with tangles of gray-black, unwashed hair, and murky eyes that supported the label underneath his picture: "Homeless Drug Addict." The shot cut back to the reporter at the ministry.

"Mr. Larson," Deb Rosen said, "claims that Brother Bartholomew offered him help for what he said was a decades-long addiction to narcotics and alcohol. But what Brother Bartholomew was offering turned out to be anything but helpful."

The video swung to Karl Larson. The street person responded to the reporter's queries in a gruff, raspy voice.

"I thought the Certain Path was about praying and stuff," Larson said. "But after a little while I couldn't do the meditation and the hours and hours of praying. And no matter how hard I tried, I couldn't stay clean and sober. That's when Brother Bartholomew began to beat me. He put me in a cell in the basement to keep me away from the booze and drugs. Then he'd beat me on my back and butt with straps and ropes and even canes. Sometimes he'd tie me up. He told me it was the only way to get the demon out. We may be homeless and desperate, but we still got pride. And we don't deserve to be beaten like dogs, even though, as Brother Bartholomew says over and over, it's for our own good."

Larson held his tattooed arms up to the camera to show they were bruised and scarred. The next shot cut from the drifter back to the outside of the ministry, where the camera followed the reporter around the perimeter of the aged redbrick building, with a red neon sign running down one corner that read, simply, MISSION.

"According to prosecutors, Mr. Larson was not the only addict subjected to Brother Bartholomew's unusual brand of aversion therapy."

The next transition showed the outside of a police station. The bottom graphic identified the officer interviewed as Lieutenant Erik Olsen of the Wichita, Kansas, Police Department.

"We have several alleged victims of Xavier Bartholomew who have come forward to file complaints. The matter is under investigation, so I cannot comment further at this time."

"And yet, in another twist to this story of good intentions gone bad," Deb Rosen's voice said from off camera, "not all of the addicts who have sought out Brother Bartholomew for help have been treated as Karl Larson allegedly was."

The man in the next shot looked to be everything Larson was not. He was bright-eyed, clean-shaven, well dressed, and smiling. The undergraphic identified him as Paul Silasky, recovered alcoholic/addict.

"I would have died if it weren't for Brother Bartholomew," Silasky said. "Same for a lot of others, too. I tried everything, NA, AA. You name the twelve-step program and I did it. Nothing worked for me until I found Brother Bartholomew. I don't consider the Certain Path's way a punishment. It's a path to freedom—a way to life."

The segment finished with the reporter across the street from the mission. The graphic shown in the upper right corner of the screen was a photograph of Brother Bartholomew, a man in his fifties with a round, cherubic face and a horseshoe head of silver hair, absent in the front, down past his shoulders in the back. He wore a bright, floral-designed shirt underneath a heavy, dark brown wool monk's robe. Chains of brightly colored beads—turquoise, reds, and blues—dangled around his neck. Some of the necklaces had ornaments attached, but none were of any religious symbol that Griff recognized.

"Community activists, social workers, and other mental health professionals have been uniform in their condemnation of the Certain Path's alleged methods," the reporter said. "Some are opposed to the ministry and its soup kitchen remaining open to the public. In the meantime, Brother Xavier Bartholomew is free on bail and back at work. A trial date is projected for sometime next year. Bartholomew and his attorney declined our requests for an interview."

YouTube faded to black. Griff pointed to the stats that showed the video had originally been uploaded four years ago, and over that time had amassed only 725 views.

"Guess a video about abusing drug addicts isn't going to sweep the world," Griff said.

"Certainly not like all those dancing overweight cats with ten million views apiece," Forbush replied.

"I think I need to try and find Brother Bartholomew and get some answers for ourselves."

"What's so important?" Melvin asked.

"Because if we're right, and Chen was experimenting on people, I would assume that the subjects were referred to her by Bartholomew."

"It's possible."

"What's possible?"

"For a man of the cloth to go bad. In *Night of the*

Hunter, Robert Mitchum—one of my favorite actors, incidentally—plays Harry Powell, a serial killer and self-proclaimed preacher, who has L-O-V-E tattooed on the knuckles of one hand and H-A-T-E on the other. Then there's Reverend Phillip Shooter in *Hot Fuzz* and, of course, Cardinal Richelieu in all the *Three Musketeer* movies and spin-offs. Those are just for starters. Now that I think about it, there's—"

"Melvin, I get the point. I want to know how these people were chosen, where they were treated, and what was done to them. And most of all, I want to know what happened to J. R. Davis. Was he just some sort of clerical error on Sylvia's part, or is he still alive?"

Griff held up Davis's lab report, distinguished from the others in the fax set by a result that did not conclude with the word "deceased."

"Could Bartholomew be in jail?" Forbush asked. "That news report was from a few years ago."

Griff surfed the Web some more.

"It says here the case against him was dropped a few months before trial. That was about two years ago. Doesn't say anything about the ministry closing down."

"And Allaire can't know about this?" Melvin asked.

"Allaire might have orchestrated all of this," Griff said. "I don't know the man well enough. He doesn't trust me, anyway. What if he ordered Chen to conduct human experiments? You'd think he would have told me if he knew Chen was dosing people with the virus, but I'm just not sure. If he's involved, he might decide I'm going to use this stuff against him. Or else he'll think I'm just setting it up to give me leverage to bolt.

For now, Melvin, nobody else can know about this—at least not until we know more ourselves. It's better to ask forgiveness than permission. Can you sneak me out of here, the way you did Angie?"

"What about our work? Orion? Our experiments?"

Griff rubbed at his eyes.

"What experiments are we going to continue, Melvin?" he asked, his voice cracking. "The ones that aren't working? The ones that never had a chance to work? I was on this job for years at Columbia, then here before they arrested me. Find a way to keep WRX3883 from killing people—that was my original assignment. And I failed. A lot of scientists fail. That's just the way it is. We fail and we fail until one day we shift gears and change direction and something works. So now, I'm being asked to do in a week or two what I couldn't accomplish in years. You tell me what I'm leaving?"

"We could lose a lot of time. It could be the end of the line for the people in the Capitol."

"I'm telling you, Melvin, it's the end of the line already. I've done everything I can think of. If this J. R. Davis really did survive his WRX infection, then we might have something. We might have that change of direction."

Forbush sat pensively for a while, then said, "I don't believe we should take the chance of trying to sneak you out in the trunk."

"Why not?"

"I think Angie and I were lucky. Now that we actually did it, I would bet eight out of ten times we'd be caught."

"Maybe they were under orders to let her go so she could be followed."

"Now that you mention it, that seems possible. I lied to the guards about a critical experiment being in jeopardy unless I got to town for some supplies we didn't have, so they might have been in a rush. Plus, I do asthma attacks well because I actually have it. The guard was rummaging through the glove compartment for my inhaler when Angie slipped into the trunk."

"So the trunk isn't going to work. What else?"

"What about the exhaust system?"

Griff saw the possibilities immediately.

"How many of the ventilation ducts have surface access outside the wire?"

"Only one," Forbush said. "We have a dedicated single-pass air exhaust discharge for the Kitchen ventilation system that pumps HEPA-filtered air to the surface. It was intentionally installed far from occupied buildings and the other air intake vents. It's interlocked with the other subsurface supply and exhaust fans to prevent positive pressurization in the Kitchen labs."

"How wide is that vent shaft?"

"Big enough to fit you inside, if that's what you're thinking."

"That's what I'm thinking."

"But not a heck of a lot bigger in diameter than that. Plus, from what I recall, after it leaves the Kitchen, the duct makes a pretty intense vertical rise. There are not many sharp bends in ductwork, or long horizontal runs, because those put a lot of strain on the exhaust fans. On the plus side, the discharge is well outside the perimeter of the base."

"So nobody would see me exit?"

"Not even if they were using searchlights."

"How do I get in?"

"First, you have to be suited, so that's going to make the work harder."

"What tools do I need?"

"A screwdriver and ratchet should do it. You'll have to remove the pre-filters first, then the HEPA filter from its housing, clear the bags from the safety and cinching straps and such, the blower too. Piece of cake."

"That's some cake. Is the exhaust system alarmed?"

"It is, but I can shut that down."

"How long will it take me from the Kitchen to the surface?"

Forbush pondered the question.

"Twenty minutes, I would guess. You're going to have to shimmy your way to the top. That will be the hard part. Keep your hands and feet pressed to the sides of the duct and inch your way up."

"Sounds tough."

"If you slip, you'll fall like you were on one of those giant water chutes. You could twist an ankle or break a bone when you hit bottom, in which case you'd never get back up to the safety grate."

"You don't sound very optimistic."

"That depends on how well you kept yourself in shape in that cell. Give yourself thirty minutes instead of the twenty I said. There's a ladder bolted into the duct at the far end. That should help."

Griff checked his watch.

"I have a couple of things I want to finish in the lab. I'll be ready to go at two this afternoon—no, make it three thirty. It'll be almost dark then. If it takes me longer than we think, I don't want you waiting around in the dark in the middle of noplace. Can I just climb out at the other end?"

"The safety grate is heavy. You won't be able to push it off without a winch pulling from the other side."

"Do we have one of those?"

"In the machine shop, I think. I should be able to attach it to the trailer hitch on my Taurus."

"Then it's settled," Griff said. "Meet me at four o'clock by the grate."

The intercom system buzzed its shrill alarm. It was loud enough to be heard even inside spacesuits and it happened whenever somebody surface-side wanted to speak to someone below. All of the phones subsurface had an instant push-button connection to the topside communication post.

"Rhodes here," Griff said into the phone's receiver.

"Rhodes, it's Sergeant Stafford. How's it going down there?"

"Let's just say that if this were easy, everybody would be doing it."

"Not me," the soldier replied. "I've already seen what that virus can do. Listen, an unexpected surprise visitor just flew in. He wants to meet with you right away."

"Who is it?" Griff asked, rolling his eyes at Forbush. "I'm really busy."

"It's the guy who, unless you can deliver, is now just a few heartbeats away from the presidency—Homeland Security Secretary Paul Rappaport—our designated survivor."

CHAPTER 49

The tension evident in Bethany Townsend's expression made Ellis uneasy. There was a look of concern about the president's physician that the speaker simply did not understand or trust. Did Townsend know about her sneaking into the Senate Chamber? Could she be aware of her role in the murder of Archibald Jakes? If so, why was Townsend the one confronting her, and not Allaire. Something did not add up, and Ellis was never in the mood for surprises.

Even more disturbing was that Townsend had come accompanied by Henry Tilden. At the physician's request, they had convened at the rostrum where their conversation would not easily be overheard. Given that Ellis had clearly declared her continuing enmity for Allaire and her belief that he was lying to everybody and using the situation for his personal and political gain, the visit from his personal doctor was unsettling.

As soon as possible, Ellis vowed, she would have to take control of the situation. Tilden was a dimwit, but Townsend was sharp, and given their limited contact over the years, something of an unknown commodity.

"We have a serious situation," Townsend began.

"That seems rather obvious, Doctor," Ellis said. "So I trust you are not here to rehash old business."

"I do have new concerns, Madam Speaker," Townsend replied. "And they revolve around President Allaire."

Ellis, her spirit suddenly taking flight, looked on gravely, mirroring Tilden's worried expression. Thanks to her connection with Genesis, and her nearly disastrous encounter with Group C, she knew specifics about the virus and its horrific physiological effects. Was Allaire suddenly infected? Had he fallen victim to his own creation? That had to be it. Destiny had taken her firmly by the hand.

"Is there something wrong with the president?" Tilden asked. "I was with him just a few hours ago. We were discussing supply shipments. He seemed fine to me. Anxious, but fine."

Ellis was pleased that Tilden had been excluded from whatever was going on, but she was hardly surprised. Clearly, Allaire considered him as much of a dimwit as she did.

"I, too, thought he was doing well," Townsend said. "But now there's been an incident."

Again, Ellis felt a rush. *Bad things should happen to bad people,* she was thinking.

"What sort of incident?" Tilden asked.

"The president went into a rage during a video conference with the virologist who is working on the antiviral treatment."

"Do you know what set him off?" Ellis asked.

"That's the strangest thing of all," Townsend replied. "Nothing really did it. It was like a switch had been thrown. Even the president admits that his outburst was disproportionate to the issue being discussed."

The virus, Ellis thought. It could be stress, but she sensed it was infection.

Then she realized a downside to Allaire's getting infected that she had not considered. Her thoughts opened on the horror she and O'Neil had encountered within the Senate Chamber. The lethal insanity of Archibald Jakes. The blood. The sickness and stench fouling the room. The wretched sounds of suffering. If Allaire was succumbing to the same malady, then this virus could be spreading faster than Genesis had led her to believe it would.

"So, does Allaire—excuse me, *President* Allaire—know you're speaking with us?" she asked. "I mean, you are his physician. Is it appropriate to be discussing his medical status with us?"

"He doesn't know that I'm speaking to you about this," Townsend admitted. "But I have another duty to perform that exceeds my obligations to any privacy standards."

"Duty?"

Ellis already knew what was coming. She had to hold on to the side of her chair to keep from floating.

"The Twenty-Fifth Amendment to the United States Constitution," Townsend said.

"Are you suggesting the situation is so dire that we must consider forcibly removing the president from office?" Ellis asked.

Of course, she now knew that was exactly what Townsend had come to discuss. Still, it was meaningful to her to hear the words spoken aloud.

"I have not approached President Allaire about transmitting to Vice President Tilden, our president pro tempore of the Senate, and yourself, a written declaration that he is unable to discharge his duties. But this is a matter we discussed soon after the virus was released."

Ellis knew the mechanics of the Twenty-Fifth Amendment verbatim. Tilden, along with either Congress, or the Cabinet and principal officers of the executive branch, could remove the president from office with a simple majority vote. The president's personal physician held tremendous influence in determining how people would vote.

"What are you proposing we do, Dr. Townsend?" Ellis asked, barely able to keep a tremor from her voice.

The stars were aligning.

"For now, nothing," Townsend said. "But Mr. Vice President, you are second in line to ascend to the presidency, and Madam Speaker, you are third. I felt it was my obligation to inform you both of the situation, as you, Henry, may be called upon to take the presidential oath of office."

Tilden grimaced in an honest display of remorse. Ellis did the same, but her apparent dismay was anything but honest.

"Let's pray it doesn't come to that," Tilden said.

"I suggest that we meet at least every two hours on the hour so that we're all on the same page," Townsend said. "If the situation with the president worsens between checkpoints, I shall simply summon you both back to the rostrum and we will decide a course of action from there. Agreed?"

"Agreed," both said.

The meeting adjourned, and Ellis set off to locate Gladstone. Her mind was on the biocontainment suit she saw hanging by the Senate Chamber door. She regretted now not putting it on, as she had subjected herself to a high concentration of infected air. Hopefully, she would not manifest signs of infection until she had shepherded the Genesis bill through Congress. The video on her BlackBerry of Group C, and the guarantee from Genesis of a treatment, should be enough to drive the legislation home in no time.

Before she could locate Gladstone, she felt a vibration against her ribs. The Genesis messaging device, secured there with masking tape, was buzzing for her attention. Ellis made a hasty change of direction and returned to the ladies' room, where she felt it safest to read and respond. The message from Genesis was simple and to the point.

They wrote: What is the status of the legislation?

Ellis typed back: Getting closer. Allaire is showing symptoms of infection. Has exhibited rage behavior that is worrisome to his personal physician.

Genesis: This is the time to strike. Get that bill passed.

Ellis: Tilden is still a veto threat.

Genesis: That is your concern, not ours. If you want

the antiviral treatment, then you will need to find a way to pass the bill into law.

Ellis stared at the messaging device. She knew what "find a way" really meant. She was third in line for the presidency, soon to be second. More than just her ambitions were at stake now. She had put her life in danger simply by setting foot inside the Senate Chamber. Now, she needed the treatment. Of course, there was a way.

Consider it done, Ellis wrote.

CHAPTER 50

Sergeant Stafford equipped Griff and Forbush with down parkas for the short walk to the bungalow where Rappaport was waiting. For Griff, it felt splendid to breathe fresh air again. One of the greatest pleasures of going down was a deep appreciation for the little things after coming back up.

The sun was a pale disc in a placid sky. It would be nearly set by the time he escaped from Kalvesta on his way to the Certain Path Mission in Wichita. Wind from the south whipped across the flat, frozen landscape and sent Griff's hands scrambling for the lining of his jacket pockets. His footsteps crunched on rime as he and Forbush trudged past the same model VH-60N Whitehawk helicopter that lifted him out of the Florence prison yard just a few days ago.

"Isn't that the president's helicopter?" Forbush asked.

"No, it's just the same model," Griff said, his voice etched with worry. "But if we don't figure out an antiviral treatment, it could be the new Marine One for President Rappaport."

They entered the topside bungalow that functioned as the facility's conference room. The sharp wind whipped the hinged door closed behind them. A portable kerosene heater in the corner of the room sputtered and gurgled while keeping the rectangular space at a serviceable sixty-five degrees. Griff left his parka on, hoping that the Secretary of Homeland Security would get the hint that there was work to be done below ground.

Four people—three men and a woman—sat waiting at a long foldout table in the center of the room. Griff figured the two men and a woman standing nearby were Rappaport's assigned Secret Service agents. Husky Sergeant Stafford and three of his team brought the total number present to a baker's dozen—just above capacity for the space.

A thin man with graying temples, sharply dressed in a tailored suit, rose from his seat at the table. Griff, hardly a newshound, had never seen photos of any of the Cabinet. He assumed the man, who moved like an athlete and looked patrician bred, was Paul Rappaport. The former governor's bearing and sharply defined features had Griff trying to recall the exact words to Creedence Clearwater Revival's song "Fortunate Son."

"Griffin Rhodes," Griff said. "My associate, Melvin Forbush."

Griff took a step forward to shake hands. Two of the agents intervened, blocking his path.

"We've got to search you first, sir," the woman said.

Groaning inwardly, Griff dropped his parka to the

floor, and lifted his arms for a pat-down. A second agent swept him with a handheld metal detector. Melvin, who had a dreamy expression that Griff took to mean he was imagining himself in any number of movie pat-down scenes, was subjected to the same treatment.

"All clear," one agent said to Rappaport.

The secretary then met them in the middle of the room. Griff extended his hand. Rappaport took it for a moment. Griff could see mistrust in the man's gray eyes.

"I'm not the bad guy here," Griff said in a near whisper.

"I know what you believe, but I also know your history," Rappaport said.

"So you know that I was framed."

The secretary did not smile.

"I know that you were arrested for stealing the virus," he said. "And I know that you're the man President Allaire has tasked with saving our government. Makes me think of the fox guarding the henhouse."

Griff's expression was one of extreme displeasure. Angie's heroism and current plight continued to dominate his thoughts, along with his impending escape from the lab to Wichita. In addition, Griff had Sylvia Chen's human experimentation and his own continued failures with Orion adding to his emotional cocktail. His ability to control his simmering anger was hanging by the strand of a spider's web.

"Mr. Secretary, what is it you want from me?" he said. "Did you just fly a thousand miles to put me in my place?"

Rappaport's grin held no mirth.

"Well, what I want, Dr. Rhodes, is to make absolutely certain you are doing what you have promised to do. I am ready to become president if I must, but I'd prefer it not come to that."

"Pardon my saying so, Mr. Secretary, but to my sense, at least, that statement isn't exactly oozing sincerity."

"That's your interpretation, Rhodes. As secretary of Homeland Security, it's my sworn duty to protect the president and this country. If that includes monitoring you and your work here, and it does, then that is just what I shall do. If my sworn duty involves taking over for President Allaire, then that is what I will do. But at the moment, all I care about is seeing to it that you do everything in your power to save those poor unfortunates in the Capitol. In that regard, I want to know exactly what you are doing down there in that little hole of yours. Because, let us be honest with each other—"

"Yes, let's."

"I don't trust you."

"So, I've gathered."

"I have brought with me some folks who will make absolutely certain I can keep a very close eye on you and your activities."

Rappaport turned and motioned to one of the men seated at the conference table behind them. The man stood slightly taller than Rappaport, and appeared equally as fit. He wore a blue blazer over an oxford shirt. The jacket had a ten-point buck emblazoned on the pocket. Unlike Rappaport, he *was* interested in shaking Griff's hand.

"I'm Roger Corum," he said, "CEO of Staghorn Security Technologies."

Forbush's expression suddenly became that of a child viewing a fireworks display.

"Wow! That's so great," he said, with his typical enthusiasm, as he gave Corum's hand a prolonged, vigorous pumping. "I've been wanting to get in touch with you guys about some security tape I have from the system you upgraded a couple of years ago. Talk about a lucky break!"

Rappaport interrupted before Corum could reply. Clearly, the secretary had no interest in communicating with Griff's associate.

"I asked Roger to accompany me here as a personal favor. I will allow him to explain our intentions."

"Why don't we all sit first," Corum said, his speech gently Southern, and his manner much more agreeable than Rappaport's.

"If it's okay with you, I prefer to stand," Griff said. "Because if we're standing, this meeting will be shorter. And every second we're not working is another second we're not working."

"Understood," Corum said. "Secretary Rappaport is interested in monitoring the activities down below in real time. Since it is impractical for him to be physically present there, he has asked that Staghorn install state-of-the-art communications equipment to allow him, and through him, the president, to remain in constant voice and video contact with your team."

"By my *team* you mean Mr. Forbush and myself. Because that's all we have."

Corum smiled genuinely at the image.

"I've worked with teams of a hundred that are probably not as effective or efficient as the two of you," he said. "Dr. Rhodes, what we'll do is replace some of our existing cameras and equipment with newer models that allow for encrypted, wireless streaming over a secure satellite network. That way we can broadcast your activity to any location on earth."

"You won't get a signal that far below ground," Forbush said.

"True as things stand," Corum replied. "Presently, the cameras are hardwired to the hub in the communications building here at the facility. We'll replace that hub with our newer model as well. With the cameras connected to the new hub we'll be able to transmit signal from the building to our satellite network. Which brings me to our next effort, videoconferencing."

"We have that already," Griff said.

"But you don't have *mobile* conferencing." Corum took out a device from his blazer pocket that was no bigger than a cell phone. "This is the TX-Mobile Communicator. We developed it for Uncle Sam. It's a handheld, private networked videoconferencing system. Inside the casing is a stand-alone sophisticated GPS tracker, built into a disc that's not much bigger than a silver dollar. It will allow us to pinpoint your exact location, even underground."

"You want us to carry that gadget around like some sort of parolee ankle bracelet?"

Griff's disgust was evident. Rappaport stepped forward.

"I expect you to do what you are told, Rhodes," he said.

"Well, perhaps you've forgotten, Mr. Secretary, but what I've been told to do is save this country, not answer to you."

"Don't get so high on yourself," Rappaport replied. "This country will continue on no matter the outcome of what you do. In a worst-case scenario, it will be incumbent on me to form an interim government. And I promise you, we'll emerge from those ashes stronger and more resolved to combat terror than ever before."

"By that do you mean all the personal freedoms you're going to revoke?" Forbush blurted out. Griff shot his friend a stunned but simultaneously appreciative look. "I've read up on your policy positions," Forbush then went on. "The walls and moats between the U.S. and Mexico. The wiretapping. The computer monitoring. The cameras. The profiling. The—"

"That is sheer nonsense," Rappaport said, speaking at least as much to the others in the room as to Forbush. "I am not going to take away any freedoms granted by our Constitution. I am committed to protecting this country and the American way of life. And if doing so requires stronger security at the borders, more use of surveillance technology, photo ID cards, profiling, and an expansion of the Patriot Act in any way necessary to combat terrorists like Genesis, then that is exactly what I will do."

"Excuse me if I don't concur," Griff said.

"Personally, Dr. Rhodes, I don't care if you support

my political philosophy or not. Now, you'll both carry this device. And you will answer whenever I request a conference."

"And if I refuse?" Griff asked.

"I shall inform the president of your subversive behavior," Rappaport replied. "Succeed, or fail, you could end up spending the rest of your life back in that prison cell. So you don't really have a choice. Do you?"

Griff resisted the urge to reiterate his "no hidden catches" deal with James Allaire as well as the urge to tackle the Homeland Security secretary to the floor and show him knuckle-to-jaw what true subversive behavior felt like. Instead, he indicated the two people still seated at the conference table.

"So are these your install folks?" he said to Corum.

The CEO smiled, visibly relieved for the change of subject.

"Staghorn is not in the business of manufacturing any of the technology we sell," Corum said. "We're more of a consortium—international general contractors for security, if you will—which is why I've brought with me the CEOs of two of the foremost companies in the world—companies that will be providing us with the equipment to get this job done." He gestured to the woman first. "This is Marguerite Prideaux, from Paris. Marguerite is with SecureTech, a French company in our vendor network. And next to her is Colin White-head, CEO of Matrix Industries of New Jersey. Yes, *that* Matrix."

The woman approached Griff and extended a fine, slender hand. She was a dark-haired beauty, dressed in a fashionable pantsuit. She had an aura about her that announced her European heritage as though it was a perfume she wore. From Griff's arrival, she had kept her intelligent, oval eyes fixed on him.

Her fellow board member was a cadaverously thin man in his forties, with the crimson spray of rosacea across his cheeks. He coughed twice as he came forward, and Griff could see the top of a Camel cigarette box jutting out from the breast pocket of his shirt. His nose was bulbous and pocked—possibly from too much drinking.

Griff shook their hands impatiently. Forbush gave each a far more enthusiastic greeting.

"So which of you can help me with my problem?" he asked.

"What problem is that?" Colin Whitehead replied, partially stifling another cough.

"I have proof that the security videotape showing Dr. Rhodes, here, stealing the virus from our lab, has been forged. I was going to contact Staghorn to get some expert opinion as to how that could have been done. But now, here you are, right on our doorstep."

Griff shot Forbush a disapproving glare. There was no time for this.

"Melvin, we have those test tubes in the centrifuge we need to extract."

"No we don't," Forbush said cheerily. "I took those out hours ago."

"Well, we have to run the test again in another three hours. Three hours from now, Melvin."

The exchange between the two was handled with all the elegance of a rugby scrum, but finally Forbush seemed to key in on what Griff was trying to say.

"Right . . . three hours. . . . We have testing to do. But Griff, I can be quick. We need this. You need this if you want to prove your innocence."

Roger Corum saved the moment.

"We'd be happy to look at whatever you have to share, Melvin. We're here for a few days—until the install is complete, anyway."

Rappaport took a step toward Griff.

"You had better not be planning anything, Rhodes," he said.

"I'm planning to work."

"I am not stupid. You think I didn't notice you and Melvin, here, trying to have a sidebar conversation in front of us? Roger, I want very much for you to meet with this fellow about the video footage, since he asked so politely. I will be contacting President Allaire and letting him know we are here and on top of the situation. Dr. Rhodes, I also intend to tell him that progress is being made."

"Tell him whatever you wish."

"As soon as I am finished with the president and some other business, we are all going to take a trip down to the lab."

"Why would you want to do that?" Griff asked, focused on the ventilation shaft, and his upcoming thirty-minute crawl through darkness to the heavy grate beyond the installation's fenced perimeter. "I mean, soon enough you'll have your cameras and recording devices in place to keep watch over me."

"I want to see for myself what it is you are doing down there," Rappaport answered coolly. "And more importantly, I want to make sure that you are down there doing it."

CHAPTER 51

Griff lay prone on the floor of the Kitchen, with a spin ratchet, a screwdriver, and a flashlight beside him. Working with any sort of tools in a biocontainment suit was like swimming in molasses—possible, but certainly no fun. The targets were the screws securing the slotted front grate of the ventilation shaft. The heavy screwdriver turned awkwardly in his gloved hand, falling again and again. Most of the lab equipment in the Kitchen was specially designed for the decreased mobility of BL-4 laboratory work, and the extra effort and concentration required to maneuver the tool had Griff's heart racing. Droplets of sweat condensed on the inside of his faceplate, reducing visibility in the already dimly lit workspace. But turn by turn he was making progress.

Two screws out. . . . Now, three . . .

One to go.

The groove of the final screw was nearly gone, and

the body was stripped, making the already difficult task nearly impossible. Griff needed some sort of lubricating spray, but there was none. The five minutes he and Melvin had allotted for this phase of the escape had already taken triple that. How ironic to have the fate of the country hinging on a tiny bit of rust. The notion brought a rueful smile.

Griff had overheard Stafford say that patrols along the roads bordering Kalvesta were being increased in response to the secretary's unexpected arrival. Any delay on his part risked Melvin being spotted by one of those patrols—assuming, of course, that Melvin ended his Staghorn meeting in time to make their rendezvous. With his anxiety escalating, Griff brought in a small hammer and chisel to loosen the stripped screw.

For want of a nail, the shoe was lost, he said to himself, tapping on the chisel to the rhythm of the proverbial poem. *For want of a shoe, the horse was lost. . . .*

Another try with the screwdriver. Griff figured he could change the angle of the blade to improve the leverage.

For want of a horse, the rider was lost. . . .

The handle shook as Griff strained to turn it. The shank slipped free of the mangled screw head, and he felt the blade tear across the fabric of his suit. Hyperventilating, and fearing the worst, he checked the puncture. The suit's several protective layers seemed to be intact.

For want of a rider the battle was lost. . . .

Griff tried another approach, gripping the sides of the vent with his gloved hands and twisting the already loose metal plate as he pulled. Home run! The trouble-some screw budged, then creaked a fraction of a milli-meter, then suddenly turned. For the moment, at least, the kingdom was saved.

The pre-filters removed easily enough, but the much larger HEPA filter looked to be a serious chal-lenge. The angle required to use the spin ratchet on the stainless steel bolts seemed designed for a contor-tionist. Sweat continued dripping down Griff's brow and stinging his eyes, until he was working nearly blind. To make matters worse, again and again his elbows displaced his flashlight.

He finally managed to unplug the connectors power-ing the fan, and held his breath. Despite Melvin's assur-ance, he still worried about the alarm. The loud rush of air being sucked up the vent stopped suddenly. The only sound was his heart pounding in his ears. An inch at a time, he worked the cumbersome fan free from the alu-minum duct. The razor-sharp edges of the filter's metal casing were a continuous threat to the integrity of his suit, but he handled them well.

Finally, he took in a single deep breath and pulled until the heavy filter came free of the duct. He let it fall to the floor of the Kitchen with a loud, satisfying crash.

Buoyed by a second wind, he removed the remain-ing components—blowers and bags—with a great deal less effort. Now, it was time to get Rappaport out of the picture. In a short while, a powerful animosity had de-veloped between the two of them. Rappaport was con-vinced of Griff's guilt and lack of patriotism, and Griff was uncomfortable around the man's arrogance and self-assuredness. In addition, more and more, thoughts were taking shape regarding the fact that until it became clear why Genesis was undertaking their reign of terror, Paul Rappaport seemed to be at the forefront of those who would benefit from it.

Griff's joints ached from his having stayed so long in such an awkward position. He crossed to the wall-mounted control panel for the Kitchen's Environment Status System—its ESS. His goal was to make the place seem even more potentially lethal than it already was.

Of the three buttons on the panel's front face, the green one was lit, and the yellow and red ones were not. Griff keyed the input code required to change environment status, and with a push of a button the Kitchen went from a green safety level to yellow. The yellow status alerted topside communication of a potential exposure risk in the labs. Nothing too alarming, like the total evacuation and shutdown mandated by red, but nothing they would risk Rappaport being exposed to, either. It would certainly buy some time. How much, Griff had no way of knowing.

He went back to the ventilation shaft and used his Maglite flashlight to penetrate the darkness of the metal tunnel, scanning for sharp edges between duct joints that could slice open his suit before he cleared the hot zone. Fortunately, the engineers had injected sealant between the joints. The passage would be relatively smooth.

With thoughts of Angie and of what might lie ahead in Wichita, he set the flashlight down. He would need both hands free to work his way up the steep rise at the far end of the system. Detaching the air hose from his suit, he positioned himself facedown on the metal and snaked his way into the blackness.

Space in the duct was unpleasantly tight. Griff worked forward in a military crawl. The shaft was roughly the diameter of the opening in an MRI machine. His back scraped against the top of it every time he arched his hips. The darkness was now total, and the accompanying claustrophobia was becoming oppressive. His helmet and face mask made the situation even more difficult and unsettling.

Breathing through his nose, eyes closed, he wriggled ahead, feeling for any incline.

Breathe in . . . breathe out . . . breathe in . . . breathe out . . .

The tube seemed interminable, the air stale. Then, just as he was wondering if Melvin had given him misinformation about the course of the system, he sensed an incline beginning. At first the rise was subtle. Griff opened his eyes, but he was still engulfed in absolute darkness.

Breathe in . . . breathe out . . .

Suddenly, the incline became more severe. The shaft bent upward at an angle that was at least forty-five degrees. Instantly, the rhythm Griff had established disappeared. Movement ahead and upward became awkward, and required every bit of his strength. Without the air hose to help cool him, his suit trapped much of his body heat. He kept himself wedged in the shaft, moving through the blackness only a few inches at a time. Fatigue became a serious problem. The climb was far more difficult than he had anticipated. He fought off the increasingly desperate urge to try crawling backward to the opening.

Visions of giving up—of just stopping and dying there—began to dominate his thoughts. He drove himself ahead by remembering the guards at Florence, beating on the soles of his feet and calling him a traitor and a terrorist. He allowed his mind to relive the electric total-body pain and the blood of his Ebola infection.

The rise in the shaft increased. Griff slid backward. Frantically, he pressed his palms against the metal, finally managing to regain his leverage. Again he shimmied ahead, his arms shaking from supporting what amounted to his full body weight. Still, he managed to inch higher. He guessed the angle of the shaft to be at least seventy degrees, now.

Angie . . . the guards . . . Louisa . . . Rappaport . . . the cell . . . Allaire . . . Africa . . .

He was nearly upright now, wedged in place, but able to use his knees for support and thrust. As Melvin had warned, this part of the ascent *was* like rock climbing. But nothing had prepared him for the consuming blackness. His forearms were on fire.

I've beaten Ebola. . . . I've outlasted Florence. . . . I can do this. . . .

Tears of pain mixed with the sweat and salted his lips. He kept his gaze fixed upward, searching for the end. Then, suddenly, his glove hit metal—the rung of the ladder! Above him, the utter darkness had given way to the gloom of dusk. He bent his head back as much as space would allow and saw the squares of the access grate, silhouetted against a darkening sky.

One rung, then another. Finally, his fingers closed on the heavy steel grate. As Melvin had warned, there was no way he would be able to shove it aside. Clutching the ladder to keep from falling back down the shaft, he cried out to the world overhead.

"Melvin! Forbush, are you there? Get me out of here! Melvin, for God's sake, help me!"

Griff feared the suit was muffling his cries. He let go with one hand and slammed the base of his palm against the grate. Nothing. Then he heard a motor engage. An instant later, one edge of the heavy obstruction was lifted by a hook he hadn't noticed, and the grate was dragged clear of the opening. Dizzy with exhaustion, Griff tried to lift himself out of the shaft. But the strength wasn't there. A pair of hands reached down and grabbed Griff by his wrists.

Melvin!

Forbush lifted him clear of the shaft, disconnected his helmet, and pulled it off.

Gasping, Griff flopped over onto his back and squinted up at the fading light. His chest was heaving, desperately sucking in the wintry air. Forbush next unzipped the biocontainment suit. Underneath it, Griff was wearing only scrubs and booties. He felt a wave of frozen air envelop him, stinging his skin. His sweat instantly cooled, forming a chilling sheen that grew colder every second. Now out of his suit, Griff began shivering.

"You made it, buddy," Forbush said. "You made it."

"Yes, he did," a deep voice said from behind his friend. "Good job, sport. Bloody good job."

A huge man emerged from the far side of Melvin's Taurus and slashed the gangly lab assistant across the back of the head with the barrel of a submachine gun. Forbush dropped like an anvil and lay on the frozen ground, rolling from side to side, moaning, and pawing at his head.

The behemoth leveled his gun at a spot between Griff's eyes.

"Welcome to the world above, Dr. Rhodes," he said. "You and I have some business to discuss."

CHAPTER 52

Matt Fink pulled a tangle of rope from the open trunk of the Taurus and tossed it by Griff's feet.

"Tie him up," he ordered.

Melvin had made it unsteadily to his knees. Through the gloom, Griff could see blood cascading around one of his ears and down his neck.

"Shit," Forbush said. "You didn't have to do that."

"I said tie him up!"

"How did you know we were here?" Griff asked, stalling, but also desperate to learn the answer.

Genesis had somehow been aware when Angie left the compound. Now, it appeared, they were once again a step ahead.

"I'll ask the questions here," the man said. "Now do as I say or I swear, I'll shoot this jerk in the eye."

"Why do you need me to tie him up? What do you want with us?"

"Do I look like someone you should be fucking

around with, sport? You're going to tell me where you are headed and why, or things are going to get mighty painful for both of you."

Griff's teeth were beginning to chatter. He rubbed at his arms to keep his circulation going. The icy wind was cutting through his thin scrubs like a scalpel.

"Didn't he bring a jacket for me?" he asked. "I . . . I need one."

"My patience is wearing thin, sport. Now, do as I say and you'll get your jacket. Don't do it and watch your friend here die a painful death while you become an icicle."

Griff quickly surveyed their surroundings. To the west was the lab—a series of tiny lights on the horizon, perhaps a quarter of a mile away. To the north and east the flat, frozen ground was interrupted only by the scattered silhouettes of rolled hay. The south, however, held some promise. In fact, the distant farmhouse, outbuildings, and enormous barn told him precisely where they were—on the vast Cahill Bar-B Ranch, home to one of the largest herds of bison in western Kansas.

During his initial time at the lab, he had actually driven past this field a number of times. Once he had stopped to walk to within just a few yards of the magnificent beasts before a ranch hand on horseback warned him that, even though herds of wild bison had given way to ranch-bred, the animals were still fast, unpredictably temperamental, and at two thousand pounds, with horns, hooves, and a massive, battering-ram head, more deadly than a grizzly.

"I've had it with you, Rhodes," the man was saying.

"You're a wise guy, and you don't care what happens to your pal, here. Well, maybe you care about what happens to yourself."

He jammed the muzzle of the submachine gun with force into Griff's kidney, sending him down to one knee. Just as quickly, Griff was up, refusing even to rub at the spot.

"Who are you?" he asked, searching for an opening, any opening, through which to attack or to run.

"I'm a bad man, sport. That's all you need to know," he said, pressing the muzzle against the back of Forbush's head for emphasis.

Like the killer who had tracked Angie to New York, this was a professional. Griff knew with certainty that there was no way either he or Melvin was going to leave this place alive.

Griff's vision had adjusted to the gloom, and he could see a portion of the bison herd itself, huddled together against the cold. His best chance, likely his only chance, was to find a moment's break and to run weaving in that direction.

"Are you Genesis?" he asked.

"Tie him the fuck up!"

"I won't do it."

Griff's shivering was becoming more intense. He had to do something while he was still able.

But before he could make any move, the huge man charged at him, lowering his shoulder and driving it hard into Griff's sternum. Griff heard the popping of his ribs separating from cartilage or breaking. The pain was explosive. The fury of the surprise attack lifted him off of his feet and sent him flying backward onto the rock-hard ground. He landed heavily, gasping, his lungs unable to take in air. Through dizzying pain, he rolled onto his stomach, and forced himself onto his knees. Then he glared up at the figure towering above him. Death for Melvin and for him was getting closer. The man's temper and intense anger were the only weapons they had left.

"I've had it with you, sport," he said. "You can just stand there until you freeze solid. I'll enjoy watching."

Teeth clenched, Griff maneuvered one leg underneath him, and was working painfully on the other when he saw movement from behind the man.

Melvin!

The gangly virologist was a specter, blood smeared across his face, rising up behind their assailant like Phoenix from the ashes. The wildness in his eyes shone through the mounting darkness like lasers.

"Okay, I'll do it," Griff cried out, grunting around the words, but still heightening the distraction. "I'll tie him up! . . . I'll tie him up!"

At that instant, with the shriek of a banshee, Forbush leapt onto the man's back, his hands clawing frantically at his face, his fingernails digging into his cheeks. The giant swung his body around, but Forbush held his grip like a rodeo cowboy on a bull. The submachine gun fell. Griff dragged himself toward the weapon, but the man kicked it out of reach. Then, in a blaze of motion, he pulled an enormous hunting knife from his boot.

"Nooo!" Griff screamed.

In a single, practiced move, the killer drove the blade up and back into the taller man's shoulder.

Still, Forbush held on, yelling for Griff to run.

Then, bellowing and stumbling awkwardly, the man whirled and buried the knife almost to the hilt at the base of Forbush's neck. Blood spewed from the wound. Forbush screamed, released his grip, and fell limply.

Griff was on his feet now, staring in disbelief at the scene. Melvin lay motionless, blood pulsing from his neck and pooling beneath him. Griff's eyes clouded over. He felt weak and disoriented, immobile and unwilling to believe his friend's wound was mortal.

Get the gun!

Griff heard the words in his mind as if Melvin had hollered them.

The gun!

Two agonizing strides and Griff had the submachine gun in his hands. He whirled and aimed at the center of the man's chest. His index finger pulled the trigger, and the assailant, who was clumsily trying to stand, dove to his right in evasion.

The gun did not erupt.

Griff aimed at the man's back and pulled the trigger once again.

Nothing.

Griff's experience with guns was a single, unpleasant session many years before at a firing range with a friend and his target pistols. Now, he panicked.

Had the gun jammed? . . . Was there a safety he needed to release?

Either way, Griff knew his ignorance was about to be lethal. The man was back on his feet, no more than ten feet away, clutching the heavy knife. Griff glanced down at Melvin, who was unmoving and silent, his eyes wide open and staring unblinking at the blackness. Dark blood was pooled on the frozen ground beneath his head.

For a moment, Griff stopped caring. He wanted desperately to charge the beast, who had perhaps killed the most harmless, gentle man he had ever known. He wanted the whole thing just to be over.

Finally, with the man moving unsteadily toward him, Griff took a single step backward and looked to the south. The plains there were divided by stretches of wood-post fencing that extended in every direction. The distant farmhouse seemed unlit—five hundred yards away, he estimated. Maybe farther.

His chest was throbbing mercilessly, but he could no longer feel the painful cold in his feet. Still, clutching the useless weapon, he shambled awkwardly across the field. The solid, frost-coated ground was pocked with divots that made every step a danger. The surgical booties made traction even worse. Now, from behind him, Griff heard footsteps crunching on the frozen ground. The footfalls were steady but uneven, suggesting the assassin might be limping.

But they were also getting closer.

"You're a dead man, Rhodes!" the killer bellowed from behind him. "This knife is going to love finding a resting place in your heart!"

CHAPTER 53

The running had brought an electric pain back to Griff's feet. Still, he drove ahead. His booties had torn away, but traction in his bare feet was no better. Every step was treacherous. His injured ribs made each breath agony, and now, it seemed, he was unable to draw in enough air. A strong gust of wind caused him to stumble, and twice he nearly fell. The uneven ground was as great an enemy as his pursuer. He could afford one fall, perhaps. Two, he knew, would cost him his life.

He was closing in on another fence—three rough-hewn rails, sixty inches or so high, with posts spaced every twenty feet. Beyond the fence was a tightly packed herd of bison, and some distance beyond them, his only hope, the barn.

Suddenly he was lurching and stumbling downhill. The land had dipped into a shallow, frozen swale that he had not seen. There was no way his aching legs could keep up with the decline, and he fell, tumbling over and over to the bottom. Skin vanished from his exposed elbows and knees. His final graceless landing drove his damaged ribs together with the force of a thunderclap. Ignoring the intense pain as best he could, he staggered up the other side of the slope.

At the top, he risked a glance backward. To his astonishment, he had kept his injured pursuer somewhat at bay, and had what he estimated to be a forty-yard lead. The barn, though still some distance away, seemed possible.

Jets of frozen breath from his mouth and nostrils filled the air in front of him. His lungs burnt mercilessly. Thirty feet to the fence . . . now twenty. Griff looked behind again. Trouble! Somehow, in the brief span since he had last checked, the man had cut his advantage in half, and was hobbling much less now. Unlike Griff, his breathing did not seem labored.

The fence came up suddenly.

Griff slowed but could not keep himself from skidding awkwardly into the sturdy rails. He cried out as his torn ribs raked across one another. His hands reflexively grasped the top railing, sending the submachine gun spiraling away. There was little consideration of trying to retrieve the useless weapon. Scaling the fence with two free hands was going to be hard enough. Griff stepped on the lowest rail and thought for a moment that his frozen foot was going to snap in half. Then, he folded himself across the topmost rail and flopped over, landing on one badly scraped knee.

The gap between him and the man who was going to kill him had narrowed even more. It wasn't going to be long. Directly ahead of him now was the herd—several dozen bison, statuelike except for the bursts of frozen vapor from their nostrils.

Unpredictable . . . More deadly than a grizzly . . . Hooves . . . horns . . . head.

The wrangler's warning resonated in his thoughts as he neared the closest of the majestic beasts. There was a slight stirring among them, but no other movement. Their heavy breathing seemed to mirror his own.

Griff moved stealthily past a huge bull, keeping his hands tightly against his sides. Risking another glance backward, he saw the silhouette of the man, bending over the spot where the submachine gun had landed. Moments later, the weapon was in his hand and he was carefully climbing over the fence. For a short time the night was eerily silent save for the snorting of the bison, the steady swoosh of the wind, and the blood from Griff's own heart pounding through his ears.

The restlessness of the herd seemed to be intensifying as he made his way among them. Their grunts grew louder as if they had begun communicating with one another. A few had dropped their enormous heads to graze at what pockets of straw remained scattered about, or perhaps as some sort of signal to the others. Always, though, it seemed as if their eyes were upon him.

Easy, guys . . . easy.

A number of the larger animals swung their heads up as Griff passed. Dagger-sharp horns turned in his direction. Dark faces, concealed by dense curls of shaggy hair, followed his movement among them.

Easy . . .

The bison's hooves began shuffling beneath their short, powerful legs. Several of them started to shift from side to side. The grunting seemed louder, the plumes of vapor more intense.

Then gunfire erupted.

Griff's antagonist was on one knee, just past the shallow swale. At first, it seemed to Griff as if the bison weren't going to react. He was a few feet into the herd. Ahead of him and to his left, still some distance away, he could see the barn.

There was another volley from the submachine gun, then another.

Griff swore out loud. Clearly he had overlooked the safety when he had control of the weapon.

At that moment, one of the larger bulls toppled over. A second snorted loudly. Several more animals shifted away from the fallen beast. All of them seemed to be milling and bellowing at once. Then the herd began to charge directly toward Griff.

Bullets continued crackling through the frigid air. Another bison keeled over. The hoofbeats of the herd became deafening. Vapor spewed out from flared nostrils like steam from fast-running trains. Griff was knocked to his left by the flank of a passing cow, and then slammed to the ground by another. He scrambled between hooves, expecting any moment to have a one-ton animal crush his skull or finish the damage in his chest.

Time slowed to a stop as the bison thundered past, legs and hooves brushing against Griff, but none of them connecting directly. Dust beaten upward from the wintry ground filled his nose and throat, choking him. The hoofbeats resonated through his chest like cannon fire. He imagined the huge killer laughing as he released the safety on his gun and laughing even harder when he decided to use it to start a stampede.

From not far away, there was another burst of gunfire. A huge animal dropped dead in front of Griff and rolled over, ending motionless with the top of its enormous, shaggy head resting against Griff's chest. Instantly, the speeding bison parted like the Red Sea to avoid the dead bull. Griff pulled his knees up. Cringing in a fetal position, he burrowed into his savior as tightly as he could manage.

Then, through the corner of his eye, he saw the stampede suddenly shift direction. The herd was pounding away from the spot where he and the dead bull lay, and racing toward the fence. They were also, he suddenly realized, headed in the direction of the man who had been firing at them.

Over the exploding hooves he heard the chatter of submachine gun fire resume. Then, as the last of the animals sped past him, he thought he heard the man scream.

With difficulty, he rose and lurched toward the barn. His feet and the muscles in his legs were on fire. Fatigued, breathless, and freezing, he had no chance to recover when he slipped on a patch of ice. He slid face-first across the frozen ground, gashing his face and sending blood cascading down his cheek. Cursing, he managed to regain his footing, but it was becoming increasingly difficult to do so.

The scene before him was grim.

Ten bison lay dead or dying on the frozen ground. The remaining animals had stopped running and formed something of a wall between him and his pursuer. Griff peered into the darkness, but could not locate the man. Then, through an opening in the herd, he spotted him, lying facedown. The gloom made it difficult to sort out whether he was dead or alive, or whether he still had his weapon, but in seconds, both questions were answered.

In ponderous, agonizing slow motion, the assassin worked his way to his feet. Even through the distance and the darkness he looked battered and broken. His left arm dangled uselessly at his side. When he took a step toward the barn, he was dragging his right leg. Still he remained upright, stumbling forward a step at a time. Griff could almost see the determination on his face. He could also see the powerful submachine gun dangling from his right hand.

The angle down to the darkened farmhouse was cut off. The barn, built on a broad, flat table of land, was Griff's only chance. The structure was quite large and seemed to be well maintained. On either side, like the towers of a medieval castle, stood steel grain silos, each at least three stories high.

Gasping, Griff made his way toward the two large front doors. If they were locked or chained, he was dead.

From behind him came the chatter of gunfire. Several bullets snapped into the barn. He was ten feet from the double doors when his heart sank. There was a heavy chain across them, in addition to a plank of wood.

Death was closing in.

Griff hunched down as best he could and zigzagged toward the corner of the barn. Blood was flowing from his cheek as he ducked around the corner. There was a door. The smooth knob, some sort of bone or plastic, was unyielding. Any moment now it would be over.

With a burst of adrenaline that took him completely by surprise, Griff rammed his shoulder against the weathered wood. The door burst open. He cried out as pain exploded from his mid-chest and his momentum carried him stumbling into the interior of the barn. Dim light through a long row of windows was the only illumination. Surrounding him were stacks of hay bales extending to the back wall, and forming, in places, natural staircases ten to twenty-five feet high. He could hide behind the bales or . . .

Griff's pursuer tripped against the doorjamb, giving him a few precious seconds of warning. His respirations filled the barn. Reacting more than reasoning, Griff carefully made his way up one of the tallest of the hay staircases. Halfway to the top his fortune took a turn.

A long-handled, four-pronged pitchfork was wedged in one of the bales.

Griff slid the tool out and used it as support to ascend to the top. The giant's labored breathing seemed to obscure the sound of his movement.

"You stupid fool," the man shouted into the darkness. "You think you can stop me?" He sent a short hail of bullets into the roof. "Nothing can stop me! I saw some blood by the door. You hurt bad? If you're not, you will be. I'm going to shoot to maim you, not to kill you. Then I'm going to use the knife I used on your friend to gut you bit by bit until you tell me what I want to know, or until you die. It really doesn't matter."

From his hiding place, Griff listened to the man's footsteps as they scraped unevenly across the barn's wooden floor, drawing closer. He forced his breathing to slow as he visualized his adversary's position.

It was time.

Griff peered over the edge as the giant cautiously approached. He could see now what devastating damage the stampeding bison had done to him. His parka was nearly torn off, exposing a fractured forearm, where jagged white bone jutted through his skin. It seemed quite possible that his leg was broken as well. The dramatic wounds would make him slow to react—or at least *slower.*

Griff gripped the pitchfork and shifted his weight, preparing to climb over the top of the hay bales and slide down the other side.

Ready . . . and . . . now!

He pushed off the highest bale, screaming as loudly as he could.

The man whirled and raised the submachine gun, ripping off a wild burst that totally missed the dark shadow flying down at him.

The pitchfork, with all Griff's weight behind it, struck home across the center of the man's chest, its lethal tines penetrating through skin, muscle, heart, and bone, before exiting through the back. The force drove him backward onto the straw-covered floor and pinned him there. Blood erupted from his mouth. He tried to say something, but succeeded only in spewing up more blood.

Seconds later, he was dead, the long handle of the pitchfork still pointing at the ceiling, quivering.

Griff took the knife and the submachine gun, which he fired successfully into a hay bale just to prove to himself that he could. Then he checked the professional killer for the ID he knew would not be there, and spent a few moments gazing down at his lifeless, battered, and broken corpse.

"I only wish it had lasted longer," he said viciously.

CHAPTER 54

Vice President Henry Tilden shifted from one foot to the other. He was standing in the middle of an orderly food line that snaked along two walls of the House Chamber. Ellis watched the man from halfway across the hall. . . . Watched and waited.

More people than ever were coughing now, she noted. Some coughed just a little bit, as if they were trying to clear a bothersome tickle from their throats. Others, including the president's wife and daughter, were suffering from a more persistent, wet hacking.

Ellis made eye contact with Gladstone, who was some fifty people in line behind Tilden. A slight nod from her and Gladstone abandoned his place. He walked past Tilden, and without offering an apology or explanation, cut in front of Supreme Court Justice Alfred Bauer. In the past, and at times during the current crisis, Ellis had witnessed the crusty Bauer lose his temper, usually without much provocation. Minor offenses such as loud talking, or even snoring, had been triggers enough to set off the already agitated, elderly judge. Ellis was counting on Bauer losing his cool one more time.

"You can't cut the line, young man," Ellis heard him say to Gladstone.

Gladstone, in response, turned to Bauer, and just as they had rehearsed said, "You can't make me leave. You're not the all-powerful justice, here."

Gladstone then turned away from the man and resumed his waiting.

"I don't tolerate that sort of disrespect, young man," Bauer snapped.

"I frankly don't care what you tolerate or don't tolerate."

Bauer took the bait and pushed Gladstone in the small of his back. Ellis's aide stumbled forward. He waved his arms wildly in the air, pretending to lose his balance, and crashed into the man standing in front of him. Then he executed a quick side step to his right, and the man into whom he had fallen responded with an angry shove into Bauer's chest. The justice countered with a wild, errant punch that missed his target, but grazed across a congresswoman's jaw.

The ensuing melee exploded like a match on gasoline-soaked rags.

Having predicted every moment of the scenario, Ellis listened to the escalating shouting and startling profanities from men and women, many of them with impeccable pedigrees. She watched as more people joined in, pushing and shoving, and calling other combatants names.

We'll teach you the right way to brawl, she was thinking. *The way we do it in the deep South.*

Punches were now being thrown. Boxed dinners were flying like missiles. A congressman was repeatedly kicking a fallen reporter in the abdomen and head. Pent-up frustration and anger, in all likelihood fueled by WRX3883, burst forth like an oil well gusher. Secret Service agents quickly rushed in to quell the mayhem. Several of them became enmeshed in it. Others extracted Allaire's wife and daughter before they could become victims of the increasing violence. Capitol Police and more agents came together to pry apart several small pockets of fighting. Noses were bleeding, now, as fists continued to fly. Congressmen and -women were on the floor along with other dignitaries, cowering or flailing with their hands and feet.

"I can't take this anymore!" Ellis heard somebody scream.

"Stop hitting me! I didn't do anything to you!" shouted another.

Ellis and Gladstone grabbed Tilden by the arms before any Secret Service agents could get to him.

"Come with us," she yelled into his ear. "There's a problem with President Allaire. Dr. Townsend wants us right away."

Tilden nodded and allowed himself to be guided out of the House Chamber into the corridor that would lead across the Capitol to the Senate wing. As Ellis had predicted, the guards who had been posted at the doors had rushed in to help quell the fight. The screaming and racket muted once the exit doors closed behind them.

Ellis was not the least surprised that her tactics were working perfectly. It was probable that no one had noticed them leaving.

"What's going on?" Tilden asked.

There was confusion and panic in his voice and expression. Ellis wondered if he was reacting to the riot, or to the notion of becoming president. Probably both, she decided. *How in the hell had he ever made it so high?*

"Townsend is waiting for us by the Senate Chamber," she said. "We've got to hurry."

"Why there?" Tilden asked.

"You saw what's going on here. Townsend couldn't meet us on the rostrum, and she couldn't risk getting together anywhere near the president. He's become paranoid about being removed from office. His doctor used the word 'dangerous' to describe him. That's her word, not mine." Ellis held up a metal tube. "I've got the documents rolled up in here that Townsend has prepared for us to sign."

Ellis and her aide walked the vice president at a brisk pace. According to the information that O'Neil had provided, Allaire was in a meeting with Salitas and would be there for at least an hour. If O'Neil were wrong about that, and by accident they bumped into the president, she would have to think fast. But she was totally capable of doing that. And besides, it was unlikely the man would venture into this wing, especially given the diversion Gladstone had started in the other.

Nice!

They led Tilden to the Senate Chamber, following

the same route that Ellis had taken earlier—down the West Grand Staircase, across the House connecting corridor, into the Senate connecting corridor, and finally up the East Grand Staircase. She knew that all patrols to this side of the Capitol had been stopped per Allaire's orders—more useful intelligence from O'Neil. Perhaps there could be room for him in her administration after all.

Ellis quickened her steps to separate herself from Tilden. Gladstone dropped back. When the Senate Chamber door came into view, she dropped the metal mailing tube to the marble floor. It landed behind her with a loud, resonating clank. Fumbling to retrieve it, she kicked it so that it would roll toward Tilden and away from the door.

"I'll get that," the tall vice president said, bending down.

Ellis stood in front of the chamber door, blocking the door handles from his line of sight. There was a plastic bucket by her feet. The lock and chain that had once secured the doors were now coiled inside it. Gladstone had done his job well. He always did. Before he started the food line riot, he had gotten the key to the Senate Chamber lock from O'Neil, along with a blue plastic temporary handcuff.

In the few moments Tilden was retrieving the metal tube, Ellis cut the plastic ties securing the door using a knife she had purloined from the food service. By the time Tilden reached her with the tube, she had already kicked the pieces of the temporary handcuffs under the door.

"If Townsend is right," she said, "you'll be taking the oath of office in a few hours."

Gladstone readied himself as Ellis held her breath and pulled open the doors. Tilden hesitated at the threshold, clearly taken aback by the commotion and the stench.

But it was too late.

Gladstone shoved him brusquely into the vast room, and Ellis quickly closed the door behind him. Then she slipped the tube through the door handles. They could hear Tilden screaming and pounding from inside.

"Open up! For God's sakes, Ursula! Open the door! Help! . . . Hey, let go of me. Let go of me, dammit!"

No patrols. No guards. No worries.

With Gladstone holding the tube in place and keeping his shoulder hard to the door, Ellis pulled the chain from the bucket and looped it through the handles. The door bucked as Tilden, still crying out, continued to push against it from the other side.

And then, quite suddenly, his screaming stopped.

CHAPTER 55

DAY 6
7:00 P.M. (EST)

Ellis gave her aide a decent head start and then followed him back to the House Chamber. Her thoughts were consumed with how close she now was to taking over the reins of leadership for the most powerful nation in the history of the planet.

The House Chamber itself had degenerated into chaos. There were clusters of people facing off against one another, exchanging verbal threats, childish insults, and furious looks. Rows of sleeping cots, which had taken the place of many of the rows of chairs, were tipped over and their bedding ripped and tossed about. The floor was littered with food cartons and was slick to walk on from spilled drinks. But even in the din of that commotion, Ellis could still hear people coughing.

She had prepared a simple explanation for her whereabouts if pressed, but she found the door through which she had reentered the chamber unguarded. Capitol Police and Secret Service agents were still too busy with crowd control. Some had their weapons drawn, though most of the security force looked bewildered and incapable of restoring order.

Ellis knew exactly how to rein in the unruliness.

It was time to bring her bill to the House floor.

The time had come to expose America to Jim Allaire's unforgivable lies.

Ellis felt she had proved herself every bit the leader that Allaire was not. She had proof now that Harlan Mackey had been executed because of the lethalness of the virus. Surely, the president had other options for dealing with the aging senator, but those options would have required him to admit his deception. In doing so, he would have made it clear to the American public that he did not trust them, and in doing so, they would learn that he was not trustworthy himself.

In contrast to Allaire, Ellis had solid reasons for what she was doing. Negotiating with Genesis and locking Vice President Tilden inside the Senate Chamber were justifiable acts under these extreme circumstances. She was born to lead, and leadership not only demanded sacrifice, but a willingness to change the rules of the game. She had done what needed to be done. True leaders, she knew, were the ones who made the hard choices and never looked back.

After a time at the rostrum working on details and watching the melee finally wind down, Ellis summoned Gladstone to her side. Her aide was pale and bleary-eyed. Never robust, he was starting to look frail. His weakened state was understandable given the hours he had spent crafting the bill and incorporating her edits, to say nothing of the stress of working to elevate her to the presidency.

"Are we ready?" she asked him.

"I believe so," her aide said. "I've made copies of the bill for every voting member and their aides, but only those who are in the House Chamber. I'm assuming Groups B and C are out of the equation."

"You assume correctly," Ellis said.

"And I used version twenty-three of the bill, is that correct as well?"

"Yes it is. Well done. Now, have you been able to locate Jordan Lamar? As architect of the Capitol, we need his support to make everything happen as I've planned."

"I haven't tried to find him yet," Gladstone said, "but I don't believe that will be necessary."

"I want those television cameras turned back on, Leland. Our dear Mr. Jordan is the only person with the authority to defy the president and restore those transmissions. It's essential the American people be made aware of the truth. They must see with their own eyes the reason why I have been negotiating with Genesis."

Gladstone peered over Ellis's shoulder.

"I'm saying it won't be necessary to find him," he explained, "because it appears he has found us."

Ellis turned to see Lamar, Bethany Townsend, and the president heading toward them. All three looked gravely concerned.

"We haven't seen Vice President Tilden in over an hour," Allaire said, without a greeting. "Have either of you seen him?"

Ellis's eyes narrowed.

"No, I haven't," she said. "Not for hours. Leland? You?"

"Nope. He was in line here when all the craziness started, but that was the last time I saw him."

"Well, keep your eyes out. He's on treatment for high blood pressure."

Ellis tried to make eye contact with Townsend, hoping she might bring up the meeting the three of them had, but the physician looked away.

Enough is enough, Ellis decided.

"President Allaire," she said, "as long as you're here, I think you should know that I've had a change of plans regarding my committee."

"I hope that change involves your disbanding it," the president said.

"Actually, my current plan is to seek cooperation from the Committee on Rules, in hopes that they will grant privileged status to a special rule for a specific legislative measure that I intend to bring to the House floor for consideration."

Allaire looked appalled.

"I've had enough of your antics, Ursula," he exclaimed. "We're involved in a deadly crisis of unparalleled scope, and you have been nothing but an impediment to resolving it."

Ellis urged herself not to become rattled.

"Well, I'm afraid, Mr. President, that the rules of the House preclude your displeasure from interfering with permitted congressional business. Besides, you are in no position to be combative with me. That will only cause you trouble. Just ask your Dr. Townsend, here."

Allaire turned to his physician, concern drawing a shadow across his face.

"What is she talking about, Bethany?"

Townsend shuffled her feet and struggled to make eye contact with the president.

"I . . . have some serious concerns about your ability to control your emotions," Townsend responded, "especially your temper." She paused to give Ellis a venomous stare. "I witnessed your outburst myself, and as is my duty to the country, I brought my concerns to the attention of Vice President Tilden and the speaker of the house."

"Why would you do that?" Allaire asked with the sting of betrayal evident in his voice.

"You know what infection with the WRX virus can do to any of us. It could become incumbent on them to initiate the proceedings."

"By proceedings," Allaire said, now straining to remain calm, "you mean my forcible removal from office."

Townsend nodded somewhat sheepishly.

"You demonstrated behavior that you, yourself, had warned me about, sir."

Ellis's inward smile broadened.

"Yes, Mr. President," she chimed in, "you never told most of us, but you warned Dr. Townsend and your inner circle about the true dangers of this virus. Isn't that correct?"

"What are you talking about?" Allaire demanded.

"Why, the virus," Ellis said saccharinely. "I'm talking about the dreadfully lethal virus you called the flu—the virus that is going to kill us all unless somebody does something drastic."

"It is not always lethal," Allaire countered.

"Oh, the fuck it isn't!" Ellis held up Gladstone's Black-Berry. "No thanks to you, but I know just how goddamn lethal this virus is. I saw what Group C has become. I even photographed it."

A primitive rage twisted Allaire's expression. Ellis took a cautious step backward.

"You had no right going into that room," he said. "I am the president. It is my job to make decisions that are in the best interest of this country. Telling the whole truth about WRX3883 would have caused a panic here and on the outside that would have endangered everyone. I could not take the chance of triggering a pandemic."

"Wrong, Mr. President. I have the inalienable right to life, same as every man, woman, and child whose survival you've so callously put at risk."

Jordan Lamar looked concerned.

"What is she talking about, Jim?" he asked. "You told us the virus wasn't that dangerous."

"He lied to you, Jordan," Ellis said. "He lied to us all. And what I propose we do is turn those network television cameras back on and show the American people exactly what it is that we're facing."

"Just what *are* we facing, Ursula?" the architect asked.

"A certain and horrible death, that's what. But this legislation I plan to present will guarantee us the delivery of an antiviral treatment."

Allaire's jaw fell slack. His look was of total dismay and disbelief.

"You're mad," he said. "Absolutely mad."

"A *no* vote to what I'm proposing would be no different than putting a gun to our heads and pulling the trigger."

"Don't listen to her, Jordan," Allaire insisted. "She doesn't have the facts. She can't deliver what she's promising."

"Is it true, sir?" Lamar asked. "Did you lie to us?"

"I did what I believed was right—for all of us."

For the first time, there was little conviction in his voice.

"The virus is going to kill us," Ellis repeated. "I have proof I can show you. And it will be a horrible death, Jordan. But I tell you again, I've secured us an antiviral treatment."

"How?" Allaire shouted at her. "How is that possible, Ursula, when the only person who could deliver a treatment is working with us?"

"We pass my bill, and Genesis will deliver the antiviral treatment. They got the virus, they have the treatment."

Allaire went pale.

"What have you done?" he managed.

"I've cut a deal with them," she said. "This bill—*their* bill—for our lives. And before you say we don't negotiate with terrorists, I want everybody to see what is going to become of us. Jordan, get this video to play for everybody inside this chamber. And I want to simultaneously broadcast it to the American people. No more lies. No more deception. The time has come to do what must be done. Let's get that broadcast going."

"Jordan, don't!" Allaire exclaimed. "Our scientist is getting close. He's nearing a breakthrough. Whatever this—this madwoman has been promised by the terrorists is a lie. I'm telling you the truth. There is no treatment yet. No cure. You will severely impede our ability to operate if you undermine my authority here."

"Give me the BlackBerry," Lamar said to Ursula. "I want to see the video myself."

"Jordan, no!"

But Lamar snatched the device from Ellis's outstretched hand and turned his back to keep the president from taking it away. The architect's shoulders slumped as he watched the horrific recording. Ellis could hear the tinny audio track sounding through the BlackBerry's mono speaker. She heard the grunts and the screams. The sound of vomiting. The gunshot.

"Mr. President, what have you done?" Lamar asked.

"Jordan, don't do it!" the president said again.

"I am the architect of the Capitol, sir. If I wish to broadcast chamber activities, the rules governing this facility permit me to do just that."

"You will be committing a treasonous act," Allaire warned.

Lamar shook his head grimly.

"Then that will be an action of which we will both be guilty, Mr. President," he said. "Madam Speaker, I'll arrange for the broadcast."

Lamar turned on his heels and quickly walked away.

"Come back here!" Allaire cried out. "Come back here this instant!"

The president grabbed the armrest of a nearby chair and with surprising, rage-driven strength, yanked it free, splintering the wood. Holding the armrest aloft, he took a menacing step toward Ellis. His face was contorted with anger. The arm holding his makeshift weapon was shaking. Then, suddenly, he dropped the club and gazed with horror at his hands.

Ellis and the others immediately saw what was upsetting him so.

His palms were now marked by an intricate design of circular swirls—lines the color of blood.

CHAPTER 56

Battered and aching as much in his heart as his body, Griff kept a vigilant lookout for police on his four-and-a-half hour drive east to Wichita. It was doubtful his disappearance from Kalvesta had been discovered yet, but as a precaution he drove the speed limit, used his turn signals, and adhered to all the rules of the road. Getting stopped for even a minor traffic transgression could lead to questions. And questions, especially the way he was looking, would lead to problems.

After cleaning up the scene of two violent deaths at the Cahill Ranch, Griff drove through the night, stopping at a twenty-four-hour truck store for some clothes, and to clean up. The trip was lonely and anguished. Angie was in a New York hospital, and now, his dearest friend was dead—gone from his life forever. Who was the man who had ambushed them and killed Melvin? How had he known of their plan? Was there anything Griff could have done to anticipate and prevent it? Mile after mile passed, and still the questions remained unanswered.

Making the tragedy of Melvin's terrible death even more painful was what Griff had done with his friend's body. When he returned from the barn to Melvin's side, he futilely checked him for any hint of life. Then, utterly worn out, he sank onto the frozen, windswept ground and wept.

Finally, he changed into the parka and jeans that Melvin had brought for him. Patrols around the lab would be more frequent with Rappaport on base. As quickly as he could manage, he emptied Melvin's pockets and as reverently as he could, lowered the body over the edge of the steep ventilation shaft. Then, with a silent prayer, he let go.

Next he drove Melvin's Taurus around until he found the killer's car—a nondescript rental with an agreement in the glove compartment that almost certainly was obtained using forged papers. The keys were on the floor. A trip back to the barn to stuff the giant's body into the trunk, and he left the car hidden in a secluded grove of cypress trees. It would be found at some point, and an all points bulletin would probably be issued, but hopefully not until long after he and Brother Xavier Bartholomew had done their business.

As Griff used the winch to resettle the heavy grate—the tombstone for his closest friend—he was thinking vengeance. The death of Melvin's killer wasn't nearly enough. He wanted Genesis. He wanted them badly. He would hunt them as intensely as he had hunted outbreaks of Marburg virus, and he would do whatever was necessary to bring them down.

Highway KS-156 was largely deserted. Griff drove with the car radio off, preferring silence and memories of his quirky assistant to news about the Capitol. Eventually, the lights of downtown Wichita came into view. He imagined Sylvia Chen driving along this same road two years before. Her research at the time, he knew, was foundering, and the rug of secret federal financing was about to be pulled out from beneath her. It was hardly a stretch to envision the scientist, frantic to keep her research afloat, arranging a meeting with a bogus saver of souls that would lead to desperate decisions and horrific choices. She was going to accelerate solving the problems of her troubled but potentially remarkable virus by testing it on humans.

Once again, at least to the extent described in her "Recipes from the Kitchen," Chen had failed to control her creation. All of her human subjects had died—all, that was, except possibly for one. It would have been disaster for her. It was hardly a stretch to imagine that soon after her failure, she had entered into a deal with the devil calling itself Genesis—a deal that would lead to the theft of her virus, the frame-up and jailing of one of her scientists, and finally to her violent death and the impending deaths of hundreds more.

Now it was time to learn exactly what she had done here in Wichita, whom she had done it to, and perhaps most important, what, if anything, she had learned.

Seething, Griff followed directions to the Certain Path Mission that Melvin had printed out and left on the front seat of the Taurus. Streetlamps shimmered like disco balls in the night, reflecting off the still water of the Arkansas River. The height of most of the office towers in the sleepy downtown would have been lost in other metropolises, but Griff's impression of the city, as announced on several signs, was that this was a nice place to live. A nice place to live unless you happened to stumble into the Certain Path Mission looking for help.

He drove past a tall highway billboard offering prayers for the government, and all the victims of the Capitol tragedy.

The Certain Path Mission was a square, two-story stone building, tucked away in a quiet neighborhood on the outskirts of Wichita. A sign on the front lawn, lit by two spots and fenced by a circle of neatly trimmed shrubs bore the ministry's name. Beside the sign stood a small, stone statue of a Native American woman whose bronze eyes gazed reverently skyward.

It was just after midnight.

Griff worked his way around the building perimeter and tried to peer through the evenly spaced windows. It was hard to imagine the self-proclaimed cleric living anywhere other than in the mission. There were no interior lights on that he could see, so after a moderately calming breath, he shrugged and rang the front doorbell. Above him and to his right, a security camera looked down impassively. He had no qualms whatever about waking the brother. From all he could tell, this was a bad man who had done some very bad things.

After a minute, he rang a second time. The heavy oak door creaked open. Xavier Bartholomew, rubbing sleepily at his eyes, peered out from the blackness. Griff had no doubt that the gesture belied the fact that the man had checked his security screen before opening the door.

"You look worn and weary, my brother," Bartholomew said, his voice a rich bass. "Have you come to purge yourself of the poison festering in your soul?"

"I have," Griff said. "Are you Brother Bartholomew?"

"I am he—the beacon to the Certain Path."

His temper on a knife's edge, and his patience nearly gone, Griff forced open the door with his knee, and moved quickly past the man, who made an unsuccessful attempt to block his entrance. Brother Bartholomew staggered back a step, his sleepy expression now one of alarm. He was in his early fifties, and had on a heavy, hooded wool cassock cinched at the waist with a tasseled cord, and well-worn Birkenstock sandals. His oily hair was streaked with gray and pulled back into a tight ponytail, which was tucked inside his robe. His eyes were dark and narrow, and he reeked of stale cigarette smoke and cheap cologne. The tawdry furnishings in the foyer and the adjacent living room reflected the man perfectly. Through the dining room Griff could see the chapel—rows of mixed folding and kitchen chairs beneath a chandelier that had probably come from a yard sale.

"You are blessed, my friend, for you have found the Certain Path," Bartholomew said, quickly regaining his composure. "I will be happy to counsel you, but to begin your journey, a sacrifice is required."

He pointed to a large wooden bucket, dangling from

a frayed rope that was knotted around a ceiling support beam. A whitewashed placard, lettered not that meticulously with a Sharpie, was nailed to the side of the bucket.

Cast your bread upon the water, and your return shall be manyfold.

It's always about the bread, Griff thought.

"I have come a long way to see you," he said, solidifying his position with several steps toward the living room. "I have questions that need answering."

Bartholomew's wariness returned.

"I see that life has dealt you some cruel blows," he said, gesturing toward Griff's fresh bruises and scabs. "For now, whatever you have in your pocket will suffice to start you on your journey of healing. Later we will determine how much of an additional sacrifice is required for your cure."

"I am prepared to make a donation to the mission, Brother Bartholomew, but only if the answers to my questions are satisfactory."

Now, the cleric was on all-out red alert.

"Exactly what sort of questions are you talking about?" he asked.

"Questions about a scientist named Sylvia Chen."

Bartholomew paled.

"You a cop?"

"Nope."

"Private dick?"

"Nope."

"Then get the hell out of here!"

Brother Bartholomew grasped a vase from the top of a small credenza and swung it at Griff's head.

Griff erupted.

Ignoring the heavy ache in his chest, he blocked the attack, sending the vase to the flagstone floor, where it shattered. Bartholomew turned to run, but Griff snatched ahold of his hood. He had not fought anyone since high school, but he hadn't felt such fury in at least that long. He twisted Bartholomew's arm behind his back and lifted it toward his shoulderblade. Then he used his knee to propel the man with force against the stone wall at the rear of the foyer. He had never had any martial arts training, but every anger-driven move seemed natural.

With Bartholomew's arm still pinned to his back, Griff applied his forearm to the nape of the man's neck, pressing his face flush against the wall. Then, leaning in close so he could be heard at a whisper, Griff growled into Bartholomew's ear.

"Is there anybody else here?"

"Yes . . . yes, there is," Bartholomew managed.

The self-proclaimed minister was breathless and shaking. With thoughts of Melvin, Griff lifted the man's arm even higher up his back. Numbed by adrenaline, the pain in his own damaged ribs was barely noticeable.

Bartholomew's arm was reaching the snapping point.

"No . . . more," he cried. "I'm alone! I'm alone! Please, let go of my arm! It's going to break!"

Griff relaxed his grip slightly. The letup in pressure was enough for Bartholomew, who countered with surprising quickness and unexpected strength. He twisted his body hard to the right, breaking free of Griff's hold on his wrist. Then he ducked and turned, separating himself from Griff entirely. Without hesitating, he dashed through a set of French doors into the chapel, and headed toward the back of the mission.

Griff, now short of breath, but hardly short of determination, cursed his stupidity and drove on after the man. There was a fire door on the far side of the chapel, and Bartholomew was now just a few feet away from it. But there was no way Griff was going to let him get there. He left his feet and dove at the back of Bartholomew's legs, buckling the man's knees and sending him skidding across the hardwood floor, knocking the chairs about like bowling pins.

Air exploded from the brother's lungs, but in seconds he was on his feet again, charging toward the fire door. On all fours, Griff caught him by the ankles, pulled him to the floor, and wrestled him to his back. Then, straddling his chest, Griff punched him in the face—once, then again. Blood burst from Bartholomew's nose, and his body went limp.

Painfully, Griff worked himself to his feet, then grabbed a box of tissues off a windowsill and tossed it down to the man.

"Tell me about Sylvia Chen," he said, breathing heavily.

"I don't know who that is."

"Bartholomew, my best friend was just murdered because of her. Mess with me about this, and I swear I'll punch your teeth in. I'm that angry."

Griff cocked his arm again, and his adversary flinched.

"Okay . . . I knew her."

Bartholomew remained on his back.

"What did she want with you?"

"She . . . she promised she could help me cure drug addiction. She told me her system would work. And . . . and she said she'd pay me to cooperate with her."

"What exactly did you do?" Griff said, as he hoisted Bartholomew off the floor by the shoulders of his robe. "I said, what did you do?"

"We tested something she was working on," he said. Tears began to stream down his red, swollen face. "I'm not a bad person. I wanted to help. She was a scientist and she said that she had a treatment she wanted to try out on . . . on some of my tougher clients. She said that together we could save many addicts from their misery."

The man was weeping piteously now, but Griff would not make the same mistake by lowering his guard.

"Did you supply her with people?"

Griff was shaking with anger.

"I . . . I did."

"Where did she conduct these experiments? Tell me, dammit!"

"Let me go," Bartholomew said in a shaky voice, "and I'll do better than tell you."

"How's that?"

"I'll show you," he said.

CHAPTER 57

Griff kept Bartholomew's arm pinned tightly against his back and followed closely behind him.

"I'm not going to run again," Bartholomew pleaded. "Promise. I shouldn't have run in the first place. You . . . you surprised me is all. Please, you're really hurting me."

"And I'm not taking any more chances."

Bartholomew fell silent and led Griff through a pair of dimly lit corridors and down a small flight of stairs that ended at a heavy oak door. The surrounding walls were concrete bricks, painted gray and in need of cleaning.

"You'll need to let go of my arm if you want me to take you downstairs."

"I'll let go," Griff said, "but you need to know that you are in even more of a fix than usual."

"How's that?"

"You and Sylvia Chen are partly responsible for the sickness and death that are going on at the Capitol.

She's dead. Murdered. Try my patience now, and I won't hesitate to hurt you, and I'm willing to bet that nobody will do anything but cheer."

With difficulty, Bartholomew looked over his shoulder. He appeared genuinely surprised.

"You're talking about the president?" he asked.

Griff tried to read through the man's words. Did he have any idea whether or not the president was involved with what Sylvia Chen had done at the Certain Path Mission? It seemed almost certain that the answer was no. Allaire, at least in terms of this aspect of Chen's work, was probably innocent. From now on, Griff decided, if he needed the man's help, he would seek it out. He would also, as soon as possible, share his growing suspicions with the president regarding Paul Rappaport.

"Those experiments you helped Chen with had nothing to do with drug addiction," Griff said. "It was part of a biological research program that I was involved in. I'm a scientist—a virologist just like Chen. The virus we were developing, that you helped her try out on people here, is what the terrorists released during the State of the Union Address."

"Oh, God. I heard on the news that it was just some sort of flu, not anything—"

"You know that it's lethal, don't you? . . . Don't you?"

The cleric bowed his head. Then he began to cry.

"I've done such terrible things," he said. "Such terrible things . . ."

His voice trailed off and his body was racked with each sob. Griff had to remind himself that Brother

Xavier Bartholomew was, in all likelihood, a sociopath, capable of turning on emotion like he would a faucet.

"If you cooperate and tell me everything I want to know, I promise to speak up on your behalf. Understood?"

Bartholomew nodded dispiritedly. Griff let go of him and took a cautious step backward, ready to react. Shaking the feeling back into his arm, the man withdrew a black string necklace that was tucked inside his robe. Dangling from it was a large, antique metal key that looked straight from the set of a horror movie. He unlocked the heavy door with a clank that resonated off the walls. Then, after a hard tug on its ornate handle, the door creaked open.

The passageway behind the door was a spiral stone staircase that was dimly lit by a light glowing from someplace below.

"Are there many places like this in Wichita?" Griff asked.

"There may be, but I've never heard of one. Apparently, the man who built this place was a little—what's the word—eccentric."

"I'll bet I could come up with a few words that were more appropriate."

Bartholomew started down the staircase and Griff followed warily. The stairs were narrow and so steep that Griff used one hand to keep his balance. The heavy, bone-chilling air grew mustier as they descended. The smooth sidewalls became exposed rock, suggesting that the original excavators had left the stones exactly as their tools had unearthed them.

Eccentric, indeed.

The stairs finally ended at a surprisingly large circular room with three dark passageways extending off of it like the spokes of a wheel. Hanging on the walls of the room, secured there by metal spikes driven into the stone, were implements of torture and pain—whips, batons, wood rattans, shackles, and chains. The space kindled memories of his cell in the Alcatraz of the Rockies.

"What *is* this place?" Griff asked.

"Believe it or not, it used to be a wine cellar. Then I transformed it into what many of my acolytes call the center of all things."

"Is this where you beat people?"

"It was aversion therapy, reserved for only the hardcore addicts and alcoholics—the ones who had failed at everything else, including AA. Whatever you might have heard, I had many, many successes."

"Okay. Is this where you conducted your—*aversion therapy*?"

"Not here."

Bartholomew flicked a wall-mounted switch that illuminated the passageway directly in front of them. A string of tiny colored Christmas lights on a long cord hooked into the ceiling lit the way.

Bizarre . . . macabre . . . alarming . . . disgusting . . .

Griff searched his vocabulary for the most apt description, and found all of them wanting.

Bartholomew ducked to pass underneath an archway, and motioned for Griff to follow. The vapor of their breathing now hung in the chilly air, and the musty odor was more overpowering the further in they traveled—the smell of fear . . . and of death. Griff shuddered. Ventilation was minimal. Beneath his parka, he had begun to perspire.

The corridor opened into a square room—an antechamber of some sort. There were stone alcoves built into three of the room's walls. Each alcove had a wooden door with a small, barred window in the upper center.

"I conducted my mission work here," Bartholomew said. "Sometimes, I kept my brothers and sisters here for days without food. Sometimes, if necessary, I would beat them. The key was to weaken their wills."

The terrible irony of the man's statement hit home with force. Griff reflected grimly on the day he first met with Sylvia Chen at her office at Columbia University, and on his decision to move to New York to work with her on the microbe she was developing. *The key is to weaken their wills.* It seemed possible she had said those exact words.

"Your brothers and sisters?" he asked Bartholomew, now.

"Those who came to me for salvation."

"Your prisoners, you mean."

"They could leave any time. The doors weren't locked. They asked for this treatment only after they failed at AA and many other programs."

Griff ran his fingertips over one of the doors and tried to imagine what it had been like for Bartholomew's tragic sisters and brothers.

"How do you explain these locks?" he asked.

Bartholomew looked remorseful.

"I added the locks at Sylvia Chen's insistence," he said.

"Explain."

"She came to me with an offer. She had researched me well, and she knew about my arrest and my ensuing financial troubles. She offered me a way to get back on my feet and continue to help people at the same time."

"So she paid you?"

Griff vaguely remembered a visit to Kalvesta a few years before from a bureaucrat with one of the government accounting offices. He wondered now if Chen had juggled her books to cover this black site operation. He also wondered if the president was in any way involved.

"She paid for everything," Bartholomew confirmed. "The equipment that was brought in. Everything."

"What equipment?"

"There were airlocks and partitions and showers and all sorts of things that I didn't understand."

"She wore a biocontainment suit when she worked down here?"

"If such a suit is what I think it is, she wore one all the time."

"And the people she worked on—your clients?"

"They were bottom-of-the-barrel alcoholics and drug addicts. They drifted in for a meal and some prayer, and often they stayed. They were lonely men and women. No family. No friends. Like I said, bottom of the barrel."

Correction, Griff was thinking, *you're the bottom of the barrel. You and Sylvia Chen.*

"So the brothers and sisters Dr. Chen worked on— they all died?"

Griff forced back a fresh surge of anger.

"They did."

"How many of them were there altogether?"

"I don't know. Six? Seven? Eight?"

Greed in action—financial and scientific.

Griff felt utterly repulsed.

"What did you do with the bodies?" he asked.

"We have a large furnace down another passage. Heats the whole building. We cremated the bodies in the furnace, then eventually discarded the ashes in a steel drum. I don't know what Chen did with the drum."

"Why are you telling me all this now?" Griff asked.

Tears streamed down Bartholomew's flushed cheeks.

"Because I've been secretly praying that you'd come," he said between heavy sobs. "I was too weak-willed to kill myself. Believe me, I've wanted to. And I've tried— more than once. So I prayed that somebody would find out the truth and come to free me from my sins. I guess that person is you."

Griff detested and pitied the charlatan with equal vigor. His intentions may have been honorable at one time. His methods and his avarice, however, never were.

"According to my information, not all of the subjects involved in Chen's experiments died."

Bartholomew nodded.

"Oh, now that I think about it, that's true. One of them escaped. I had given in to Chen and started coming down here and wearing those biocontainment suits, as you called them. I was inexperienced at working in those horrible things and didn't set the lock properly on his cell. Chen blamed me for the mistake."

"Why didn't the guy turn you both in after he got out of here?" Griff asked.

"That wasn't ol' J.R.'s style. He looked out after J.R. and no one else. Besides, he was already wanted for robbing a convenience store someplace at gunpoint. The man had a heavy habit. I mean heavy. Habits like that need constant feeding."

"What do the initials stand for?"

Bartholomew did not answer immediately. His cards were almost played out, and Griff could see him trying to calculate some sort of deal. Griff could no longer hold back his anger. He lunged at Bartholomew, seizing him by the front of his robe and slamming him backward against the stone wall.

"Tell me his name!" he rasped.

"Johnny . . . Johnny Ray Davis. He called himself J.R., though, like the guy from TV."

Griff felt his pulse begin to race. The blank space beside the man's name in Chen's notebook was no accident. It was certainly possible that he had escaped before being exposed to the WRX virus. But then again . . .

"Do you know whether Chen ever gave J.R. the virus?" Griff demanded. Bartholomew hesitated and Griff slapped him across the face with all his strength. Then he lifted his hand to do it again. "My patience is gone, you fraud. Answer me!"

A trickle of blood had formed at the corner of Bartholomew's mouth. Even in the dim light, Griff could see his handprint in scarlet on the man's cheek.

"He . . . he was here for more than a week, so I suppose he got the virus. In fact, I'm sure he got it."

"And he didn't get sick?"

"Not so far as I know. He was well enough to pick the upstairs lock and then steal a bunch of stuff from my desk before he took off."

"Jesus," Griff whispered, his heartbeat now a jackhammer. "Do you know where he is?"

Bartholomew looked at him with feigned bravado.

"What's in it for me?"

"Your life," Griff snapped, fiercely grasping the man by the throat.

Bartholomew managed a nod of surrender, and Griff let up.

"He's in prison. El Dorado Correctional Facility. Now ain't that a kick. He escapes from this cell here, and winds up in El Dorado."

"What's he in there for? . . . I said, what's he in there for?"

Griff could see the end of what resistance remained in the man.

"Murder. Double murder, in fact," Bartholomew said. "Bastard's there on death row."

CHAPTER 58

The El Dorado Correctional Facility, situated east of the town of El Dorado, was a sprawling complex of brown cement buildings seemingly designed to compete with its desolate surroundings.

Following Brother Bartholomew's admissions, Griff had contacted the president. It was time to trust him. Beyond funding Sylvia Chen's research, Griff was convinced that James Allaire had no connection with the way she had conducted it. Allaire's response to Griff's report regarding the Certain Path Mission and J. R. Davis was to galvanize all the resources at his disposal. Clearly, the man understood that time was running out for all those in the Capitol.

Now, Griff's military escort, organized in amazingly short order, passed through two perimeters, one made of chain-link fencing, and the second of tightly strung wire. Both were topped by razor wire.

Griff's limousine driver checked his watch.

"Normally takes forty minutes to get here from Wichita," he said through the partition. "We did it in just a little over twenty."

Overhead, three Apache helicopters hovered, kicking up dust while their crews kept watch in all directions. The El Dorado security team met Griff's black armor-plated limousine at the gate, and then escorted the caravan into the correctional facility's main parking lot. A moving wall of Humvees flanked each side of the limo. Ambulances and police cars, along with a fleet of motorcycles, also participated in the transport team that was filling most of the available parking spaces in the expansive prison lot. Clearly, Dr. James Allaire was not a president of minimal action, especially when his life and his family's were at stake.

Griff stepped onto the tarmac and shielded his eyes from the early morning sun and the chopper-generated winds. A SWAT team joined with the military police and the correctional officers from the El Dorado facility. Griff suspected that their orders were to safeguard him from assassination. It was good to see that Allaire was finally giving Genesis their due.

The circle of armed security surrounding Griff parted to allow a lone man to approach. He wore a dark suit and had thinning hair on top, and an ample belly below. His face featured a neatly trimmed gray and brown beard. The man shook Griff's hand vigorously and shouted to be heard above the helicopter's whirl.

"Warden Jay Tobert, Dr. Rhodes," he said. "Welcome to El Dorado. We'll get you processed and with the prisoner as quickly as possible. I hope you've had a chance to review the files that you requested?"

Griff nodded. He'd been given the faxed pages by one of the MPs and read all about Johnny Ray Davis on the drive to the maximum-security penitentiary. Charged with the shooting death of a husband and wife during a failed carjacking, Davis was sentenced to die. Despite an initial plea of innocent, the evidence included in the file was irrefutable. Forensics and ballistics linked Davis to the crime. Several reliable eyewitnesses sealed the case for the prosecution.

Griff swallowed hard as he glanced at the stone walls and steel bars. It was one thing to be reminded of time done in prison, but something far worse to be back inside one, regardless of the reason. The familiar feelings of hopelessness and despair returned as though they had never left.

"Reception is waiting for you," the warden said. "We'll go to the Tower East building first to get you cleared. Then we'll be heading over to our Commons building. That's where you'll meet Davis."

Griff followed Tobert while the battalion of security followed him.

"Looks like you've got some friends in pretty high places," Tobert understated on their walk to Tower East. When Griff just nodded, the warden continued to fish for information. "Not every day the president of the United States calls me to request special access."

"Not every day," Griff echoed.

"I understand that the Wichita police arrested this Bartholomew fellow on his way out of town."

Again, Griff nodded.

"He tried to run," he said. "Guess he panicked after I made the call to Washington. I imagine you'll be hosting him here at some point."

"We do good keeping our prisoners where they're supposed to be. Haven't had a successful rabbit since I became warden. Good thing, too, because if Johnny Ray ever busted out of here we'd have a heck of a time catching him."

"Why's that?"

"Boy's a natural runner," Tobert said. "I'd guess he could run straight to California without stopping or getting winded. Guy never gets tired jogging in the yard. And I mean never."

"Well, I don't know what'll happen to Bartholomew now that he's in custody," Griff said. "But I hope it isn't good."

Griff also hoped that Allaire would follow through on his promise to investigate Paul Rappaport. That part of their short phone conversation had been anything but pleasant. He had called the president's emergency number from Bartholomew's cramped, cluttered office at the Certain Path Mission.

"Rappaport shows up and Melvin is killed," Griff had said to Allaire. "Murdered by someone working for Genesis. Explain to me how Genesis knew about our plan?"

"I can't," Allaire said. "But you had no right jeopardizing our objective by sneaking out of Kalvesta, Rhodes. You've gone rogue on me and I don't like it one bit."

"Pardon my saying so, Mr. President, but I don't

much care what you like. What I care about is what you do. And I need you to do something for me."

"What?" Allaire said.

"Two things, actually. I want you to treat Rappaport as a suspect. Have him watched. Put a tail on him. Wiretap his phones. Get ahold of his computers. Put the CIA, NSA, FBI, and any other letters you can think of on him. Put a dossier together that will detail what he's had for breakfast every morning for the last ten tears. I'm convinced it's him, and somewhere along the line we'll find that he's tipped us off to that. He's the force behind Genesis. He did this to become president."

"You think he arranged to have his own daughter robbed while she was taking a shower?" Allaire asked. "You think he would arrange to traumatize her by cutting up her underwear and spreading it across her bed, just so he could get me to appoint him the designated survivor?"

"Anybody who did this to you and the others at the Capitol is capable of anything," Griff had replied. "The setup for the release of WRX3883 has been going on for a long time. The whole Genesis thing—the blackout in New York, and those explosions—were just a prologue leading up to the State of the Union."

"I'll think about it," was all Allaire had said. "What's the second thing?"

"Have Sergeant Stafford go out with some men to the ventilation shaft to retrieve Melvin's body. He was a hero. If you ever get out of this, he deserves a Congressional Medal of Honor, or whatever the civilian version is of that."

"Consider it done. Now get to that prison and this time keep me posted about what you're doing."

Griff was replaying that conversation in his mind when he was startled by a loud buzz. He stiffened at the sound. The heavy metal door unlocked and the noise stopped.

"It's hard coming back to prison, huh?" the warden commented, evidently aware of Griff's history.

"You have no idea," Griff said.

"Well, thankfully, you're right about that."

Griff went through the screening process without incident and followed the warden into the prison yard. The helicopters continued to circle overhead like the buzzards in his recurring Ebola dream. Crossing a patch of barren ground, they entered the Commons building. The corridors there were quiet and deserted.

"I've got 'em on lockdown for as long as you're here," Tobert announced proudly.

"Thanks. I'm sure that won't win J. R. Davis any popularity prizes."

"He can take care of himself. Truth is, I think most of the guys are scared of him."

The warden opened a door marked ATTORNEY'S ROOM and motioned Griff to follow him inside.

Griff was surprised to see only a foldout table in the center of the room, with a plastic chair on either side, but no Plexiglas divider to separate the lawyers from the convicts. He took a seat at the table facing the door. Four guards stood behind him.

The door buzzed and then opened. Three more guards entered, escorting a man in an orange prison jumpsuit.

His ankles and wrists were shackled. Two of the guards assisted the convict in getting seated. Faded tattoos of women covered the outsides of both his arms. His jet-black hair was buzz cut, his narrow face horselike, and his upper lip had been gashed at some point and sutured carelessly, so that the edges of the vermillion border did not meet. The result was what amounted to a permanent sneer.

But the most striking feature of Johnny Ray Davis's countenance—the one that struck Griff almost immediately, were his eyes.

The right one was sky blue . . . and the left was chestnut brown.

CHAPTER 59

"Johnny Ray Davis?" Griff asked, though he'd already seen photos of the pale-skinned convict.

"It's J. R. Who're you?"

Davis had an odd twang that Griff placed somewhere between Midwestern and Creole.

"Griffin Rhodes. Griff. I'm a virologist."

Davis stiffened. A fearful expression chipped away some of his tough-guy persona.

"You with that woman from the mission in Wichita?"

"I was at one time. She's dead now."

"Good. I tried to get those fuckers busted for what they done to me," he said. "Her and that bogus preacher. I called the police, but I couldn't leave my name. It weren't just me, you know. There were others, too. But the police ain't much for listenin' to the ramblins of a junkie. Know what I mean? Hey, you got a smoke?"

"Sorry."

"Then how about you send someone to get me some?"

The killer already knew that whatever was going on, he had some leverage. Griff warned himself not to underestimate the man. He turned to the warden, who had felt it was in his best interest to remain in the room and oversee the most important prisoner visit of his career.

"Can you do that?" Griff asked him. "Cigarettes?"

"Marlboro Reds," Davis clarified.

"You'll get what you get," the warden snapped.

A guard exited the room to get the smokes without his needing to be prompted.

Griff leaned across the table.

"What did they do to you, J. R.?" he asked in a low, sympathetic voice.

Griff could see the gears turning in the convict's head. Davis was clearly not ready to give away anything for free.

"What's this all about?" the man asked.

"I need to know what happened to you at the Certain Path Mission," Griff said.

"Why?"

"It's important."

"What's in it for me?"

"Special privileges," Griff said.

It was the first thought that came to his mind. The warden gave him a disapproving glare.

"That wasn't part of any discussion I had," he said.

Impatient and exhausted, Griff glowered back at him.

"I'm sure the federal government will find a way to subsidize you for any added cost or burden."

The warden grinned, and so did Davis.

"Federal government, eh?" Davis said. "You mean, like the president?"

"That's right."

"So it ain't just rumor."

"What isn't?"

Davis sat up straighter and tapped his feet on the floor in a quick rhythm.

"Rumor going round the cells is that the president himself personally arranged this little meeting."

"Who told you that?" Tobert demanded.

Griff decided in that moment that in any clash of character or intellect between prisoner and jailer, his money was on the prisoner.

"Hey, easy there, warden," Davis said. "The cons and guards talk. We learn things, they learn things. So is it true? Did the president send you?"

"He did."

"This have anythin' to do with what's goin' on in Washington?" Davis read the surprise in Griff's expression. "We got newspapers in the library, you know. Not all of us are as dumb as we look. Some of us can even read."

"It is about the Capitol."

Davis looked contemplative as he traced the scar on his lip with a nicotine-stained fingernail.

"Special privileges, huh?"

"Now, tell me what happened at the Certain Path Mission."

Davis fell silent. He stared at Griff through his two different-colored eyes and remained silent until the guard returned with his cigarettes and an ashtray, lit the smoke, and handed it to him. The convict jostled with his irons to slip the butt into his mouth. Then he took a long, hard drag and exhaled a plume in the warden's general direction.

"They tested on me," he said. "The lady in a white suit, like a spaceman, I mean space*woman,* sprayed stuff in my face. She injected me, too. And almost every day, she drew blood outta my arm."

"Did she tell you what it was she injected?"

"Said it would help me get clean off drugs," Davis said. "But it didn't take the cravin's away none. Once I heard her and that fake asshole monk talking about burnin' bodies. But the police didn't think much of my report, like I told you. That Chinawoman and the monk are the ones what should be sittin' here, not me."

"Did they do any other experiments on you?"

"She asked me stuff."

"What kind of stuff?"

Davis thought for a beat.

"She gave me a stack of cards," he began. "Each card had a number on it, from one to ten, or sometimes a shape, like a star or a circle. Then she'd tell me to pick up a card and study it. I weren't allowed to show her the number, see, but she asked me what it was. Sometimes she told me that I had to lie about it, like if I had a four, I'd tell her it was a seven, or something. You see?"

"Go on," Griff said. "You're doing great."

"But then she'd ask me if I was lyin' to her. Well, of course I were lyin' to her," Davis said with a laugh.

"She told me to. That were the instruction. But here's the rub—the real weird part. Sometimes, she said to me that if I admitted to lyin' about the number, she'd burn my arm with a solderin' iron."

"So you were supposed to tell her that you weren't lying about your card number, even though you did."

"That's right," Davis said. "Simple. No, I'm not lyin', it's really a seven, so don't burn me."

"And what happened when she asked if you were lying?"

"I was sort of woozy—half asleep, if you know what I mean. But I do know that I told her the truth. I mean the real truth. I admitted to her when I 'uz lyin', and I admitted to her when I weren't."

Davis looked down at his cigarette, clearly upset at what he was remembering.

"You admitted to lying even though it meant you'd get burned?"

Davis turned his wiry arms over and showed Griff a series of crisscross scars that covered both forearms and extended nearly up to his biceps. The scars were almost certainly burns. Griff felt his stomach turn and his heart begin to race.

This was it!

"Did you even try to lie to her?"

"Every time," Davis admitted. "I knew how bad that damn iron burned. But she'd ask me, 'Johnny Ray, tell the truth now. Are you lyin' to me about that number?' Sometimes, I'd shake my head no, but then I'd answer yes. And then she'd burn me. And we did it over and over again."

Davis, clearly distressed by the memories, asked the guard for another smoke.

Griff could only stare at him. Not only did he survive his WRX3883 exposure, but the virus in his body had actually worked on the will center. For all of Chen's shortcomings, the test she had devised was truly brilliant—brilliant and elegantly simple. Johnny Ray Davis lacked the willpower to lie, even though he knew the consequence of telling the truth would be extreme pain.

Then Griff felt a knot developing in his gut. He knew that he desperately needed this man's blood. He needed to study it, to figure out what had allowed him to live when all the others had died. But he also knew using Davis's serum would be tantamount to the most egregious violation of his own code. He had committed his life's work to testing on computer models, not animals. But Orion kept failing him, and time was running out. To make his program work, he needed to feed it better data. And the data that he needed was coursing through the arteries and veins of the man seated across from him.

Did it matter that Johnny Ray Davis was a convicted double murderer? Did it matter that Griff wasn't the one who had exposed him to the virus and tested its effects? Sooner or later, every drug intended for use in humans or animals needed to be tried in humans or animals. Where should the line be drawn?

Help me, Louisa. Help me know.

"I need your blood," Griff suddenly heard himself saying.

Davis treated the request the way he might a ten-dollar cigarette trade. "How much blood?" he asked.

"All of it."

Davis coughed out a thick cloud of smoke and stubbed away the last embers of his Marlboro.

"How's that possible?" he asked.

"It's called plasmapheresis," Griff explained. "We'll replace your blood with a substance called albumin, and where necessary, a fresh supply that matches your blood type. Hospitals do it all the time."

"What's this for? You tryin' to figger out why I'm still alive?"

"Yes, that's exactly what I'm trying to figure out."

"Why do you think I didn't die?"

"If I had to guess?"

"Yeah, if you had to guess."

"You're heterochromic," Griff said.

"I'm hetero what?"

"Your eyes. They're two different colors. It's a genetic marker. Often accompanies other genetic deals. That's why I need your blood. I need to see what's different about it—what else besides the gene for your eye color. Because to be honest, you should be dead."

"My sister's eyes're just like mine."

"I'm not surprised."

"Well, ain't that just a peach," Davis said. "You need my blood. But you can't just gut me like a fish to get at it, can you?"

"No, I can't."

"But what you're really sayin' is that the president hisself needs my blood."

"I have paperwork you'll need to sign to authorize the transfusion," Griff said.

"Not so fast, amigo," Davis answered. "You know that I'm innocent. The bastards are gonna fry me for a crime I didn't do."

Griff's mind flashed on the photographs of the brutally murdered husband and wife that were included in the case file he had reviewed.

"I'm not here to judge you, J.R.," he said. "I'm here to take your blood."

"Well, I thought you should know that I 'uz innocent before I tell you what it's gonna cost."

"You want money?"

Davis laughed sharply and lit another smoke.

"No, you stupid prick," he said. "I want you to call your buddy, Mr. President, and get him to issue me a full presidential pardon. You can have my blood all right. But I'll be a free man before I give you one innocent drop of it."

CHAPTER 60

The Kitchen was like a ghost town. Griff's biosuit was isolating enough when Melvin was around. Now it merely enhanced his inestimable sadness and loneliness. Each procedure felt like the last one he would be able to perform. Even with the crisis in the Capitol, and the ticking bomb of WRX3883, thoughts of Angie were the only thing keeping him on task.

After Chad Stafford and his men had retrieved Melvin from the ventilation shaft and returned to the compound, Griff had spent some time alone beside the plastic bag containing his friend's body. His family in West Virginia had opted for cremation and a memorial service sometime in the future. Griff promised Melvin's sister and mother that if the president survived the crisis in the Capitol, he would be there to honor the man who had done so much to save his life.

Now, he knew that he needed to have the help of his gangly, oddly obsessed soulmate one more time—as motivation to press ahead with the analysis of Johnny Ray Davis's serum, and the incorporation of the new data into the program he had named after Orion, the hunter.

Griff barely spoke on the Army helicopter flight from El Dorado back to Kalvesta. He kept running the Led Zeppelin song "Dazed and Confused" over in his mind. It had been thirty-six hours since he left the lab— thirty-six hours of minimal sleep, of watching his closest friend be murdered, and of being battered in body and spirit.

Dazed and confused.

The president had taken almost no time at all to pardon Davis for his crimes—proof of how critical things had gotten for the seven hundred waiting in the Capitol for news that they might not die. Griff had left the now ex-convict at the hospital, where he'd undergone the plasmapheresis. The legacy of WRX3883: grisly death after grisly death, and now a double murderer set free.

Paul Rappaport was still at Kalvesta, and was there to greet Griff when he deplaned. The two men shook hands, but Griff did nothing to hide the coldness he was feeling.

You're Genesis, you son of bitch, he thought. *I know you are.*

Rappaport appeared relatively calm.

"We're counting on you, Rhodes," was all that he said as Griff started his journey downward.

You're counting on me to fail, Griff said to himself. *But win or lose, I'm going to bring you down. And when I do, there's going to be a photo of Melvin Forbush in your coffin.*

Sergeant Stafford coordinated the security detail assigned to cover Griff, and barked out instructions that kept his team on constant alert. Stafford and some troops accompanied Griff down to the lab level. Because of the exposure risk, they guarded only the entrance to the Kitchen, not the Kitchen itself. Griff passed into the restricted area alone, carrying with him, in a large cooler lined with icepacks, six liters of Johnny Ray Davis's anticoagulated blood.

Carefully, Griff decanted some plasma into four test tubes and set each tube in one of four wells of a large centrifuge. The instrument whirled in excess of three thousand revolutions per minute, separating cellular debris from the serum.

Seven hundred lives rested on his finding an elusive antigen, or some unusual enzyme in that serum—something that had allowed Davis to survive, while others exposed to WRX3883 had died. Seven hundred lives were running out of time.

Griff used gel electrophoresis to separate the treated serum into DNA, RNA, and protein molecules for further analysis. Police forensics used the technique to amplify DNA for their criminal investigations, but Griff was interested in every component of the serum—most specifically, something unique to J.R. Davis.

Hours passed. Frustration and apprehension grew. Fatigue became a mortal enemy. Then, suddenly, it was there.

Interleukin 6.

Davis's serum contained ten times the normal level of the protein Interleukin 6.

Ten times the norm.

Griff checked and rechecked his technique and his calculations. He felt a vibration at the base of his neck and down his spine. He knew the sensation well. It occurred whenever an idea had begun to take hold and grow.

What, exactly, was it that the warden said about Davis? Griff tried to recall. The man could run straight to California without becoming winded—something like that. Never gets tired jogging in the yard. . . . Never.

It had been a simple, off-topic conversation that Griff had nearly forgotten about. But suddenly, when viewed in a different context, that comment took on an enormous new significance.

Griff knew a great deal about the IL-6 protein. It was secreted by T-cells and functioned in part to stimulate the body's response to trauma—burns, tissue damage, and such. He was also aware that IL-6, for reasons still unknown, became elevated during periods of physical stress. He conducted some quick research on the Internet and found a study of Fuchs heterochromic iridocyclitis that linked patients with the different-colored irises to elevated levels of IL-6 in the blood. The Fuchs variant of heterochromia was associated with viral illness, probably measles.

Griff began to wonder what would happen if he added an adjuvant to Orion—a biochemical booster that amplified IL-6 production.

But which one?

More research online. More poring through his grad school notes and his files of articles.

Bless you, Melvin, for keeping everything in order. Bless you, old friend.

One possibility kept arising: antisense oligodeoxynucleotides, more commonly called ODNs. The odd name was also known by geneticists as "negative sense." Sense and antisense proteins were increasingly being used to battle complex diseases such as AIDS, asthma, and even muscular dystrophy. In theory, a synthetic strand of the nucleic acid could bind to messenger RNA and effectively alter its behavior.

Griff powered up his computer. He modified Orion's programming to include an ODN adjuvant that stimulated IL-6 production from the body's lymph nodes and spleen. In his program, Griff magnified the production of IL-6 until the levels cranked out by the body treated with ODN matched those found in Davis's blood.

Ten times the norm.

Side effects of the treatment were not a concern. With a WRX infection, the only thing worse than the inevitable death were the days that preceded it.

Adding the antisense/ODN adjuvant to his Orion program took more than four hours. Griff had barely eaten or slept in two days. Still, with the excitement of the discovery, he found that his focus was sharp. His brain was pulsating with possibilities.

Work, baby! . . . Come on, deliver for Papa!

When the programming was complete, Griff sat in silence for a time, with his finger poised above the Return key, set to execute Orion's "run" sequence. Images of the Capitol and Jim Allaire tumbled through his thoughts along with those of Angie and Melvin and Louisa and even Moonshine. Finally, his jaw set, he held his breath and pressed the key.

Orion was programmed by Griff to terminate computation the instant it failed. No reason to waste computing time processing a dead-end treatment. The longer Orion's program processed, the greater the probability of success. Over the years of working in Sylvia Chen's lab, Griff had run thousands of simulations that churned through thousands of preprogrammed assumptions, subroutines, and over a hundred thousand lines of complex code. In all that time, Orion had never run for longer than ten minutes.

Griff watched the digital clock on his computer monitor as it counted the time.

Two minutes passed . . . then three . . . then five.

Griff could feel the adrenaline rushing through his circulation.

Eight minutes . . . nine . . .

At the ten-minute-and-zero-second mark, Orion's program terminated with the abruptness of a racecar hitting a wall. Griff knew without having to read through the output what had happened. His system had failed once again.

Four more hours.

Griff tweaked the levels of the adjuvant to drive the IL-6 levels from ten times normal up to thirty, always in increments of five. He ran a test for each change that he made.

Every time, Orion's treatment simulation failed, and always at the ten-minute-zero-second mark.

Beneath his suit, Griff was sweating profusely now. He was exhausted to the point of delirium. But time was continuing to spill away for the people in the Capitol. He refused to quit—to believe that he and the system he so believed in had failed.

Then, like a lantern approaching through fog, an idea came to him.

What if IL-6 levels were just a part of the solution? What if there was something unique in Davis's serum itself that would make the treatment work?

Griff altered Orion's programming so that in addition to the antisense/ODN booster, it incorporated an exact replica of the DNA, RNA, and proteins found in Davis's blood.

Then, once again, his eyes fixed on the counter, he initiated the program.

Once again, Orion began to synthesize a blocker against the growth of the WRX virus.

At the nine-minute mark, Griff felt a tremor of anticipation begin. At nine minutes and forty-five seconds he began to hyperventilate—short, shallow, rapid respirations.

He closed his eyes, waited for as long as he could stand, then looked at the timer.

Eleven minutes and forty-eight seconds, and Orion was still running.

In all, it took twenty-five minutes for the program to complete. Griff, flushed with excitement, waited for the output to compile. When the data finished processing, he sank into his chair. He'd been so conditioned to expect failure that when success finally had occurred, he did not exactly know how to feel.

Angie was the key. If she had not succeeded in New York, none of this would have been possible. Because of her, they had an antiviral treatment. He wished he could call and tell her, but with Rappaport listening in, he wasn't certain the idea was a good one.

Then Griff began to wonder. Orion had worked. At least, according to the computer it had worked. The data said the drug would be a success, but he had no empirical proof—no infected subjects that he had cured.

What should be done next?

The laboratory had an extensive supply of biological and synthetic agents to work with. He checked the reagent case and confirmed there was enough antisense/ODN on hand for him to perform at least one test.

Then he asked himself if he really needed a test to prove that his treatment worked. Wasn't his computer model proof enough? Wasn't that the point of his work? Hadn't he found a way to develop and test drugs that spared animals from the agony and torture of experimentation?

He studied Orion's output files again, imagining himself standing at a crossroad. But unlike the crossroad immortalized in song and story, Griff suspected the devil was waiting for him regardless of which direction he chose. He closed his eyes and waited for the answer to come. Soon, his thoughts became filled with noise. It took time for him to recognize the hideous sounds—they were the screams of monkeys, dying in Hell's Kitchen from an accidental overdose of WRX3883.

In that moment, Griff knew exactly what he had to do.

He stood up from his workstation. His legs were barely functional from sitting for so long. He carefully retrieved living WRX3883 virus from the cultures that Melvin had maintained, and used a syringe to mix the virus with a hundred milliliters of saline solution. In theory, his computer models alone should be enough proof that he had succeeded.

In his heart, though, he knew that was not enough.

Perhaps one day Orion would be used to jump-start a movement that would reduce or, better still, eliminate animal testing in both virology and other areas of medical and product research. But for now, the certain path to an antiviral treatment, no matter what his computer spit out, was to work with an infected host.

Moving as in a dream, Griff disconnected his air hose and unzipped his biocontainment suit. He removed his helmet and gratefully wiped the sweat from his face. Then he set the syringe down on the table and prepared a single dose of Orion's theoretical antiviral treatment—a mixture of Johnny Ray Davis's serum and a powerful IL-6 boosting adjuvant. He had the perfect test subject to prove all of his theories and validate all of his work.

He had himself.

CHAPTER 61

Griff knew that calls made from the phone system in the Kitchen were being monitored around the clock, but he didn't care. Rappaport was about to learn that there might have been a breakthrough, but Griff would figure out what to do about that when it became a certainty. He moved the intercom over to his workstation, put it on speaker, dialed # 9 for a long-distance line, and called Angie's cell phone. If she didn't answer, he would try a call to her nurses' station to get a message to her to call about a family emergency.

His biocontainment suit lay crumpled in a ball by his feet. Win or lose, the die was cast.

Two rings and Angie answered. She sounded as if she might have been sleeping. Griff glanced up at the wall-mounted clock. It was twelve fifteen in the morning Kansas time, one fifteen Eastern.

"Hiya, lady," Griff said, leaning back and savoring

air that wasn't coming into a helmet via a tube. "Greetings from the heartland."

"Griff! I've been hoping each call was you. Allaire and his doctor have been in touch with me, and they've sent specialists in and put some guards outside the door and in here, but I was wondering when I'd ever hear your beautiful voice again. You don't sound like you're speaking from behind a mask, though. Where are you? What's going on? You got news?"

Griff smiled at the phone, wishing she could see how happy she was making him. The rocket-fire questions continued. Always the reporter. He held off answering for as long as he could, content just to listen to her. The elevation in his spirit confirmed two things he already knew: He loved her as much as ever, probably more, and he was right in needing to hear her voice before he injected himself with the virus.

"Angie," Griff cut in finally, "tell me how you're doing. You sound okay."

"I'm fine. Really. Tired is all. That may have something to do with that I'm not sleeping regularly. Instead, I drop off for twenty minutes here and twenty there, but no real REM sleep, if you know what I mean."

"I do, yes. When this is all over, we're going to this South Pacific island that's covered from one end to the other with mattresses. I read about it in *National Geographic*. Sealy, Serta, Tempur-Pedics, all the best brands. Any word on a discharge?"

"Looks like today. Sometime this afternoon. I want to get back there to you guys. I miss you both so much."

Angie read Griff's silence almost immediately. "Something's the matter. What is it?"

More silence. Griff's eyes begin to well and he wondered if he was going to be able to speak.

"It's Melvin," he finally managed. "He's dead."

Now the prolonged silence was from Angie's side of the line.

"Tell me," she said after a while.

Griff shared an abbreviated version of the events following her injury up to the plasmapheresis on J. R. Davis.

"Oh, I'm sorry, Griff," she said when he had finished. "I am so sad and so sorry. What a terrific fellow he was. I know how close you two were. And I'm glad you got the man who killed him."

"Thanks. As soon as we can, we'll go visit his family in West Virginia."

He looked over at the loaded syringes on a metal tray by his desk. It seemed almost wishful to be talking about their future.

"I do have a bit of good news," he continued.

"Tell me, tell me."

"Thanks to you and Melvin, I believe we've done it. According to Orion, I've got a workable antiviral treatment."

He had hoped there would be more exuberance in his voice, but Angie understood and the excitement in her voice filled in for his lack of enthusiasm.

"Oh, Griff, that's wonderful! I knew you could do it. I knew it!"

Griff hesitated. It was time to tell her.

"I still don't know for certain that my conclusions will work."

Not surprisingly, Angie sensed what was coming.

"I don't understand."

"Just that. All I know at this point is what Orion has told me, and he looks suspiciously like a computer."

There was prolonged silence.

"Griff, what are you going to do?" she asked finally.

He could hear the apprehension in her voice.

"I need to be certain that I'm right, Ang," he said. "We have a limited supply of Davis's serum. He's probably someplace a thousand miles away by now. The people in the Capitol are in serious trouble, and it's getting worse fast. If we go there with what I have, and Orion is wrong for whatever reason, there's no time to come back here and fool around."

"Griff, I don't like where this is going."

"I need you to be with me, Angie. I need you more than you could ever know."

"Griff, please . . ."

"I'm going to dose myself with the virus, and then I'm going to give myself the treatment."

"No! There has to be another way."

"If it doesn't work, then I'll leave you my notes and the serum. I don't trust anybody but you with this information. You'll come to Kalvesta with another research team and pick up where I left off. Maybe there'll still be some people left in the Capitol we can help."

"Try it on an animal—a monkey, a chimpanzee. If you're wrong, you'll die."

"But I'm not wrong," Griff said.

"What do you mean? I don't understand."

He sighed.

"All these years I've been telling everyone who would listen that computers can supplant animal testing. It's been my mantra—the one thing since my sister died that allowed me to work in virology. I've thought about this, Ang. It's time to trust the program I've spent so much of my life developing. It's time and it's right. Now please, I need you to understand."

"I . . . I do understand," she said.

Griff could hear her crying. For a time, he cried with her.

"It's going to work," he said. "It has to."

"I love you, Griff," she sobbed. "I've loved you since the first day we met."

"I love you too, Angie," he said. "Just think about that island in the Pacific. All those palm trees growing up through those double-thick pillow-top mattresses."

"Hammocks, too?"

Griff picked up the syringe filled with WRX3883 and saline.

"Hammocks, too," he said. "All over the place."

He had premixed the antiviral treatment based on the data from his only successful Orion test. He and Orion had calculated there would be enough serum for seven hundred and thirty doses.

"What are you doing? Talk me through it, Griff," Angie said. "Please, talk me through it."

"I'm cleaning the puncture site on my arm with alcohol. . . . I'm fine, honey. I love you. . . . I've got a vein, a real good one."

"I love you, Griff. Everything's going to be all right. Tell me everything is going to be all right."

"I'm in. Everything's going to be all right. You told me on the houseboat not to just sit there drinking beer and fishing. You were right. This is where I'm supposed to be, doing something that matters. . . . Okay, I'm going to inject."

"Griff . . ."

"Here it goes."

Griff slid the needle into the bulging cord, snapped off the tourniquet, and depressed the plunger. Since he had chosen to go the IV route, using a large, concentrated quantity of virus, symptoms would not take long to develop. Griff took in a few deep breaths. Could it be that his chest already felt tight? Was that anxiety or was the virus already taking hold?

"Griff! Talk to me."

"It's in," he said. "I'm doing fine."

"How long will you wait?"

"Twenty minutes. Then I'll inject Orion's treatment."

"Twenty minutes. . . . God, what am I going to do for twenty minutes."

"We could tell ghost stories," he suggested.

"Not funny."

"Just sit with me, Angie. Just breathe into the phone. Just say something every now and then. Be with me. Be my lover. Be my friend. That's all I need."

Griff closed his eyes and listened to every sound that she made. The rustling of her hospital bedsheets. The beeping of some machine in the background. Her sighs. Her sobs.

His chest was getting tighter. There was wheezing now, too. He could hear it and feel it. Breathing deeply and deliberately through his nose, he picked up the syringe containing the antiviral serum. Orion had been pleased that J. R. Davis's blood was AB negative. Griff wondered if that was related in any way to the interleukin excess and the heterochromia. Linked genes, perhaps.

"Talk, Griff. Talk to me!" Angie demanded.

"It's in. I've got the treatment inside me. We just need to wait, now. Want me to call you back?"

"You big jerk. How long do we wait?"

"A couple hours I suppose. Close your eyes, Angie. I'll wake you up."

"I've got my phone plugged in so I can stay on the line. I won't fall asleep."

"It's okay if you do."

Griff sat at his desk, staring at the black plastic intercom and wishing it were she. His eyes felt heavy, but he suspected it would be impossible for him to sleep. The tightness was no better, but it did not seem much worse. For an hour they spoke only intermittently. They talked about Melvin, mostly, and what Angie had been through in Chinatown. And they talked about Africa.

Somewhere in the second hour, Angie fell asleep. They had been quiet for a stretch and then Griff heard the pattern of her breathing change. Instead of waking her, he just listened. An irritation had developed in his throat, and he cleared it with a small cough. He didn't want to think about the scene when he first arrived in Statuary Hall at the Capitol, but there was no way he could stem the flood of images. He wondered if by now, he should have been feeling sicker.

He continued to listen to Angie as she slept.

It was nearing five in the morning—six, Angie time. Griff took his vitals on the hour. No change. He reached for the pen and notebook where he kept those records. Something about his hand caught his attention. Something that had not been there just a short while before.

Trying to will what he was seeing not to be so, he turned his hands over and held them up. His heart sank. Suddenly, the tight band around his chest intensified and his breathing became more labored.

Covering most of each palm, not unlike the bull's-eye symbol for the popular department store, were intense, slightly irregular, concentric, scarlet circles.

"Everything okay, darling?" Angie asked dreamily. "I think I fell asleep."

"Yeah, Ang," Griff said, still staring in utter dismay at his palms. "Everything's fine."

CHAPTER 62

DAY 9
6:30 A.M. (CST)

The sharp knock on Paul Rappaport's front door awakened him from a fitful sleep. Time was running out for the seven hundred in the Capitol. He felt certain he had been dreaming about how he would have handled the disaster had he been in Jim Allaire's position, but he couldn't recall any of the details. With the possibility of starting a pandemic very real, would he have made the heroic choice Allaire had made—essentially opting to sacrifice himself, his family, and many, many of his friends and supporters in exchange for keeping the country and possibly even the population of the world safe?

Unless the rebel, Rhodes, came through—and Rappaport strongly doubted that was going to happen—it would not be long before the call came summoning him to D.C. to assume the presidency. His mouth went dry at the prospect.

"Come in," he called, pulling on a terrycloth robe.

Janet Fox, the Secret Service agent covering him on the graveyard shift, slipped inside. She was dressed for the high plains winter in ski pants and a furlined parka, but still looked cold.

"Mr. Roger Corum and two others are here to see you, sir," she said. "They say it's important and confidential. I've taken them next door and sent for backup to help me check them over."

"That won't be necessary, Janet."

"I'm afraid we have our orders about that, sir. Straight from the top."

"Oh. I understand. Do what you have to do. I won't get in the way."

"Hopefully things will get better at the Capitol soon, sir."

"Hopefully so."

But I don't see it happening.

Rappaport had showered, brushed his teeth, and brewed himself a cup of coffee when Fox returned. He wondered what could be happening at this hour that was so important to the Staghorn people.

At last report, five or six hours ago, Corum and his technical crew were making rapid progress, and would probably finish establishing their state-of-the-art security and monitoring system by the end of the day. The final task would be the most important—installing monitoring cameras inside the Kitchen. If Rhodes failed, the system would still be put to good use.

One of Rappaport's first acts as president would be to beef up the Kalvesta facility as the jewel in his administration's bioterrorism research and counterinsurgency force. That division of his new-age army would be only the beginning of an all-out war to secure national borders, keep out illegal aliens, and quash terrorism—a comprehensive approach that would dwarf all such efforts to date. Allaire had done a half-decent job battling a complex problem, but Paul Rappaport would go down in history as the president who made it safe to live in America.

After Janet Fox assured him that the officials from Staghorn Security were "clean," she led them in and directed them to the conference/monitoring area set up in one of the large front rooms. In less time than Rappaport believed possible, Corum and his team had mounted three digital touch-screen maps to the bungalow walls. The maps allowed the Homeland Security Chief to track threats against the United States from any number of terrorist organizations, domestic or international.

In the room across the hall, there were several computer workstations, and two satellite phones, one of which had a dedicated connection to the Hard Room at the Capitol. Marguerite Prideaux and Colin Whitehead followed Corum to the conference area, each carrying a mug of coffee. Their expressions were grim.

"What's going on?" Rappaport asked once the four of them were settled in around his small table.

"We were in the process of getting the communication hub online with the new monitoring equipment," Corum said, "when one of Marguerite's workers picked up a transmission from the laboratory's intercom phone system. Here, have a look."

Corum handed Rappaport a stack of printed-out pages. The three security experts waited patiently while the secretary of Homeland Security read. When he finished with the transcript, Rappaport set the pages face-down in front of him.

"What do you make of this?" he asked.

Pallid, cachectic Colin Whitehead answered for the group. He was an Ivy League intellectual—Yale, Rappaport thought he remembered.

"We aren't sure," Whitehead said. "We've had to shut down all laboratory video feeds in order to get the new board and the updated equipment installed. All we can monitor for about another three or four hours are conversations within the various rooms down there, and also the phones."

A coughing jag cut Whitehead's explanation short. Rappaport heard the mucus rattling in the man's chest and grimaced. Ivy League or not, he detested smokers. The stench was bad enough, but he found the weakness of the habit even more reprehensible. Once his antiterrorism program was underway, with all that it entailed, he would turn his attention to shoring up borders and intensifying the war on drugs. Included in that war would be a jihad against smoking and smokers.

Marguerite Prideaux picked up where Whitehead had left off. Her French accent was pleasing to the secretary, as was her shapely body, and her self-confidence.

"It seems the virologist working at this moment down below us believes that he has a cure for the infection in your Capitol building," she said. "And he has now intentionally exposed himself to the virus to prove it."

"And do you believe from this conversation you recorded that he has a cure?"

Corum spoke up again.

"We unfortunately don't have the video to confirm what is going on in the lab right now, but the answer to your question is yes. He sounds quite confident, actually."

"I can still call down to Rhodes, yes?"

"Of course. The intercom will reach him in any room, and because he might still be helmeted, and wouldn't hear as well over the rushing air, lights will flash all over to tell him there's a call."

"You people think of everything," Rappaport said.

"Competition is fierce in our field," Prideaux replied. "We must stay always one step ahead."

"I feel exactly the same about politics," the secretary said, chuckling. "Listen, for the time being, I'm going to assume Rhodes is onto something. But he's as slippery as a greased eel, and I don't trust him. I'm going to call down on the intercom and see if I can get some information from him. Meanwhile, see if you can get the video monitors working in the lab ahead of schedule. I don't have the least desire to go down there and put on one of those biosuits. If Rhodes survives what he's done, I'll have to confirm it, and then get in touch with the president. Getting a direct look at him will help."

CHAPTER 63

DAY 9
2:00 P.M. (EST)
Angie's headache was not nearly as bad as the doctors had predicted it might be. There was a mild throbbing above her eyes where the fracture was, but nothing more—at least not yet.

As instructed in the fax from Griff, she had taken the subway from the station across the street from the hospital, but switched trains four times, twice to backtrack to previous stops. At each station, Angie subtly surveyed the crowd for anybody whom she had seen before. Her throat was dry and tight, and her heart beat like a drumline, but still she maintained what she thought was a calm, measured exterior. In a previous incarnation as an investigative reporter, she had learned a good many tricks of the trade of how to follow or avoid being followed. Some of those she employed now.

Convinced that she was alone, she finally took a cab from Columbus Circle to Penn Station, and boarded the Acela, the express train to Washington. The first-class car was nearly full, but she had managed to get a single separated by a table from another single.

The instructions in the fax had been explicit in every respect, but reading it left Angie concerned. After their long, loving early morning on the phone together, she had expected to get a follow-up call from Griff telling her that things were still going well with the treatment he and his computer program had created. Instead, a few hours after their conversation had ended, she had a surprise visitor—Wu Mei, the stunning young charge nurse from the Riverside Nursing Home.

Mei was overjoyed to find Angie ready for discharge, and shyly handed her a small box of Chinese candy and a manila envelope containing the fax. Griff had been meticulous in his preparation, and had clearly chosen this route of delivery as the one he could trust more than any others. The cover page with the fax explained that this was an emergency, and that Wu Mei was to be called immediately to bring it to Angie Fletcher at Lower Manhattan Hospital.

To Angie, he wrote that communication from now on would be face-to-face only. No phones. No texting. No e-mail. Her job was to deliver the fax to General Frank Egan at the Capitol, who would then bring it in to President Allaire, and return with orders for her. Until she reached Egan, she would essentially be on her own.

The fax was specific enough, especially given that Griff knew that one or two people at the nursing home might read it. Still, there was a coldness to his writing—a detachment that made Angie uncomfortable. Something was wrong, either with him or around him. She could feel it in her heart. He hadn't called her back, and after saying any number of times over the phone that he loved her, there was not one word of concern, caring, or encouragement. The end of the fax asked Allaire to call him after reading it.

Something was wrong with him.

The Acela was smooth and fast, and several times during the trip to D.C., Angie actually dozed off. The fax was on her lap in a briefcase she had bought in a leather store near the hospital. At Griff's instruction, she had purchased a courier's security chain and had it attached from the handle of the case to her wrist.

General Egan was waiting for her at the Capitol. Minutes later, she was assigned two FBI agents to babysit her until he was done meeting with President Allaire. One of them was a hot, gum-snapping African-American chick in a miniskirt and thigh-high boots, and the other was a stocky brunette wearing jeans, horn-rimmed glasses, and a backpack, and looking to be no more than twenty.

The two agents settled in with her at a nearby coffeeshop.

An hour passed, then two more. The undercover FBI agents were clearly accustomed to waiting. They chatted, read, and even napped. At one point, over the phone, they reserved a room for Angie at a nearby hotel. A while later, they took her out to buy a small suitcase, some clothes, and some toiletries. Finally, General Egan summoned them back to the Capitol. Then, the head of the Northern Command dismissed her bodyguards and brought Angie into his small but well-equipped field office.

"First of all, tell me," she said. "Is Griff all right? There's something about the way he wrote that fax that makes me think there's trouble."

"No one said anything to me about there being a problem."

You're a lousy liar, Angie quickly concluded. *Why aren't you telling me the truth?*

Griff was sick, she concluded. The antiviral serum had failed, and he was ill . . . or worse.

Damn him for not telling me. Damn him! Damn them!

"You've read the fax, Ms. Fletcher," Egan said, "so you know what the president is planning to do at our safe house."

"I think the idea is brilliant. I want to be there when it goes down."

"We discussed that possibility, and I'm afraid the president has rejected it."

"Then you let me go inside there and speak to him myself."

"I understand you've been in the hospital with quite a nasty head injury."

"I'm going to be there," she said, pointedly ignoring the inference.

"We can put you in the surveillance van. It will just be a couple of blocks away."

"Genesis murdered two dear friends of mine and now the man I care more for than anyone in the world may be sick. I'm going to be there in that safe house when Griff's plan starts unfolding. And when this whole thing is over, I'm going to tell the stories of Melvin Forbush and Gottfried Sliplitz, and most of all of Griffin Rhodes. You tell President Allaire I deserve that."

Egan looked somewhat bewildered. Then he excused himself and left the office.

Griff was ill, she thought as she sat there grim and angry. The serum hadn't worked the way he anticipated, and now he was sick. But he was determined not to go down without taking Paul Rappaport with him. They had to let her be there.

Angie was working through her response to being turned down by Allaire when Egan reentered his office.

"Okay, Ms. Fletcher," he said, taking his place at his small desk. "You're in. It's your story. Now, here's what you've got to do. . . ."

CHAPTER 64

The intercom conversation with Griffin Rhodes was about what Rappaport had anticipated—as icy as the Kansas morning, and as informative as a weather report. Yes, his computer program seemed to have succeeded in creating a program for an antivirus treatment, and yes he trusted his work enough to try it out on himself. Now, there was nothing to do but wait. He would be running tests on himself throughout the day, and as soon as he was confident things were still going well, he would notify Rappaport as well as the president. And finally, yes, he was aware that time was of the essence.

That was all.

Rhodes was impossible to deal with.

Frustrated and anxious, Rappaport did an hour of calisthenics and weights, caught up on some correspondence, and wandered over to the Staghorn Headquarters to check on progress with the video monitoring. There were technical delays, he was told, before their people could be suited up and sent into the hot zone. Another four hours, Corum told him. Maybe five. Marguerite Prideaux made him some tea, but then had to leave when one of her team reported on the technical problems.

Rappaport returned to his office, and called to check in on his daughter, who was still living at their home and was absolutely paranoid about the Secret Service presence there. She was also upset that the latest series of meds weren't working, and she wondered if she should be back in the hospital.

After terminating their conversation as quickly as he could, Rappaport decided to check in on Rhodes again. He was crossing to the intercom when the satellite phone on his desk chirped, announcing an incoming call. He quickly pushed the key sequence required to connect with it. Then he put it on speaker and set his feet up on the desk.

"Secretary Rappaport," he announced.

"Paul, it's Jim. We need to talk."

Rappaport felt himself tense.

Is this it?

"I may have some important news for you as well," he said.

Allaire went on as if he hadn't heard.

"A few minutes ago, I called Dr. Rhodes to check on his progress."

"And you learned that he had dosed himself with the WRX virus."

"You know?"

"Sir, I've been preparing a report for you. A few

hours ago, Staghorn Technologies intercepted a lengthy, unauthorized communication from the Kalvesta labs to the cell phone of Angela Fletcher, the reporter who disappeared from here. She's—"

"In Manhattan. I know." Allaire's voice had a weakness to it—an odd quaver, as if he had aged.

At that moment, there was a knock on Rappaport's door.

"Excuse me for just a moment, sir," he said. "Someone's at the door. Come in."

One of the day-shift agents stepped inside and announced that Roger Corum was there, that he had been checked over next door, and that it was important. Rappaport nodded to show him in.

The head of Staghorn entered, holding up another transmission.

"It's Roger Corum, sir, the CEO of Staghorn Security."

"I suspect what he is there for has something to do with why I'm calling. Mr. Corum, is this regarding the conversation I just had with Dr. Rhodes?"

"Yes, sir, it is. I have a transcript of it in my hand."

"Remarkably quick work. Rhodes said there was no safe line down there in the lab. I guess he's right. Just leave it there, Mr. Corum. The secretary can read it over after we've spoken."

"Yes, Mr. President."

Corum mouthed the words *good luck,* and backed out.

"I've been told Staghorn has highest clearance," Allaire said.

"Yes, sir. I feel strongly that they can be trusted with whatever is in this transmission."

"Excellent. Gary will brief you," Allaire said. "You're on speaker."

After a beat, the secretary of defense took over.

"Paul. You holding up all right?"

"Very worried about you all, Gary."

"With good reason. But there may be a glimmer of light at the end of the tunnel. One that isn't an approaching freight train."

"Go on."

"I may be repeating things you already know, but at oh one hundred hours, Griffin Rhodes ran a successful computer simulation of his antiviral treatment program named Orion. Following that simulation, Rhodes intentionally and very bravely injected himself with a high concentration of WRX virus to prove that it would work on those of us who have been exposed here in the Capitol."

"Did the treatment involve the blood he came back with from the inmate at El Dorado?"

"*Ex*-inmate," Salitas said. "President Allaire pardoned him. The bastard wouldn't cooperate if he didn't."

"I would have done the same thing you did, Mr. President."

"Thank you," Allaire said.

"He's the only known survivor of a WRX exposure," Salitas went on. "Rhodes mixed his serum with a chemical called an adjuvant, that's used to boost the level of a specific blood protein."

"And was the treatment a success?"

"It was not," Salitas said flatly. "Within hours of dosing himself with a purposely massive amount of virus, Rhodes developed shortness of breath, cough, and curious markings on his palms that we know are symptoms and a sign of mid-stage infection."

"Good lord," Rappaport said.

"We're in a very dire situation, Paul. We believe most of the population in Group C is now deceased, locked inside the Senate Chamber. Group B, in Statuary Hall, is worsening. And the president, who is in Group A, is showing signs of viral spread as well. Like Rhodes, red markings have appeared on his palms. And his temper is becoming more labile."

"This is terrible," Rappaport said, wondering about the light in the tunnel Salitas had spoken about.

"To make matters even worse," the defense secretary said, "we can't find the vice president."

"Henry's vanished?"

"He's been missing for a couple of days. We're still looking, but so far, nothing."

"Do you think he left the Capitol?"

"We haven't dismissed any possibility. On top of everything, that harpy Ursula Ellis has convinced the architect of the Capitol to resume television broadcasts from inside the House Chamber."

"She's done what!?"

"It appears she's been in touch with Genesis. Don't ask us how. She's been an obstruction on every level. In fact, she's drafted legislation which she claims Genesis wants to have passed."

"Legislation? What are you talking about?"

"A bill," Salitas said. "Like a real, legal bill. Most of Congress is here, so they can do it. She's distributed the bill, it's been debated for days, and now she's pushing for a vote. Apparently Genesis are some sort of ultra left-wing whackjobs. An ACLU on steroids. The legislation they are demanding will repeal the Patriot Act, make wiretapping illegal, and dismantle almost every advancement we've made in bolstering our national security."

"We can't let that happen!"

"It very well might," the president said, taking over the line once more. "Ellis is prepared to share what she knows about the virus with the American people. I did my best to hold back the truth. I wanted to avoid a panic. It appears now that decision will be used against me."

"Why does she want this bill passed?"

"If it passes," Allaire said, "Genesis is promising they'll deliver her the antiviral treatment. She'll be a hero. And with Henry missing, if I die, she won't have any trouble taking over."

"Is that true about Genesis having a treatment?"

"No, of course not! Whoever the hell they are, they're playing her like a rented fiddle. Why? Stalling, I'll bet. Stalling until . . . until we're all dead."

The weakness in Allaire's voice had become even more pronounced.

"Isn't there anyone who can reason with her?" Rappaport asked.

"Gary here, again," Salitas said. "Ellis won't listen to reason. She's crazy for power. She's even got Bethany Townsend, the president's doctor, watching his every move for signs that he's not fit to remain in office. Jim is ready to veto Ellis's bill. But at the moment it looks like she's going to outlast him."

"My God!"

Again, Allaire took over.

"I might not be president long enough to stop its passage. Paul, the situation is truly at its most desperate. But there is a ray of hope."

The light.

"I'm listening," Rappaport said.

"The communication we received from Rhodes included a summary of his research data. He believes his mistake was in the ratio of the adjuvant he used to the amount of serum. He's convinced a fifty percent greater amount of this protein is required in order to be effective against the virus—the ratio is something his program sent out that he misinterpreted. His only mistake, he's calling it."

"Can't Rhodes just give himself another treatment with that added boost?" Rappaport asked.

"Too late," Allaire said. "The massive dose of virus he shot into himself is overwhelming the treatment. The virus is already mutating—causing new symptoms. He's bleeding from his nose, just like many of the people here. He admits it was overconfidence to inject such a large amount, but Rhodes is certain that a fifty percent increase will work for most, if not all of us."

"So what's the next step, Mr. President?"

"The serum is the key," Allaire said. "But it is also unique. We can't get another batch."

"How can I help?"

"The FBI and the CDC are setting up a lab to prepare a new batch of treatment according to the specifications given to us by Rhodes."

"Where?"

"One of our safe houses here in Washington. Gary will give the address to you. We need you and the Secret Service people guarding you to bring the serum to that lab. Genesis has been a step ahead of us at every turn, so secrecy has got to be your highest priority."

"I understand. Consider it done, Mr. President."

"Paul, this is it for us. This is the only chance we have. I don't trust anybody but you to handle things. We're sending three choppers in to get you. The pilots will know what to do from there."

"I won't let you down, Jim. How do I get the serum out of the lab?"

"Rhodes decontaminated the cooler containing the serum and is leaving it for you outside the door into the lab. You can retrieve it without having to put on a biocontainment suit."

"What about Rhodes?"

Again there was a long pause.

"Rhodes is already quite ill," Allaire said finally. "According to his estimates, he'll be dead in a matter of a few hours."

CHAPTER 65

DAY 10
12:00 MIDNIGHT (EST)

Angie checked her watch and paced about the dimly lit living room like a caged lioness. She drew in several calming breaths, but could do little to slow her excitement. She passed the time by mentally drafting her story, featuring Griff as the hero and Paul Rappaport as the mastermind behind Genesis. The prize at stake: the presidency of the most powerful nation on Earth.

The brownstone, she was told, was one of several safe houses in the metro D.C. area used by the FBI, the ATF, and the CIA. The understatedly elegant building, situated on a quiet street in the Adams Morgan neighborhood, had been used in the past to bait and trap spies, extortionists, arms dealers, child molesters, and con artists. Every room was bugged, and there were high-tech hidden cameras throughout. A few blocks away, a surveillance van would be serving as backup.

Angie would be safe, they assured her, but she had

her doubts, especially when she was given a pistol—a Glock 19, they said, and a brief course in its use. The gun, a perfect fit for her, was somewhat reassuring. She had seen what Genesis was capable of, and believed that no place was truly safe from them.

For the thousandth time, she wondered about Griff. No one had told her anything. This was his plan, but he wasn't there. He had requested that Allaire call him as soon as he had read the fax. What, exactly, had he told the president in that conversation? Was the story of the serum needing modification one that he had conjured up, or was it the truth? At the moment, it seemed to be at least a half truth, in which case, Griff might already be dead.

Rappaport believed he was transporting the serum that, when modified in the laboratory upstairs, was the last hope for the president and all those trapped inside the Capitol. If he was Genesis, he would either appear with a story of having been forced at gunpoint to give up the serum, or he would fail to show up altogether. Either way, according to the Constitution, he would be next in line for the presidency. Another possibility was that he had already made a switch, and that what he was delivering was a well-concocted sham, short in one crucial ingredient, but a good enough replica to mislead the biochemists upstairs. After all, nobody but Griff knew what he and his computer model had put together.

The furnishings in the richly appointed rooms were well suited for an upscale sting—armchairs upholstered with plush fabrics, a bedazzling chandelier made of brass and crystal, and fine oriental rugs that framed a deep fieldstone fireplace. This was a home that could have belonged to any high-ranking diplomat or well-connected politician.

Angie fingered the compact pistol in the pocket of her skirt. She had little experience with guns, but she also had a fierce love of life and suspected that she would use this one if hers depended upon it.

A panel of one wall opened up silently, and the three FBI agents whom she had been with since being brought to the house returned to the room.

"They're here," one of them said.

Through the tall bay windows, Angie watched a black Lincoln Town Car pull to an abrupt stop at the curb outside. Three Secret Service agents quickly exited the vehicle. One of them opened the Town Car's rear door and Paul Rappaport stepped onto the curb. The Homeland Security secretary, wearing a stylish overcoat, held one handle of a large, blue cooler. A muscular agent had taken hold of the other. Angie took a few photos with her new digital SLR camera as the two men made their way up the cement outside stairway. The other two agents took up positions near the Town Car.

Angie waited behind the brown leather sofa, which faced the room's only door. The door opened without a knock and the Secret Service agent stepped inside, his gun drawn. After a check of the room, he holstered his weapon and signaled for Rappaport to enter. The secretary spotted Angie immediately.

"What're you doing here?" he asked. "Where are the chemists? The lab?"

Rappaport pulled the cooler tight to his body and

took a cautious step backward. Angie snapped a series of pictures.

"Upstairs," she said, "waiting for you."

"What are you doing here?" Rappaport went on. "I was told you were in a New York City hospital."

"I got better," Angie said. "And now I'm writing this story. Hopefully, it will have a happy ending."

"Hopefully," Rappaport said, his eyes narrowed with suspicion.

"Pardon the camera, but people like pictures."

Angie peered through the camera's viewfinder and let out a terrified gasp. Two powerfully built men, dressed in black, wearing black ski masks, carrying pistols, had appeared behind Rappaport. High-tech gas masks dangled from their belts.

"Look out! Behind you!" Angie cried out.

But her warning came too late.

One of the men grabbed Rappaport across the throat, and before he could move, had the muzzle of a heavy pistol pressed up against his temple. The agents in the room were a beat too slow to react. Another intruder moved in quickly and snatched away the cooler from Rappaport's trembling hand, just as three more masked men burst into the room, each carrying a submachine gun.

"Drop your weapons," the man holding Rappaport demanded, "and no one dies."

Two of the agents had their guns out, but the numbers were bad. Angie had her hand in her skirt pocket, wrapped around the Glock. It seemed unlikely she could pull it out, fire it, and hit anyone before she was blown to bits.

"We have what we want," one of the intruders snapped, his accent heavily Hispanic. "Do as we say, or you'll all die. Weapons over there. On the floor. Lock your fingers behind your heads. Now!"

Angie hesitated. A burst of machine gun fire erupted from close range, the bullets screaming past her head and slamming into the wall. For a moment, she was certain her heart had stopped. She ducked, hands covering her head, and screamed as she dropped to the floor. The other security people and Rappaport were already down, their weapons thrown aside. When she looked back, all five intruders had gas masks on. They were unimaginably quick and well organized.

A canister was dropped on the rug in the center of the room. Angie and the others began to cough as the foul-smelling vapor stung their lungs. Her eyes were watering profusely, and her throat seemed as if it had closed off. Gloved hands grabbed her from behind. Before she could scream again, a patch of duct tape was pulled across her mouth, and her hands were secured behind her. The whole operation had taken less than a minute. Then, the room went completely black.

Angie came to almost as rapidly as she had gone out. She felt the acidy burn of bile as it worked its way up her throat, and shuddered with a new fear that the tape covering her mouth would cause her to choke to death on vomit.

She rolled to one side, breathed slowly and deeply through her nose, and focused her thoughts on an image of Griff that she had conjured up during their phone conversation from her hospital room. She pictured him down in the Kalvesta lab, bravely and confidently injecting himself with a virus as deadly as any he had hunted down in Africa. From his courage, Angie found strength of her own to remain calm.

All around her, agents were gagging and coughing. Moments later, there was a commotion from the doorway. Her hands were untied, and the numbness in them began to abate. The room was crowded now with police, soldiers, and FBI agents, so numerous that they struggled to move about freely.

"I can't believe we blew this," one of the agents who had been with Angie said. "They moved like frigging Delta Force. How in the hell did they get in so easily?"

"The two guards outside are dead, both shot in the head, probably with silencers. We didn't hear a thing until a volley of machine gun fire from up here. By the time we left the surveillance truck and made it over, they were gone."

"Rappaport!" Angie coughed out the words when an FBI agent pulled off the tape covering her mouth. "Where is Paul Rappaport?"

"He's right here," the agent said. "He was tied up like the rest of you."

"The cooler . . . the serum . . ." Angie struggled to get the words out. She was hyperventilating and her eyes still stung from the smoke. "The cooler," she managed again.

The FBI agent just shook his head.

"Whatever was in that cooler," he said, while helping Angie to her feet, "went out the door with the guys who took it."

CHAPTER 66

DAY 10
1:00 A.M. (EST)
Destiny!

Ursula Ellis knew she was on the brink of history. She stood at the rostrum of the House Chamber and gazed out at three hundred frightened and bewildered faces. But she was their leader now—their shepherd. She had lost the battle of the election, but now, thanks to her destiny and to Genesis, she was going to win the war.

She took a deep breath, inhaling the feelings of the moment, and the events just ahead. The Committee on Rules, facing what she had called "our lives or this bill," had granted privileged status to her legislation.

She motioned Leland Gladstone to her side. He was carrying the communication device Genesis had given her.

"Have they responded to us yet?" she asked.

"Nothing," Gladstone said. "Do they know the vote is now?"

"I told them. They'll come through. I'm sure of it."

"Maybe we should hold off until they've delivered the treatment."

"We've come way too far," the speaker whispered, sensing a nugget of concern form in her gut. "Just keep trying to reach them."

It had been two days since Gladstone distributed copies of the bill to each voting member of Congress capable of casting a ballot. Over the time since then, Ellis had heard disgust from every corner of the chamber. One congressman tore the twenty-page piece of legislation in half. Another had tried to set it on fire before the Capitol Police intervened.

But from what she could see before her now, not a single congressman looked interested in protesting the bill—not after she had showed them the videorecording she had made inside the Senate Chamber; not when everyone understood James Allaire's perfidy, and the nightmare that lay ahead for them; not when they knew that without her—without this bill—they were going to die, and die horribly.

A heavy silence followed her re-showing the grisly Senate Chamber video, but clamor erupted seconds later. The noise level rose. Hands were raised high—politicians begging Ellis for a chance to be heard.

They want to vote for my bill. They want to live.

Ellis let the commotion continue unhindered for several minutes. Thanks to Lamar, the eyes of the world were upon her. The television cameras that Allaire had ordered shut down were broadcasting once again. The American people were strong. Ellis put more faith in them than Allaire ever did. They needed to witness history as it unfolded.

Rumor had reached her that the president was failing rapidly. By the time the bill was passed and Genesis delivered the antiviral treatment, it would likely be too late for him. Ellis adjusted the microphone and turned up the speaker volume. Then she snapped her gavel down on the rostrum three times, and the room fell silent.

"I would like to begin this House vote on my special legislative measure by addressing the citizens of the United States of America, and those around the world watching tonight's broadcast. I have requested that these proceedings be shown worldwide because the government of the United States of America is about the people, and for the people, and we will not abandon the most sacred and essential tenet upon which our country was founded, even if the truths we reveal this day are as horrible as the tragedy we now face."

Ellis paused and reminded herself to stick to the way she had rehearsed the speech she and Gladstone had written.

"This will be the unfinished State of the Union Address," she had told her aide, "only this time it will be me who will be delivering it."

Destiny.

"To my friends and colleagues in Congress," she went on, "I realize the bill before you has come as a shock. Many, if not all of you, know that some of the points enumerated in it deviate from my well-documented views. But I have been offered an awesome opportunity—the opportunity to save the lives of many of the most important leaders in our nation.

"Genesis, the vile and traitorous organization responsible for the acts of terrorism that have plagued our country, have released a deadly virus upon us, claiming that their position must be heard. It is not a trade I condone, but it is one I reluctantly endorse. Genesis has offered us a treatment that will deliver us from the horror befalling the unfortunates you have just witnessed again inside the Senate Chamber. The price is high—your passage of this legislation. But I, for one, choose life!"

Comment erupted throughout the chamber. Ellis silently polled the Supreme Court justices seated before her, searching their eyes for judgment. That she saw no disparagement bolstered her resolve. It helped her that one of their court was prominently featured in the video from the Senate Chamber.

"I have brokered an agreement with terrorists," Ellis said. "That is true. But we are a democracy and—"

At that instant, the doors leading across the Capitol to the Senate wing burst open, and President James Allaire strode in.

CHAPTER 67

Wide-eyed, Ellis fixed on the president as he ascended to the rostrum and moved forward until he was only a few feet from her.

"You're finished, Madam Speaker," he said loudly enough to be easily heard through the PA system. "You have done as much damage and created as much chaos as the terrorists. And it ends now!"

The president signaled to Sean O'Neil, who was still beside the door that Allaire had come through. One by one, a small procession of sick and hobbled men and women began shuffling into the House Chamber. Their complexions were ashen. Many of them were smeared with blood. Some of them were clearly disoriented, bewildered, and agitated. They coughed as they marched. Some had to stop to breathe. Those who were too weak to walk unaided were assisted into the chamber by Secret Service agents and the Capitol Police.

At virtually the same moment, a second, larger

procession entered the chamber from Statuary Hall. This group, headed by a muscular African-American man with a military bearing, wearing only surgical scrubs, was in less frightening shape than the other, but they were still obviously failing.

The final two people to enter the chamber came from the Senate. They walked shoulder to shoulder, although one of them moved with great difficulty and needed to be supported by the other. Vice President Henry Tilden, the weaker by far of the two, was a phantom—battered, stoop-shouldered, and gaunt. His face was badly clawed and smeared with dried and drying blood. Supporting Tilden was a tall man in a blue biocontainment suit. Glare off the faceplate of his helmet made it impossible for Ellis to identify him. He held a blue plastic cooler in his gloved left hand.

"What is the meaning of this?" Ellis shouted into the microphone. "Those are the sickest of all of us. You are bringing death into this room. People around the world are witnesses."

Allaire's expression was one of disgust.

"No, Ursula. What they are witnesses to is your madness. Vice President Tilden and others are prepared to swear that it was you who locked him in the Senate Chamber to die or be killed."

The crowd erupted into a chorus of angry and confused shouts. Allaire banged Ellis's gavel to settle them down. He then continued, still extremely shaky, but managing to address the assembly with the mannerisms of a president.

"These people have been brought out from the Senate

Chamber, and those from Statuary Hall, because we now have the means to treat them—and all the rest of us as well."

"Lies!" Ellis screamed. "He's telling all of us lies. The madness is in this man! He is badly infected with the virus and is about to be relieved of his duties as president. Ask Dr. Townsend, his physician. She knows that the virus has attacked his mind."

"Yes, the virus is affecting me more each hour," Allaire said. "And yes, I chose to refrain from broadcasting its terrible effects. But I did so to keep all of you from panicking while we worked around the clock to find a cure. I did not mislead you because I wanted to deceive, but because I felt in my heart that I had a duty to protect you."

"Don't believe this insanity," Ellis bellowed. "The bill must be passed if you want to live. The cure is with Genesis, and only I have access to it!"

Allaire glanced over at his wife and daughter.

"Genesis, whoever they are, doesn't have any cure, Ursula," Allaire said, patiently. "They never did. They are thieves and terrorists. They don't have the technology, or capability, to deliver treatment for a virus this complex. My administration created this nightmare in the misguided hope that we could do away with all forms of torture. We developed the WRX virus, and we are the only ones capable of stopping it."

"You're lying. . . . You're lying . . . ," Ellis kept repeating, but there was no longer any force behind her words.

"Genesis needed to buy time, Ursula. Time for us all

to die. So they played you. They used your pathetic lust for power to turn you into their puppet. We have the cure. That's why I have brought all these brave people back into the chamber—to prove to you that soon the infection will be a thing of your past. Soon we can begin to repair our lives. And we have one person to thank for that."

Allaire gestured to the man in the biosuit, who made his way slowly up to the rostrum. Then the man released the clasps and Velcro holding on his helmet, and eased it off, exposing himself to the contaminated air they were all breathing.

The man had a worn, grizzled face, but his eyes were bright. It took a few seconds for Ellis to place him. But when she did, it was as if an icy hand had gripped her heart.

The man was Griffin Rhodes.

CHAPTER 68

One by one, at intervals of five minutes, three rented sedans pulled in through the rear garage doors of the S&S Trading Co. Five men, all in black, exited the garage through an inner door and entered the large storehouse on the street side.

Waiting anxiously around a makeshift biochemistry lab, complete with immunoelectrophoresis, mass spectrometry, and a chemist, were Roger Corum, Colin Whitehead, and Marguerite Prideaux.

The leader of the mercenaries withdrew five large glass jars from the cooler, each one carefully labeled and containing a slightly opaque straw-colored liquid. The group of them then joined two other men dressed in black, one of whom was operating an impressive pair of videoconferencing screens. On the screens, waiting at their desks in opulent offices, were Song Xi in Beijing, China, and Ibn al-Basarth in Riyadh, Saudi Arabia.

The four men and Prideaux, each worth tens of

millions, formed the secret international cartel which called itself Genesis. The group had been Corum's brainchild, as was taking the names from the Old Testament. Their organization had one goal and one goal only: profit. After this operation was complete, and Paul Rappaport was sworn in as president, there would be no need for Genesis to continue to exist. The American people and their new leader would take care of the rest.

"So, any trouble?" Corum asked the head of the squad.

"Two casualties on their side is all," the man replied matter-of-factly. "Unavoidable."

"No problem. Is Rappaport okay?"

"Fine. He was just as clueless and frightened as the rest of them."

"So," Song Xi asked, in near-perfect English, "Secretary Rappaport still has no idea that Genesis is all about getting him and his policies put into the White House?"

"Not only him and his policies," Prideaux replied, "but thanks to the work of Genesis, an American public ready to cooperate with them, and expand the country's security system to the tune of billions of dollars."

"Tens of billions," Whitehead corrected, punctuating the words with a cough.

"And of course," al-Basarth said, "who better to provide the new identification system, and surveillance cameras, and anti-alien barriers, and electronic monitoring, than our companies—already leaders in our fields."

"I'll bet my own government won't be far behind," Xi said. "I think the world is ready for a little isolationism. Paranoia equals profit. Who first said that?"

"I did," Corum, Prideaux, and Whitehead answered in unison, and all of them laughed.

"How are we doing?" Corum asked the chemist, a man named Falicki.

Falicki had worked for him before. In fact, it was he who first put Corum in touch with the late Matt Fink. There would be no need to silence Falicki or any of the men. Their salaries would see to that.

"Almost there."

The computer printer chimed, and soon began to spit out results from the mass spectrometer analysis, taken from the serum that Paul Rappaport had brought with him to Washington from Kalvesta.

His brow furrowed as Falicki studied the readout.

"Well?"

"It appears this is the authentic antiviral treatment," the chemist announced. "The serum contains the properties we expected to find, as well as the adjuvant we knew the virologist had included. I would like to be certain that what is contained here is the precise drug that your Dr. Rhodes injected himself with, but this is as close as we are going to get. Insofar as I can determine, I believe this is the real deal, Roger. Congratulations."

Corum flinched when he heard a loud pop behind him. He turned to see a now beaming Prideaux holding an open magnum of champagne with foam gushing out its mouth.

"Zees eez cause for celebration, *non*?" she said,

purposely adding a dense French accent, when in truth she had very little.

Whitehead applauded and everyone in the warehouse joined in. There would be no last-second miracle cure for James Allaire and his administration. The doomsday survivor had been aptly chosen. The decision to get Rappaport, himself, to request the undesirable position by putting stress on his mentally ill daughter had been brilliant, Corum reflected. Absolutely brilliant.

"Xi, Ibn," Corum said to the men watching the events via video, "if you have any celebratory drinks nearby, I suggest now is the time to pour them. Along with Mr. Whitehead and Mlle. Prideaux, we are soon to appear on lists of the wealthiest men—and women—in our countries."

Prideaux handed over the magnum to the head of the mercenary force and passed out flutes she had purchased in the package store. Then she raised her glass toward the two grinning men half a world away. The group assembled in the old warehouse did the same, and Song and al-Basarth responded in kind.

"To the trade show in Las Vegas, and the evening when the visionary Roger Corum first brought us all together," Prideaux said while hoisting her glass.

"To the trade show," everyone sang out.

"Speech, Roger," Whitehead demanded.

Corum stepped forward, glass raised once more.

"I think we owe Speaker of the House Ellis a few moments of grateful silence for being such a perfect foil, and for obviously not being aware of the folk tale of Br'er Rabbit and Br'er Fox."

"What is this folk tale?" Song asked.

"Well, Br'er Fox was about to eat Br'er Rabbit when the Rabbit started crying and carrying on that the Fox could do anything he wanted to, up to and including having the rabbit for dinner. 'But please,' the shrewd rabbit begged, 'just don't throw me in that there briar patch.' Well, Br'er Rabbit had caused Br'er Fox so much grief over the years that Fox decided he could always catch another meal. But he could not always cause his nemesis such terrible and feared discomfort."

"But, of course," al-Barsarth said, "the patch was precisely where this Br'er Rabbit wanted to go."

"In fact," Corum said, "he had a lovely vacation home there. By presenting the foolish, off-the-charts left-wing bill I crafted, Speaker Ellis was in essence throwing us in the briar patch. If Genesis was for it, when Rappaport took office all the world would be against it."

"To Br'er Rabbit," Song said, raising his glass.

"Br'er Rabbit," all the others echoed.

"Now," Corum said, after the laughter had died down, "it is time we disposed of the contents of these jars."

With the help of Prideaux he brought the serum to an industrial-sized double sink against one of the walls.

"Five jars," the Frenchwoman said. "One for each of us. Xi, I'll do the honors for you, and Roger will represent Ibn."

So saying, she removed a label across the top that read: STERILIZED. Then she unceremoniously dumped the contents down the drain.

After a second pouring, Corum moved to the sink.

"Ibn, this is yours," he said.

As the last of the golden liquid spilled from the bottle, something metallic dropped out of the bottom and fell, with a soft clink, into the steel sink. Corum reached down and picked up a dollar-sized, gold-colored disc, an eighth of an inch thick.

"Oh, holy shit! It's a homing device. One of ours—"

Corum's words were cut short by a series of loud explosions at the front of the warehouse. Pulverized concrete, debris, and large, deadly fragments of metal siding instantly penetrated the room as the front wall and part of the ceiling burst apart. The prolonged blast of powerful sonic waves that followed the explosions shattered all the glass in the room and knocked everybody within it to the floor. A rolling wall of dust engulfed them.

Some were coughing, some were dead, others were writhing in pain from gashes and broken bones. Then the soldiers stormed in.

Lights and lasers mounted atop assault weapons penetrated the dense cloud of dust and debris. Dozens of soldiers followed the winter wind into the warehouse, some pushing mobile spotlights.

"Hands behind your head!" General Frank Egan cried out, brandishing his pistol. "Get down, arms behind you, or we'll shoot you dead! I swear we will! Get down!"

One mercenary whirled and got off an errant shot. The hailstorm of automatic weapon fire that slammed into his body sent him dancing off the floor like a marionette. After that, resistance vanished. Wrists and ankles were secured, and weapons were collected.

As the soldiers stepped back, Angie entered the warehouse and joined Egan at the center of the room. Monitoring the conversations from the surveillance van, she had sorted out that Corum was the leader of Genesis and that Paul Rappaport was an unwitting dupe, chosen because of his well-known reactionary politics.

The army information specialists provided her with brief, printed dossiers on Corum, his company, and every person whose name was mentioned during the celebration. They even managed file photos of him and Colin Whitehead.

Amazing.

Dazed, Corum tried to get up. He had been gashed in his back and one arm, and it looked as if the other arm was broken.

"Stay down, Corum," Angie barked. "Stay the hell down or I'll shoot you. You have no idea how much I want to, and I promise I will! My name is Angela Fletcher. I work for *The Washington Post,* and guess what? You're gonna be in the papers."

One of the dead men, lying near Corum, Angie recognized as Colin Whitehead. The dust had largely settled or been blown away by the wind. She nudged the soldier watching Corum.

"Turn him over, please," she said.

The soldier used the steel toe of his boot to lift against a spot between Corum's ribs. The CEO let out a pained groan and rolled onto his back. Angie snapped a photo of him and then several of the room.

"This is my payment for services rendered," she said to Corum. "I get to write all about you and your greedy cronies, and Griffin Rhodes is getting the satisfaction of knowing that the antiviral serum the president ordered Rappaport to bring east was a fake that Griff put together in his lab and topped off with the homing device you made for him to wear. It wasn't easy. In fact, it took him almost as much time to concoct that fake serum as it did to make the real deal."

"Fuck you," the CEO rasped.

"You killed my friends. You killed dozens and dozens of good, innocent people. You terrorized the country. Who in the hell did you think you were? What gave you the right?"

Corum's smile was nasty, showing blood-stained teeth.

"I'm just a man," he said, coughing up a glob of blood. "A man with a dream."

"A dream of causing death?"

"Even if I don't benefit directly now," Corum said, "my industry will. My heirs. My employees . . . It's commerce. Commerce at its purest."

"Paul Rappaport is not going to be the president," Angie said. "He'll be pleased that we have a recording of you talking about how you were using him—setting him up because of his conservative philosophy. Setting him and the American people up essentially to work for you and your gang of thugs."

Corum tried to speak, but coughed more blood.

"It doesn't matter now," he finally managed. "Piles of money will go into the security industry regardless. That's something of a legacy for me."

"But it won't go to you or to any of your companies. I'll see to that."

"Does that give you any satisfaction, Ms. Fletcher?"

"You know what, you pathetic creep," Angie said. "It kind of does."

CHAPTER 69

DAY 10
2:00 A.M. (EST)

Griff stood at the rostrum, looking out over the nearly seven hundred survivors, all of them infected to one degree or another with the WRX virus. The moment in the lab when he saw the concentric red circles on his palm was among the most frightening, soul-crushing he had ever experienced, not only because his research had failed, and people were going to die, but because he had seen Angie for the last time. For nearly an hour he had sat there in his office, motionless, staring at the wall, and planning what he might do to end his life as soon as symptoms of the virus began to become manifest.

Then, suddenly, the miracle began to unfold.

Over another hour, the dreadful markings began to vanish, until finally, after nearly three hours, they were gone altogether. By then he had already contacted the president by fax through Angie, and had asked him to begin laying the trap that was going to confirm or disprove Paul Rappaport's involvement with Genesis.

The mood inside the House Chamber was an odd mix of bewilderment and buoyancy. Some in the vast room were hugging. Some were crying. And some were merely standing motionless, staring up at the strange tableaux.

Ellis stood frozen on the stage, her eyes looking furiously at Griff. Several of the Capitol Police force had moved in close to her, awaiting orders from their chief or from the president. Griff had helped the weakened vice president into the speaker's chair. Then he opened the cooler and extracted a large jar of opaque serum and held it aloft for all to see.

But before he could speak, a man's voice hollered out from somewhere near the middle of the crowd.

"Get in line! There might not be enough!"

Suddenly, driven by primal survival instincts, and in all likelihood by the effects of the virus as well, the crowd began to surge forward.

"Wait!" Griff cried into the microphone. "Everybody stop! There's enough. There's enough for each of you."

But his words had no effect. People, some violently shoving, others already on the floor crawling, had reached the stairs to the rostrum. The police moved in and the Secret Service began to form ranks about the president and vice president.

But before any of the people reached Griff, three ear-splitting bangs stopped the milling crowd and silenced the hall. Leland Gladstone was standing behind him. The still-smoking barrel of the gun he had fired into the air he now held against Griff's temple.

Ellis's aide quickly ripped the cooler from Griff's hand and handed it to her. The Capitol Police surrounding the speaker moved away.

"This is yours, Madam Speaker," Gladstone said. "You've worked too hard for it. We can't stop now. We mustn't stop now."

Ellis took the cooler from her aide, and pulled out one of the sterilized jars. The chamber remained silent, all eyes fixed on the precious serum. Ellis faced the assembly while Gladstone, wild-eyed, continued to shift the gun toward anyone who moved.

"You have all been fooled," Ellis cried out. "And you continue to be fooled. What is this?" She shook the bottle for emphasis. "You're going to let this charlatan inject you with this when I have promised you the real treatment? You are going to trust this . . . this hermit, and not me? Haven't I shown you the truth? The truth about Senator Mackay? The truth about the Senate Chamber? Haven't I done my part to expose the lies of this president? And yet you still rush for this concoction? Either the content of this jar is useless, or it will quicken our deaths. But I can assure you of one thing— this is not a cure! Only Genesis has the cure. Only Genesis and the bill I've presented can save your lives, not this bottle of lies."

Allaire, who had been ushered off the stage by the Secret Service, pushed himself through the cluster of bodies surrounding him.

"You need to stop this, Ursula," he said in a calm voice. "What you have there cannot be replicated. Surely you want to save the lives of all these good people. You need to give the serum back and allow us to administer it. You must."

"I must save these people from you!" Ellis cried out.

Gary Salitas, who had been on his cell phone, leaned over and whispered to the president. Allaire turned to the crowd.

"I have just been informed that the gang of terrorists calling itself Genesis has been captured. Several of them are dead. The rest are on their way to jail." He shifted his attention back to Ellis. "They admitted that they were using you, Ursula. They have no serum."

Some cheered, others continued to stare at the speaker.

Allaire's announcement was the final straw for her.

"Lies!" she shrieked. "All lies."

She raised the bottle above her head and hurled it into the crowd, where it shattered on the carpet. A second jar disintegrated against the head of a tall, balding man, sending a gruesome mix of blood and serum cascading over him.

Before anyone could move, she had thrown a third jar, this one smashing on the metal frame of a bed.

There was a gunshot, loud and echoing. Ellis's head snapped back as the bullet tore through her, exploding out the back of her skull. Blood, brains, and bone splattered over the rostrum as she crumpled to the floor by the seat that had been hers for so long.

Gladstone, his eyes widening, still with the gun in his hand, took a shot in the center of his face, the bullet following a path almost identical to the one that had killed Ellis. He instantly fell lifeless across her body, his blood mixing with hers.

A short distance away, Sean O'Neil held his smoking pistol, preparing for the follow-up shot that would not be necessary.

Allaire rushed to Griff, his expression panicked.

"You said the serum couldn't be replicated," he said. "You said this was a one-time deal. Can you possibly stretch out what's left? Can you make it be enough for all of us?"

Griff raised his hands to quiet the crowd. Then, as the cries and commotion settled down, he turned to the president and grinned.

"President Allaire," Griff said into the microphone, "the antiviral treatment that I developed cannot be replicated. That is true."

"No! Don't let us die!" somebody shouted.

Others echoed the fear, and again the frightened, emotional crowd began to unravel.

"Please," Griff called out to them. "You've all been through enough. Please listen." An uneasy silence returned. "The serum cannot be replicated," he continued, "so I could not trust myself to be the one to bring it here. Genesis had too many eyes and ears for me to believe they could not get to me, which is why the mixture I carried into the chamber was a ruse, not the antiviral treatment I developed." He nodded toward the door to the Senate Wing and a solidly built man in a biocontainment suit stepped forward. "Let me introduce to all of you Sergeant Chad Stafford of the United States Army—the one person I knew we could all trust with our lives. The serum in his backpack is enough for every one of you."

Applause and cheers started in the back of the crowd

and rolled toward the soldier like thunder. In addition to his backpack, he held an assault weapon at the ready. People moved aside to allow him to pass as the cheering grew even more intense. All business as usual, Stafford climbed the rostrum stairs and stood next to Griff, who turned to the man and shook his hand.

"Glad you found the place okay," he said.

EPILOGUE

The Inn at Coco Island, American Samoa, was unlike any vacation destination in the world. Built on stilts, ten feet above the vagaries of the South Pacific winds and tides, on the eastern end of the island, the inn was the only structure on the two-square-mile atoll, save for the home of innkeeper Jarvis H'malea, located on the far west end. The inn had only one suite—six rooms. It was owned by a consortium of Vegas casino heads and serviced by H'malea and his family. Rental was $50,000 a week, with a minimum stay of two weeks.

The closely guarded guest list at the Inn at Coco Island read like a who's who in entertainment, business, and sports, and the ability to pay the tariff and sea plane fare did not guarantee an applicant a vacation there. The fine, white sand was legend, and the palms were reputed to produce the largest, sweetest coconuts to be found anywhere.

In the ten years H'malea had been the steward at the inn, he had successfully honored demands—dietary and otherwise—from some of the most eccentric, uncompromising men and women in the world. But the request from the two guests flying in now was unique—a king-sized mattress, placed in a grove of palms, on a small bluff facing east toward the sunrise.

The new E. S. Kluft Beyond Luxury Sublime mattress had been flown to Pago Pago from the Kluft factory in California, brought over to the inn by boat, and paid for, H'malea's Vegas contact had told him, by some sort of special act of the United States Congress. At first, H'malea was sure the man was pulling his leg, but that was before the mattress, with a pricetag in the mid-forties, was off-loaded.

The seaplane materialized as a dot in the perfect late morning sky. H'malea, thumbs in the beltloops of his khakis, strode along the pier past indescribably blue water with visibility of over two hundred feet. His two guests had requested nothing more than peace and quiet, and, of course, the mattress, but they would have access to SCUBA equipment, kayaks, small sailboats, a hot tub, and a luxuriously stocked wine cellar and kitchen, with or without H'malea's skill as a chef.

The drone of the engine could be heard now as the pilot banked smoothly into the light southerly breeze. H'malea knew of the events at the U.S. Capitol, and that the passengers had been central in keeping the death toll down and in saving the lives of the president and vice president, as well as close to seven hundred others. But he knew few of the details. Nor would he bother Angela Fletcher or Dr. Griffin Rhodes to fill him in.

On board the seaplane, Angie looked down from her seat by the pilot.

"I told you I didn't like large groups of people, Dr. Rhodes," she said into her mouthpiece. "What is that mob doing down there on the pier?"

"I'll speak to him about crowd control," Griff said.

Three weeks had passed since the last of the victims of WRX3883 had been treated and, after a day, sent through decontamination, out of the Capitol, and back to their lives. Although he would have preferred his role remain anonymous, Griff knew that would never be the case. Angie had spent most of the time at her keyboard, writing a series of articles for *The Post* and a proposal for what her new literary agent said would be the book of the century.

Before Angie began her writing, though, and before Griff accepted his newly acquired celebrity; and before he submitted to extensive debriefing from the president and his advisors, including Homeland Security Secretary Paul Rappaport, the two of them bundled into her silver Miata and drove to a small farm near Beckley, West Virginia.

"Melvin were never much for keeping in touch," Kyle Forbush told them over a lovingly prepared dinner of pork, beans, boiled greens, and homemade bread, "but he called from time to time and came home every other Christmas or so. We knew from early on that he were more, I don't know, unusual, than the other boys his age. If he had stayed and worked in the coal mine like we expected him to, chances are he would have been beaten to a pulp in the first month. He did his last year in high school living with my sister in Morgantown, and then put hisself through bug school—that's what I called it—working in a video store. He were a real nice boy and a good son. We're sad to hear of his passing."

Forbush and his wife knew surprisingly little of the events at the Capitol, but they were pleased and impressed that President Allaire and the senators from West Virginia had declared an upcoming Wednesday Melvin Forbush Day, and would all be traveling to Beckley to celebrate.

The pilot swooped in with practiced ease, and tied up at the pier. Thirty minutes later, Griff and Angie were alone on their mattress, wearing nothing but sunscreen.

"Considering that I made this place up," he said, "it's hard to believe it really exists."

"I'm proud that you allowed Congress to do something for you in addition to the medal and the citation. I'm also pleased that because our trip is privately donated—a little from each of them and from the Cabinet—I don't have to write an exposé about it. I'm also glad the president paid for the mattress himself."

"It's a little out of character for me to say he owes me," Griff said, stroking a wisp of her hair from her forehead, "but he does."

In a contrite, impassioned speech to the world, Allaire had come completely clean about the WRX3883 virus and his role in developing it. He admitted to making choices under pressure that he might otherwise not have made, including the unjust imprisonment of the man who had subsequently saved his life and that of his family and so many others. He also promised his quick resignation should public opinion demand it.

In an affirmation of honesty from politicians, his next approval poll was the highest of any during his presidency.

Griff and Angie made love that afternoon, and again that night beneath an unending sea of stars. Days passed during which they slept and healed, and swam and ate and read, and drank coconut milk. Over that time, they spoke almost nothing of Kalvesta nor the Capitol.

On the fifth or sixth day, they were surprised by the appearance of a thin, white and tan dog—thirty pounds or so, and an indefinable mix of breeds. He ambled between the palms, and settled down for an hour just off the foot of the Kluft Beyond Luxury Sublime mattress. He allowed himself to be patted, and nuzzled them without being intrusive. Then, in no particular hurry, he left the way he had come. The next day, he returned and departed in the same way . . . and the next.

On the tenth day, after breakfast and well before their visitor made his appearance, Angie moaned happily and nestled herself tightly against Griff's chest.

"I haven't asked you because you never brought it up," she said, "but have you given any more thought to Allaire's offer to have you take over as the director of the CDC?"

"It's in Atlanta," he replied.

"I know that, you big goof. I would move there if you took the job."

He kissed her on the mouth.

"And I would move to Washington for you. In fact, that's what I'm going to do if you want me to. It would only be for four years, but that will be enough time for you to finish your book and for us to decide if it's appropriate for us to lend our gene pools to the world."

This time she kissed him—long and deeply.

"Now that would be something to write about," she said, beaming. "But what do you mean, four years?"

Griff's tanned face crinkled in the grin that Angie loved the most.

"I've been saving something for you," he said, "and this seems as good a time as any to spring it on you. I made a deal with Allaire."

"A deal?"

"At the moment, he's coping with a presidential-sized load of guilt, so I decided to take advantage of it. If you say yes, you're looking at the newest member of the President's Cabinet—the first secretary of the Department of Animal Welfare."

Angie threw her arms around him.

"Oh, baby, that's incredible! Absolutely wonderful news. Do you know what the job will entail?"

"I was sort of hoping you'd help me fill in the blanks on the trip home."

"My brain's already exploding. You can deal with cruelty and exotic pets, and zoo standards, and the feeding and housing of premarket hoofed livestock and chickens, and a tax credit for neutering and spaying, and of course experimentation, and—"

"Hey, not until the ride home."

She held his face close to her own.

"Okay," she said, "I'll think of something we can do in the meanwhile. One thing, though."

"Yes?"

"Have you considered that creation of this post will put you squarely at number eighteen on the ladder of presidential succession?"

That evening, Jarvis H'malea made his scheduled every-third-day visit to the inn. He seemed especially pleased that there was nothing either of his guests needed that he hadn't already provided for them.

"Tell me something," Griff asked, after the steward had shared some grilled sea bass and a delicious bottle of chardonnay with them on the verandah, "your dog has been a welcome visitor at this end of the island almost every day. What's his name?"

"I have no idea," H'malea replied. "And he's not my dog. In fact, if he stays on Coco Island much longer, he's going to be the death of me."

"Explain," Angie said. "Where could he possibly have come from?"

"A few days before you showed up, *he* showed up. Strolled into our house just like he always lived there. No boats are allowed inside the reef, and of course, no one other than guests are permitted on the island. But I can't prevent boats from anchoring outside the reef. Almost certainly, the dog came from one of them. I sent several radio messages, and my wife has been listening for one ever since, but there's been nothing. Not a word. And for the last four days there's been no one anchoring."

"So why is he going to be the death of you, Jarvis?" Angie asked.

"I can't breathe when I'm within five feet of him.

Some sort of allergy, I guess. I can't stop wheezing and coughing. Say, I don't mean to sound forward, but as you can tell, I'm desperate. I don't suppose you two would like to take him along with you when you leave."

Griff and Angle took only seconds to conduct a silent poll.

"As a matter of fact," Griff said . . .

Read on for an excerpt
from Michael Palmer's next book

OATH OF OFFICE

Coming soon in hardcover
from St. Martin's Press

PROLOGUE

I'm finished.

I can't believe this has happened again. I just blew
up at one of my patients. The last time, when I screamed
at Calvin Summers for continuing to smoke despite a
massive heart attack, my medical license was suspended
for six months, and I had to go away for treatment. The
board of medicine said there was no excuse for that
kind of behavior from a doctor, no matter how pure my
motives.

Now it's Mabel Jennings. She just stormed out shouting at me that she was not going to tolerate that kind of

abuse, and that she was going to contact the board as soon as she got home. My office staff heard her. The patients in the waiting room heard her.

What am I going to do?

I'm alone in my office. Her tires just screeched on the pavement as she sped out of the parking lot. I can just picture her at the wheel, her face all pinched and angry. The door to the hallway is closed. I can't just sit here like a lamb waiting to be dragged to the slaughter, especially when I didn't do anything that wrong. I love my patients, but there's not a chance in the world the board would understand that. They won't care that Mabel Jennings is eating herself to death.

Hypertension . . . type 2 diabetes . . . ankle edema . . . varicose veins . . . arthritic knees . . . hiatal hernia . . . carbon dioxide narcosis. . . .

They won't know how many times I begged her to change—how many diets; how many referrals; how many discussions. They won't see that I had every right to scream at her the way I did. I have to do something to save myself—to save my career.

I gaze at two pictures of my family on the corner of my desk. My favorite is the one taken in springtime—Joanne and our three daughters, huddled together on our front porch swing. The girls are raven-haired beauties, just like their mother. The milkman's kids I'd often half joke, because they don't look much like me. The other picture is of Chloe, my youngest. I know I'm not supposed to have a favorite child, so it feels horrible to admit to myself that I do.

Must do something.

Everything I've worked so hard for is in danger. My breathing is coming hard—shallow and more rapid. It's like I'm trying to suck in molasses. I know exactly what's going on inside me. Chemical signals from the amygdala area of my brain are in rapid-fire mode, instructing my heart to beat faster. Adrenaline is being pumped into my bloodstream like rocket fuel.

Witnesses.

Everyone out there is a witness to what happened. They will all be called before the board. That would be the end. A lamb to the slaughter. I must do something to prevent them. I don't remember unlocking my desk drawer and bringing out my pistol. I haven't even seen the Smith and Wesson Sigma SW40VE in at least a year. But it is here in my hands.

I unlock the safety. Everyone out there in the waiting room will testify as to what they heard. And that's all it will take to finish me off. I took an oath when I became a doctor to do no harm, and that's an oath I have kept. Nobody cares about my patients the way that I do.

Can't believe this happened. . . . What choice do I have? How else can I save my career . . . my family?

If no one is there to corroborate Mabel's allegations, it will be her word against mine. He said, she said. The board would never pull a doctor's license on a flimsy claim like that—especially one as dedicated to his patients as I am.

Must do what's fair.

No witnesses.

I open my office door and step out into the hallway. The fluorescent overhead lights are hurting my eyes.

With the Smith hanging at my side, I head down the corridor into our newly furnished, patient waiting area. My heart is pounding against my sternum. Blood is churning in my ears. The room has begun to spin.

I wish there were another way.

Two women are in the waiting area—Margaret Dempsey and Allison Roundtree. They both look disturbed by what they heard. I wonder if they were talking about just leaving—deserting my practice and transferring their records to another doctor—probably to my partner, Bud.

Sunlight in the foyer is illuminating dust motes circling in the air. Small details, yet so clear. I double-check that I've got two additional clips tucked inside the pocket of my white coat.

No witnesses.

Ashley is sitting behind the reception counter, looking distressed. The new nurse, Crystal, is behind her. Ashley is thirty. Two kids. Her glasses hang over her breasts, suspended by a gold lanyard that sparkles against her tight-fitting black sweater.

Details.

There is no another way. I need to protect my career.

For a moment I feel uncertain . . . confused. Then my resolve returns. Must act before they see the gun.

I raise the Smith.

I'm doing this for us, Joanne. It's the only way to save the children—to save you and our way of life. Any doctor threatened like I am would handle things the same way. The first shot explodes in my ears. The gun recoils.

I fire again and again and again. Suddenly, there is blood everywhere.

Glass shatters.

Ashley looks up at me wide-eyed.

I shoot her in the forehead. She flies backward and lands on top of Crystal. I feel calm now. In control. I'm a doctor, and I always will be. I begged her to lose weight. I had every right to yell at her. In fact, I didn't even really yell—just raised my voice a little. I walk with determination back down the hallway and turn toward our tiny kitchen. Teresa and Camille are there. They were undoubtedly discussing what to do about me when they heard the shots. Now they are on their feet, screaming.

My office manager tries to speak, but I can't make out what she's saying. My finger tightens, then loosens, then tightens again. The Smith spits fire. Theresa is hit in the throat, Camille in the chest. The women crumble like rag dolls. Camille tries to get up. A shot to the back of her head settles her down. I replace the clip in the Smith.

Almost done.

Back to the hall. Bud is in his office. He may not have heard what went on with Mabel, but maybe he did. Bud was never much of a doctor to begin with. He'll probably be ecstatic when they pull my license and tell him to take over my patients because I'm never going to be allowed to be a doctor again.

His office door swings open just as I arrive. Two feet separate us. I can smell his fear. For a moment, I hesitate. I can't get my brain around things. My thoughts are without focus. Is he going to be a witness or isn't he?

"John, what in the hell?—" Bud cries.

I empty the entire clip into his chest and face. His blood splatters over me. Fragments of his bone cut into my skin. I want to tell him it's all Mabel Jennings's fault, but it's too late. I slump against the wall, breathing heavily. They never would have understood. They never would have cared how much being a doctor meant to me.

Suddenly, I stop.

My God, I've done something very bad. Now the board of medicine will be hard-pressed to let me keep my license at all. I've made a terrible mess of everything. I replace the clip a final time. Then I close my eyes and press the barrel of the gun to the side of my temple. I picture Chloe in my mind. I'm going to miss her the most of all.

Wondering how it all unraveled so quickly, I pull the trigger.